WHERE WAS THE BABY?

Rounding the corner, Jesse caught her breath at the wreckage that had been made of the living room. She'd worry about it later. After she'd gotten Amanda. After she held her baby, sweet and safe in her arms.

Clutching the bannister for support, Jesse scrambled up the stairs. In the soft glow of the early morning light, the nursery was just as serene, just as secure as before.

Jesse raced across the room, her bare feet noiseless on the deep carpet. The side of the crib was up, just as she'd left it. Her arms were outstretched, hands already reaching, as she came up beside the bed. And in that instant the nightmare began.

The crib was empty. Amanda was gone.

■　■　■

NIGHT CRIES

LAURIEN BERENSON

HarperPaperbacks
A Division of HarperCollinsPublishers

This is a work of fiction. The characters, incidents, and dialogues are products of the author's imagination and are not to be construed as real. Any resemblance to actual events or persons, living or dead, is entirely coincidental.

HarperPaperbacks *A Division of* HarperCollins*Publishers*
10 East 53rd Street, New York, N.Y. 10022

Copyright © 1992 by Laurien Berenson
All rights reserved. No part of this book may be used or reproduced in any manner whatsoever without written permission of the publisher, except in the case of brief quotations embodied in critical articles and reviews. For information address HarperCollins*Publishers,*
10 East 53rd Street, New York, N.Y. 10022.

Cover photography by Joe Burleson

First printing: December 1992

Printed in the United States of America

HarperPaperbacks and colophon are trademarks of HarperCollins*Publishers*

❖ 10 9 8 7 6 5 4 3 2 1

ACKNOWLEDGMENTS

Any new endeavor requires help, and I must gratefully acknowledge the assistance of two special agents of the FBI, one in New Haven and one in Bridgeport, both of whom wished to remain anonymous, but who were kind enough, and patient enough, to answer my numerous questions. Thanks also goes to the officers of the New Canaan Police Department, who provided the same function.

With many fond memories, this book is dedicated to the class of Composition 205, Vassar College, 1971–1972, and to its teacher, Colton Johnson. Thanks for the push.

And to my mother. Thanks for the shove.

O<u>NE</u>

Something was wrong.

Jesse Archer's eyes snapped open, sleep abruptly gone. She lifted her head from the pillow and gazed around the night-darkened room, looking for . . . what? The window beside the bed was half-open, its silky curtain undulating silently as the moist night breeze lifted it inward. A shaft of moonlight reflected off the row of perfume bottles atop her dresser. Her running shoes lay in a heap where she'd kicked them the evening before.

All was quiet, yet Jesse's heart was racing. Then she heard the noise again.

It wasn't exactly a creak, more a low whine. Whenever the humidity was high, the window in the back wall of the living room stuck. Pushed, it protested. Now as she strained her ears to listen the sound shivered through the house once more.

Slowly, stealthily, the window was being forced open. Someone was coming in.

Jesse's hand scrambled to the night table. Often she left the cordless phone there, but the tabletop was empty.

Six months earlier she wouldn't have hesitated. She'd have thrown open the backdoor and raced like hell into the deep cover of the dark night because there was nothing in the house that was worth facing an intruder for. Now there was. Her four-month-old daughter, Amanda, was asleep in the second-floor nursery.

Jesse's first instinct was to race to her daughter's side, a compelling impulse, but impossible. The only access to the second floor was a flight of stairs on the other side of the living room. Directly across the intruder's path. No, the kitchen with its wall phone and its sharp, shiny knives was her only hope.

Jesse sat up and slipped her legs from beneath the covers. Maybe she was mistaken. Maybe what she'd heard was no more than the house settling, or the window sash swelling with moisture from an approaching storm. Please God, she wouldn't mind being wrong. She'd always had an active imagination. Maybe she'd conjured up a problem where none existed at all. . . .

The scraping sound was soft, but undeniable. A moment later there was a quiet thump. A pair of feet landing on her living-room floor. Now there was no mistake. She wasn't alone in the house.

Jesse stood unsteadily. The long white nightgown slithered down to her calves, diaphanous in the moonlight. She gathered up the hem, then knotted the fabric tight across her hips. She had to be ready for anything.

At the bedroom door she hugged her body close to the wall. The sound of her own breathing echoed in her ears. Sweat gathered under her arms, and ran in trickles down her sides. She blinked once, then twice, trying to clear her vision.

The small square hallway that stood between her and the kitchen was dark and empty. Jesse heard footsteps in the living room, then a muffled thud. A hoarse voice muttered, "Shit!"

He was coming closer.

Jesse leaped through the doorway and into the kitchen. It was a race she'd run a thousand times in her dreams, flying weightless through misty fields, and never stopping once to look back. Breathless, she dodged around the counter. The phone was on the wall between it and the cabinet above. Her hands were shaking so badly she could hardly lift the receiver. Moonlight, so bright on the other side of the house, was nonexistent here. She couldn't see the numbered buttons.

Nine, lower right-hand corner. She pushed down hard and heard a queer tone. That wasn't right. Abruptly she remembered. There were four rows on this phone, nine was in the third. Her fingers fumbled over the instrument, then finally found the lever to disconnect.

It seemed like forever before the dial tone returned. This time Jesse found the right button. Quickly her fingertips skated across the board to the opposite corner. As they punched the first "one" she heard him in the hall. Instinctively she dropped to her knees behind the counter. The receiver was still clutched in her hand; the call incomplete.

For an endless moment there was only silence. Jesse edged slowly upward until she could see over the top of the counter. A figure filled the doorway, dressed in black and barely visible in the gloom. For several panicked seconds Jesse couldn't find his head. Then she realized there was a ski mask over his face.

She wasn't able to see his eyes, but when his head turned, she knew he was looking around the room. Any minute now he'd notice that the phone was off the hook. Any minute now he'd charge around the counter and—

And do what? Jesse's usually vivid imagination refused to supply an answer.

Her knees began to wobble and she clutched at the counter for support. She dared not change position lest the movement catch his eye. Nothing must draw his attention, not down here, and especially not upstairs. Thank God her daughter was a sound sleeper. Please, Amanda, Jesse prayed, don't make a sound. Don't let him know you're there.

The weight of the telephone receiver, still clutched in her hand, mocked her silently. Three more seconds and she'd have been able to complete the connection. Three more seconds, and cars with flashing lights and loud sirens could have been speeding to her rescue. Instead there was only silence. Silence, and the shadowy figure of a man, now taking his first step into the room. Somehow he knew she was there and he was coming for her.

He reached the other side of the counter. His hand, encased in a black glove, trailed aimlessly across the top. It passed within inches of Jesse's nose and she shrank back. A startled gasp escaped from between her teeth. The tiny sound seemed impossibly loud in the quiet room. Immediately his head swung around, and for a brief, startled moment their gazes met.

"No!" Jesse screamed. She sprang to her feet, adrenaline pouring through her veins. The receiver in her hand felt as heavy as a club, and she swung it wildly, just missing the man's arm as he leaped back.

He landed on both feet, immediately balanced, watching as she held the plastic implement up in front of her like a shield. Jesse raised her other hand, fist clenched. Her knees were bent, her feet braced.

And still he stood there watching.

He had her cornered. He had all the time in the world. And they both knew it. Fear, its taste sharp and metallic, coated Jesse's tongue. Why didn't he do something? Goddammit, why didn't he move?

And then he did. One minute he was facing her across the counter, and the next—Jesse hadn't the slightest idea how—he had braced one hand on the waist-high barrier and simply vaulted over it. Suddenly he was beside her.

Again she swung the receiver, but this time he didn't even bother to dodge. He caught her arm and snapped it around. He wasn't that much taller than she, but Jesse's strength felt like nothing compared with his. He bent her wrist back, squeezing hard, and her fingers opened. The receiver dropped to the floor with a clatter.

A wail, part anger, part despair, was torn from her. Jesse wrenched her hand loose. Ignoring the knife-edged pain that shot up into her shoulder, she fell upon him, raging with fists and feet. The blows landed, but made little impression. The sweat suit he wore was thick and bulky. Jesse felt the soft give of fabric and knew she wasn't hurting him at all.

It was as if he was merely toying with her, deflecting her blows, or tossing them off, letting her struggle until she was spent. Jesse opened her mouth, gasping for air. What was the use? In the end everything would be the same, all she was doing was prolonging the inevitable. Maybe it was better just to get the whole thing over with. But even as the thought crossed her mind an image of her sleeping child followed it, and Jesse knew she couldn't give up.

Her hand came up to claw at his eyes, but he snatched it out of the air, his fingers closing over her fist and trapping it between their two bodies. Then he angled closer to obliterate the space between them, so that Jesse was forced to lean back, her spine stretched over the counter at an impossible angle. Her free arm was twisted to one side; her fingers scraped the smooth Formica for purchase and found none.

She'd felt pain before, but nothing like this. Her feet left the floor, dangling in the air as she tried to raise them. Anything, anything, to relieve the pressure on her spine. Still he continued to shove her down until the edge of the counter dug between her vertebrae, and streaks of white-hot light flashed before her eyes.

She could feel his breath, hot and moist on her face. Through the holes in the mask, she could see his eyes. Cold, black slits: they were flat, emotionless. At the sight of them whatever hope she'd still clung to shriveled and died. Oh God, thought Jesse, he was going to kill her.

Abruptly her fingers connected with something on the countertop. A wire—but to what? Through a haze of pain she tried to remember. The bottle sterilizer. She'd had it out the night before. Her hand scrambled over the wire, drawing it in like a lifeline. There was a scraping noise, then her fingers closed over something solid and heavy.

He heard the sound, too, and turned to look, just as she lifted the sterilizer and swung it with all her strength at his head. If his reflexes had been slower, she'd have had him. Instead he arched backward and the blow glanced off his chin.

Jesse heard his jaw snap shut. She felt his cry of rage. It was an awful, guttural sound, more animal than human, and chilled her to her soul. A horrible thought skimmed the edge of her subconscious. What would he do to a tiny baby?

The back of his hand sent the sterilizer flying. It hit the kitchen floor and skittered across the tile before coming to rest against the wall. He raised his hand again and Jesse knew he was going to hit her.

As if in slow motion, she watched the black glove descend. Incredibly long seconds passed before the flat of his hand made contact with her cheek and sent her head reeling. Blood spurted inside her mouth, filling her senses with its sickly taste.

She never even saw the second blow coming.

TWO

It was the pain that brought her to.

Slowly Jesse's eyes opened. For a moment she saw only patches of light and dark; then things swam into focus. She was sitting in one of the cane-backed kitchen chairs, her chin resting on her chest, her head lolling on a neck that felt too weak to support it. Her hands had been tied behind the chair's rigid back; her ankles were bound to its legs. Her nightgown was tangled and torn. Blood stained its bodice.

With effort Jesse raised her head. Her spine, throbbing at the spot where she'd been braced across the counter, seemed to compress beneath its weight. An attempt to move her arms brought only another spasm of pain. Her wrists were tightly lashed together, fingers tingling as though cut off from their supply of blood.

In a rush the horror of the nightmare returned. Was Amanda safe?

She heard a crash from the direction of the living room, then a moment later a soft, fluttering noise it took her a minute to identify. Pages, being flipped through rapidly. What was he looking for? Money? She didn't have that much. And what she did have certainly wasn't hidden between the pages of a book. She heard a series of thumps and the tinkle of glass breaking.

Please God, please don't let him make enough noise to wake up Amanda, Jesse prayed. Whatever he took, whatever he did to her, she'd survive as long as he didn't hurt her baby. With any luck he might never even realize Amanda was there at all. Of course he'd notice the stairs. But maybe he'd assume they went up to an attic. . . .

She was drifting. Determinedly Jesse stiffened her spine and a jolt of raw pain skated across her nerve endings. The shock of it cleared her head, helping her to focus. The green digital clock on the microwave read 2:45.

Jesse closed her eyes hard, then opened them slowly. She was fading again and she couldn't allow that to happen. She looked down at her nightgown and saw that the hem had come unknotted, leaving it tangled around her thighs. Above that was a long, jagged rip. It started at the neckline and traveled halfway down the front. On one side the torn material gaped open lewdly, exposing her breast.

When had that happened? Jesse stared at the tear with horrible fascination. What else had he done?

She shuddered violently, overcome by a wave of revulsion. She felt the imprint of his hands crawling over her skin; imagined those flat, black, lifeless eyes looking at her, staring at her exposed body. . . .

And then suddenly he was there.

Jesse wasn't sure just what made her glance up, but when she did, he was standing in the doorway. He didn't say a word, didn't make a sound.

"What do you want?" she asked. Her voice quavered like a petulant child's.

He hadn't been looking at her, but now he did. Or at least Jesse thought he did. Behind the mask it was hard to tell. In this light she couldn't see his eyes, only the two holes where they should have been.

He crossed the room in three short strides. Jesse watched every move. The police would ask for a description. She had to pay attention. She had to believe that she would get through this and would be there to answer questions. Because if she didn't believe that, then there was nothing left to cling to.

Jesse jumped as he yanked open a drawer, pulling too far, so that it reached the end of the runners and fell to the floor with a crash. Silverware scattered in all directions. He left it and went on to the next.

Finally he found what he was looking for. He held up a long, sharp-edged carving knife, turning the implement in his hand as though testing its weight. Jesse felt herself go cold all over.

He turned to face her as Jesse'd known he must. "Please," she whispered. "You can have anything. Anything you want from the house. Just take it. But please don't hurt me."

He took a step toward her, then another. Jesse's eyes never left the blade. Fascinated, hypnotized, she watched as the shiny steel edge came closer and closer. When he stopped, the tip was only inches from her nose. Oh God, Amanda, I tried. I love you so much. Whatever happens, I'll always love you. . . .

He lifted his hand and the flat of the blade scraped across her cheek. Jesse jerked her head back, eyes open wide and wild with fear.

Once again the blade rose.

This time he slid the tip into her hair, lifting the light brown strands, sifting through them, and letting them fall. For a moment he seemed to consider what he was going to do. Then his other hand came up, grasped the locks where they lay heavily on her shoulders, and held them out. There was a quick, upward thrust of the knife, a stinging in the side of her scalp, and the hair came off in his hand.

Tears gathered in Jesse's eyes. "Please," she whispered, but the word had no meaning, no power. Nothing had any power save the man in black. He could do whatever he wanted and they both knew it.

Ignoring her plea, he snatched up another hunk of hair and hacked at it roughly, then let it fall to the floor. Jesse felt another yank as he chopped off the back.

Shaking, miserable, she felt the long strands slither down her body and gather at her feet. There wasn't anything she could do, anything she could say. She accepted that fact now, just as in some perverse way she'd accepted him. Whatever was coming, she just wished he'd get it over with.

A loud clatter brought her up with a startled jerk. He'd tossed the knife into the sink. It skidded on the stainless steel, bounced once, then lay still. Before it had even settled, he'd spun around and left the room.

Several long minutes passed, time Jesse spent listening for sounds, anything that would give her a clue as to what he was doing. Three-sixteen, blinked the green numbers on the digital clock. Three-seventeen, three-eighteen. The living room seemed quiet, but so did the rest of the house. Surely she'd have heard him above her if he'd gone upstairs, wouldn't she?

Then finally there was a sharp, metallic click, followed almost immediately by another. Locks being flipped back. With a *whoosh* her front door opened. Another, and it slammed shut.

Jesse held her breath, sitting rigid in the chair. It didn't seem possible that he'd actually gone.

But as the minutes slipped by, hope stirred. She began to play a game, her eyes focused unwaveringly on the clock. If ten minutes passed without his return, she'd accept that he was gone. But when the first ten minutes were up, she found herself waiting another ten. Then ten more after that. Slowly, gradually, she began to believe. By the time the lighted green numbers flashed 3:48, Jesse's shoulders sagged with relief.

The nightmare was truly over. She and Amanda

were safe. Jesse drew in a deep breath and let it out slowly, savoring the simple luxury.

She had to get loose, had to get to Amanda. Never had the urge to hold her sleeping child in her arms been so strong.

Jesse twisted in her chair, pulling against the ropes that bound her wrists. They burned into her skin. Desperately she wiggled her fingers, trying to inch one hand free, but the ropes held firm.

The telephone! The receiver, dangling by its cord the last time she'd seen it, had been replaced. He must have done it while she was unconscious. She could knock it off with her head, Jesse decided. And push the buttons with her tongue. But first she had to get there, and that meant dragging her bruised and aching body across four feet of silverware-strewn floor. The task seemed insurmountable.

But what other choice did she have? Who else was going to come and save her? If there was one thing she'd learned in the eleven months since Ned left, it was to depend on nobody but herself. Besides, what if the man in black changed his mind? What if he came back?

The thought motivated her as nothing else could have. Pulling with what little strength she had left, Jesse lifted the chair slowly, painfully, off the floor. Inch by inch she dragged it toward the counter. Sweat beaded at the sides of her brow. She gritted her teeth and ignored the pain. Inch by painstaking inch.

She was almost there when the back of the chair caught on a half-open drawer. Jesse was exhausted and off balance; the small jerk was all it took to send her sprawling. Her knee hit the floor with a jarring thump that brought hot tears to her eyes. She pitched forward, then onto her side, and came to rest on a bed of discarded silverware.

Jesse let her eyes close. All she wanted to do was sleep. How easy it would be to just let go and leave all the pain behind. . . .

"No," she said aloud, the word hardly more than a whisper. She had to get to Amanda.

Her fingers scrambled in their bonds, reaching for leverage. Instead they came up with something cold and flat. As her fingertip scraped over the sharp edge, Jesse laughed out loud. The sound was brittle and edged with hysteria. She'd found a knife.

It took her ten minutes just to line the blade up along the rope. Then, the first time she'd tried the awkward sawing motion, the knife slipped from her fingers and dropped to the floor. Another twenty minutes passed before she was ready to try again. In silence, punctuated only by an occasional grunt, Jesse worked.

Gradually the room around her went from dark to gray, then lighter still as the first amber streaks of dawn came up over the horizon. Just as she'd begun to believe it might never happen, she felt the rope loosen. She yanked her hand and felt it give. Frantically she began to saw once more. At last, with a small pop, the rope broke.

Jesse gasped as her arms snapped free and blood returned painfully to the numbed limbs. She rubbed her hands together desperately, massaging her swollen fingers and forcing the feeling back into them. As soon as they were able to function, she grasped the counter and hauled herself to her feet. Once she was standing, it was a simple matter to lift the chair and slide her legs free.

Jesse set the chair aside and started for the stairs. Rounding the corner, she caught her breath at the wreckage that had been made of the living room. Furniture was overturned, prints torn from the wall, statues broken. Averting her gaze, she made her way through the debris. She'd worry about it later. After she'd gotten Amanda.

Clutching the banister for support, Jesse scrambled up the stairs. To her relief nothing here seemed to have been disturbed. In the soft glow of the early-morning light the nursery was as serene and secure as always. Clouds and rainbows danced across the pale yellow walls. A mobile of laughing clowns hovered in frozen animation above the crib. The rocking chair with its needlepoint cushion waited by the window for Jesse and Amanda to come and rock.

Jesse took in the scene in a moment's time. Then she was racing across the room, her bare feet noiseless in the deep carpet. The side of the crib was up, just as she'd left it. The colorful bumpers were still in place. Her arms were outstretched, hands already reaching, as she came up beside the bed. And in that instant the nightmare began again.

The crib was empty. Amanda was gone.

THREE

Day One

In a voice that was flat, devoid of feeling, Jesse made the call to the police. Shock coated her emotions like a thin veneer, insulation against the horror of the night's events. Later the pain would come, she was sure of that. For now there was only numbness.

The waiting began, but not in the kitchen. The memories there were all too vivid. Nor, Jesse discovered, could she face the living room. Finally she wandered into the bedroom and sat down on her bed. She thought about getting dressed, but couldn't seem to find the energy. Just sitting there seemed to require all her strength.

It was time for Amanda's breakfast. Right now they should be sitting by the window in the kitchen, where the morning sun fell in golden streaks.

Amanda would lie nestled in the crook of Jesse's arm, her plump hands clutching at the bottle greedily as she drank. When she'd finished, Jesse would offer rice cereal. Amanda would stick out her tongue and smear the cereal in her hair. Then they'd both laugh at the mess she'd made. . . .

No! Jesse sat up straight, willing the image away. She couldn't think about Amanda right now, because when she thought about her daughter, she couldn't seem to breathe. She'd felt loss before, but nothing like this. Never like this. No matter what, she had to stay in control.

Looking for distraction, Jesse gazed around the room, then stopped, suddenly, staring at the reflection in the mirror above the dresser. For a moment she almost didn't recognize herself. Her head, shorn of its long, thick hair, looked strangely small and defenseless. Tufts stuck out at odd angles, framing a face that was red and puffy. A dark bruise ran down the side of one cheek. Her lower lip had split open, and swollen to twice its normal size.

Even her eyes looked different, huge and dark. And haunted.

When the doorbell rang, she climbed slowly to her feet. She felt old. Yesterday thirty had seemed like a good age, but then she'd never before feared what the future might bring. Now she did. The change was as simple, and as devastating, as that.

There was a patrol car parked in the driveway, and two uniformed officers standing on the front step. Jesse opened the front door and stepped wordlessly aside. They looked at her, then exchanged a glance. One, a freckled blond who looked as though he might have graduated from high school the week before, hurried back to the car.

The other officer was older, probably midtwenties. He was a neatly turned out black man with enviable posture and a pleasant face. "Officer Rollins, ma'am," he said. "May I come in?"

Jesse nodded, clutching at the nightgown that still gaped at her throat. Too late she realized she should have at least made the effort to put on a robe. There was a closet next to the front door. She opened it and pulled out a down vest, slipping her hands through the overlarge holes, then snapping it down the front.

When she turned back to Officer Rollins, he was staring at her trashed living room in dismay. Cranford, Connecticut, may have grown into a thriving city in recent years, but the police, Jesse suspected, were still more accustomed to dealing with speeding drivers and teenage drug pushers than anything like this.

The officers let her tell the story her own way, taking notes but asking few questions. As she reached the end another car pulled up outside. Since Jesse's Honda and the patrol car filled the small driveway, it slid into an empty spot on the street.

"That'll be Detective Maychick," said Rollins. He went and stood by the door.

The detective came straight in; no niceties, no formalities for him. He was older than either of the two officers, with short, straight, dark hair and a face that had settled into lines of permanent disgruntlement. For his bulk he moved with surprising grace. An athlete who had let himself go to seed. Mentally Jesse drew a line from broad shoulders to equally broad hips. A paunch, partially contained by a too-tight belt, took up the space in the middle. Unlike the officers, he was wearing a suit. It was dark blue and boxy, as nondescript as the brown Ford Fairlane he'd parked outside.

"Jesus," he said to Rollins as he took in the scene. The undertone carried clearly across the room. "Why didn't you tell me it was a rape? We need to get a woman officer out here."

"There was no rape," Jesse said quietly. Maychick turned to look at her. She lifted her chin and met his gaze. There was something reassuring about him. He looked strong, and dependable, the kind of man who would endure. The kind of man who could find her baby. Or was she only seeing what she wanted to see?

The detective took out his ID. Jesse examined it only briefly before handing it back.

"Tell me what happened."

"I've already told the other two officers."

"Tell me again."

"You're wasting time," Jesse said angrily. "Time that could be spent trying to find the maniac who took my baby!"

Ignoring her outburst, Maychick sat down on the couch. He patted his pockets absently as though searching for a cigarette and sent a pointed look in the direction of the two uniformed officers. Immediately they withdrew, leaving Jesse and the detective alone in the living room.

"Look Ms. Archer." Maychick's tone made it clear he was not the sort of man to whom patience came naturally. "The fact is, nothing we do or say this morning is going to be a waste of time. In order to find your baby, we have to know which direction to start looking. To figure that out we need to know everything that went on here last night."

Resigned, Jesse righted the armchair across from the couch and sat down. She began to talk, the words coming haltingly. Maychick let her finish without interruption. Then, when she was done, he began to ask questions.

"Can you describe the man?"

Jesse shook her head. "It was too dark. He was wearing a ski mask over his face, and something bulky—a sweat suit, maybe—on his body. Everything was black. I could hardly see him at all."

"Must have been hot," Maychick muttered. He made a note in a small pad. "Height?"

"Not very tall. Five-eight, maybe five-nine."

"Weight?"

Jesse shrugged helplessly.

"Fat? Skinny?" Maychick prompted.

"I don't know."

"Okay. How about his hands?"

Jesse felt consumed by frustration. She'd thought if she could just make it through the night, everything would be all right. But it wasn't all right. It wasn't even close.

"He was wearing gloves," she said softly.

"All the time? Ever take them off?"

"Not that I saw."

Maychick didn't look pleased. "We'll get someone up here to dust for fingerprints anyway. You never know. How about his voice?"

"He . . ." A wave of inadequacy washed over her. "He didn't say anything."

"Never? Not one word?"

Again she shook her head.

Maychick snapped the notebook shut and slipped it into his pocket. He looked like a man who wanted a cigarette, badly. Jesse knew the feeling well.

"You have any idea who did this to you?"

She raised startled eyes to his. "You mean, someone I know?"

"It's not unusual. More often than not crimes like this are committed by someone the victim knows."

"No," Jesse said firmly. "The man who was here last night was a stranger."

Maychick started patting his pockets again. This time he came up with a worn, slightly bent cigarette. He placed it between his lips but didn't light it. Jesse wondered if the cigarette could possibly be as stale as it looked. There was an ashtray on the side table and she started to reach for it, then changed her mind and slid her hand back into her lap. The small flicker of his eyelid assured her he'd missed neither action.

"The women's movement aside," he asked, "is that Miss or Mrs. Archer?"

"Mrs. At least for now."

"Your husband around?"

"He lives in White Plains."

"Separated?"

"We're working on a divorce."

"Friendly or unfriendly?"

Jesse sat very still. Her legs were aligned from knee to ankle; her fingers lay clasped in her lap. She could spend hours answering that one question alone.

"Well?"

"Unfriendly," she said shortly.

"Your husband ever beat you?"

She glared at him in outrage, but Maychick didn't seem to notice. Several moments passed before Jesse realized he had no intention of ending the silence.

"How many questions are you going to ask?" she snapped.

"As many as I need."

"And do I have to answer them?"

"That's up to you. You said you wanted us to find your daughter. I'd like to know if your husband ever knocked you around."

"No!"

"Is the baby his?"

Jesse drew a deep breath. "Biologically, yes."

"Meaning?"

"I didn't find out I was pregnant until after we'd already separated. When I told him, he said it was my decision. I could do whatever I wanted, it didn't make any difference to him."

Maychick's cheeks sucked in as he drew on the unlit cigarette. "So you went ahead and had the baby on your own?"

"Yes."

"Does he have visitation?"

"He could come if he wanted, I wouldn't keep him away. So far he hasn't."

"He pay support?"

"No."

"You realize we'll be checking all this out."

Jesse looked at him in surprise. "Do you think I have any reason to lie to you?"

"I don't know. Do you?"

The man's calm was infuriating, thought Jesse. He was a smug, supercilious—

"Do you?"

"Of course not!"

"Good." Maychick stood. As though with no particular destination in mind, he began to wander around the room. He looked at everything, but was careful not to touch. Finally he stopped beside the fireplace. On the mantel was a silver-framed picture, one of the few things left standing amid the wreckage. An infant with large blue eyes and silky blond hair smiled out at him. "Is that the baby?"

"No." Jesse dug her hands into the pockets of the down vest. Her fingers balled into fists. "I had another child before. She died."

Maychick's brow lifted.

"In the hospital. Complications due to a premature birth." The words sounded so cold and precise. They were the ones the doctor had used to describe the situation, the ones that had stuck in Jesse's mind even after the image of the tiny baby she'd lost had begun to blur and soften around the edges.

"Which hospital?"

"St. Simon's." Jesse was tired of answering questions. Tired of being made to feel as though she'd done something wrong. She added pointedly, "Two blocks down, one block over. On Newfield."

Maychick glanced at her over his shoulder. "I know where it is."

"I'm sure you do." She'd almost hoped he'd take offense at her tone, but the detective didn't even seem to notice.

"I guess that's all for now. If you don't mind, I'll just take a look around."

"I thought that's what you were doing."

The cigarette waggled up and down in his mouth. Maybe she was getting through to him after all.

"The rest of the house—kitchen, bedroom, bathroom. That's it for the first floor?"

"That's it."

"Nursery upstairs?"

"Yes."

Maychick nodded to himself, details falling into place in his mind. "While you're sitting there, Ms. Archer, I want you to start thinking of names."

"Names?"

"We're going to need a list—friends, acquaintances, who picks up your garbage, who mows your lawn. Anyone who's been here in the last six weeks or so. You had your sink fixed, I want to know about it. You had a boyfriend in—"

"I just had a baby!"

Maychick dealt her a pointed look. "I'm only trying to cover all the bases. Anything, no matter how small, could be important. The more complete a list we can get from you, the better. I'll send Officer Rollins back in to help you with it."

The statement didn't seem to require an answer, so Jesse didn't bother supplying one. Through the front window, she watched another car pull up outside. A man carrying a black leather case stepped out. Rollins met him in the driveway and they walked around to the backdoor.

Across the street, the curtain on Mrs. Manetti's front window lifted, then abruptly fell. No doubt the Portland Road gossip mill was grinding into action. By midmorning the entire block would know that something was going on at Jesse Archer's house.

Maychick reappeared in the doorway from the hall and Jesse realized she hadn't noticed him leave. She wondered how long he'd been gone. How long had she been sitting there, propped up in that chair, breathing in and breathing out, going through the motions of being alive because she couldn't think what else to do?

"We're dusting for fingerprints now," said Maychick. "And we'll need to take yours as well. It shouldn't take long."

And then what? Jesse couldn't imagine them gone, the house empty, nobody there but herself and her thoughts. But she was going to have to imagine it. More than that, she was going to have to deal with it.

Jesse cleared her throat, and was pleased when her voice came out sounding strong and sure. "What happens now?"

"You talk to Officer Rollins, if you're ready."

"No," Jesse said distinctly. "I mean after that. What are you going to do about getting back my baby?"

"We have a lot of avenues to pursue—"

"Don't feed me jargon like I'm some sort of a moron." Jesse straightened in her chair. For the first time all morning she began to feel just the tiniest bit like her old self, like a woman who had fought rather than run, for the sake of her child. "Tell me what you're going to *do*."

If anything, Maychick looked slightly annoyed by her interest. He might have been assigned to the case, but that didn't mean he had to waste any of his time explaining things to her.

"For starters, we've already notified the FBI. They're sending a team down from their Bridgeport office. Meanwhile, my men are going to be talking to your neighbors, finding out if any of them heard or saw anything. After that I'm going to interview your ex. You say he has no interest in the child. Maybe he says differently." Maychick's calm, dispassionate stare dared Jesse to object. She bit her lip and remained silent. "And next we're going to consider the possibility that the kidnapper may come to us."

"What?"

Maychick saw the fear on her face. Absently he hooked his thumbs into the waistband of his pants and hitched them up. His paunch lifted, then settled, with the effort. "If, as you say, the man who came in here last night and took your daughter was a stranger, then there's a good chance he'll be looking for some money to give her back. If that's the case, he'll be in touch."

"But I don't have any money. I mean, I do—enough to live on certainly, but not enough to interest anyone in taking Amanda."

"You're assuming that whoever took the child knows that."

"All he'd have to do is look around. There are plenty of mansions in Fairfield County. This isn't one of them."

"I'll bet you still paid better than a hundred fifty for it."

"So?"

"The way some people see it, that's plenty. Your average criminal, all he's looking for is opportunity. You offered it to him, it's as simple as that. For all we know, taking the baby may have been an afterthought. Maybe what we have is some young punk, decides to break in here, mix the place up a bit. He sees the child, thinks maybe there's an extra buck in it, grabs her, and runs."

"Do you really think so?"

"Mrs. Archer, right now I don't think anything. I'm open to any and all ideas. By the way, we've put a trap on your phone, along with a tape recorder on this end. If anyone calls, pick up quickly, try to keep them talking for as long as possible. We'll do what we can to trace the call."

"But I . . ." Slowly Jesse shook her head. The thought of someone—that maniac—holding her daughter for ransom was almost inconceivable. "Yes, of course."

Maychick nodded toward the doorway. "Officer Rollins is waiting. Are you ready to talk to him?"

Jesse looked up. "I'm ready. And after that I want to do whatever else I can to help."

Maychick had started for the hall. Now he turned and paused. "You really want to help, Ms. Archer—if I were you, I'd pray."

FOUR

Officer Rollins was a slender young man with skin the color of café au lait and close-cropped hair that angled sharply into a flat plane on top. Jesse watched as his gaze shifted up, down, anywhere but directly at her. Was it a sympathetic response, or simply more of the offhand cynicism she'd seen in Detective Maychick?

Rollins crossed the room and took Maychick's seat, opposite Jesse on the couch. He balanced a pad of paper on his knee and set his pen at the top, ready to begin. "Did Detective Maychick explain to you what we're looking for?"

"The names of everybody I know."

"I guess you might look at it that way." Rollins started to smile, then decided against it. "The best thing is just to take it slow. That way you won't leave anyone out."

The first few names came easily—friends, neighbors, a colleague from work. Remembering what Maychick had said, Jesse also supplied the names of the services—garbage pickup, minimaid, lawn care—whose representatives were in and out frequently.

Finally, under Rollins's careful prodding, she began to fill in the small details—the approximate dates of two UPS deliveries, the painters who'd restained her house in June, the handyman who'd chopped down and hauled off a dead tree.

As they talked the other policemen worked around them, examining broken china, taking pictures, and dusting for fingerprints. With quiet efficiency the officers sorted through the debris and discussed their findings. Jesse watched their faces, their eyes, looking for hope or a spark of revelation, but found neither.

More than an hour passed before Rollins was finally satisfied. He folded the sheet of paper and tucked it away carefully in his pocket. "Maybe there's somebody you'd like me to call for you?" he offered as he rose to his feet. "You know, relatives or something?"

Jesse didn't even have to think about it to know that the idea was impossible. She hadn't seen her parents since Ned moved out—their choice, not hers. Even the birth of their granddaughter hadn't been enough to overcome their stern disapproval at her supposed failings. Considering her situation now, this hardly seemed the time to hope for their forgiveness.

"No," she said softly. "But thanks."

Rollins waited while she was fingerprinted, then went off to join Maychick in the kitchen. Jesse was debating whether or not to follow when the doorbell rang. She started to rise and found she had to brace both hands on the arms of the chair to complete the move. A cacophony of aches and pains, her entire body protested.

Before she could reach the front door, it was shoved inward, propelled by a short, round-faced woman with a headful of moppetlike curls. Kay Samuel looked like an overage Shirley Temple—at least that was how Jesse tended to think of her. Her neighbor's high-pitched voice and determinedly optimistic outlook on life only completed the picture.

"Jesse, I saw a police car out front. Is everything all ri—" The question died abruptly as Kay took in the condition of the room, Jesse's battered appearance, and shorn head. Her face paled with shock. "My God, what happened?"

"Amanda . . ." Jesse began, then found she couldn't finish. She turned away and sank back down in her chair.

"What about Amanda?" Kay's voice rose. "Is she all right?"

Jesse shook her head.

"Jesse, what is it?"

"She's gone."

"Gone?"

"Someone broke in last night." Jesse had neither the desire nor the energy for a full explanation. "When he left, he took her."

"Oh no . . . Do the police know who did it?"

Shaking her head, Jesse waved vaguely toward the doorway. "They're working on it now."

As if on cue, Maychick appeared in the hall. "We're all done in here," he announced, looking back and forth between the two women.

"Detective Maychick, Kay Samuel," said Jesse. "Kay's a neighbor."

Maychick nodded in acknowledgment, but his hand was beckoning at the two of them impatiently. "If you two could step into the kitchen, my men will just finish up a few things in here."

"Sure," Kay agreed, already in charge. As though Jesse was an invalid, Kay took her friend's hand and helped her to her feet. Once in the kitchen, she sat Jesse down by the window, then went directly to the coffeepot on the counter.

Maychick remained in the room with them and Jesse realized he was assessing Kay. When Rollins turned in his list, Maychick would find Kay's name at the top of it. As Jesse's best friend, she was a frequent visitor.

"Jesse told me Amanda's missing," Kay said as she finished with the coffeemaker. "What can I do to help?"

"The police will be doing everything in their power—"

Always impatient, Kay didn't wait to listen to Maychick's platitudes. "How about making fliers and distributing them in the neighborhood? Or what about milk cartons?" She frowned thoughtfully. "I wonder how you'd go about getting Amanda's picture featured?"

"Milk cartons are for older kids," said Jesse. "Ones that have been missing for months."

She stopped abruptly. Until that moment it hadn't occurred to her that Amanda might be missing for months, any more than she'd been able to consider the notion that her baby might not come back at all. When Kay placed a mug of coffee on the table in front of her, Jesse wrapped her chilled fingers around the cup gratefully. Despite the mugginess of the late-spring morning, despite the down vest she wore over her nightgown, she was shivering and she couldn't seem to stop.

She looked up and found herself the object of both Kay's and Maychick's scrutiny. The detective's stare held speculation; her friend's sympathy. And something else. Anger, Jesse decided. She had a sneaking suspicion she was about to become her friend's latest cause.

"Did I hear Mrs. Archer say you live on this street?" Maychick asked Kay.

"Um-hmm. Number one sixty-nine. The gray house at the end of the block."

The unlit cigarette Maychick had toyed with earlier had disappeared; now he began rifling through his pockets once again. Obviously there was something about asking questions that made him feel deprived. "The police will be going door-to-door in the neighborhood, but since you're here, I may as well ask you now. Did you see or hear anything unusual going on last night?"

"What time?"

"Between two and three-thirty, maybe a little later."

Kay looked at Jesse and shook her head. "I'm sorry, I was asleep. Of course I'll ask George about it, but I'm sure if he'd noticed anything he'd have mentioned it this morning."

"George?" asked Maychick.

"My husband."

The detective nodded. "Anyone else live in the house with you?"

"The twins, Michael and Kevin. They're four." In other circumstances she'd have pulled out pictures. "But as far as I know, they were asleep, too."

"All set, detective," one of the officers called from the living room.

"Be right out." Maychick turned back to Jesse. "Like I told you before, there's a trap on your phone. Officer Rollins is going to wait here with you in case a call comes in. He'll know how to help you with it, so listen to what he says."

"Of course."

"There's one last thing, Ms. Archer. Have you spoken to the baby's father yet?"

"No," said Jesse, surprised by the realization that the thought of calling Ned hadn't even occurred to her. Maybe she was finally beginning to heal after all.

"Any particular reason why?"

"That jerk probably wouldn't even care." Kay snorted derisively. She was well acquainted with tales of Ned Archer, as Jesse had moved into the small house on Portland within weeks of her husband's desertion.

"Your opinions are noted," said Maychick. "But he still ought to be notified. Do you want me to make the call?"

"No, I'll do it." Mentally Jesse relegated the task to later, to some future time when she'd begun to function again.

Maychick nailed her with a look. "Make sure you do. I'll be heading down to White Plains to talk to him. It'd be better if you gave him the news first."

"Sure," Kay broke in. "And Jesse's life might have been a little better if he'd stuck around when she needed him."

"Leave it alone, Kay," Jesse said quietly. "I'll take care of it."

Maychick started to go, then stopped again as something else occurred to him. "You probably ought to see a doctor, make sure nothing's wrong other than what you can see. If you want, I'll run you over to the emergency room now, get it taken care of."

Jesse glanced up. Without thinking, she lifted a hand to her head to brush back her hair. Too late she realized there was nothing there. Self-consciously her hand dropped back down to her side. "I'll be all right."

"It's up to you," Maychick said with a shrug. He pushed the kitchen door open.

"Detective?"

He paused on the step.

"I want you to keep me informed. If you get any information at all, I want to know what it is."

"Yeah." Maychick let the screen door swing shut behind him. "Sure."

"There he goes," said Kay, watching through the window as the detective strode toward the street. "America's sweetheart."

"I don't care if he's the Son of Sam," Jesse said grimly. "As long as he can find Amanda."

Kay changed the subject by lifting the coffeepot and carrying it over to the table. "Ready for some more?"

"No . . . but thanks." Jesse laid a hand on Kay's

arm. "I mean that. I really appreciate your being here right now."

"That's what friends are for. You know if anything happened to the twins, you'd be the first person I'd turn to." Abruptly Kay frowned, a sudden thought crossing her mind. "Look," she said slowly, "I know you and your parents don't get along very well, but maybe I should call them anyway. You never know—"

"Yes, I do." Jesse drew in a breath and let it out in a long sigh. "My parents don't deal with crises. They don't believe in them. According to my father, the only way to get into trouble is to bring it on yourself."

"But—" Kay was clearly unconvinced.

"But nothing. My parents have never been tolerant people, but after my brother died in Vietnam, they changed, became even more rigid. Nothing I did was ever good enough.

"When my first baby started fading . . ." Jesse closed her eyes. "When it began to look like she wasn't going to make it, my mother came up and stayed with Ned and me. She saw how it was, she knew what I was going through. And after all that, when Christina finally died, the only thing I can remember her saying was, 'I managed to balance motherhood with a career. I don't know why it should be so difficult for you.'"

Kay gasped, but Jesse didn't seem to hear her.

"Not only that, but during that whole time my mother never once showed any emotion over what was happening. Christina was her granddaughter, dammit! I don't know if she cried for my brother. If she did, she didn't let me see. But she didn't cry for Christina. . . ." Jesse's voice was barely louder than a whisper. "And neither could I. My own daughter . . ."

Silently, Kay reached over and took Jesse's hand. Wrapping her fingers around her friend's, she squeezed hard.

"Now you're wondering," said Jesse.

"About what?"

"Why I'm not crying now."

"I am not. People respond to pain in their own way. Just because you aren't hysterical doesn't mean you don't have feelings."

"I can't cry now," Jesse said determinedly. "Because if I do, that will make it real. I'll have to admit that Amanda's really gone. I mean, rationally, I know it's true. But emotionally . . . I just don't believe it at all. Like maybe she's really at the day-care center, or upstairs in her crib asleep. I just keep thinking that any minute I'm going to get up and walk through that door and there she'll be, sitting up and grabbing at her toys."

Jesse turned her face up to Kay's, her eyes huge and stricken. "Oh God, I'm just so scared, and I don't know what to do."

"The police will find her, Jesse." Kay's arms circled her shoulders and hugged fiercely. "You've got to believe that."

At the sound of a discreet knock, the two women separated slowly. Officer Rollins was standing in the doorway.

"Ms. Archer? There's a car pulling up outside, probably the FBI. Did Detective Maychick tell you? We notified them this morning."

"Yes . . . Yes, he did." Jesse straightened, trying quickly to compose herself. For once she was grateful that the policeman couldn't seem to meet her eye.

"Their involvement is standard in cases like this," Rollins continued. "They'll want to ask you some questions, then begin an investigation of their own."

"I'll come right in," Jesse said, rising. Abruptly she realized she was still wearing her nightgown, the down vest snapped haphazardly over it. "On second thought, please ask them to give me five minutes. I just want to slip on some clothes."

"Sure, ma'am, no problem."

"Unless you think I could be of any help, I'll leave you to them." Kay looked around the kitchen and shook her head. "Call me when they're gone. As soon as they've seen everything they want to see, I'll come back and clean up."

"You don't have to do that." Even to Jesse's ears the protest lacked conviction.

"Sure I do. I've seen the way you clean house. With this mess I'm the best hope you've got."

Jesse tried for a smile and failed utterly. "Thanks."

"You're welcome," Kay said, then added firmly, "Call me." She pushed open the screen door, strode down the driveway, and was gone.

Moving stiffly, Jesse made her way into the bedroom. She paused in the doorway as sunlight, glinting off the perfume vials on the dresser top, caught her eye. Without thinking, she glanced at the window beside the bed. The curtain was hanging still. Below it her running shoes lay tumbled where she'd left them. Nothing had changed, and everything had.

Would it ever be the same again?

FIVE

It took Jesse only a minute to shed her nightgown and pull on a T-shirt and a pair of cotton pants. She might not be presentable, but at least she was dressed. On her way back out, she stopped in the bathroom. Carefully averting her gaze from the mirror, she splashed cold water on her face, wincing as it stung her bruised flesh.

As she patted her face dry Jesse could hear the low rumble of voices in the other room. The Federal Bureau of Investigation—the very name sounded daunting. She walked into the living room half expecting to find Efrem Zimbalist Jr. sitting on her couch.

He wasn't, but two solemn-looking men were. As Jesse stepped through the doorway they rose together. Both men were tall, one slender, the other more solidly built. Both wore dark blue suits, crisp white shirts, and conservative ties. Their hair was short and neatly styled, their faces clean shaven. They looked like bookends, or matching toy soldiers, Jesse couldn't decide which.

The slimmer one was also younger, and wore a pair

of narrow-rimmed, tortoiseshell glasses. He stepped forward and offered his hand. To his credit his gaze didn't even flicker at her appearance. "I'm Special Agent Phillips," he said. "And this is Special Agent Harvey."

"Jesse Archer." Her hand was enveloped in a firm handshake.

"If you don't mind, Special Agent Harvey will have a look around while I ask you a few questions."

"Certainly, go right ahead."

As only two pieces of furniture remained upright in the living room, inevitably once again Jesse found herself seated in the chair, this time facing Agent Phillips, who had taken a place on the couch. One more time she was taken through the now-familiar territory she had covered with the police that morning.

"You know, I've given this information twice already," she said finally. "Couldn't you just get my statement from Detective Maychick?"

"We find it's more thorough if we conduct our own separate investigation," Phillips said patiently, as though it was a question he was used to answering. "Much of the same ground gets covered twice, which means there's less chance of anything being overlooked. Now, about your place of employment."

With a sigh Jesse resigned herself to the process. "I work for National Brands."

"Corporate headquarters in White Plains?"

"Yes."

"Position?"

"Group product manager."

"For how long?"

"Six years at NB, one in my current position."

"Salary?"

Jesse bristled, not for the first time, at the casual presumptuousness with which her private life was laid bare. "Is that really relevant?"

"It may be." Agent Phillips smiled reassuringly.

"The more background information we have to work with, the better."

"I make in the high five figures."

Without comment Phillips wrote the information down. Government jobs being notorious for their poor pay, Jesse wondered if that sounded like a lot to him.

"What sort of arrangement do you have for your daughter while you're at work?"

"She goes to day-care, Piper Ridge in north Cranford."

"Hours?"

Jesse squirmed in her seat. "They're not really set yet."

Phillips glanced up questioningly.

"After Amanda was born, I took a three-month leave of absence, so I've really only been back at work since May fifteenth. At the moment, until she gets settled in, I've been dropping her off at eight and picking her up at four. Eventually, of course, the hours will have to be lengthened. . . ." Slowly Jesse's voice trailed off as she realized what she'd said.

Without thinking she glanced toward the kitchen where the wall phone sat, still as silent as it had been all morning. She dreaded the idea that it might ring at any moment, the thought that that maniac might be holding her daughter hostage—goods in exchange for money—as though she was nothing more than a commodity to be used for his own gain.

Even more she dreaded the idea that it might not ring at all.

Briefly Phillips's gaze followed hers. Though he must have guessed the direction of her thoughts, he didn't say anything. Instead he simply waited until she'd turned back and he had her full attention once more.

"Are you in contact with any of the other mothers at Piper Ridge?"

"What do you mean?"

"You know, play groups, gymboree, that sort of thing."

Jesse looked at him in surprise. "You must have children of your own," she guessed.

For the first time Phillips's expression warmed. "Not exactly, but close. A niece and a nephew. They're five and seven now, but I remember back when they were small. My sister was into everything."

Jesse's hands clasped in her lap. "Amanda's not involved in any of those things yet. To tell the truth I think she's just too young for outside activities. Besides, it's always seemed to me that a play group for four-month-olds is really more of a support group for mothers."

Why did she sound so defensive? Jesse wondered. Though Agent Phillips certainly hadn't said as much, she suddenly felt as though her parenting skills were being questioned. "Unfortunately I don't have time for play groups, and neither do the other mothers at Piper Ridge. That's why we use day-care, because we have to—not because we want to."

"I see."

Did he? Jesse realized she was beginning to resent the way Phillips had of taking careful note of everything she said while at the same time being equally careful not to comment about anything. Maybe it was part of his job not to have an opinion.

"Does you sister work?" she asked.

Phillips seemed surprised by the question. He hesitated for a moment, as though debating whether or not to answer it. "Part-time," he said finally. "While the kids are in school."

"But when they were younger, she stayed home?"

The agent nodded. "She thought it was better."

"I do, too," Jesse agreed. "Your sister was lucky to have a choice. I don't."

Phillips cleared his throat and quickly moved on. "That brings us to your husband." He looked down and consulted his notes. "Ned Archer?"

"What about him?"

"You're separated?"

"Yes."

"But not divorced?"

Going through this once with Maychick was bad enough. Why did she have to do it all again? "Only for lack of a court date."

"Has there ever been any disagreement about custodial rights?"

"None. He doesn't want Amanda, I do."

"You're sure of that?"

Jesse shot him a glare. She knew he wasn't baiting her on purpose, but that was how she was beginning to feel. "Not all fathers take the two A.M. feeding and carry pictures in their wallets."

"I'm making you uncomfortable," Phillips said mildly.

"Yes, you damn well are."

"Believe me, that wasn't my intention."

"Then stop insinuating that this is all my fault."

Phillips slipped off his glasses, using his thumb and forefinger to massage the sides of his nose. "I'm sorry if I led you to think such a thing."

Deliberately Jesse waited until he'd settled his glasses back in place so that he was able to look her straight in the eye when she began to speak. "There's something I want you to understand," she said firmly. "I'm a good mother. No, dammit, I'm a great mother! If you knew how much I wanted Amanda, if you had any idea how much she means to me—"

"I'm sure you love your daughter very much," Phillips said quietly.

"Then why are you asking me all these questions as if I'm the one who's done something wrong?"

"Believe me, it's just routine. In order to help you it's imperative that we find out as much as we possibly can."

Jesse seldom lost her temper, but neither was she

accustomed to being alternately bullied and patronized. She was tired, battered, aching, and her daughter was missing; and nothing anyone had done so far seemed likely to change any of that.

"Imperative," she snapped. "I'll give you an imperative. Find my daughter! That's the only thing that matters."

Phillips looked at her for a long moment. "Maybe we should take a break." He closed his notebook and rose to his feet. "I'll go see how Special Agent Harvey's doing. When you've calmed down a bit, we can continue."

He strode across the room, then paused in the doorway and looked back to where she was still sitting in her chair. "We really are trying to help, you know," he said quietly. Without waiting for her reply, he continued on into the kitchen.

In silence Jesse watched him leave. She lifted her legs into the chair and wound her arms around her knees, hugging them close. Curled into a tight ball, she realized she was shaking again.

The shrill ring of the telephone cut through the quiet of the house like a clarion call. Agent Phillips was instantly beside her, helping her to her feet. When they got to the kitchen, Officer Rollins was standing beside the phone. He lifted the receiver and handed it to her.

"Hello," Jesse said haltingly. With a smooth whir the tape recorder clicked on.

"Jesse Archer?"

"Yes."

"This is Rita Hollings calling from the *Cranford Journal*—"

"I have nothing to say." Jesse replied quickly, biting down on her lip.

Immediately Agent Phillips reached out and plucked the receiver from her hand, listening for only a moment before cutting in. "This is Special Agent Samuel P. Phillips of the FBI. Ms. Archer has no comment at this time. The police will be happy to keep you apprised of any developments in the case. In the meantime I'm sure you can understand our need to keep this line open. Thank you."

Phillips settled the receiver back in the cradle with finality. "Just what we need," he muttered, then turned and saw Jesse's face. It was ghostly pale. "Are you okay?"

"Yes . . . fine." Jesse shook her head. She felt faint, and there was a strange roaring in her ears. "I just thought . . ."

Phillips took her arm and helped her to a chair. His hand, braced gently between her shoulder blades, guided her head downward until it was between her knees.

Blood was returning to her head in a rush. She closed her eyes, took several deep breaths, and decided she was well enough to sit up.

Phillips looked at her critically. "All right now?"

"Much better. Thank you."

"You're welcome."

Phillips glanced past her toward the phone, his expression thoughtful.

"If he was going to call, he'd have done it by now, wouldn't he?" asked Jesse.

"It's hard to tell. Sometimes they . . . they make you wait on purpose."

"Why?"

He looked away uncomfortably. "So that when the call comes, you'll be anxious, ready to do whatever they say."

"Bastards."

"My sentiments exactly." Phillips nodded toward the living room. "Let's get on with it, shall we? This is one bastard we're going to nail."

The rest of the day passed much the same as the

morning had. Agent Phillips asked questions; Jesse answered. By the time he finished his interrogation, she was sure he knew everything there was to know about her, except perhaps her shoe size and the name of her second-grade teacher. Quietly and efficiently Agent Harvey completed his work while Officer Rollins, buoyed by endless cups of coffee, continued his patient vigil beside the silent phone.

It was late afternoon before Agents Phillips and Harvey were satisfied with the information they'd compiled. With relief Jesse saw them to the door. "I want to keep in touch," she said. "Where can I call you?"

"We'll be setting up a command center at the Cranford Police Station. Until the investigation is concluded, that will be our headquarters. Phone me anytime. If I'm not there, leave a message and I'll get back to you."

As the two agents walked out to their car, Jesse saw Kay coming up the street. "You didn't call," Kay said as she approached. "And then it occurred to me what an idiot I was—of course you wouldn't want to use the phone." She paused, then added carefully, "Have you heard anything?"

"No, nothing."

Kay frowned, then hurried on: "I've got another hour before the twins get back. I asked Denise to keep them late, just in case. Until then I'm all yours."

"Come on in. But do so at your own risk. I know what the place looks like and I haven't got the slightest desire to do a thing about it."

"Who asked you to?" Kay took Jesse's arm and led her to the couch. "Sit, relax, don't move. You look like you're about to shatter into a million pieces."

Kay had always been perceptive. It was one of the reasons they got along so well—they understood each other without always having to talk about it. But now Jesse found it disconcerting to be the object of Kay's concern.

"Maybe I am," she said quietly.

"I'll bet you haven't had anything to eat all day."

"I'm not hungry."

"Of course not. I'll heat up some soup."

"I don't want any soup—"

"It'll make you warm," Kay said firmly. "From the inside out. Besides, it'll give you a good excuse to sit while I clean."

Too tired to argue, Jesse gave in. Several minutes later she took the steaming mug Kay offered her, sipping at it without interest as she sat and waited. The room around her faded from view; it might not have even existed at all. The only thing she cared about now was the telephone, and the possibility—her only hope, really—that it might ring.

She heard Kay working in the kitchen, but couldn't seem to concentrate on the thought. Even when her friend dragged the vacuum cleaner and a large trash bag into the living room and began to work around her, Jesse remained oblivious. Humming to herself, Kay righted and dusted the furniture, picked up broken china, and collected the books that were scattered around the floor. She rehung one small painting; a print whose glass had shattered she leaned against the wall. Finally she decided she'd done the best she could.

Kay put away the cleaning tools and headed for the door. Still Jesse hadn't moved. The soup, barely touched, sat on the coffee table, making a ring.

"I'm leaving now, Jess," Kay said.

Jesse looked up, blinked slowly. "Already?"

"It's almost six. The twins are due home at any minute. But listen, if you want me to go collect them and then come back—"

"No," Jesse said quickly. "That's all right. I'm fine, really."

"You're sure?"

There didn't seem to be any logical way to answer that question. Jesse settled for a nod.

"I hope you don't mind, I fed your Officer Rollins. He looked hungry."

"No . . . I . . . Thanks."

"Don't mention it." Kay looked at Jesse and frowned. "Listen, try and get some sleep, okay? It'll be good for you."

"Sure," Jesse agreed. As the front door swung shut she rested her elbows in her lap and propped her chin in her hands. Doubtless there were things she ought to be doing, but she hadn't the slightest idea what.

Usually at this time of night she'd be watching the news and feeding Amanda her dinner. They'd sit together on the bed, with Amanda propped up a bank of pillows; Jesse discussing world events as Peter Jennings revealed them, and Amanda gurgling delightedly at everything she said.

But now, without her daughter, nothing seemed important enough to bother with. Indeed, nothing seemed to have any meaning at all.

In the house the shadows lengthened, until finally darkness came. Officer Rollins walked through the rooms, switching on the lights. "Why don't you go on to bed?" he said.

Jesse shook her head. Now that it was dark, she couldn't imagine going back into that bedroom, that bed. The last time she'd fallen asleep there she'd awakened into the middle of a nightmare. No, she'd stay in the living room, thank you. With the lights on.

"What time is it?"

"Almost eight o'clock."

Jesse digested that information. The day was almost over. "He isn't going to call, is he?" she said quietly.

Rollins's eyes were filled with sympathy. "It doesn't look that way."

"How much longer will you wait?"

"Another hour or so, I guess. After that . . ." Rollins shrugged, but didn't finish the thought. Jesse knew what he meant. After that it would be time to give up, to accept the fact that whoever had Amanda had something much more complex in mind than a simple exchange for money.

"Officer Rollins?"

"Hmm?"

"Would you do something for me?"

"Be happy to." He seemed relieved at the idea that he might finally be of service.

"Upstairs, in my daughter's nursery . . . I can't face going up there right now, but there's something I'd like to have. In the crib there's a doll with blond hair and a pink dress. It's Amanda's favorite. Would you mind bringing it down here for me?"

"Not at all."

A moment later Rollins delivered the pretty baby doll into Jesse's hands. She'd thought Amanda too young to choose a toy as her favorite, but as soon as Jesse'd given the doll to her, Amanda had giggled gleefully and clutched it to her. They'd seldom been separated since.

Now, cradling the doll in her arms, Jesse began to hum softly under her breath. The sweet strains of a lullaby, the same one she used to rock Amanda to sleep, filled her head. Slowly she lowered her head and let her eyes drift shut. Darkness veiled her thoughts like a shroud. Embracing the doll, clasping it to her like a child, Jesse finally slept.

SIX

The baby arrived in the dead of night. The woman stayed up, waiting what seemed like hours, to receive her. But when she came, she was perfect, as perfect as the room that awaited her. The woman had been preparing for this moment for weeks.

She'd painted the nursery a soft shade of pink, and the cradle she'd chosen was an antique, carefully refinished, then rubbed till it shone. The woman had crocheted the soft blanket herself, and hand-stitched the delicate sheets, tiny pink rosebuds on a background the color of heavy cream. The miniature dresser was stenciled with bunnies. The cushion on the small chair beside it matched. There were damask curtains hanging at the window, and a closet filled with lace dresses waiting to be worn. It was a room fit for a princess: it was just what the woman wanted it to be.

She unwrapped the baby's swaddling blanket, protection against the damp night air. Even in sleep the infant's tiny fists curled, her plump legs kicked. She had spirit, all right. Yes, she would do.

Slowly the woman removed the baby's clothes, her

fingers fumbling over the unfamiliar task. The soft flannel nightgown was stripped away. The disposable diaper followed. Now the baby was naked, as she'd been born. That was as it should be. For what was this night if not a rebirth, a time of new beginnings?

With gentle fingers the woman explored every detail of the child. She felt a sense of wonder, and awe as well, that a baby so beautiful could exist, that a child such as this should come to her.

Her fingers skimmed over a ticklish spot and the infant gave a startled cry. Her blue eyes opened, blinking in surprise at the unfamiliar touch. With soothing words the woman lifted the baby to her. The child turned her face inward, hungry lips reaching, seeking. But there was no pliant nipple waiting, no warm sweet smell of milk. Instead she found only a cotton shirt that scratched her cheek and the scant comfort of a strange voice, strange hands.

She began to wail in earnest now, her cries defiant and impossibly loud. The woman shushed her, but to no avail. She began to rock, swaying back and forth on her feet. And still the baby cried. She sang one song and then another; not lullabies, but deep, bluesy hymns, the only songs she knew. And still the baby cried.

The woman didn't know what to do. She didn't know how to make the baby stop. It wasn't supposed to be like this. Everything was supposed to be perfect. She loved this child, and the child must love her.

The woman's hand came up, fingers stumbling over the buttons of her blouse. She parted the material and pushed it aside, then did the same for her bra. The baby lay cradled in the crook of her arm. Hesitantly the woman guided the infant to her breast.

There was no milk, but there was the warmth of flesh against flesh, the comfort of a nipple to fill her mouth. Gradually the baby's protests quieted. Slowly her eyes closed.

With a fierceness born of devotion, the woman hugged the sleeping child to her. "You're mine," she whispered. "We'll be together always, you and I. Forever and ever. You're mine, little girl, you're mine."

SEVEN

Day Two

Dawn came and went as the morning sun shifted slowly across the living room. By the time it reached the chair where Jesse slept, it had been up for several hours. She felt the warmth on the back of her neck first. The soft skin, always covered before by her hair, prickled with the unfamiliar sensation.

Slowly she opened her eyes. Still groggy from sleep, Jesse blinked in confusion. Why was it light out? Had she slept through Amanda's five A.M. feeding? Surely the baby's hungry cries would have awakened her. They always had before. . . .

Frowning, Jesse lifted her head and looked around. The movement brought a spasm of pain that shot through her shoulder and up her neck. With it came the terrible knowledge that had been hovering at the edge of conscious thought. No one had awakened her because there was no one else in the house. Since early yesterday morning—twenty-four hours now—Amanda had been missing.

Throwing back the light blanket that covered her, Jesse scrambled to her feet. Her body was sore enough to protest every move. When Amanda's doll tumbled to the floor beside the chair, the effort to bend down and retrieve it brought a grimace to her face. Leaving it, Jesse hurried out to the kitchen.

Officer Rollins was obviously long gone. The only sign that he'd been there at all was the rinsed coffee mug, drying in the dish drainer. A note from Kay was tacked, eye level, on the refrigerator. "I checked back in while you were asleep. Amanda's in our prayers, and you are, too. If there's anything else we can do, CALL!"

As her gaze skimmed over the green, glowing digits on the microwave, Jesse realized that she'd lost nearly twelve hours. The whole night had passed, and still there was no news. Frustration flared first, followed quickly by anger. How could her body have betrayed her like that? She should have been up. She should have been doing . . . something. *Anything*.

Jesse closed her eyes and drew a deep, steadying breath. It should have filled her, but somehow it didn't. Her body remained empty, as hollow, and as fragile, as a cast-off shell.

She lifted both hands, fingers grasping the counter in a grip solid enough to concentrate on. It was then that Jesse realized the message light on her answering machine was blinking. For a moment she couldn't seem to move, neither toward it or away. The possibilities were paralyzing. The kidnapper? Detective Maychick? Another reporter?

Then she hit the playback button and the machine spun to life. She was holding her breath, her hands unconsciously clasped as if in prayer, when the beep sounded and her husband's voice filled the room.

"What the hell is going on?" Ned demanded. "Jesse, where are you? Do you realize I've spent the last hour being grilled by a policeman? Detective Paycheck, or something like that. He has this crazy idea that I've got the baby. You put him up to it, Jess, don't tell me you didn't. You're not going to get away with this kind of harassment. Get back to me immediately."

Jesse straightened and headed for the coffee machine. There was nothing like a dose of her soon-to-be ex-husband to get her up and running. Talk about egocentric. Had he even stopped ranting long enough to realize that if she didn't have Amanda, and he didn't have Amanda, then their child was missing? Or, in his haste to make accusations, had that salient fact passed right by him? The baby, indeed. Was it possible he didn't even remember his own daughter's name?

All right, so maybe she should have called him. In fact she seemed to remember making a promise to Detective Maychick to that effect. But on the other hand she'd been busy with far more important things to worry about than Ned Archer's precious sensibilities. Was it her fault they were so far removed from each other that she'd forgotten all about him?

As she rounded the counter, Jesse's eye caught an unexpected flash of color: Amanda's plastic seat. Someone, probably Kay, had tucked it away in the corner. Any other morning it would have been out on the table. Amanda would have been settled there, cooing and batting at the large plastic keys that hung from the chair's handle as Jesse made them both breakfast.

"Ow!" Jesse barked as she banged her shin on the cabinet. Abruptly the vision cleared. The kitchen was empty, and silent as a tomb. How could a routine only four months old already be so ingrained? How could the absence of one tiny baby leave behind a void this huge?

Jesse snatched open the door to the broom closet and tossed the seat inside, out of sight. So much for answers. Working by rote, she dumped out the stale remains of yesterday's coffee, rinsed the pot, and set up a fresh brew.

She would have to talk to Ned, that much was clear. But nobody said she had to hurry. It would have been bad enough trying to explain what had happened before Detective Maychick went to see him. Now she wouldn't even know where to begin.

Of course Ned would blame her. He'd blamed her for everything else that had gone wrong in their lives, why should this be any different?

The machine perked, then filled. Absently Jesse poured herself a cup and drank it where she stood.

She could imagine what Ned was going to say. *You thought you were superwoman, didn't you? You thought you could do it all. Most women wouldn't dream of raising a baby all by themselves, but not Jesse Archer. She can do anything.*

The irony of it was, there had been a time when she'd thought she could have it all. She'd been younger then, and newly in love, entrenched in a fast-track career that would take her straight to the top. At the time anything had seemed possible.

But not anymore. Now she knew better. She hadn't been able to save Christina, and she hadn't been able to save her marriage. And if it wasn't bad enough that she'd taken the failures to heart, both Ned and her parents had been right there, all too eager to point out who was to blame.

So now Ned was on the warpath again. What else was new? Ever since he'd left, he'd done his best to make her life miserable. And unfortunately for her Ned's best was pretty damn good. When the divorce petitions had first been filed, he'd requested alimony. Two weeks ago her lawyer had informed her that Ned had lost his job and was now demanding interim support. One more thing to hammer out in court.

Or to be more precise, thought Jesse, one more twist of the screws. No matter that from her point of view the problems with their marriage had been as much his fault as hers. As far as Ned was concerned, he'd been wronged. And he was determined to have his revenge.

The question was, just how far would he go?

Jesse finished the last bit of coffee in a long gulp as she contemplated the possibility of her ex-husband's involvement in her baby's disappearance. Yesterday she'd dismissed the notion out of hand. Ned had no interest in Amanda, and thereby had no reason for wanting to abduct her. But that logic had one basic flaw: it totally overlooked Ned's capacity for malicious game playing. Could he possibly be enough of a bastard to use his own daughter to achieve his ends?

Anxious now to find out what Detective Maychick might have learned in his interview, Jesse reached for the phone. Surely if there'd been any real news, good or bad, the detective would have called. On the other hand, from what she'd seen yesterday, Maychick didn't seem like the sort who'd go out of his way to keep her informed.

Which only meant that she'd be the one to chase after him, Jesse decided as she picked up the receiver and punched out the number. Okay. She'd dealt with recalcitrant workers before. She'd deal with Detective Maychick, too.

If she ever got the chance. According to the officer who answered the phone at the Cranford Police Department, Detective Maychick was in a meeting. If she wished to leave her name and number, he would pass on the message as soon as possible. Jesse did, then broke the connection and dialed again, this time to Amanda's day-care center, where she told the director that her daughter would be away indefinitely. That call complete, she made a third, to her boss at National Brands.

"I get two weeks' vacation this year, Gus. I'm taking it, starting today."

"Very funny, Jess. What's the matter, you need the morning off? The timing isn't perfect, but I guess we can spare you for a few hours—"

"Two weeks, Gus. I need the time."

"Don't we all?" Gus asked, then paused. "Look, is something wrong?"

"Very wrong," Jesse said heavily, then quickly forestalled his next question. "It's personal."

"Can I help?"

"You can give me the time off."

"Do I have a choice?"

"No."

Gus took only a moment to weigh his options. "In that case consider it done."

"I've been working pretty closely with Laurel on the Frooties launch. She'll know where all my notes are."

"She can't take your place, Jess."

"Someone will have to."

"Are you okay?"

"No."

"Right." A brisk beat hummed through the line. As usual Gus was drumming his fingers on the receiver. "Will you be home if we need you?"

"Maybe, I don't know."

"Okay." The drumming stopped. "You take it easy. We'll try to cover things on this end. And Jess?"

"Hmmm?"

"Whatever it is, good luck."

She carried the sentiment with her into the bedroom, where she pulled off her clothes and headed for the shower. Gus might be miffed, but there was nothing he could do. For all the same reasons that Ned resented her commitment to her job, she was too good an employee to give ultimatums to.

Six months ago the thought of taking off on the eve of a national launch would have been inconceivable. Now she didn't even have to think twice. Laurel and Gus would do the best they could to cover for her. With any luck that would be good enough. And if not, well, who the hell cared whether or not Middle America got its Frooties by July 1 anyway?

Steam and hot water took the edge off her soreness.

By the time Jesse finished her shower and went to brush her teeth, she could raise her arm above shoulder level without wincing. At least as long as she didn't look in the mirror.

The day before the bruises had been red. Now, examining them dispassionately, Jesse saw they were shades of green and yellow. All in all it wasn't an improvement. The swelling in her lip had gone down. The skin beneath her eye was turning black. Makeup would help. With her head haphazardly shorn she looked like a refugee from some war-torn, third-world nation. The worst part was, she looked better than she felt.

A quick rummage through the top of the coat closet turned up three gloves, two mittens, and a moth-eaten beret. She fared better in the junk drawer of her dresser. The first scarf she found was too small, but the second was large enough to cover her hair and knot under her chin. The addition of sunglasses did the rest. She didn't exactly look normal, but she'd seen rock stars who looked worse.

It was a ten-minute drive to the police station. Once there she was made to wait another fifteen minutes until Detective Maychick was ready to see her. A uniformed policeman escorted her to his office, which turned out to be a square box of a room, tucked away at the end of the corridor.

Maychick's desk was cluttered with papers and files. A basket in one corner, labeled "incoming," overflowed onto the floor. Though the presence of a peeling leather border indicated there was a blotter underneath, Jesse doubted the detective had seen it in months. Three coffee mugs lined one side of the desk. Two were old enough to have left rings. The odor of old cigarette smoke lingered faintly in the air, but the only ashtray Jesse saw was clean and pushed to one side.

As she entered the room Maychick grasped the arms of his desk chair and heaved himself to his feet. His suit today was brown, cut to the same nondescript lines as the one he'd worn the day before. Though it was early, he'd already loosened his tie and unbuttoned the top of his shirt.

"I got your message, Ms. Archer." His version of courtesy satisfied, Maychick settled back in his seat. "You didn't have to come down. I'd have returned your call just as soon as I had a chance."

Jesse glanced around and saw a wooden, straight-backed chair pushed up against one wall. Though the detective hadn't offered her a seat, she took it anyway. "I placed that call over an hour ago. What if I'd had something to say that was of vital importance to the investigation?"

"Then I assume you'd have found a way of conveying that fact to the officer who took the message."

Hands knotted in her lap, Jesse bit back a sharp retort. Yesterday his gruff manner had seemed like a sign of authority. At least that's what she'd tried to make herself believe. Today, however, there was no getting around the fact that he felt she was wasting his valuable time. That being the case, she'd cut straight to the chase.

"It's been twenty-four hours since Amanda was taken, Detective Maychick. I know you've managed to light a fire under my ex-husband. Have you accomplished anything else?"

Maychick crossed his arms over his chest. She didn't have to be an expert in body language to know what that meant.

"As a matter of fact we have. In cases such as these there are certain prescribed methods that the department follows. Any one of these procedures might be likely to turn up a clue that would point us in the right direction. My men have devoted the last twenty-four hours to working in those areas."

Jesse's lips pursed in irritation. He might as well have been reading from a cue card. "What exactly might those procedures be?"

"For starters, we're asking questions. We've already

spoken to all the neighbors on your street. Today we'll spread the circle a little wider."

"Did you find anyone who saw anything?"

Maychick leaned back in his chair and shook his head. The chair creaked loudly beneath his weight. "Too bad, too. I thought we might have had a shot—nice family neighborhood like that. Some of these areas you go into, even if people saw, they don't talk. Here, I figured that would have been different. Of course, on the other hand, the fact that it's a quiet neighborhood worked against us, too."

"How?"

He shuffled through some papers until he'd found what he wanted. "According to my notes, you said the man left your house at approximately three-thirty A.M."

"That's right."

"In some parts of town people would still be up and around then. So far, on Portland Road, we haven't even found an insomniac."

"But you'll keep looking."

It was a statement, not a question. Maychick treated it as such. Frowning, he set the paper aside. "Also, we had a roadblock on your street last night from two A.M. until dawn."

"What would that accomplish?"

"We wanted to see who'd pass through. Who knows? Maybe someone's on their way to the early shift at the hospital and takes that route every day."

He had to know what her next question was going to be. But that didn't stop him from making her ask it. "And did you find anyone like that?"

Again Maychick consulted his notes. If he'd simply let her see them, Jesse could have saved them both a lot of time.

"Three cars," Maychick read. "No regulars. We'll try one more time tonight."

One more time. The words had such an air of finality about them. "And then what?"

"And then we'll continue to explore other avenues. We have the list you gave Officer Rollins yesterday. There are people working on setting up interviews now." Maychick picked up a pen and began to doodle. "If you like, we can run through the list again now, just in case you might have forgotten anybody."

"Officer Rollins was very thorough," said Jesse. She wasn't above flattery if it would help. "I think the list is complete."

"I couldn't help but notice you didn't list many friends. Services, yes." His drawing became a large arrow, with smaller ones shooting off from it in all directions. "Visitors, no."

"I work, Detective Maychick. I have to support myself and my child. On top of that I spend as much time with Amanda as I can. That doesn't leave much room in my life for anything else."

"I don't know. I guess it's just hard for me to imagine a young woman like yourself with no social life at all." Maychick's shrug was deliberately casual. "Then again your neighbors bear you out."

Shocked, Jesse could only stare. "You've been questioning them about *me?*"

"We've been asking them about everything and everyone." Maychick tore the doodle off his pad and wadded it up. "That's what a thorough investigation is." He held his pen poised above the clean sheet of paper. "If you have anything you want to add to your statement, I can take it down now."

"I went through the sequence of events three times," Jesse said evenly. "I hardly think I forgot anything."

"You never know, sometimes things occur to you later. Things that maybe didn't seem so important at the time. If there's anything you haven't told us, Ms. Archer, it's better we hear it from you than your neighbors."

Outrage bubbled up within her. "You can't possibly mean that you think I had something to do with my own daughter's disappearance." Jesse's hand flew to her face, her hair. "Do you think I did this to myself?"

"Stranger things have happened." Maychick met her glare without a flinch. "At the moment I'm not ruling anything out."

Discomfited, it was Jesse who looked away first. Usually she wasn't a fidgeter. Now, as the focus of Maychick's scrutiny, she couldn't seem to sit still.

"I understand you talked to Ned," she said.

He left her hanging long enough to indicate that he'd noted the change of subject. "Your husband? Yeah, yesterday afternoon."

"And?"

"He has an alibi for the time period in question. We'll be checking it out."

"He got the impression you thought of him as a suspect."

Maychick lifted a brow. "I guess that means you finally got around to calling him."

The rebuke hit home—as it was no doubt intended to. "Actually, no. He left a message on my machine."

"Well, when you do talk to him, tell him the same thing I told you. Right now we're looking into all the possibilities." Maychick reached for a piece of paper and slid it to her across the desk. "Your statement was typed up yesterday. I'll need you to read it and sign it before you go."

She'd say one thing for Detective Maychick. Subtle, he wasn't. Fishing in her bag for a pen, Jesse scanned the paper he'd handed her: a flat, emotionless recounting of the events two nights earlier. Satisfied it was accurate, she scribbled a signature on the bottom.

By the time she was done, Maychick was already on his feet. "Anything happens," he said, ushering her to the door. "We'll be in touch."

Jesse paused, resisting the light pressure of his hand on her arm. "And if nothing happens?"

"It will." Maychick swallowed heavily. "It always does."

EIGHT

Detective Maychick's dismissal was so persuasive, Jesse was out the front door and halfway down the stairs before she remembered she had another option. The day before Agent Phillips had mentioned that he was going to be setting up a command center somewhere in the police station. Turning back inside, Jesse had to ask three officers before she found one who knew where it was.

Tucked away at the end of another hall, Phillips's office was the same size and shape as the other she'd just seen. That, however, was all they had in common. While Maychick's work space was close and cluttered, this one was neat almost to the point of sterility. There were no papers on the desk, no files scattered around. Nor was there any sign of Agent Phillips.

The door was partway open. Jesse pushed it further and walked inside, wondering whether it made sense to wait. Just because Agent Phillips had set up a temporary office in Cranford didn't mean he would be there every day. Maybe leaving him a note would be better.

Unsure, Jesse scanned the empty office once more.

Two days ago she'd considered herself a decisive person. Now nothing she said, or did, felt right.

Voices outside in the hallway had her retreating back to the door. Agent Phillips appeared, a briefcase in one hand, a cup of coffee in the other. "I'll get back to you," he said to a uniformed officer who kept on walking. Then he turned and saw Jesse.

"Ms. Archer." Phillips started to smile, then seemed to think better of it. Edging past her, he set both coffee and briefcase on the desk, then shrugged out of his suit jacket and slung it over the back of his chair. "How are you?"

"I'm . . . all right."

Ignoring her response, he looked from the bruise on her mouth to the slightly stiff set of her shoulders. "You want to take off your sunglasses?"

Jesse did, lifting her chin defiantly.

"See a doctor?"

"No."

He muttered under his breath and dragged the visitor's chair away from the wall. "Sit. Want a cup of coffee?"

"No, thank you."

Phillips sipped at his own mug and grimaced. "Just as well." He sat down himself, unbuttoning his cuffs one by one, then rolling his sleeves up over his forearms. "If you're here because you want to know that we're doing everything possible to find your daughter, let me start by assuring you that we are." He snapped open his briefcase, pulled out a file, and set it on the corner of his desk. "I know that the last twenty-four hours probably seem like a lifetime to you, but in that time we've opened a number of avenues of inquiry."

"I know." Jesse realized her fingers were clasped together tightly in her lap. Deliberately she eased them apart. "I spoke with Detective Maychick a few minutes ago. He told me about the questions and the roadblocks and the interviews."

Phillips flipped the switch on his computer. "Did

he explain about the National Crime Information Center?" He looked up in time to see her frown. "No? Come here then, I'll show you."

Together they bent over the screen. "The NCIC is a national network based in Washington, D.C." He punched a few keys and called up the file. "A missing-child record was entered for Amanda yesterday, which means that her description has been distributed nationwide. It's also been hooked into the On-Line Law Enforcement System in Connecticut. If anyone should report having seen her, we would find out about it within minutes."

"She's only four months old," Jesse said quietly. "What are the chances of someone really noticing a baby that age, much less recognizing her from a description?"

"Not as great as we might wish," Phillips admitted. He saved the file and the screen went blank. "Still, it's a good system, and the more wheels we set in motion . . ."

Silently Jesse nodded her agreement. Still, she couldn't help wondering. Was that all there was? The afternoon before Agent Phillips had seemed so competent, so confident. Now a whole day was gone. She was happy that wheels were turning, but surely there had to be something more.

Aware suddenly that he'd stopped speaking, Jesse looked up. Agent Phillips was simply watching, and waiting. "We *will* find your daughter, Ms. Archer," he said, when he had her attention once more. "You've got to believe that."

"Do you?"

Jesse had expected a glib reply. Instead Phillips pondered his answer for several seconds. "I believe we will do everything in our power to bring Amanda home to you," he said finally. "And that's a damn impressive team on your side. In the meantime I want you to do something for us."

"Yes? What is it?"

"Keep turning things over in your mind. See if you

can come up with anything, no matter how small, that might get us started in the right direction."

"But I told you—"

A wave of his hand silenced her objection. "This wasn't only an abduction, Ms. Archer, it was an attack against you. Maybe, even though you don't realize it, you know the reason. Someone singled you out. We need to know why."

Jesse didn't have an answer for that. When Phillips reached over and turned off the computer, its sudden silence only underscored her own. Instead she settled for changing the subject.

"There's one more thing I need to ask."

"Shoot."

"Detective Maychick interviewed my ex-husband yesterday. Will you be doing the same?"

Phillips picked up his coffee cup and took a long, slow sip. "No, I won't."

"Why not?"

"It has to do with jurisdiction. Kidnapping is a matter for the FBI. Domestic squabbles aren't. If the local police become convinced that your daughter's disappearance has to do with a custody argument, I'll have to bow out of the case."

"Then you're not investigating him at all?"

"Not at this time, no."

"But that's not fair."

"As it happens I agree with you. But that's the way the system operates." "Yesterday you told me you were sure your husband wasn't involved. Have you changed your mind?"

"No . . . That is, not exactly. I'm sure Ned doesn't want custody of Amanda."

"But?"

"But I know he's very angry with me." The words came out in a rush. "I'm just not sure how far that anger might cause him to go."

"Did you tell that to Detective Maychick?"

"No."

"Why not?"

Jesse lifted her head. "He thinks Ned has an alibi."

"Your husband isn't my province, Ms. Archer, but I'll mention your feelings to the detective."

Phillips's hand came up, his thumb and forefinger massaging the ridge of his nose beneath his glasses. Jesse had seen him make the same gesture yesterday. Was it a sign of frustration, or was he just taking some time to think?

Then he looked up and the glasses settled back into place. "One more thing—yesterday you mentioned that you have parents living in Pennsylvania. Have you spoken to them yet?"

"I haven't had a chance." The excuse was inadequate, but Jesse had no desire to explain. "We're not a terribly close family."

Phillips's skeptical expression said clearly what he did not. How close did you have to be to share something like this? Amanda was their granddaughter. Surely they deserved to be involved.

"I should have called." Jesse found herself answering the unspoken rebuff. "I'll do it this morning, as soon as I get home."

"Actually, since you haven't done so already, I'd just as soon you didn't." Phillips opened a desk drawer, pulled out paper and pen, and jotted down a note. "Instead I'll get in touch with the Philadelphia office and send someone out to see them."

"Why would you want to do that?"

"The fact of the matter is, a stranger may have done this to you. But it would make more sense if it was someone you knew. Especially when families aren't close, disputes such as this have been known to happen."

"No." Jesse shook her head firmly. "My parents and I may not agree on a lot of things—"

"Like how to raise a child, perhaps?"

Perceptive, wasn't he? Jesse's head was still shaking. "It doesn't matter. My parents are not violent people.

There's no way they could have been involved in something like this."

"Not even if the end result had turned out a bit differently than they'd envisioned?"

"Not even then." Jesse's conviction was absolute. She leaned down and retrieved her purse from the chair beside the desk. "You will keep me informed of anything that comes up?"

"Certainly." Like Detective Maychick, Agent Phillips walked her to the door. Unlike the detective, Jesse got the impression he was sorry to see her go. "Feel free to call, as often as you like. It doesn't have to be something important." He contemplated her bruised face. "Have you had anything to eat yet today?"

Jesse shook her head.

"Yesterday?"

"Not really."

"Do yourself a favor. Get something down, whether you want to or not. You've got to heal as well. You won't do your daughter any good if you don't stay strong."

"I'll try."

"Do better than that."

That brought her up short. "Pardon me?"

"There are a lot of things I like about my job," said Phillips. "And one I don't. In my work I see a lot of victims, people in the midst of catastrophe. Yesterday you impressed the hell out of me. You were mad, and you didn't care who knew it. With all that bastard had done, he still hadn't managed to knock the fight out of you. I can't tell you how much I admired you for that. Don't lose that feeling. It'll help us more than you can imagine."

For a moment Jesse didn't know what to say. Yesterday her hopes had been higher, and her anguish that much closer to the surface. Today, confronted by the excruciatingly slow pace of the investigation, she'd felt herself growing numb, blocking out the things she couldn't seem to deal with.

Now, however, with Phillips's words, she felt

renewed strength flowing through her. Of course she would work for her daughter's return. Of course she would believe. Amanda would be coming home. The question was when, not if.

"Thank you," she said simply.

Jesse meant to drive straight home, call Ned, have it out with him, and get it over with. At least then she'd know if her suspicions had any merit. At least then she could stop worrying about what Detective Maychick might, or might not, overlook. But somehow, as she turned her car onto Portland Road, she found herself stopping at the gray house on the corner.

Kay's station wagon was sitting in the driveway. Jesse pulled in and parked behind it. The kitchen door was standing open. Jesse knocked lightly on the screen, then stuck her head in. Kay was sitting at the table, engrossed in a pile of papers.

"Hi! Come on in." Kay dropped her pencil and leaped up. "How are you feeling?"

"Okay." Jesse tried for a smile. "All things considered."

"Has there been any news?"

"Not yet."

"Is there anything I can do?"

Jesse shook her head. "The police seem to think they have things well in hand."

Kay's brow lowered at that, but she didn't comment. Boxes were piled haphazardly about the room. She steered Jesse around them and found her a seat. "Book fair," she said. "Don't pay any attention. How I let the Young Women's League rope me into running this thing, I'll never know."

"Go on. You love it."

"Maybe." Kay sighed. "It's a curse."

"Where are Kevin and Michael?"

"With the baby-sitter for the morning. It was the only way I was going to be able to get any work done at all."

"Oh." Jesse swallowed her disappointment. Of course she'd wanted to see Kay. But after twenty-four hours in a house as silent as a tomb, she hadn't realized how much she'd been looking forward to the twins' cheerful, noisy distraction. "Well then, I won't get in your way, either. I just wanted to stop by and say thanks for everything you did yesterday."

"Don't mention it. I mean that. And don't even think of leaving. You look like you could use some company. And as it happens, I was just about to take a break."

"But—"

"But nothing." Kay stood over her, hands propped on her hips. "Have you ever won an argument with me yet?"

"I'm sure I must have won at least one."

"I doubt it."

"Only because I lack your gift for talking people to death."

"If you've got it, flaunt it." Kay walked out to the middle of the room and began stacking the boxes to move them out of the way.

"Want some help?"

"It's done now." Kay eyed the space she'd cleared. "Here, slide that chair over."

Jesse did as she was told.

"Now sit back down."

"Why would I want to do that?" Jesse eyed her friend warily.

Kay, rummaging in the drawer beside the sink, tossed her answer back over her shoulder. "Because this way you won't have to go around wearing a scarf over your head for the next six months."

It was a useful drawer to have, Jesse decided, for it yielded both a pair of scissors and a comb. "Have you ever cut anyone's hair before?"

"Sure," Kay say breezily. She undid the scarf and tossed it aside. "I do the twins all the time."

"Kevin has a buzz cut."

Kay fluffed what remained of Jesse's hair. "No

problem, so do you." Jesse's hands flew to her head. Gently Kay disengaged them. "Trust me."

"Now, why would I want to do a thing like that?"

"That's the spirit." Kay began to snip. What she lacked in finesse, she made up for in enthusiasm. Within minutes she'd smoothed out the worst of the spikes and layered the choppy ends. "A few years ago we'd simply have dyed this green and put a ring in your nose," she said when she had finished.

"Puh-lease." Jesse reached for the mirror Kay held out and studied the effect. She'd never had short hair before, and never particularly wanted it, either. Still it could have looked worse. "That's not bad."

"Not bad?" Kay snatched the mirror back. "Considering what I had to work with, it's a miracle." The mirror, scissors, and comb were tossed back into the drawer. "Now, how about some lunch?"

"I don't want to put you out—"

"Good. You can slice the tomatoes."

Calmly and efficiently Kay put Jesse to work. There was such an air of normality to the small tasks—opening a can of tuna, mixing in the mayonnaise—that Jesse was able to lose herself in them. Grief had stripped the color from her world and left it gray. Now, though she didn't forget, for a few minutes she was able to set the emotion aside. Brief though the respite was, it left her feeling revitalized.

They pushed the papers aside and ate at the kitchen table. The meal was quick. Even so, by the time they finished eating, then piled their plates in the sink, Jesse found herself growing restless.

"I should be going," she said as a loud shriek sounded from outside.

"Chicken." Kay laughed. "Do my ears deceive me, or have the little dynamos returned?"

The screen door flew open, banging against the wall. "We're home!" Michael yelled as Kevin bounded into the kitchen and wrapped his greasy hands around his mother's waist. "Are you glad to see us?"

"Of course I'm glad to see you." Kay leaned down for a smooch that left a long streak of dirt across her cheek. "I'll be even more thrilled once you're cleaned up. The powder room's that way. Don't forget to use soap."

"Hey, cool!" cried Kevin, opening the nearest box. "Books!"

Michael leaned in for a look. "Are they kid books or what?"

"Not until you wash your hands. Now march!"

The twins' baby-sitter appeared in the doorway. She was a chunky woman with short blond hair and solid features. Early forties, Jesse guessed. Maybe a bit older.

"Halfway down the block they ran on ahead," the woman said through the screen. "I'm not as young as I used to be."

"You're not the only one," Kay replied. "Come on in. Let me find my wallet." Her purse was on the counter. She began to rummage through it. "Jesse, Denise Connelly. Denise, this is Jesse Archer. You may have bumped into each other here before."

"Possibly," said Denise, staring with obvious interest.

For a moment Jesse was startled by the woman's scrutiny. Then she remembered what she looked like and lifted a self-conscious hand to her face.

Denise just kept talking. "You're the lady with the new baby. Kay said you might be calling me when you wanted to start getting out again."

"Yes." The word stuck in Jesse's throat.

The twins came rushing back, and she turned away. She'd wanted to see the boys; but now, as they attacked the boxes with four-year-old exuberance, it suddenly seemed an effort to exist from one moment to the next. She'd thought they'd be a source of comfort. Instead they were a devastating reminder of what she'd lost.

Blindly Jesse reached for the screen door and shoved it open. She was halfway down the block before she realized she hadn't even said good-bye.

NINE

There was another message from Ned on Jesse's machine when she got home. In the interim between the two calls he seemed to have calmed down. Now, however, he was convinced she was purposely dodging him. "I'm not going to keep leaving messages," Ned finished by saying. "I'll be home all day, so get your butt in gear and get down here."

Nothing like a little charm to smooth the way. Jesse'd see Ned, all right. She had to. But nobody said she had to hurry.

She set the machine to rewind, then wandered over to the window that faced the small backyard. Outside, everything was lush and green, plants thriving in the wake of the wet spring. One corner of the yard was cleared, the dirt turned over. She'd meant to plant a garden, but somehow never found the time.

Time. For years it had seemed like there was never enough. Now, suddenly, it was all Jesse had left.

The plot in the corner was brown and dry and as barren as she felt herself. She'd planned to grow all of Amanda's vegetables. She'd bought several how-to books, and even some seeds. But somehow she'd never gotten around to planting. Between her job and her baby the work had simply never gotten done.

Jesse stood and stared at the empty plot. Maybe it was no wonder Ned had walked out. If she was too busy to manage a garden, what did that say for the amount of time she'd had to devote to her marriage? Not that she was willing to shoulder all the blame. Ned had known when they met that her career was important to her. And yet, it was clear now that he'd expected her to change.

And if she had? Jesse wondered. If she could have been what Ned wanted, where would they be today?

In the beginning it had all seemed so easy. Four years ago she'd been National Brands' youngest product manager, riding high on the crest of a successful new product launch. Nothing in her personal life could approach that kind of satisfaction. Maybe she'd even stopped expecting it to.

Then she'd met Ned Archer, and overnight everything had changed.

To give Ned credit, he'd softened her hard edges. He admired her drive while feeling no compunction to emulate it. For Jesse, who'd been indoctrinated early with the idea that work was everything, Ned's attitude was a refreshing change. It was he who'd encouraged her to loosen up, he who'd given her the freedom to relax and simply enjoy.

Within weeks Jesse knew she was in love. Looking back now, she could see that things had moved too fast. But at the time it had all seemed perfect. Even her parents approved. Two months after their first meeting Jesse and Ned were married in a small ceremony on Christmas Eve.

It didn't take long for Jesse to realize that their life together wasn't going to be nearly as smooth as she'd imagined. Ned was smart, but he was immature. He was also lazy, and not above relying on his looks and charm to slide by. In spite of that, when Jesse earned a promotion and a raise to go with it, Ned couldn't seem to understand how her career had passed his own.

That was when the tests had started: silly, little trials Ned devised, which he seemed to think would measure the depth of her devotion to him. One time when Jesse was working late, he'd called and claimed to be sick, requesting that she pick up some medicine. Only when Jesse arrived home and found him waiting did she realize that he was timing the minutes until her return. Another time he'd planned a barbecue of his own on the day of Jesse's company picnic, then blithely told her to choose.

Yet in spite of all that she'd still thought the marriage could work. No relationship was perfect; every couple she knew had their ups and downs. Besides, there were still times when she and Ned were together, when they were as attuned to each other as they'd been on their first day together. They were simply ironing out the kinks, Jesse told herself. A good marriage was something to be worked at, not taken for granted; and she intended to give their relationship all the time it needed.

It was Ned who'd first suggested they have a baby. Even now Jesse found herself wondering whether he'd really believed she wouldn't see through to his real motives. But if he'd secretly hoped motherhood would wean her away from her career, so what? She adored children and had always hoped to have several. The idea seemed like the perfect solution for them both.

Jesse conceived quickly, but there were problems with the pregnancy. The demands of her job placed her under a lot of stress, as did Ned's continuing discontent at home. Though she'd always been a smoker, Jesse gave up the habit as soon as the pregnancy was confirmed. Still, her doctor warned her that under the circumstances there was a good chance she wouldn't carry the baby to term.

Her water had begun to leak in the twenty-fifth week. Immediately Jesse had been admitted to St. Simon's Hospital. She was put on drugs to stop her contractions, but several days later when an infection developed, the baby had to be delivered anyway.

At birth Christina weighed less than two pounds and the doctors were not optimistic about her chances for survival. She was placed in an incubator and fed intravenously through needles attached to her skull. For the first few days Jesse remained at the hospital day and night, monitoring her daughter's progress and doing anything she could to help.

Ned's initial visit lasted four hours; his second less than two. Christina had the best medical help available, he argued. And aside from that they were barely allowed even to touch her. Why did Jesse need to spend so much time at the hospital, doing little more than staring at their daughter inside her plastic cocoon, when she could be home, with him, recovering from the delivery?

Torn between the two most important people in her world, Jesse tried to reach a compromise. Days, when Ned was at work, she spent her time at the hospital. Nights, when he was home, she was there for him.

Two days before the end of her third week Christina died. Jesse was devastated; and in the painful weeks following their daughter's death she and Ned turned to each other for comfort. For a time it seemed as though the cracks in the marriage had been healed.

All too soon the illusion faded. Jesse wanted to get pregnant again immediately. Ned, however, was adamantly opposed. He had not yet recovered from Christina's death, he claimed. Nor was he willing to go through something like that again.

Soon Jesse found that the best way to keep the peace was to bottle her feelings up inside. Lacking another outlet, she lost herself in her work. And in the process she lost Ned as well. One day while she was at work he simply packed up his things and left.

Once again Jesse had found herself adrift. She'd worked through the desolation that coated her days and, when her attempts at reconciliation were firmly rebuffed, resigned herself to being alone. She'd adjusted because she had no other choice. She'd taken her half of the proceeds from the sale of their house and moved into the little Cape Cod on Portland Road. And when, two months later, she'd discovered she was pregnant, she'd adjusted again.

It was her new neighbor Kay Samuel who'd counseled her through morning sickness, and taken her to shop for a layette. Seven months later it was Kay who'd held her hand and breathed with her as she lay on the delivery table at Cranford Hospital and delivered a healthy baby girl. And in that moment Jesse had known that whatever came before, *this* was worth it.

Amanda. She was all that mattered. Jesse closed her eyes and willed her thoughts outward. Where are you, baby? I'll find you, honey. I swear I will.

She hadn't seen Ned in almost a year. If she'd had her way, she'd never need to see him again. But then so few choices seemed to be hers these days.

The trip to White Plains took less than twenty minutes. Though she'd never been there before, Jesse found Ned's apartment complex with little trouble. She drove through slowly, checking from door to door until she found the number that matched Ned's address. There was an empty space just beyond. Jesse pulled in and parked.

Ned must have been watching out the window. To her surprise he opened his door and stepped out on the stoop. She saw that his hair was longer than it had been and that he'd lost a little weight. Aside from that, nothing else had changed. His eyes were still the same warm shade of brown that she remembered. He still had that cocksure, confident swagger to his stance.

And he could still make her hot just by looking at her.

Oh God, thought Jesse. So much else had passed between them, how could the physical attraction still remain?

Much sooner than she was ready, Jesse found herself climbing out of the car to greet him.

"I see you got my message," he said when she reached the stairs.

"Both of them." Jesse lifted a hand to brush back her hair and came up with only air. Though Ned was staring, his eyes didn't meet hers. It took Jesse a moment to realize that he was looking at her bruises.

"The detective told me you'd had a hard time. He didn't say it was that bad."

"I'm okay." Jesse willed it to be true.

Ned pushed the door open and led the way. "Come on in." His voice was softer, warmer, than Jesse'd heard it in years. "Let's talk."

TEN

The apartment was smaller than it looked from the outside. Even so, it was sparsely furnished. Most of the pieces, Jesse recognized; they'd come from the home she and Ned had shared. His leather recliner was right where she'd have expected it to be—opposite the large-screen TV. The couch was an old one they'd had in their basement; the bookshelves, Scandinavian modern, were new. Cheap carpeting covered every inch of the floor. Jesse guessed it had come with the rental.

"Sit down." Ned gestured vaguely in the direction of the couch. "Can I get you something to drink?"

"No thanks."

Avoiding the bad spring in the middle, Jesse perched in one corner and folded her hands in her lap. They were as correct, and as uncomfortable, with one another as strangers. Except for that brief, unwise, and hopefully undetectable spurt of attraction outside, was this all that was left?

"So, aside from . . . you know, how have you been?"

"Fine." Jesse stopped, amended. "Okay. Better on the days I don't have to see the lawyers."

If Ned caught the subtle dig, he chose to ignore it. "Yeah, me too."

Already Jesse was squirming in her seat. This was impossible. She'd never been good at idle chat, and the situation could hardly have been more awkward. But how could she ever hope to assess Ned's motives unless she drew him out?

"How's the job search going?" she tried.

"You heard about that?"

How did he suppose his lawyer would angle for interim support without explaining the circumstances? "From my lawyer. I'm sorry."

"These things happen." Ned flashed her that cocky, lopsided grin that, in the past, had always made her stomach flip. "You know me, I've never exactly been nine-to-five material."

"No," Jesse agreed. At least that was one thing they couldn't dispute. "Are you looking in the same field?"

"Actually, at the moment, I'm not looking at all." Ned stood up and strolled into the kitchenette, folding back the louvered doors above the counter so that they could continue to talk as he pulled a beer out of the refrigerator. "Sure you don't want anything?"

Jesse shook her head. "Why aren't you trying to find another job?"

Ned flipped the pop top, tilted back his head, and took a long swallow. "You know, Jess," he said finally, "that was always the biggest difference between us. You knew exactly what you wanted and were hell-bent on getting it. Me, I'm thirty-two years old and I've been working for ten years at a succession of jobs that have bored me silly. Now just seems like a good time to take a little vacation, that's all."

"But—"

"Let's not start, okay? I don't want to argue, and I don't want to talk about work." Ned came back in and sat down in the recliner, balancing the open can of beer on the chair's broad arm. "Tell me what happened the other night."

"I'm sure Detective Maychick filled you in."

"He gave me the facts." Ned's gaze dropped to a patch of reddened skin on her throat. "I'm beginning to realize there were some details he left out."

Jesse ducked her head, shielding her neck from his view. She made the telling as quick, and as painless, as possible.

"He hurt you."

Jesse jumped at the nearness of Ned's voice, the graze of his fingers across her battered flesh. Somehow, while she'd been speaking, he had moved to sit beside her on the couch. When had that happened? "We struggled," she said, leaning away to put more distance between them. "I fought back."

"Yes," Ned agreed softly. "You would."

He was the only man Jesse had ever known who could caress a woman with his voice. He hadn't used that tone with her in years. The last thing she needed was for him to start now. "He was stronger than me. I lost consciousness. When I woke up, he had tied me up."

"You weren't raped."

"No." To Jesse's relief Ned drew back. He'd always known just how far he could push her. Was that what he was doing now?

"Did he . . . touch you?"

"I don't know." Jesse shivered slightly. The revulsion was still too near the surface to be contained. "When I awoke, I'd been moved. My nightgown was ripped. I don't know what happened in between."

Ned lifted a hand as if to touch her again. Jesse flinched, the small movement totally involuntary, a reaction more to the topic than to him. Noticing, Ned let his hand drop to his lap. "What about your hair?"

"He cut it off with a knife. Kay trimmed it for me this morning. She did the best she could."

"It looks fine. Just different, that's all. Who's Kay?"

"A neighbor . . . a friend."

Ned rose and went back for another sip of beer. "Are you this jumpy with everyone, or is it just me?"

Jesse nailed him with a stare. "Just you."

"Good."

"Really? Why?"

"The baby's gone, Jess. I'd hate to think that you were coming apart as well."

Sudden anger propelled her to her feet. "Maybe I *am* coming apart, Ned. God knows, I have every reason to. Because until I get Amanda back, I won't ever feel whole." Jesse threw up her hands and paced across the room. "How you can be so unaffected is beyond me. Amanda isn't just *the baby*. She's *our* daughter."

"Of course she is." Ned reached out a hand as she passed by.

Angrily Jesse shrugged him off. "You've never even been to see her."

"I didn't think you'd want me to come."

His words stopped her, where his touch hadn't. "Whatever gave you that idea?"

"The fact that you never invited me, for starters."

"How many men would feel that they needed an invitation to visit their own daughter?"

"In my situation, plenty."

"I called you after she was born. I told you her sex, and her weight, and her name. I said that our differences shouldn't affect her, that you'd always be her father."

"You also said that you didn't need any support or help of any kind, that you were perfectly willing to raise her alone."

"Of course I said that." Jesse glared at him. "What else was I going to do? You didn't want a wife, and you certainly didn't want a baby. You'd gone out of your way to make that perfectly clear."

"It's always black and white with you, isn't it, Jess? People either agree with you, or they're wrong."

"That's unfair!"

"Unfair?" Ned lifted a brow. "I'll tell you what's unfair—siccing the police after me like I'm some sort of criminal. What did you tell that detective to make him think I was behind this mess?"

"Nothing!"

"Come on, Jess, there must have been something. He wouldn't have come up with the idea all by himself."

She drew in a deep breath, feeling, all at once, incredibly tired. Why had she ever thought it would be possible to communicate with Ned like a civilized human being? She might get the information she sought, but she was going to have to fight for it. And after all that had happened, she wasn't sure if she had the strength.

"As a matter of fact Detective Maychick did find you all by himself. He says that in cases like these the crime is more likely to have been committed by someone the victim knows."

"You don't know anybody but the people you work with," Ned said rudely. "Why doesn't he go sniffing around there?"

"I believe he's looking for people who have a motive for wanting to hurt me."

Ned finished off the last sip of beer, took a bead on the trash bin in the kitchen, and lobbed the can over the counter. The shot bounced off the wall, missing by a foot. The can rolled noisily across the floor.

"Or me," he said.

Irked by the childish antics, Jesse didn't catch on right away. "What did you say?"

For a man who'd just missed an easy shot, Ned's smile was positively smug. "Don't tell me there's something your Detective Maychick failed to tell to you?"

"Are you going to answer me, Ned, or do I have to call him and ask?"

"Keep your pants on, it's not that big a deal."

"It is to me."

"All right then, here it is." There were two stools beneath the counter. Ned dragged one out and sat down. "Much to my surprise, when the detective was here he mentioned the possibility that someone might have been trying to get at me through Amanda."

"That's crazy!"

"He didn't seem to think so."

"But anyone who knew you at all would realize what a stupid idea that is."

"Says you." Ned leaned back casually against the counter. "If I do say so myself, Maychick seemed rather taken with his own logic."

"So what?"

"So who do you know that's mad enough to do something like this?"

"That's exactly my point," said Ned. "Nobody. In fact I'd say the real question is exactly the reverse."

Jesse narrowed her eyes, waiting to hear him out and knowing, already, that she wouldn't like it.

"What have you been up to, dear wife, to get us all in this sort of trouble?"

She'd have argued with the endearment, but there were more important battles to be won. "Give me a break. You know perfectly well what I've been up to. I've been having your baby, that's what."

Striding past him, Jesse entered the small kitchen. A well-aimed kick sent the empty beer can careening out of the way as she opened the refrigerator and helped herself to a diet soda. Jesse knew he was watching her; she didn't care. Taking her time, she held the chilled can up to one heated cheek, then the other. Finally she flipped open the top and took a sip.

"So," she said casually, "I hear you have an alibi."

"Umm-hmm."

"Are you going to tell me what it is?"

"Frankly it's none of your business. But since I'm sure you'll find out anyway, I may as well tell you. As it happens, I was out drinking with friends."

"All night?"

"A good portion of it."

"Most bars close at two."

"Am I on the witness stand?" Ned inquired. "Or we still pretending this is a friendly chat?"

If pleading would have moved him, Jesse wasn't above it. Anger came out first. "No more games, Ned. Just tell me."

"All right. You asked for it. I brought someone home with me that night: a woman. As far as where I was at two A.M., you might say my time was very well accounted for."

He wanted a reaction from her; Jesse was damned if she'd give him the satisfaction. Of course she'd known there must have been other women. It had been more than a year. So why was she suddenly so annoyed? Proximity to a fool, probably.

"You know how it is, Jess." Ned spread his hands, the eternal little boy, innocent of all wrongdoing. "Too bad you haven't found someone to keep you warm at night. Maybe then none of this would have happened."

"You're disgusting."

"You never used to think so."

"Times change." Jesse strode to the couch and picked up her purse. "I know you much better now."

Ned rose to placate her. "I'm not trying to hurt you, Jess. I'm only being realistic."

"What you're being," Jesse snapped, "is childish." She walked past him to stop at the door. "You may be interested in playing this silly game of one-upmanship while our daughter's life is in jeopardy, but I most certainly am not." Her hand reached out, fingers grasping the knob. "I'm sure our lawyers will be able to handle any further communication."

"Jesse, wait."

She drew the door open, but didn't walk out. Ned had come up behind her. "What?"

"Before you go, one last request?"

"Maybe. What is it?"

"Show me a picture."

Jesse looked at him blankly.

"Of the baby . . . of Amanda. Lately—ever since Detective Maychick was here, I've been wondering what she looked like."

You never wondered before that? Jesse wanted to ask, but didn't. This was the first real interest Ned had shown in his daughter, and she wasn't about to turn it away. Someday Amanda would need a father's presence in her life. If this was the beginning of that relationship, she'd nurture it for all it was worth.

Opening her purse, she drew out her wallet. There was a small photograph inside. In it Amanda was sitting propped up against a pillow, her arms encircling the baby doll that was almost as big as she was. Jesse gazed at the happy picture for a long moment before finally handing it over.

"She's so small," Ned said in wonder.

"But getting bigger every day. That picture's two weeks old. Already she looks different."

"I guess that doll's big enough. I can hardly tell the two of them apart."

Jesse swallowed heavily. "Amanda loves that doll, it's her favorite. Don't worry, she'll grow into it."

"Of course . . ." Ned cleared his throat. "Of course she will." He took a last, lingering look at the picture before passing it back. "She's a beautiful baby, Jess."

"Yes." Jesse slipped the photo back in her wallet and put it away. "She is."

"Must take after me."

"Actually I've always thought Amanda took after me."

"You would." Ned pushed the door aside and

walked out. "I'm surprised you recognize my part in her at all. You always were like that, Jess. You always thought you could handle things all by yourself."

"That's not true." Jesse followed him out. "I needed you, Ned."

"You needed me to be who you wanted, not who I actually was."

Was that true? Jesse wondered. Or was Ned simply slanting things once again to highlight his innocence? After all this time it shouldn't have made a difference, but it did. Ned was standing with his back to her, hands resting on the rail, as he looked out over the parking lot. The urge to touch him was sure and strong. Deliberately Jesse pulled herself away. Now was not the time to reopen old wounds, when fresh ones still needed tending.

Without another word she walked past him and down the stairs. She had almost reached her car before he spoke. "Jess?" he called. "Whatever happens, let me know."

She turned and found herself squinting upward into the late-day sun. She couldn't see his face, but she could imagine his stony expression.

"I will," she said softly, then added again, louder, "I will."

E LEVEN

Jesse returned home to a house that was just as she had left it: empty and silent. There were three messages on the answering machine—sympathy calls from Laurel and Gus at work, as well as one from her secretary. Jesse had no idea how they'd found out. Later she'd call and thank them for their support. For now, though, her thoughts were filled with Amanda.

How was it possible that there could still be no news? Children, even tiny ones like Amanda, didn't just vanish. Someone must have seen or heard something. Why hadn't the police found them?

Jesse glanced in the refrigerator, but couldn't summon up an appetite. Wandering into her bedroom, she switched on the radio. Rush hour was gearing up; the deejay was giving a commuter traffic report.

There'd been days when her schedule had been determined by those reports. Some days the right decision on a route could save her half an hour. How important that had seemed then. How trivial it was now. If she had another chance—*when* she had another chance—she'd do things differently.

Well, now she had plenty of time. What was she going to do with it?

Back in the living room Jesse found her cause. Though Kay had straightened the night before, the room still looked just slightly off kilter. It needed Jesse's familiar touch to pull it back together. And all at once she knew it was important that it be restored, that all sign of the intruder's presence be obliterated.

The realization filled her with a sense of purpose. In so many ways recently she'd felt powerless; this, at least, was something she could control.

Jesse started at one end of the room and worked her way to the other. She rearranged furniture and reordered books. Kay had leaned a print against the wall. Jesse rehung it, cracked glass and all. A trace of fingerprint dust remained on the windowsill. She swiped at it with her palm, then cleaned her hand on the seat of her pants.

At some point most of the mantelpiece had been swept clean. The area was carpeted; nearly everything seemed to have survived. Kay had retrieved the pewter candlesticks and the small teak duck and placed them on an end table. Now Jesse picked up the familiar pieces and placed them back on the wooden ledge where they belonged.

Christina's picture was already there. There should have been another matching frame on the mantelpiece: Amanda's picture. Jesse scanned the room, trying to locate it. Kay had snapped the shot outside on the first warm, sunny day of spring. She'd captured the baby's wide-eyed delight and Jesse's laughing reaction to it. The photograph was Jesse's favorite; looking at it never failed to make her smile.

Remembering the state the room had been in the day before, she realized the picture could be almost anywhere. Most of the surfaces in the room were clean. They'd been dusted for fingerprints, then, thanks to Kay, dusted again. The next most logical place to look was the floor.

Jesse poked beneath the couch and peered under every chair. The fireplace was empty, she saw that at a glance. Lifting the cushions turned up nothing but lint. The picture was not in the room.

Maybe the frame had been broken and thrown out by mistake. With the amount of wreckage there'd been, it was certainly possible. But though the garbage bag in the kitchen turned up plenty of glass shards, the frame was nowhere to be seen.

Jesse picked up the phone and dialed Kay. "I have a question."

"Anything. Just ask."

"Do you remember the picture you took of Amanda and me last April?"

"Sure. The one on your mantelpiece, right?"

"Right. Yesterday, when you were cleaning up around here, did you run across it?"

Kay thought for a long moment. "No," she said finally. "I don't think so. I do remember there was one picture on the mantel. That wasn't it?"

"No, that's Christina. I've looked all over, but I can't find Amanda's picture anywhere."

"Do you want me to come and help?"

"No, of course not." Jesse was well aware that Kay had the twins to feed and put to bed. "I'm sure it will turn up."

Jesse replaced the receiver, walked back into the living room, and sat down in the chair where she'd spent the night before. The blanket was still there, as was Amanda's doll. Her movements slow, almost dreamlike, Jesse picked up both and clutched them to her.

It was only a photograph. And it probably would turn up. It wasn't gone forever, just missing. Like Amanda.

Jesse drew her knees up into the chair and hugged herself into a tight ball. Her thoughts floated, casting bright images that danced before her eyes. Amanda, two months old and bundled up as though it were January rather than April. Kay laughing as she removed the baby's hat. Jesse laughing even harder as she put it back on.

"For goodness sake," Kay had said. "She's not that fragile. If you aren't careful, you'll smother her."

"I want to smother her." Jesse lowered her face to Amanda's and rubbed their noses together. "I want to smother her with love, and attention. I want to give her the best of everything so that she'll never be cold, or lonely, or hungry, or afraid." She lifted her eyes to Kay's. "Do all mothers feel this way?"

"Mostly." Kay grinned. "Don't worry, you'll get over it."

"Ha!" cried Jesse. "Never!" It was then that Kay had taken the photograph, capturing mother and daughter, laughing together on the sun-dappled day.

Jesse willed the memory away. "I didn't do so well, Amanda, did I?" she whispered. The words sounded loud in the empty room. "I hope someone's keeping you warm tonight. Don't worry, honey, it won't be much longer. . . ."

Her voice trailed away as the shivering started, tremors racking her body as though she would never be warm again. Jesse wrapped the blanket around her, but it wasn't enough. Numbness had carried her through the last thirty-six hours, but now that blessing was gone. Pain sliced into her, its edge white hot and more shattering than she could ever have imagined.

By the time the tears started, they were almost a relief.

TWELVE

A baby ought to have fresh air and sunshine. Though the woman had never had a baby of her own, she was quite sure of that. Maybe that was why the child wasn't sleeping nights, why she awakened at all hours, crying—wailing really—and needed to be rocked back to sleep.

She should have gotten a rocking chair, but she hadn't thought of it earlier. Now, in the middle of the night, the woman sat on the floor beside the cradle, pushing it gently with her fingers so it swayed to and fro.

Even crying, the baby was beautiful, her long dark lashes spiky with tears, her tiny pink bud of a mouth pursed in outrage. The woman had dressed her in a nightgown made of satin and lace. She'd had the gown for years, tucked away in tissue and waiting for this time, this child.

"How old is the baby?" the shopkeeper had asked when she bought it.

"Small," the woman had replied, picturing her perfect child in her mind. "Very small." She'd always known that someday there would be a baby to wear such a dress. Someday she'd have a baby to call her own.

Even after two washings the lace collar was stiff. It left a ridge of reddened skin along the baby's neck. The woman smoothed the rash with her fingers as she lulled the baby back to sleep.

Actually she didn't mind sitting up. At least, with the baby, she had company. Ever since she was little, she'd had a problem sleeping nights. The darkness seemed to go on and on forever. Leaving the lights on helped, but it couldn't change what she knew inside.

The memories were always there, undimmed by time or distance. Sometimes, even now, she thought she heard the sound of her father's heavy tread upon the stairs. So many years had passed, and still it wasn't enough. Dread would gather in the pit of her stomach. In an instant she was ten years old again: frightened, alone, and utterly defenseless.

Sometimes she was lucky. Her father passed her room and went next door. Relief would flood through her, followed quickly by guilt. She'd jam a pillow over her head, but still she heard. The thin plasterboard walls didn't muffle much—not the scream of the belt as it snapped through the air, or the sound of her brother's ragged sobs. She'd huddle beneath the covers and cry herself to sleep with the shameful knowledge that, at least for one more night, she was safe.

Then there were the other times, the times her father came to her. At first, when she was younger, she hadn't understood. Her father didn't care. He overrode her objections with threats and brute force. "What am I doing with a sniveling coward for a son and a big strong daughter like you?" he would ask, his rough hands grabbing at her soft skin, that impatient, hungry look in his eyes. "You owe me, little girl. You owe me. . . ."

Mornings after she'd have a sore body and downcast eyes. Nobody would look at her too closely. Nobody would want to see. They were all experts at hiding, and staying out of the way. Her mother was the best of all.

The woman had hated her mother for that. Maybe she still did. But along the way she'd learned one thing: she wasn't going to be a pale shadow of a person like her mother had been. She was going to control her own fate, not sit back and let life screw her. She had her dreams, and she was going to make them come true. After all she was entitled, wasn't she?

And now, with this baby, it was starting to happen. A new beginning for them both. Soon they'd be where no one could ever touch them again. But first there were more immediate concerns.

They would have an outing, the woman decided. Just a short one, but it was better than nothing. She'd dress the baby in a frilly summer smock, lay her in the carriage, and push her to the corner. The child would have to be covered, and on a warm afternoon such as this that was a shame. But there really wasn't any choice, because no one must see her. No one at all must know.

Of course it would be safer to keep her indoors, but that was no way to raise a baby. And this child was going to have the perfect upbringing, just as she was going to be the perfect mother. She hadn't been able to save her brother. And she hadn't been able to save herself. But now she had a little girl of her own, and everything was going to be just fine.

Carefully the woman maneuvered the buggy out the front door and down the steps. Lulled by the movement, the baby was quiet. Out in the sun the woman adjusted the carriage's sliding top so its interior was hidden in shadow. At the end of the short flagstone walk she looked both ways, then headed east, toward the park.

Behind her, at the house next door, the curtain in the front window rose, hovered a moment, then fell back into place. Singing softly under her breath, the woman never even noticed.

THIRTEEN

Day Three

For the second morning in a row Jesse awoke in the living room. This time, however, there was no confusion; she knew, even before opening her eyes, what was wrong. The sense of loss was so strong, so immediate, that even half-awake, her body ached with the emptiness.

Amanda. Where was she? What was she doing? Who was feeding her? Who was holding her?

Without a baby to attend to Jesse was dressed and out of the house in twenty minutes. This time she didn't even bother calling the police station; she simply got in her car and drove down.

As soon as she was through the reception area, she saw Detective Maychick. He was standing beside a desk, braced, stiff-armed, above the officer seated there. Even from across the room the detective looked harried and impatient. Catching sight of Jesse, he seemed to shake his head. Or was he merely responding to something the officer had said?

"You here for me?" he asked as she approached.

Jesse was tempted to give him the answer the question deserved. Instead she merely nodded, then regretted her restraint when Maychick made no move to break away from his other conversation. "Is there somewhere we can talk?"

Maychick still didn't look around. "Keep trying," he said to the officer. "Something'll click."

He turned abruptly and started away. After a second Jesse followed. Dodging between the desks, she found herself half running to keep up. "Is that officer working on my daughter's case?"

"No." Maychick never slackened his pace. "There was a stabbing near the Town Center last night." He waited until they'd reached his office before turning around to face her. "Look, Ms. Archer, I understand how you feel, but you don't have to keep coming down. We're already doing everything we can."

Of course she had to keep coming to the police station. If she didn't, where else would she go? How else would she find a reason to get up in the morning? Leaning a hand on Maychick's desk, Jesse took a moment to catch her breath. "The roadblock last night—"

"Zip. A washout. To tell the truth, on a road like yours it was a long shot. That doesn't mean we're out of ideas. We've talked to some people, we'll talk to some more. I know it's hard, but you're going to have to try and be patient."

Patience was for the plodding and methodical, like Maychick. Not for Jesse. Not in this lifetime.

"I can't be patient. Right now I can't even remember how. Every second my daughter is gone is another second too long. I know you think you're on top of things, detective, but I can't understand why nothing's happened yet."

"These things take time."

"Time?" Her voice rose. Maychick looked past her

and out the door as though checking how far the volume might carry. "You've had two whole days, and you're no closer to finding Amanda now than you were in the beginning. In fact, as far as I can tell, all you've done is ask a lot of questions."

"I'm not Kojak, Ms. Archer." Maychick folded his arms over his chest. "Or anyone else you've seen on TV, solving crimes in under an hour. I'm sorry to have to tell you, but that's what real policemen do. They ask questions."

"And then what?"

"We hope that somebody gives us the wrong answers."

Jesse shook her head sharply, refusing to believe that was all. "It's been too long. Surely there must be something else that can be done."

"As a matter of fact there is. And if you hadn't come flying in here like gangbusters, I'd have told you about it right off." A newly opened pack of Marlboros sat on the desk. Maychick tapped one out and rolled it between his fingers. "Starting at noon today, we're going to be running your daughter's picture during the news breaks on TV. Local and New York stations both. We've set up a hot line with an eight-hundred number to field incoming calls."

"What are the chances—"

Maychick stopped her with a look. "To be perfectly honest I don't know what the chances are. Nobody does. Every time's different. But at this point the more people who get involved, the better."

Jesse nodded, feeling somewhat mollified. At least this was something tangible: something she could see, and hear, and understand. "What picture will you be using?"

"The one you gave us the other day." Maychick's eyes narrowed. "You said it was a good likeness."

"It is." The other picture—the one Jesse had lost—was older, and less clear. She couldn't imagine why the police might have taken it, but there was no harm in asking. "You didn't happen to see another photograph—one of Amanda and me both? It was in a small silver frame. . . ."

"Are you asking if one of my men helped himself to something from your house?" Maychick's voice was as cold as the expression on his face. He didn't give her time to reply. "Because if you are, the answer is no. That's not the way we do things, Ms. Archer. Not at all."

"I wasn't trying to accuse anyone of anything. I just thought perhaps you might have needed another picture for your investigation. Or, barring that, that maybe you'd noticed it somewhere in the house."

"Tell you the truth it wouldn't have stuck in my mind if I had. When I looked around your house the other day, I was looking for something that didn't belong, not for something that did."

"Yes, of course." Jesse jammed her hands in the pockets of her pants, feeling like an idiot. Were she and the detective forever destined to misunderstand one another? "Well, in that case I won't take up any more of your time."

Maychick waved dismissively. He was already turning away to yank open a drawer in his file cabinet. "Like I said before, Ms. Archer, we'll be in touch."

Jesse let herself out and followed a maze of hallways to the other end of the building. Luck was with her, and Agent Phillips was in his office when she arrived. At her tentative knock on the half-open door he looked up and smiled.

"Come on in," he said, rising to greet her.

"I just came by to check and see if anything . . ." Jesse's voice trailed away. With Detective Maychick she always felt compelled to justify her presence. Agent Phillips, however, seemed to require no such explanations. He was already taking her arm and leading her into the office.

"Here, let me find you a seat." The only extra chair in the room was piled high with books and folders. Phillips transferred the stack to the floor, then dragged the chair over next to his desk. "That's better." He pointed downward, then watched as she sat. "You look better, too. Body beginning to heal?"

"Slowly."

"Give it time." Phillips walked around and took his own seat. "You fixed your hair."

Jesse lifted a hand, fingered through the wisps. Would she ever get used to not having what was no longer there? "A friend trimmed it for me. She did the best she could."

"I like it."

The compliment was warm and direct. Jesse might have thought he was teasing, but the words sounded much too genuine. "Thank you."

"You're welcome." Looking down, Phillips shuffled through the papers on his desk. "I'm glad you came. We've turned up some information I'd like to discuss with you."

"Yes?"

"It's nothing conclusive. And it may well turn out to be nothing at all. Remember you told us you'd had your house painted the beginning of last month?"

Jesse nodded.

"Well we ran the painters' names through the computer. That's pretty routine, we've done it with every name you gave us. But in this case something came up. One of the assistants who worked on your house, a man named Andy Meehan, was arrested in Colorado eight years ago."

"For what?" Jesse felt herself starting to wobble and realized she was balanced on the edge of her seat. Deliberately she forced herself to sit back.

"It seems he kidnapped his own son away from the boy's mother, who had legal custody, then crossed into the state of Nevada with him in an attempt to hide out."

The color drained from Jesse's face. "Did they get the boy back?"

"Six weeks later. Apparently the kid got tired of life on the run and called home. His mother alerted us and we picked him up."

"Was he all right?"

"Fine—just happy to be going home. Meehan didn't hurt him or anything, just said he wanted to get to know his own son. Once the boy was back home, the mother declined to press charges."

Jesse thought for a moment. For three days the painters had been all over her house, but she hadn't paid that much attention to any of them. As usual she'd been too busy. Each member of the crew had had his name stenciled on his pocket. Andy, she seemed to remember, was a slight man with curly brown hair and wire-rimmed glasses that balanced on the edge of his nose.

"Where is Mr. Meehan now?" she asked quietly.

"That's just it, we don't exactly know." Phillips noted the expression on Jesse's face and frowned. "It's not that he's missing, or anything like that. Just that people who hire on jobs free-lance like he does can be a little harder to track down. I'm sure we'll be in touch with him shortly." He waited a moment, giving her time to deal with that, then added, "There's something else."

Jesse's fingers curled around the lip of the seat. "About Mr. Meehan?"

"No, one of your coworkers at National Brands. Laurel . . ." He stopped, scanned through his notes.

"Benning."

"Yes, Laurel Benning." Phillips found the paper he was looking for, and went on. "She and her husband have been trying to have a baby for six years. Unsuccessfully."

The word hung in the air like a condemnation. Jesse breathed in deeply and expelled a sigh. It wasn't only her life that was being laid bare, but those of her friends as well. It didn't seem fair. None of it did.

"I know," she said finally. "Although I'm surprised Laurel would tell you that. She's a very private person. I wouldn't think she'd think it was any of your business."

"Like you didn't, you mean."

Jesse heard the censure in his voice and wondered if it was justified. He suspected everybody. Wasn't there anywhere lines could be drawn?

"You want us to find your baby."

Jesse looked up. "Of course."

"Then right now everything that concerns you is our business. Don't tie my hands by deciding for me what you think is important."

"But I've known Laurel for years, and Peter, too—"

"Precisely." Phillips nodded, his point made. "We'll be investigating them along with everyone else."

FOURTEEN

Driving home, Jesse tried to remember everything she knew about Andy Meehan. It wasn't much. The man had been all over the outside of her house for three days. Why hadn't she paid more attention?

Because he'd been the quiet one, Jesse decided. George, who ran the crew, was always giving orders. She'd heard the other assistant talk back once or twice, but not Andy. He just went along with whatever he was told to do.

In fact the only time she'd heard him say anything at all was once when she'd been leaving the house to run some errands. She'd been holding Amanda in her arms; he'd been jockeying a ladder into a different position near the door. Seeing the baby, he'd braced the ladder carefully against the house while she went by.

He'd said something, made some perfectly generic comment about how cute Amanda was. He'd even reached up as if to touch her, then looked at his grimy hand and pulled it back self-consciously. The whole encounter hadn't even lasted a minute. And until now she'd forgotten all about it.

But then why should she have remembered? Lots of people had commented on Amanda, just as they probably commented on every other new baby they saw. Andy Meehan had certainly seemed harmless enough. But that only showed how little Jesse knew. The man had been arrested for abducting a child once before. And what had he been doing in the eight years since? What if he'd been looking for another child to replace the one he'd lost?

Deep in thought, Jesse missed the turnoff for the supermarket. Needing to cash a check, she stopped and circled back. Before everything had happened, she'd been planning to go to the bank. Now there was barely enough money in her wallet to put gas in the car.

Inside, Jesse wandered up and down the aisles. She threw a loaf of bread in her basket and followed it with a dozen eggs. Usually she was very organized, carrying a list and buying everything on it. Today, however, she hadn't the slightest idea what her cupboard lacked, nor did she care. Milk, bread, eggs—they seemed basic enough. She picked them up and took them along.

There was a short line at the check-cashing counter. Joining the end, Jesse slung the shopping basket over her arm and wrote out her check while she waited. A stocky man with thinning sandy brown hair was on duty. Jesse had been in often enough to recognize him as the assistant manager. He was fast and efficient at processing approvals; and after only a few minutes' wait it was her turn.

Jesse laid the check and her driver's license on the counter. When he didn't pick them up right away, she glanced up to see what was wrong. To her surprise the man was simply standing there, staring at her curiously.

"I'm so sorry, Ms. Archer," he said. "I just heard about your daughter on the news bulletin."

Jesse stiffened. Looking past him, she could see that he had a small black-and-white TV set balanced on the stool behind the counter. At the moment a game show was in progress. A winning contestant jumped up and down with manic glee. Her eyes slid away, came back to the watery brown ones opposite her. He was still staring.

"Thank you," she said quickly, wishing he'd just get on with it. Her tragedy was private. She had no desire to discuss it with someone she didn't even know. Jesse pushed the check and ID toward him across the counter.

Unfortunately the assistant manager didn't take the hint. "Do the police have any leads?" he asked.

"No," Jesse said shortly. She didn't want to be rude, but what business was it of his? Probably he was only trying to be kind. But if he really wanted to help, why didn't he just cash her goddamn check?

Still he ignored the papers on the counter. Jesse finally snatched them up and thrust them into his hand. Why hadn't Detective Maychick prepared her for this? Why hadn't it occurred to her that once her daughter's name and face had been flashed across the TV screen, she would have to deal with the morbid curiosity of virtual strangers?

"Please," she said. "Could I just have my money?"

"Of course." Processing the approval, the man gave her a sympathetic smile. At last he began to count out her money. "Listen, if there's anything I can do to help—"

"Thank you," Jesse broke in. Her fingers scrambled over the bills. She wadded them up and thrust them in her purse, uncounted. "I appreciate your concern."

Even as she edged away she felt the nearness of the people behind her in line. Had they been listening? Would they start asking questions next? It was bad enough that Amanda was gone. Must her anguish be made public as well?

Stepping quickly away, Jesse headed for the checkout counter. It wasn't her imagination, people *were* staring. She ducked her head, but still she felt them looking, wondering.

The store wasn't crowded, but all at once it seemed to close in around her. She had to get out of there. The express lane was closed, the chute beside it empty. Jesse dumped her basket on the conveyor belt and ran.

The parking lot was vast. Head lowered, she stumbled blindly across the hot tarmac. Inside, her car was stifling, but she rolled up the windows anyway, then locked the doors. Still she didn't feel safe. Pulling out of the lot, she began to drive. She was going too fast, but she didn't care. Somehow, somewhere, she had to leave them behind.

Those eyes, staring, glaring at her, from all directions. What did they want? Why couldn't she make them stop? Her privacy had been stripped away, and the last of her dignity with it. Was there nothing left to call her own? Carefully she eased her foot off the gas pedal. The car glided to the side of the road and stopped. The shivering wouldn't stop. Violation, that's what she'd felt. Just like three nights earlier.

She thought she'd put it behind her, but now she knew the panic had only been lurking beneath the surface, waiting until she was most vulnerable to strike. Oh God! How could she be strong for her daughter when she couldn't even be strong for herself?

Somehow Jesse got the car started again. There was a park nearby, with a baseball diamond, a lake, and tennis courts. It was the most normal sort of place Jesse knew. It was exactly what she needed.

She found a bench by the lake and sat, staring out over the water. At first geese came up, looking for handouts; finally they got the message and waddled away. Gradually the panic that had gripped her receded. Slowly a semblance of calm returned.

By the time she was ready to go home, she was resigned. Whatever it took, whatever else happened, she'd get through it. Not because she wanted to, but because she had to, for Amanda's sake. Self-pity was simply a luxury she couldn't afford. Maybe later, but not now.

It was late afternoon by the time Jesse arrived home. To her surprise the Samuels' car was parked by the curb. She caught a fleeting glimpse of George sitting behind the wheel, and the twins in the back, before realizing that Kay was standing on the small porch outside her front door. Jesse pulled into the driveway and rolled the car to a stop.

"There you are." Kay hopped down and started across the yard. "I was just about to give up."

"What's the matter?" Jesse was already scrambling out. "Is something wrong?"

"No, of course not." Quickly Kay closed the gap between them. She took her friend's arm and squeezed it. "Nothing's wrong, Jess, calm down."

"Sorry. It's been that kind of day."

Kay's gray eyes were filled with sympathy. "Actually that's why we're here. George and I are on our way out for pizza."

Automatically Jesse started to refuse. Then she glanced at her empty house and contemplated the alternative: another evening alone, another night filled with endless hours, jagged thoughts, and that awful, aching sense of bereavement.

"Wait!" She reached inside the open window of the car and grabbed her purse. "I'm coming with you."

It was the first time Jesse had actively sought company in days. Now, sitting sandwiched between the twins in the backseat of the car, she found to her relief that nothing was required of her at all. Conversation flowed in fits and starts. The boys argued, Kay threatened, George grinned complacently at his wife, then tossed Jesse a wink. Life as usual in the Samuel family.

In the noisy family restaurant Jesse realized with a sudden pang just how much she'd been missing. Between coping with her job, her divorce, her child, she'd cut herself off from just this sort of impromptu gathering. There'd been no room in her life for frivolity lately. Indeed, at times, just keeping things together had seemed like enough. Now, sitting back as the conversation flowed around her, Jesse realized that when she got Amanda back, there were some changes to be made. Maybe those play groups Agent Phillips had mentioned would be a start.

Though she wasn't the slightest bit hungry, Jesse managed to eat almost two pieces. When he thought she wasn't looking, Kevin snuck the last crust off her plate and polished it off himself. Predictably, having terrorized the table during dinner, the twins fell asleep in the car on the way home.

As he pulled into the driveway and turned off the car, George turned to Jesse over the backseat. "Let me just help Kay get the boys inside and then I'll run you home, okay?"

"Don't be silly." Jesse disentangled herself gently from Michael's sleeping grasp. "It's only the other end of the block. Not even a two-minute walk." She sketched a wave to Kay, who was heading inside with Kevin. "I'll be fine."

Still, George didn't turn away. When Kay flipped on the porch lamp from inside, it threw his face into stark relief—half light, half shadow. "It's not good for you to be alone," he pressed. "Let me just—"

Jesse found herself fumbling for the door handle and sliding out of the car. Though she and Kay had been friends for months, she'd never really gotten to know George, and now wasn't the time to start. "Really," she said, starting away down the driveway. "I'm all right."

The sun had been setting when they left the restaurant. Now, fifteen minutes later, it was fully dark. There were no street lamps on Portland, and Jesse picked her way carefully down the driveway to the cracked and pitted sidewalk. She'd made the walk between the two houses many times; lately, usually with Amanda in her stroller. But never had she done it at night.

As usual the street was deserted. For the most part the residents were older couples who kept pretty much to themselves. Though many of the houses had lights on inside, their shades and curtains were drawn. Not even a flicker escaped to light her way.

A line of older trees graced the narrow strip of grass between sidewalk and road, their skinny branches reaching down into the path of the unwary. Aware of the problem, Jesse kept to the inner edge of the walk, until she stubbed her toe on a brick border one home owner had planted around his yard.

"Damn!" Jesse bent down only briefly to massage her injured foot. But when she straightened again, it was with the sudden, uncanny knowledge that she was no longer alone.

Slowly Jesse turned. By now her eyes were adjusted to the dark. Still they saw nothing move. No sound was carried on the breeze. So why was the hair on the back of her neck crawling?

Jesse scanned the street in both directions. She'd come too far to turn back. Her own house was closer than the Samuel's at the other end of the block.

Stepping out boldly, she fought to maintain the appearance of calm. Her arms dangled at her sides, fists clenching and unclenching with each stride. Once, then again, Jesse stopped to look behind her. Still she saw nothing. The walk had always seemed so short before. Now it was endless.

A flash of silver caught her eye and Jesse whirled around, a scream gathering in her throat. It was only a small patch of light, reflecting off a car fender. But her mind refused to process that fact. Instead, once again, she saw the knife, just as it had been three nights earlier, lifted above her head and poised to strike.

Fear rose and eddied around her. She had to get away before it was too late. Jesse jumped back as a branch snatched at her hair. She swatted it away and heard it snap behind her. Breath clawing like fire in her lungs, she spun away and began to run.

FIFTEEN

Jesse's house was dark. When she'd gone out earlier, there'd been no need to leave a light on. Even so, it looked like a haven. If only she could get inside.

A rut in the sidewalk snagged her heel. With a cry Jesse went sprawling. The concrete jarred her knees and scraped the skin from her palms. Scrambling for her purse, she left the shoe behind and kept running. Her fingers dived inside the bag and found her keys, holding them ready.

As she reached the edge of her yard Jesse heard a noise from across the street. A car was parked in the shadows there. Its door opened. Light flickered briefly as a man wearing dark clothing stepped out.

Her nightmare was back; this time it was real.

"No!" Jesse screamed as he shut the door and the light vanished. She couldn't see if he was moving toward her. She couldn't see him at all.

Jesse raced up the stairs and onto the porch. She grabbed the doorknob with a shaking hand, her fingers fumbling with the key. She heard quiet footsteps behind her as he crossed the street. Then he reached the grass and the sound muffled.

Praying, swearing, her breath coming in gasps, Jesse jammed the key into the lock. She turned the knob and it gave. As the door opened she stumbled forward and all but fell inside. Whirling, she slammed the door shut behind her and drove the chain lock home.

She raced into the kitchen. This time she would make it. This time she would not be too late. She grabbed up the receiver and punched out the three digits. The single ring seemed to last forever.

"Nine-one-one Emergency Officer McNulty."

"I need help. There's a man outside. . . . He's coming after me. . . ." Jesse gave her name and address. Help was on the way. Her heart was pounding so wildly she could hardly hear what the officer was saying.

"Stay on the line," he repeated. "Miss, stay on the line. . . ."

Sinking down to the floor, Jesse let the receiver dangle from nerveless fingers. She had no strength to hold it up, no breath left to talk. Here, between the cabinets, she was hidden from the windows. Was he out there watching, hoping she'd turn on a light? What if he came around and tried the backdoor?

Her horrified gaze flew to the kitchen door with its intricate glass paneling. One good punch could break any one of the small panes. He'd need less force than he'd used to knock her out.

Jesse started as a branch slapped against the house. Or had one been broken underfoot? She curled up into a ball and pressed herself into the cabinets. There'd been no escape before. Why should she be foolish enough to believe there'd be one now? He was coming after her once again, and this time . . .

Lights!

One moment there was only darkness and the next they were there, filling her driveway, illuminating the front of the house. Moving slowly, almost afraid to hope, Jesse pushed herself up. Over the top of the counter she saw a police cruiser parked in her drive-way. Two officers were getting out, their stances wary, their fingers braced on their holstered guns. One headed in each direction around the house.

Weak with reaction Jesse sagged back against the counter. For the moment, until her strength returned, standing seemed like effort enough. Finally, as the police radio squawked outside, she reached over and flipped on the lights, then went to the living room and did the same there. Inside and out she turned on every light in the house.

Bright and familiar, the yard lost its menace. Jesse looked out and saw that the officers had completed their tour around the house. One was standing beside the patrol car, talking into the radio. The other had started off down the sidewalk. She went to wait by the front door and saw that the car that had been parked across the street was now gone.

One of the officers stepped up onto the porch. By the time he reached the door, Jesse had it open.

"Officer Rooney, ma'am. Everything seems to be okay out here. We had a report of an intruder outside the house. Are you sure nobody came in?"

"Yes. At least I think so."

The officer stepped past her into the living room. "If you don't mind, it's better if I have a look."

He went from room to room, peering into closets and under the bed. Feeling safer in his presence, Jesse trailed along until he went upstairs to the nursery. Then she waited at the bottom of the steps until he came down.

"Right," he said. "Everything's clear. Are you sure there was someone outside?"

"Oh yes." Jesse moved back to stand beside the window. "There was a car parked across the street—over there. A man in dark clothes got out."

Rooney followed the direction of her pointing finger. "I don't see any car there, ma'am."

"Not now! Before, when I came in."

"Are you sure it wasn't just someone visiting in the neighborhood?"

"Well . . . no."

"I see." The officer pulled out a small pad. "Can you tell me what the man looked like?"

"I didn't see him." Jesse's voice was ragged with frustration. "I mean, not really. It was dark outside, and so was he."

"Did you happen to get a license number?"

Jesse shook her head.

"How about a description of the car?"

"It was a sedan . . . I think. A dark color, maybe navy blue, or brown."

Rooney snapped the pad shut and put it away. "Well whoever it was you saw, he seems to be gone now."

The other officer appeared in the open doorway.

"Find anything?" asked Rooney.

"Only this." The man held up his hand and Jesse saw that he had her shoe.

Frowning, Rooney turned back to Jesse. "You're sure it was a man you saw?"

"Yes, I'm sure," Jesse said firmly. She felt her cheeks redden. "Actually that's my shoe."

"Really?" Rooney glanced down at her feet, noticing the state of her footwear for the first time. He looked at the other officer. "Where'd you find it?"

"Outside, on the sidewalk. Two doors down." He reached in and handed the shoe back to Jesse. "Careful, ma'am, the heel's broken."

"Yes, I know." By now the red was spreading up into her hairline. Jesse bent down and slipped the flat on.

Rooney retrieved his pad and tried again. "How did your shoe get outside?"

"I was wearing it." Jesse knew he had to ask the questions, but did he have to make her feel like such an idiot while he did? "I had been out with some friends. They live at the other end of the block. I was walking home. That's when I realized there was someone out there."

"You mean he wasn't in your yard?"

"No." Jesse shook her head. "Not then."

"Was he following you?"

"Not exactly."

"Well, what exactly was he doing?"

"He was in his car," said Jesse. "And then he got out." Now, with the light and the officers surrounding her, it was impossible to recreate the terror of the moment, or the certainty that the man had been after her.

"He was in his car," Rooney repeated slowly as he wrote. "And then he got out. And then?"

"He started toward me." At least she thought he had. Actually it had been too dark to tell, but somehow she didn't think the officers would appreciate the distinction.

"Did he speak to you?"

"No."

"Try to touch you?"

"No, he didn't get that close. I saw him coming and I ran."

"You ran inside and you called 911."

"Yes."

"So you never really saw where the man went—if, for example, he went to one of your neighbors' houses?"

"No." Jesse bit her lip, knowing how unconvincing she sounded. "I didn't look outside at all."

"I see." The two officers exchanged a glance. Once again Rooney tucked his pad away. "Whatever the man was doing out there, ma'am, everything is safe now. You keep some lights on, okay? And be sure to keep these doors and windows locked." The other officer stepped down off the porch. After one last look around the room Rooney followed.

"Thank you for coming," Jesse called after them, standing in the doorway. "I feel much better."

Rooney reached the driver's side of the cruiser. "Close that door now, and lock it. Don't worry, ma'am, you'll be fine."

Jesse followed his advice, then stood by the window, watching as the police car moved away silently down the road. Finally she let the curtain drop and turned to face the living room, which was still ablaze with light. Put the way Officer Rooney had, her fears sounded groundless, even foolish. She'd never been paranoid before; now she didn't know what to think. Had she conjured up the illusion of menace earlier, or had it really existed?

With a sigh Jesse reached out and flicked off the closest lamp. No matter what Officer Rooney thought, there had been a car. And a man in black, too. That much she was sure of. Unfortunately, beyond that, the officer was probably right: her imagination had run away with her, and she'd not only let it, she'd nudged it along.

Enough, Jesse decided. She was going to bed. Not only that, but she'd be sleeping in her own room. With the lights on maybe, but in her own bed. She'd been passive long enough. It was her house and her life. It was time to retake control.

Crossing to the other side of the room, Jesse switched off another light and picked up the blanket lying crumpled in the chair where she'd spent the two previous nights. Briskly she folded it into a small square and tucked it beneath her arm. She'd thought Amanda's doll would be on the cushion, but it wasn't. Nor did she see it on the floor.

Jesse lifted the chair and looked beneath it. Still no doll. She was sure it had been there the night before. She'd been holding it when she fell asleep. That morning she'd gone straight to the shower. Had she carried the doll with her and set it down somewhere?

It didn't take long to search the rest of the downstairs. Unlike the missing picture, the doll was large. Not only that, but while the photograph had probably been lost in the wreckage three days earlier, she'd had the doll only last night. It just wasn't possible that it had disappeared.

Thinking back, Jesse retraced the steps she'd taken that morning, opening closets and dresser drawers, then even looking outside in the car. The longer the search was unsuccessful, the more her determination grew. The doll had to be there somewhere, it was simply a matter of finding it.

Half an hour later Jesse was back in the living room where she'd started. The doll wasn't in any of the four rooms she'd searched. Only one possibility remained.

Unwillingly her eyes were drawn to the stairs. She hadn't been up to the nursery since the night Amanda was taken. The room was filled with her daughter's presence. She couldn't bear the thought of seeing it empty. Now, though, she had to know.

Leaning heavily on the banister, Jesse mounted the steps one by one. From the landing she reached around and turned on the light in the nursery. The ballerina lamp on the dresser cast a muted glow over the soft yellow walls. Impressions came and went. The rocking chair, the changing table—everything was as she'd left it.

Jesse only had eyes for the crib.

Slowly she crossed the room, her feet sinking deep into the thick cream-colored carpet. Reaching the crib, she rested her hands for a moment on the side and took a deep breath before going farther. Her elbow jostled the mobile above the bed, stirring the dancing clowns to action. Its tinny song seemed loud in the quiet room.

As the music played around her Jesse bent down and looked inside the crib. Her hand flew to her mouth to cover a startled scream. A baby was sleeping there. For a brief, wondrous moment she thought it was Amanda. Then her heart plunged as she realized it was the missing doll.

Its dress was gone; in its place was a nightgown. With a shock of recognition, Jesse realized it was one of Amanda's. Tiny bunnies hopped across the bodice. Pink satin ribbons were tied in a bow beneath the chin. A soft cotton blanket had been swaddled around the doll's body. Lying there, its eyes closed as if in sleep, the doll looked just as Amanda had, the last time Jesse had seen her.

Jesse's hands fell away from the slatted sides. Weak-kneed, she stumbled to the rocker and sank down into its hard seat. Her eyes closed; colors danced behind them. What in the world was going on? How had the doll gotten inside the crib? Why was it dressed in her daughter's clothes?

The doors had been locked when she arrived home. Not only that, but the police had just been there. They'd searched the house thoroughly and found nothing. But what was the alternative?

Heart pounding, Jesse flew back down the stairs. One by one she checked each window. All were locked, just as she'd left them. She'd given that madman an opening once, she wasn't about to make the same mistake again. And yet . . .

She hadn't had the locks changed. There'd seemed to be no point; that hadn't been how the intruder had gained access. But when was the last time she'd checked on her spare key? One was in her purse; she'd used it earlier that evening. The other should have been tucked in a corner of the utensil drawer in the kitchen.

Three quick strides carried her into the other room for a look. Frowning, Jesse yanked open the drawer. The corner where the key should have been was empty. Then she remembered: its contents had been scattered onto the floor along with everything else.

Someone, probably Kay, had replaced them. The key could have been put anywhere.

Quickly Jesse rifled through the drawer, then turned to one beside it. Three drawers down, on the end, she found what she was looking for. Her spare house key was right up front, tied to its familiar piece of colored yarn. Jesse picked it up, folded her fingers around it, and squeezed tight. One problem solved, but she still needed answers.

Nothing in her life made sense anymore; it was as though everything was spinning wildly, just beyond her control. Granted she'd been obsessed with her daughter, but could the fixation truly have pushed her that far? She'd had the doll the evening before. Was it possible that sometime during the long night hours she'd gone up to the nursery with it herself?

Had she done that? *Could she have done that?* And why didn't she remember?

SIXTEEN

Day Four

The next morning Jesse called the Cranford Locksmith first thing. No answer. Pulling out the rest of her phone books, she tried Greenwich, Norwalk, and Darien, all with the same result. She might be able to get her locks changed, but it wasn't going to happen on a Sunday morning.

Jesse headed for the police station.

"Heard you had a little excitement last night." Detective Maychick was seated behind his desk.

Jesse could only imagine what the patrolmen might have told him. "There was a man outside my house."

"So Officer Rooney said. Dark and shadowy, right? No height, no weight, no eye color?"

"If someone came after you with a knife, detective, would you stand around long enough to take in the details?"

"Knife?" Maychick looked up quickly. "The report didn't mention anything about a knife."

Too late, Jesse realized her error. "For a moment I

thought I saw something that looked like a knife. It turned out I was wrong."

"Let me get this straight. You got close enough to see what he was carrying, but not to see his face?"

"Actually," Jesse found herself stammering. "We weren't very close at all. As soon as he got out of his car, I ran."

"A very prudent course of action under the circumstances."

Was it her imagination, or was there an edge of sarcasm to his tone? "I thought so."

"'Course it would have been more prudent if you'd have gotten a license number."

"Unless I didn't survive to give it to you."

Maychick gave her a long look. Jesse returned it full measure. After a minute the detective glanced away. "Officer Rooney said they were extra careful looking around, on account of the trouble before."

"I appreciate their concern." Jesse helped herself to the chair.

"That's their job, Ms. Archer. They said everything checked out okay. You agree?"

Coming down, Jesse'd planned to tell Maychick about the doll. Now, however, in the face of his obvious skepticism, she couldn't think of a way to tell what had happened that wouldn't make her look foolish or, even worse, hysterical. How could she begin to explain something she couldn't even understand herself?

"Yes," she said finally. "I agree."

"The rest of the night was quiet?"

"Yes."

"Good. Since that's over with, I've got some news here. I don't know whether or not you'd be interested."

"Of course I'm interested. What is it?"

Maychick patted his pockets and came up with an open pack of cigarettes. "As of last night it doesn't look as though your husband's alibi is going to hold water."

"What do you mean?"

"We checked with the people he said he was with Wednesday night. They were all in a bar, all right. Both his buddies and the bartender will vouch for that." Maychick shook out a cigarette and tapped one end lightly on the top of the desk. "Trouble is, the lady he claims to have taken home with him doesn't agree. She admits she joined him at his table for a few drinks, but that's it. We know when he left the bar, and he would have had to hustle to get from White Plains to Cranford. The timing's awfully tight, but the point is, he could have made it."

Even as she listened Jesse found herself shaking her head. Call it instinct, or maybe woman's intuition. Whatever the reason, now that she'd seen Ned, she simply could not believe that he was behind Amanda's disappearance.

"Shake your head all you like," Maychick said bluntly. "To me it spells opportunity. Don't think I'm not going to consider that."

Leaving the detective's office, Jesse moved automatically toward the other side of the building. Checking in with Maychick was a necessary chore; seeing Agent Phillips gave purpose to her day. Unlike the detective, Phillips never seemed to resent her intrusions or the time he took to explain how the investigation was going. Now, once again, he had something new to show her.

"Names." Phillips gestured toward the sheet of continuous paper that dangled from his printer. "Lists of people to talk to, places to go. We've got almost two pages now, with more coming in all the time."

"But where? How . . .?"

"Detective Maychick told you about the hot-line number, didn't he?"

"Yes."

"This is the initial response."

"That's fantastic!" Jesse strode across the room,

lifted the sheet of paper, and scanned the list of names and addresses. "All these people called in after seeing Amanda's picture?"

"Yes, they did, but . . ." Jesse's face was alight with enthusiasm. Phillips hated to be the one to dash her hopes.

She let the paper drop and spun around. "But what?"

"It's only been one day, of course, but nothing that's come in yet seems especially promising."

"Why do you say that?"

"For starters, more than a few of the names on the list are already familiar to us. Any case that's advertised as this one has been invariably draws the usual collection of crackpots and weirdos. You'd be amazed how many people out there think they know where Jimmy Hoffa's buried or whatever happened to the Lindbergh baby."

"All right," Jesse said slowly. "So maybe you disregard the names of the habitual callers, what about the rest?"

"As you know, we're on the local stations, but we've also had some network coverage as well. Unfortunately most of the people who've called so far seem to have caught a broadcast that came out of New York. The majority of the tips are coming from places like Queens or Lodi, New Jersey. That doesn't mean we can rule them out, but it's certainly less likely than a call coming in from Fairfield County."

Jesse went back for a second look at the list. "You mean none of these people live in Connecticut?"

"One or two. We'll be checking those out first. In the meantime I just don't want you to get your hopes up, that's all."

Jesse turned back to face him, determination evident in the set of her shoulders, the thrust of her chin. "My hopes *are* up, Agent Phillips, and you may as well know that. I have to believe Amanda is going to come

home, because I can't bear to believe the alternative.
Maybe you won't find her this afternoon, and maybe
not tomorrow, but someday . . . soon . . . I will have
my baby back."

Phillips stared at her for a long moment. "I guess
maybe I deserved that."

"I guess maybe you did." To hell with his sheepish
expression, Jesse wasn't about to give an inch. "Tell
me about Andy Meehan."

"Ahh . . ." Phillips walked behind the desk and sat
down.

"Ahh? What does that mean?"

"It means there isn't anything to tell yet. I don't
have any more information now than I did yesterday."

Impatience shot through her, leaving her voice
sharp and shrill. "How is that possible? The man had
a job. Presumably he has a home. He can't just have
vanished."

"You're right. That's why it's only a matter of time
before we find him."

Jesse'd noticed it before. The louder she got, the
calmer Phillips became in return. It was beginning to
make her crazy. Didn't the man ever break loose and
yell?

"Maybe my daughter doesn't have that kind of
time."

There didn't seem to be an answer to that. Phillips
didn't even bother trying to supply one.

"Maybe I should hire a private investigator," Jesse
said. In truth the thought had just occurred to her.
She had no idea whether it had merit or not.

"That's up to you," Phillips said evenly. "But I
don't see what a PI could do for you that we aren't.
There are several agents working on the case, and
believe me, we're covering every possibility. Not only
that, but through the computer system we've got the
resources of the entire U.S. government working with
us as well."

"Yet despite all that you can't even find one simple housepainter."

Phillips wove his fingers together on top of the desk. "It's not that we can't find him, just that we haven't yet. We will, believe me. I know it's hard, but you have to be patient and give us time to do our jobs."

"I don't want to be patient!"

"Sometimes that's what it takes."

"Well, I hate it!"

Phillips looked up then, meeting her gaze with his own. "So do I, Ms. Archer. So do I."

Jesse left the police station and drove across Cranford to Old Greenwich. It wasn't something she'd planned to do; if she had, she'd have called ahead. Instead, on this bright, sunny, Sunday morning, she could only hope that Laurel would be home.

The Bennings' neighborhood was similar to the one Jesse and Ned had lived in before their separation: streets of proper Colonial houses, set back from the road and surrounded by tree-filled lawns. Young professional couples on their way up. Five years ago the yards would have been neat, well tended, and empty. Now they were strewn with swing sets, sand forts, and discarded tricycles. The once-quiet neighborhood was filled with the sound of children at play.

Jesse pulled into the Bennings' curved driveway and coasted to a stop beside the front door. It looked as though she was in luck; two cars were parked around back, by the garage. As she got out and headed up the steps, Jesse wondered what she was going to say.

Did she want to apologize for Phillips's intrusion upon their lives? Did she want to explain? Or was she there to satisfy herself that Laurel couldn't possibly have anything to do with Amanda's disappearance? And if that was the reason, what kind of friend was she? Jesse lifted the heavy brass door knocker and let it fall. She could answer that question in one word: desperate. Friendship was all well and good, but first she was a mother.

Laurel was taller than Jesse, and skinny as a post. She answered the door wearing a T-shirt and short shorts. Her long dark hair was wrapped up on top of her head in a towel, and she was holding a cup of coffee in one hand. By Jesse's estimate she'd been up all of fifteen minutes.

"Jesse?" Laurel looked once, then again. "Good God, it *is* you." She stepped back and drew the door open wide. "What are you doing here? Come on in."

"I'm sorry to just stop by like this—"

"No problem." Laurel waved away the apology and started for the back of the house. "I was just reading the paper. Peter's getting ready to go play golf. Come on back and get some coffee."

The back of the house had been redone, the kitchen expanded to encompass a sun porch. Windows formed two walls and part of the ceiling. In the alcove the *Sunday Times* was spread out over a sun-drenched, glass-topped table. As Laurel poured another cup of coffee there was a clatter from above. A moment later Peter appeared, galloping full tilt down the back stairs. He waved at Jesse, grabbed a muffin off the basket on the counter, and kept going.

"Late," he said by way of an explanation as he rushed out the door. "See you later, hon." A moment later they heard a car start, then take off down the drive.

"Don't say it." Laurel pushed the paper aside, sat down, and motioned Jesse to a chair. "There's a law in Fairfield County. If you're going to play golf, you have to wear pastels."

"Pastels, maybe. But hot pink?"

"Better than Greenwich green. I swear that color always reminds me of toxic waste." Laurel folded her hands on top of the table. "You didn't come to talk about Peter's taste in clothing."

"No."

"You cut your hair."

"Actually . . ." Jesse started to explain, then thought better of it. "Yes."

"I like it."

Manners, they'd all had them drummed in since birth. Laurel wouldn't dream of giving her real opinion of Jesse's hair, any more than Jesse would dream of calling her on it. "Thanks."

"We're missing you at work. The Frooties launch . . . Oh hell." Laurel stopped. "You don't want to talk about that, either. We heard . . . that is, the police told us about your baby. God, I'm sorry, Jess. Is there anything I can do?"

Jesse shook her head. "The police are working on it. They have a lot of leads, but it takes time to track them all down. I was told they talked to you."

"Everybody. Friday, at the office. The FBI came, can you imagine? Talk about panic." Laurel chuckled. "Gus thought they were after him for tax evasion."

Jesse choked on a sip of coffee. "Gus Worthington doesn't pay his taxes?"

"Who knows? When he figured out what was really going on, Gus just laughed it off. Said something about a bad shelter. Anyway they asked us lots of questions. We were all dumbfounded, I'll tell you that. I mean, when Gus said you were going to be out for a while, I thought you had the flu. I never even imagined something like this could happen."

"Neither did I."

"We all feel awful. Peter, too. He just wasn't thinking when he ran through like that. We'd love to help. You're sure there's nothing we can do?"

"I don't think so, no. But thanks." Jesse looked down, fiddling with her coffee cup. There didn't seem to be any delicate way to bring up the topic she'd come to discuss. Finally she just blurted it out. "Agent Phillips knows you've been trying to get pregnant."

"I should think he would. I told him so."

"He's planning to investigate you and Peter."

Laurel swallowed suddenly. "Not too hard, I hope."

Jesse felt an unexpected prickle of fear. "Why?"

"It's none of their business, that's why." Laurel stood up and walked over to the bank of windows. Her back to Jesse, she stared out. "I mean, we want to help, of course we do. That's why I answered his questions. In our place I know you'd do the same. But enough's enough." She spun back around, her arms crossed tightly over her chest. "Tell him to lay off, Jess. Send him in another direction."

"I can't do that."

"Can't? Or won't?"

"The police have their own ideas. It isn't up to me what they do."

"But you could tell them. . . ."

"What?"

"That you know me, that you know Peter."

"I already did."

"And?"

"They told me crimes are often committed by someone the victim knows."

"Shit!"

Half of Jesse felt sorry for Laurel. She could understand how her friend felt. Lord knew, her privacy had been all but shattered. She had to put up with the intrusion; Laurel didn't.

But the other half couldn't help but wonder if Laurel's reaction wasn't a bit out of line. Was what she was feeling normal annoyance, or was it possible she really did have something to hide?

Laurel was frowning, her features drawn tight. "Why did you come here today?"

"To see you."

"To see if we had your baby?"

"No!" Guilt had Jesse jumping to her feet. "How could you even say such a thing?"

Laurel threw up her hands. "I don't know. Dammit, I don't know anything anymore. I've just been under so much pressure lately. You're right, I'm sorry, I never should have said that."

"No," said Jesse. "I'm the one who's sorry." She looked at her friend closely. Laurel had always seemed optimistic about life, so carefree. What kind of pressure was she talking about? "Is it the launch? Because if it is—"

"God no!" Laurel snorted. "That's the least of it. There are other things. . . ." She drew in a deep breath and slowly let it out. "We found an adoption agency in Chicago. They say they'll have a baby for us within three months."

"But that's great news!" Jesse's delighted smile came, then went. "Why didn't you tell Agent Phillips?"

"I couldn't. I want this baby, Jess. And I'm not going to let anything queer our chances. This isn't the kind of place you send the FBI to." Laurel frowned at Jesse's expression. "You don't have to look at me like that. It's nothing illegal, or anything. It's all state-regulated."

"Three months," Jesse commented. "That doesn't seem like a very long wait."

Laurel sank down into her chair. Her head was lowered, she stared intently at her hands. "These babies cost a little more, that's all. I'm thirty-eight years old, Jesse. I want to be a mother *now*. Peter and I have the money, and we're going to pay."

"But surely Agent Phillips—"

"Don't tell him, Jess. I mean it."

"Or what?"

Laurel didn't answer. Manners forgotten, she didn't even look up when Jesse left. Their friendship had lasted six years. Now it would never be the same. How complicated life was becoming suddenly. Everyone had secrets. Everyone had something to hide.

And Jesse was finding out more than she'd ever wanted to know.

$\textbf{S}$EVENTEEN

Jesse drove straight home. She wasn't sure what to do next, but she did know one thing: she wasn't going to spend the rest of the day sitting around waiting for the hours to pass. From her living-room window she could see almost all the way down the block. As usual the street was quiet. No one strolled the sidewalks; only an occasional car passed through.

Aside from Kay and Mrs. Manetti across the street Jesse had met few of the neighbors. She supposed she could hold her job responsible, but busy or not, she'd never been the type to jump right in when meeting new people was involved. Besides, from what she'd seen, most of the neighbors were older than she, people who had retired from their jobs, whose children had grown and gone. No doubt they didn't have much in common, except perhaps their appreciation for the low-key serenity of the small residential street.

The police had questioned her neighbors already, as had the FBI. Neither had managed to learn a thing. Jesse might not either, but it was better than sitting home wondering.

She started with the house next door. Standing on the stoop, Jesse could hear the TV playing loudly inside. She knocked once, then again. After the third try the door was finally opened.

A tiny woman with thinning gray hair and a large hump between her shoulders had one hand braced against a walker and the other on the door. She looked up at Jesse with clear green eyes. "Yes, may I help you?"

Jesse felt like an idiot, remembering that third, impatient knock. "Yes, I'm Jesse Archer. We haven't met, but I live next door."

The woman angled her head upward. "So you do. I'm Mary Stewart. People used to call me Mrs. Stewart, but I'm too old for that now. Mary will do. You're the lady with the baby and no husband."

"Yes, actually." Jesse swallowed. She hadn't expected to hear her life summed up exactly that way. "I am."

"Amazing what women can do nowadays. In my time you had to go away when that happened. Some say the new way's an improvement, but I'm not so sure."

"Mrs. Stewart—Mary—I wonder if I might ask you a question?"

"You can try." Mary enjoyed a dry laugh. "I'm not sure how much good it'll do you."

"Four days ago, Wednesday night, a man broke into my house—"

"I know all about that."

Hope was irrational, but it flared anyway. "You do?"

"Surely do. The police came by the next day, some nice men in suits, too. Asked a lot of questions and didn't tell me a thing. 'Course I may be old, but I'm not stupid. Three police cars sitting outside your neighbor's house, it's not hard to tell where the trouble's been."

"Even though you already spoke to them, I was wondering if you might have remembered anything since. Any tiny scrap of information, anything at all . . ."

"I told the police, and I'll tell you. I was asleep. 'Course I don't sleep as well as I used to, but then I don't hear as well, either. Some nights you could run a brass band through here, and it wouldn't bother me none." Mary tipped her head back carefully. "What's all the fuss about? Don't you have insurance? I got robbed myself in forty-one. Nobody likes it, but there's not much you can do about it, 'cept put it behind you and go on. Anyways, I figure I'm safe now. Not much left around this old place anybody'd want anymore. You ask me, take that insurance money and have yourself a ball."

"I'm afraid that's not possible," Jesse said quietly. "The burglar didn't take my things. He took my daughter."

"Well, I'll be damned." Mary's fingers wrapped like claws around the top of the walker as she began to back away from the door. "Dear, you'd better come in and sit down."

"No," Jesse said quickly. "Thank you, but I can't. I've got to keep going. I want to talk to everybody on the street."

"Good idea." Mary nodded. "That's the thing to do. Talk to the Findleys. Maybe they have something to say."

"The Findleys?"

Mary gestured vaguely down the road. "Number 228 was where they were. Moved on now. They got robbed once. Did you know that?"

Jesse shook her head.

"Nineteen-eighty-eight or thereabouts. 'Course their kids were in college then, nobody was about to take them. Mabel Findley now, she might have given the boy away. . . ."

"Thank you," said Jesse. "You've been a big help."

Mary reached to a table beside the door, and came

up with a pad of paper. "Put your name and phone number on here. If I see or hear anything, I'll let you know."

Jesse took the pad and quickly scribbled the information. "I'd appreciate it." She paused, then added, "And if you ever need anything, you let me know, okay? Remember, I'm right next door."

Mary gave her a long, considering look. "I just might do that."

"Good." Jesse smiled. "I wish you would."

No one was home at either of the next two houses. At the one after that Jesse found out why. Mr. Barberi was out front, tending his geraniums. As she approached he stood up, brushed off his hands on the front of his pants, and introduced himself.

"The Newtons now, their daughter is graduating from college this weekend." He shaded his eyes with his hand and looked back the way she'd come. "And the Jacksons, they're off on a cruise. Been away all week and have another week left to go. I'm taking care of their mail, that's how come I know."

Jesse explained what she was after, but beyond the whereabouts of the other two families Mr. Barberi had nothing to add. She thanked him and kept going. It took several hours, but she made the circuit of the entire street. At each house Jesse introduced herself and explained the purpose for her visit. Some of the neighbors were sympathetic, some were curious, and some were obviously titillated by their proximity to all the excitement. Several tossed out bits of information at random, trying to be of help.

"I saw something," said Mrs. Manetti, across the street. "I told the police about it, too."

"What was that?"

"A van. I saw it that night, parked right over there." Mrs. Manetti pointed toward the end of her driveway.

"It was there Wednesday night?"

"That's what I said, didn't I?"

"What time?"

"Just about supper time." Mrs. Manetti nodded firmly. "That's what time it was. I was in the kitchen and I saw it out the window. I said to Ralph, look at that van parked right in front of our house. Nobody we know drives a green Dodge van."

Supper time? That was much too early. "Did you see what time it left?" Jesse asked.

"Not that I was looking, mind you, but I did. The reason I noticed was that when I came back to do the dishes, it was gone."

"Oh."

"What's the matter with that?"

"I was hoping you might have seen or heard something later, like maybe two A.M.?"

Mrs. Manetti propped her hands on her ample hips. "Now, what would I be doing looking out the window at that time of night I'd like to know?"

Jesse thanked her for her trouble and moved on. At the last house on the street a sprightly man who introduced himself as Bill Custer answered her knock. "Talk to the Renfrews," he told her, nodding wisely. "There's trouble around, you can bet their grandson's in the middle of it."

"The Renfrews?" Jesse had covered the entire road without coming upon anybody of that name.

"Next block over." Custer pointed around behind his house. "Where the houses back up to ours. You ask about that boy, he's always up to something."

"Mr. Custer, did you tell that to the police when they were here?"

"Well, of course I did. I'm a citizen, aren't I?"

Hot, tired, her feet aching, Jesse was finally forced to concede defeat. If there was any information to be had from her neighbors, she didn't know what it was. Three long hours of work had turned up only three minutely interesting facts, all of which the police supposedly already had.

As she reached the backdoor to her own house, the phone inside began to ring. Weariness gone, Jesse thrust open the door and hurried in. She'd left her telephone number all up and down the street. Maybe someone had remembered something important. Or maybe it was Detective Maychick. . . .

As the machine was about to click on she grabbed up the receiver. "Hello?"

"It's about time," said an accusing voice. "Do you realize I've been trying to reach you for two days?"

Jesse drew in a breath and raked her fingers back through her hair. She'd recognize her mother's shrill tone anywhere. Calm, Beth Ross's voice was smooth as a purr; angry, it could peel paint.

"Hello, Mother." Jesse walked around the counter and settled into one of the cane-back chairs, girding herself for what was to come. "I've been out a lot. Why didn't you leave a message on the machine?"

"If I wanted to talk to a machine, I could call the phone company. When I call you, I want to talk to you!"

After a promising beginning like that, Jesse held out little hope for the rest of the conversation. "So . . . how are you?"

"I'll tell you how I am. I'm shocked and I'm upset, that's how I am. How would you feel if the only news you'd had about your daughter in months came from the FBI?"

"That was your choice." Even now, would they still have to rehash the same old battles?

"To be grilled by the authorities like a common criminal?"

"No, to pretend I didn't exist. I wasn't the one who issued ultimatums. I wasn't the one insisting that I find a way to get Ned back, or else."

"Well, what else was I going to do?" Beth Ross demanded. "As I recall, you were much too busy ruining your life to listen to anything I had to say. How else was I supposed to get your attention?"

Jesse allowed herself the luxury of a long sigh. Obviously some things were never going to change. "Did you call to fight with me?"

"Of course not. I called to find out what in the world is going on. I'll have you know that a man from the FBI came to see us. The *FBI,* Jesse! Can you imagine what the neighbors must have thought?"

"Probably not a thing, unless you told them about it."

"Don't you smart-mouth me, miss. According to them my granddaughter is missing. At first Howard and I didn't even believe them. We were sure they had us confused with someone else. Do you want to know what Howard said?"

Jesse rubbed a hand wearily over her eyes. "What?"

"She was always such a good child, our Jesse. How could she have gone so wrong?"

Abruptly she straightened in her chair. "Dad said that to the FBI?"

"Of course," Beth sniffed. "Can you imagine? They seemed to think we might have been involved. As if Howard and I are kidnappers!"

Jesse could only hope the comment never made its way back to Detective Maychick. Other mothers might have called to offer what comfort they could, but not Beth. She'd called seeking reassurance of her own.

"I'm sure after they spoke to you, the agents realized you had nothing to do with Amanda's abduction," Jesse offered.

"Well, I should hope so. But what I want to know is how could something like this have happened? Your brother never got into scrapes like this. Really, Jesse, some people just seem to invite trouble—"

"If you continue that thought," Jesse said softly, "I'm going to hang up."

There was a long moment of silence from the other end before Beth finally spoke. "I'm not saying this was your fault, dear."

"Then what exactly are you saying?"

For once Beth seemed to be choosing her words with care. "That perhaps some of the decisions you've made haven't exactly been the best."

"Like getting a divorce."

"That's one."

"We've been over this before, Mother. Ned left me."

"You could have tried harder to get him back."

Jesse blew out an exasperated breath. "I could have built a ship and flown to the moon, too."

"Sarcasm doesn't become you, Jesse. It never did."

"There's no use arguing about this. What's done is done."

"Maybe, maybe not. There's nothing like a crisis for bringing a family back together."

Was that a peace offering? Jesse wondered. After all, her mother had made the first move.

"So?" Beth prompted.

"So . . . what?" Jesse was unsure what was required of her.

"Have you spoken to Ned? Are you getting back together?"

She should have known. Every time the record spun, it was bound to play the same tune. "Yes, I've spoken to Ned. But that's all. We've both built other lives. We don't have anything in common anymore."

"Nothing in common?" Beth demanded. "What about three years of marriage and a baby the two of you created?"

"We've been over this before, Mother. Our marriage had problems—"

"All marriages have problems. You work them out, and then go on."

"We did work them out," Jesse snapped, tired suddenly of the whole conversation. "We filed for divorce."

Beth's long sigh conveyed itself clearly through the wire. "You used to be so much more reasonable."

"I used to be younger. Now I know better."

"You may be all grown up, but you still don't know everything, miss. Not by a long shot." Beth's voice began to quaver. "It's so unfair. I never had a chance to know my other granddaughter. Now this one is gone, too."

Jesse knew she should be more understanding, but somehow the emotion refused to come. "You had four months."

"What's four months? I thought I had all the time in the world. Why haven't the police found that baby yet? You answer me that."

"They're working on it."

"You're sure they're doing everything they should?"

"Yes, Mother." The last thing Jesse wanted was to get into a discussion of what was, and wasn't, being done.

"Maybe if we came up—"

"No," Jesse said quickly. She could just picture such a visit with its endless recriminations. "Don't."

"What do you mean, no? We're your parents, Jesse. In times of need families pull together."

Funny, that wasn't the way it had happened in the past. Nor the way things were bound to turn out now. "It's not a good idea. You saw yourself when you tried to reach me, I'm out a lot. There wouldn't be anything for you and Dad to do."

"But we want to help."

"Right now there's nothing you can do."

Beth thought about that for a moment before taking off in another direction. "I must say I was impressed with that young man from the FBI. I imagine their agents do a very good job." There was an undercurrent of excitement in her voice, as if the drama was unfolding in someone else's family and she was merely an interested bystander, lucky to have the inside track.

"I'm sure they do."

"Now, you're sure you don't want us to come . . .?"

"Positive."

"It's only four hours by car, even less if Howard sleeps and I drive."

"Mother—"

"Don't take that tone with me, miss. I can tell when I'm not wanted."

Like mothers everywhere, hers knew exactly which buttons to push. "It's not that I don't want to see you, just that now isn't the best time."

"But that's exactly why we should come."

Jesse's finger hovered over the disconnect lever. Her mother would argue until they were both blue in the face, or until she won, whichever came first. "Good-bye, Mother."

"Jesse, wait!"

"I'm hanging up the phone, Mother. Good-bye."

"I should think you'd be glad to have the company under the circumstances. After all, that neighborhood you're in could be better."

"How would you know?"

"Well, I . . ." Beth paused. "You only have to look at what just happened to realize that."

"I suppose." Jesse frowned. "Look, I appreciate the call. And I'll let you know just as soon as I have any news."

"Yes, of course," said Beth. "And if you change your mind . . . Maybe I could come by myself. Howard could manage without me for a couple days."

"No, Mother. Good-bye."

"Oh, all right," Beth said huffily. "Good-bye."

No sooner had Jesse replaced the receiver than the phone rang again. Irritably she snatched it up. "Mother, I told you—"

"Mrs. Archer? Jesse Archer? This is Rita Hollings calling from the *Cranford Journal*."

"Oh." Jesse flushed. "I'm sorry, I thought you were someone else."

"We spoke briefly the other day, and I apologize for that. Obviously my timing wasn't the best."

"That . . . it's all right."

"Of course the paper's been covering your story, but all we have so far is the facts. I'd like to explore the human-interest angle. And of course a feature story on our front page will reach an awful lot of people."

"You want to interview me?"

"Yes, if you're willing."

"When?"

"As soon as possible."

Jesse didn't even have to stop and think. A feature story on the front page of the *Journal* would just about finish off what little privacy she had left. Then again she'd be willing to give up a great deal more than that if it would help get her daughter back.

"How about now?"

"Perfect," said Rita. "I'll be there in twenty minutes."

EIGHTEEN

Ruby Saunders was knitting on her front porch. It was much cooler outside the house than in, and besides, by late afternoon the light was better. She'd done the front of the sweater and one sleeve. Now she was midway through the back. With any luck her grandson wouldn't have another growing spurt before she sent it to him in the fall.

Or maybe the family would come and visit this time. After all, it had been almost a year. Her daughter was good about calling regularly and she sent cards and letters, too. But that wasn't the same as having everyone over for a big family dinner. That wasn't the same as giving her grandchildren a hug. When was the last time she'd cooked a turkey anyway? Or even a roast for that matter? Hardly any reason to, when there was only one mouth to feed. Drat that son-in-law of hers anyway for taking that transfer to Minnesota.

Not that the money he made wasn't good. No, her daughter had picked herself a good provider, and a fine husband, too. But then what else would you expect, after she'd had her mother's example to follow?

Forty-two years Ruby Saunders had been married. November would have made it forty-three. But Bob had always liked fine whiskey and a good cigar, and no one was ever going to tell him differently. In the end, the doctors said, the combination had killed him.

So now here she was, sixty-eight and alone. Sitting on the porch and knitting sweaters like some old lady with nothing better to do. Most days she stayed inside and enjoyed the soap operas. But now the damn fool TV was busted. Turn it on, and all she got was snow. She'd walked outside and had a look and, sure enough, the antenna didn't look right, hanging off to one side at a crazy angle.

Ruby had called the repairman and he'd said he'd fit her in as soon as possible. But when was that supposed to be? Already she'd been waiting going on three days. The man had sounded no older than her grandson. That was the trouble with the younger generation these days. They'd had things too easy, and took too much for granted. Unreliable, every last one of them.

When she went inside, Ruby told herself, she'd call again. That was the only way to get things done. Make enough noise, and sooner or later they'd have to pay attention.

Just because she was old, folks thought they could take advantage. Sure, her eyes weren't what they used to be. Lately, reading was just too much of a strain. That's why she relied on her TV. How else was she to know what was happening in the world? And she did want to know. The body might be slowing down a bit, but the mind was just as sharp as ever.

A van drove slowly down the road out front. Ruby watched its progress with interest. When it turned into the driveway next door, she rose slightly and hitched her chair in that direction without missing a stitch.

A man opened the door and got out. He didn't look like anybody she knew. He glanced around, almost furtively, his eyes scanning up and down the street.

Without knowing quite why she did so, Ruby ducked her gaze, watching as the long thin needles scratched their way through another row.

When she looked up again, the man was gone. Must have gone inside, she decided. She hadn't heard him knock, or ring the bell either. Probably he had a key. Which was odd, considering she'd never seen him around before.

And if he'd been a fixture in the neighborhood, she'd have known. Rheumy eyes and all, Ruby Saunders still didn't miss much.

Of course who was to say the woman next door couldn't have a gentleman caller? Nothing odd about that. Hell, Ruby'd be glad to have one herself, if she knew where to get one. Problem was, all the men her age were too old. And the younger ones didn't seem interested.

Now, wouldn't that be something, Ruby asked herself, if the woman next door was courting? That might explain her strange behavior lately. Not that she was standoffish, but the woman had a tendency to keep to herself. Now she'd been just about holed up inside that house for days. And the last time she'd been out, it was to walk down the block pushing a baby carriage.

A baby carriage, could you imagine that? There'd never been a baby in that house before. Ruby was sure of that. Of course she'd seen some people who did their marketing in carriages like that, but she didn't think her neighbor was one of those.

Only minutes later the man reemerged and climbed back into his car. If that was a date, Ruby decided as he drove away, it was a damn short one. But then what did these young kids know about romance anyway? All they wanted was instant gratification. Fast food, fast cars, supersonic jets. She'd heard of speed reading. For all she knew, there was some newfangled equivalent called speed dating.

Ruby chuckled at that, juices gathering in her dry

throat. Any minute now she'd get up and go inside for a drink.

A squeal of tires at the end of the block drew her attention as a low-slung red car came barreling down the street. Immediately Ruby leaped up, the knitting falling to a heap at her feet. "Hey!" she yelled, shaking her fist as the car sped past. "Slow down!"

The car reached the end of the street, turned the corner, and was gone. "Idiots," Ruby muttered. With effort she leaned down and retrieved her work. "Damn teenagers!"

The road was a shortcut to downtown and they all came through like that. Sometimes they even threw litter out of their cars, soda cans and fast-food wrappers that hit the pavement and bounced wildly, spraying their contents in all directions. Sometimes at night, just for the hell of it, they drove through with a baseball bat and smashed the mailboxes.

It was a miracle nobody had gotten hurt. Children played in these yards, and animals, too. Somebody had to look out for them, and Ruby had appointed herself to do the job.

If she was younger, she'd show those kids a thing or two. Before her eyesight faded, she'd have taken down their license-plate numbers, all right. Then when she called the police, she'd have something tangible to give them. Not like now when she reported what had happened and they said they couldn't help her.

Sometimes she called once a week. In the summer it was even more often than that. "I know my rights!" Ruby would insist to the officers who answered the phone. "These kids disturbing the peace. They're creating a general nuisance."

"We're sorry," the officer would reply, "but unless you know who they are, there's nothing we can do."

"You could set up a roadblock," Ruby had suggested, pleased with her own logic. "Or send over an officer to stand guard." So far the police had done neither.

But she was nothing if not patient, Ruby thought as she went inside to call again. Someday the police would sit up and take notice. If she made enough noise, they'd have to, wouldn't they?

NINETEEN

As she had promised, Rita Hollings arrived in no time. "I brought a photographer with me," she said, breezing in as soon as the door was opened. "I hope you don't mind."

"Well . . . no" Jesse hadn't thought of that. "I guess not."

"Good. We'll need a picture of the baby as well." Rita glanced around with the air of a woman who was used to being in charge. She chose a place to sit, hunkered down, and pulled a pen and a pad of paper from her voluminous pocketbook. "Of course I'll see that it's returned."

"I'd appreciate that." Jesse opened a drawer in the end table, thumbed quickly through the stack of photographs, and handed one over.

"Pretty baby." Rita glanced at the photo briefly then tucked it away. "Her name's Amanda, right?"

"Right." Jesse heard the sound of a camera, clicking away behind her, and tried not to look.

"Does he make you uncomfortable?"

"Yes."

"Only a few more then." Rita sent the photographer a look. "It's worth the trouble. Pictures will give the story texture, make it seem more real. I don't suppose you'd like to pose in the nursery?"

"No."

"How about the kitchen?"

"Bottle in hand?" Jesse asked wryly.

"Something like that."

"I don't think so."

"Okay then," Rita said easily. "We'll leave it for now. Just out of curiosity what have you thought of our coverage so far?"

Jesse frowned at that. She supposed she should have been expecting the question. Usually she read the paper at night when she got home. For the past several days there'd been too many other things on her mind; she hadn't seen it once.

"To tell the truth I haven't read it."

"None of it?"

"No."

Rita looked at her curiously. "Can I ask why?"

"It's bad enough living the story. I don't need to read about it, too."

"Right. Well, then let's get on with it."

Jesse had thought she'd have to retell the whole story; but as Rita had mentioned on the phone, she had the facts. What the reporter wanted now was to create an emotional impact by exposing Jesse's anguish and fears, and weaving them into a drama that the reader would be unable to put down. Her questions were probing, and to the point. More than once Jesse stopped, shook her head, then forced herself to answer.

"Why do we have to mention that I was beaten?" she asked, when the subject was broached for the second time.

"It's part of the whole picture. And besides, it'll do wonders for the sympathy vote. Trust me, it never hurts to jerk a few tears. Move people and they'll remember you."

"I don't want them to remember me."

"Oh yes, you do." Rita's gaze was steady and unwavering. "Until you get your daughter back, you want my readers to think of nothing else. Because the more people who care about what happens to Amanda, the greater the chance that she'll be found."

An hour later Rita was finished. After promising that the interview would appear in the next day's paper, she and the photographer left. Alone in the house, Jesse walked from room to room and turned on lights. Though the sun wouldn't set for another hour, shadows were already beginning to lengthen. It seemed like the coward's way out, but the extra illumination held a multitude of memories at bay.

Back in the living room Jesse lowered herself gingerly into a chair. Her bruises were healing nicely; still, after spending the afternoon on her feet, she felt sore, and tired to the point of exhaustion. Even if Agent Phillips hadn't stressed the idea, she'd have known that it was vital she keep up her strength.

What had she done so far to that end? Eat almost nothing and sleep even less. No wonder she felt as though she had nothing more to give. Tonight that was going to change. For Amanda's sake, if not her own, she'd cook and eat a real meal, then sleep for eight hours, or even more if she could manage it.

In the kitchen Jesse took a rib steak from the freezer and put it in the microwave to defrost. She debated over the hour a baked potato would take to cook, then realized it would give her time for a hot bath before she ate.

The potato washed and in the oven, Jesse stripped off her clothes and filled the tub with hot water. A box of Epsom salts was in the cabinet. She tossed in a handful, then added bubble bath as well. If she was going to soak, she might as well do it right.

Steam rose from the tub as Jesse lowered herself into the scalding water. Bit by bit the stiffness eased from her muscles, replaced by a feeling of languor. For the first time in what seemed like forever she felt relaxed. Her eyes slipped closed as she willed herself to contemplate nothing more pressing than the mound of bubbles floating past her nose.

Later—Jesse had no idea how much—she awoke with a start. The bubbles were gone and the water had cooled considerably. Scrambling up, she grabbed a towel from the hook on the back of the door and dried herself vigorously. The clock on the table beside the bed revealed that she'd been asleep for almost two hours.

Jesse slipped on a nightgown, covered it with a robe, then went to rescue the potato. Predictably it had cooked itself into a small, wrinkled lump. She set it on the counter to cool, then turned her attention to the steak. It was soggy, but still edible. With any luck, there'd be lettuce and tomato in the crisper. The combination might not provide a real meal, but it was close enough.

Jesse left the steak on the counter and went outside to light the grill. Inspecting what was left from last barbecue, she dumped in some more coals, sprayed on lighter fluid, and tossed in a match. Immediately hot blue-orange flames licked up into the night.

Twenty minutes, she decided, banking the coals with a stick. There was no hurry to go in and get the steak. Instead she waited in the backyard, enjoying the tranquil solitude of the warm summer night.

One of the reasons she'd purchased the house was the yard. Though small, it was fully fenced, affording her the illusion of privacy. Clutching the robe around her, Jesse tilted back her head. The sky was filled with a cavalcade of stars.

She gazed at them for a moment, then squeezed her eyes shut. "Star light, star bright. I wish I may, I wish I might, have my wish come true tonight. Oh please," she whispered, sending a fervent plea out into the night. "Please God, bring my baby home!"

Jesse opened her eyes slowly. The breeze was picking up. Leaves rustled in the branches overhead. Absently she poked at the coals, tucking them tight around their glowing red center. She heard the sound then, so faint at first that she could barely make it out.

A cat? Jesse listened to the weak cry. No, not a cat . . .

The sound was stronger now and she felt her heart constrict. A baby—somewhere a baby was crying. The timbre seemed achingly familiar. It spoke to her, tugged at her, demanded that she listen. The stick fell from Jesse's fingers and clattered to the flagstone below. It wasn't just any baby she heard; it was Amanda.

She didn't know how she knew. Was it mother's instinct or desperation? The sound receded once again and Jesse found herself rising up on her toes and straining to hear. The cries were softer now, barely distinguishable from the whisper of the wind itself. It didn't matter. That was Amanda's voice.

Amanda was calling out to her, calling for her mother to come and save her.

As if in a trance, Jesse began to walk. All her senses were attuned to the sound, all her faculties devoted to divining its source. She was around the front of the house before she even realized she'd moved at all.

The cries seemed louder there. The street was dark, deserted. She looked to the left first, and then the right. The wind hit her full in the face, carrying its sounds with it. The decision made, she went with it.

The pavement was rough beneath her bare feet. Jesse didn't feel the pain. When her robe tangled around her legs, she bunched it up and tucked it into the belt, mindful of nothing save the ebb and flow of the capricious cries.

At the end of the street there was only silence. Amanda was close, she could feel it. Her daughter needed her, Jesse couldn't let her down. "Give me a clue, dammit!" she yelled. "Show me which way to go!"

Nothing answered her. Even the breeze had died. Distraught, Jesse refused to let go. How could she when she felt her daughter's presence so very near at hand? Amanda had called out to her. Even now she was somewhere within reach, waiting for her mother to answer her cries. But where?

Blindly Jesse began to run. She raced the length of the block. Heedless of traffic, she darted across the road and past the next stretch of houses. Lights were on, windows open. She heard television babble and CD songs. But in the space of a heartbeat Amanda had vanished.

She had to be there somewhere, Jesse told herself frantically. She just had to be.

At night the streets all looked the same. One block blended into the next as Jesse refused to give up her search. She passed bright houses and parked cars, skimmed over gutters and lawns alike. Around a blind corner a bicyclist nearly hit her. Jesse never even noticed.

Breathing became an effort as oxygen tore like fire through her lungs. The rhythm of her stride faltered and then broke. Jesse ran on energy while it lasted, and adrenaline after that. She ran until only will alone kept her going.

And still she heard . . . nothing.

As she rounded a corner out of the darkness, her eyes were seared suddenly by a wall of unexpected light. Across the street lay the emergency entrance to St. Simon's Hospital. An ambulance was parked by one door; the wide, well-lit driveway was bustling with activity.

Shocked, gasping for breath, Jesse stopped short as an awareness of her surroundings rushed over her. It seemed as if she'd been running for hours. The breeze was gone; she didn't have to listen to know the cries were, too. St. Simon's Hospital was blocks from her house. How could she have come all that way?

Turning, Jesse retreated quickly back out of the circle of reflected light. At some point during the flight her robe had flapped open and now she quickly pulled it shut. Her hair, dried by the wind, curled wildly about her head. Her feet, torn and bloodied by the chase, began to throb. She was crazy to be out on the streets dressed like this. What was the matter with her?

Hastily Jesse took her bearings and turned to head for home. She didn't even want to think about what had happened. Later she could examine her actions and wonder. Now the only thing that mattered was getting home and bringing this horrible night to an end.

As she reached the corner a patrol car pulled to the end of the hospital driveway. After scarcely a moment's hesitation it turned in Jesse's direction. Head down, not daring to look, she willed it to go on by. Instead the car slowed to match her speed, then stopped all together.

Jesse quickened her pace, but when she heard the car door open, she knew it was no use. She paused, then turned as the beam of a powerful flashlight played up and down over her. For a moment she was blinded, then the light switched off, leaving her blinking helplessly in the semidarkness.

"Officer Rollins, ma'am," said a disembodied voice. "Are you all right?"

It was only a moment until her sight was restored and Jesse could see the officer, leaning against his open door and gazing at her with concern. She drew herself up and tried for some semblance of dignity. "Yes, of course." A hand came up to smooth back her disheveled hair. "I'm fine. I was just out . . . walking."

"Should have brought your shoes," Rollins observed. "Did you realize your feet are bleeding?"

"Are they?" Jesse asked, and wondered who she thought she was fooling.

"Maybe you'd like me to give you a lift home?"

"No, I'm fine. Really."

"Pardon me, ma'am, but you don't look fine. Why don't you just climb in the car and I'll run you by your place? It won't take but a minute and then you can tend to those feet."

Clearly further arguments were not going to win her cause. Jesse walked around the car and Rollins settled her in the front seat.

"Anything happen you want to tell me about?" he asked as he slid once more behind the wheel.

"No," Jesse said quickly. "Nothing happened at all. Like I said, I was just out walking." It was a toss-up which way he'd think her more foolish—telling the truth, or sticking to this ridiculous story. Either way he was bound to wonder.

"If you say so."

Rollins remembered where her house was without being told, and they didn't speak at all after that. In her driveway Jesse scrambled out, clutching her robe around her. "Thank you for the ride. I appreciate it."

"No problem. Make sure you see about those feet now. They don't look too good. You wouldn't want to get an infection."

"You're right. I will." Jesse paused, knowing there was a request she had to make. "Look, if you didn't have to tell Detective Maychick about this, I'd appreciate it."

Rollins gazed at her for a long moment, then finally shrugged. "Nothing to tell. Lots of people like to walk out their troubles. Even me sometimes. Don't you worry about a thing."

Jesse smiled tremulously. "Thank you."

"Don't mention it." He backed the car carefully out of the driveway and disappeared down the road.

The front door to the house was locked; Jesse didn't have a key. She went around back, pausing on the patio only long enough to separate the coals and close the grill.

She'd lost her taste for food. Sleep was what she needed now. Eight long hours of deep, dreamless oblivion.

Inside, she dumped the steak in the garbage, then headed into the living room to turn off the front light. Officer Rollins had been right, her feet did need care. There was some ointment in the medicine cabinet—

Jesse rounded the corner and a scream bubbled up in her throat. A man was sitting by the window. He rose to meet her, arms outstretched, hands reaching. Even as she spun away she knew it was too late.

Darkness rushed up around her as she began to scream.

TWENTY

"Jess, stop it! It's me." Hands grasped her roughly and spun her around. "What's the matter with you?"

There wasn't time to think, only act. Instinctively her fist came up, connecting hard against his jaw.

"Shit, Jess! Cut it out!"

It took a moment, but the angry words finally penetrated. As did the voice. Jesse's eyes widened. "Ned?"

"Ahhh Jesus." He backed away, rubbing his aching chin. "Who else did you expect?"

"Nobody," she snapped, turning on the nearest light. Damn, her hand was killing her. She watched with satisfaction as Ned stumbled to the couch and sat down. It served him right. "I wasn't expecting anybody. How dare you come in here and scare me half to death!"

"I wasn't trying to scare you." Ned poked his tongue around his lip experimentally and found a small trickle of blood. "I was waiting for you. Dammit, did you have to hit me so hard?"

"If you'd announced yourself rather than pouncing on me like that, I wouldn't have hit you at all." Frowning, Jesse crossed the room and sat down beside him.

"Here, let me see." As she'd suspected, the damage was minimal. "Don't be such a baby, it's barely a scratch."

"Easy for you to say. You weren't on the receiving end."

"Oh, for Pete's sake." Jesse rose and started for the kitchen. "Sit there, I'll be right back."

She wet several towels with warm water, then found the antiseptic ointment in the bathroom. Back in the living room, while Ned dabbed at his lip, she attended to her feet. Finished, she looked up to find him watching her with interest.

"What the hell happened to you?"

"It's a long story."

"I'm listening."

"Don't bother." Jesse gathered up the towels and set them aside.

"If you're not going to talk to me, this is going to be a very long night."

"Or a very short one."

Ned frowned at her tone. "I realize that you're feeling a little defensive right now, but I really think we need to talk."

"What about?"

"Us."

"*Us?*" She almost laughed. "There is no us, Ned. You took care of that."

"Maybe I was wrong."

Jesse turned and stared. "What?"

"I said, maybe I was wrong."

Deliberately Jesse leaned back to put some distance between them. "I doubt it. As I recall, you were never wrong."

"You're not going to make this easy, are you?"

"No."

"I didn't think so." Ned looked at her for a long moment. "But it has to be said. Ever since you came to see me, I've been thinking. Things aren't over between us, Jesse. Maybe they never will be."

"You're crazy." Jesse leaped up. Agitation had her pacing across the room. "You're imagining things."

"No, I'm not. You were all over the place at my apartment. You jumped every time I came near you. You felt something, Jess, or you wouldn't have run away. Are you going to tell me I was imagining that?"

"Yes."

"You never were a very good liar."

"And you were always too full of yourself."

"Maybe." Ned grinned. "It's one of my virtues." Sitting back, he spread an arm across the top of the cushion. "Would you come here and sit down? All that moving around is making me crazy."

Jesse eyed the seat he had in mind for her. "Thank you, I'd rather stand."

"Still running?"

"No. Just much too cautious to spring that trap."

"Then you admit it."

"What?"

"You do feel something for me."

"Of course," Jesse said sweetly. "Irritation and impatience come immediately to mind."

Ned crooked a finger in her direction. "I dare you to come closer and say that."

"Grow up!"

"I'm trying." Ned plowed his hand back through his hair. "Jesus, Jess, I'm trying."

From across the room Jesse contemplated her husband in silence. There was an ulterior motive there somewhere; there had to be. She knew from past experience that he was a master at manipulation. But what was he after now?

"Ned," she said softly. "Why are you here?"

"I had to see you. After I saw you the other day, I knew I couldn't just let you walk out of my life again."

Obviously he'd forgotten who'd been the one to do the walking. "It took you forty-eight hours to figure that out?"

"Actually I came yesterday."

Jesse's head snapped up. "When?"

"Late afternoon. You weren't here. I parked across the street and waited. You didn't show up until after dark."

Stunned, she sank down in the chair. "Last night, the man in black—that was you!"

"I'd been waiting for hours," Ned said plaintively. "And then, when you saw me, you looked like you'd seen a ghost."

"I thought you were the kidnapper! You nearly scared me to death!"

"I called your name. Didn't you hear me?"

"No, I didn't hear you. I was probably too busy screaming. For Pete's sake, why didn't you come out into the light and identify yourself?"

"In case you haven't noticed, there are no lights on this road. Besides, before I'd gone a dozen steps, you were inside the house. I didn't know what the hell to do. I went back to the car and figured I'd give you a few minutes to calm down."

"When the police arrived, you were gone."

Ned threw up his hands. "What else could I do? I wasn't about to wait around for Detective Maychick to roust me again. The minute I saw all the lights coming, I got the hell out."

"Leaving me to explain to two very skeptical patrolmen that it wasn't my imagination, there really had been someone out there. Dammit, Ned, don't you ever think ahead? How could it not have occurred to you that I'd be frightened?"

"For one thing I didn't expect it to be dark when you got home." Ned stopped, shook his head. "No, scratch that. The answer is, you're right, I should have behaved differently. Of course you're feeling vulnerable right now." He rose from the sofa and crossed the room. Squatting down before Jesse's chair, he rested his arms on her knees. "I was wrong, and I didn't think. I'm sorry, Jess. Will you forgive me?"

"Well, I . . ." Surprised by his sudden capitulation, Jesse needed a moment to find the words. "I guess so." She wanted to remove his hands, but there was no where else to put them. Simply pushing them away seemed somehow churlish.

"Gracious as always. That's my girl."

"I'm not your girl, Ned."

He angled his weight back until he was resting on his heels. "You can fence with words all you like. In the end it'll be the same."

"What will?"

"You still care for me, Jess. You can say you don't, but you do. Why else would you have come to see me after all this time?"

That did it; she was glad she'd hit him. This time she did push his hands away. "Don't flatter yourself," Jesse said as she rose from the chair. "I didn't go to your apartment because I wanted to see you. I went because I needed to find out if you knew anything about Amanda's disappearance."

"Don't be ridiculous. You know I'm not a kidnapper." Ned followed her into the kitchen. "Where are we going?"

"If you're going to be here much longer, I'm going to need coffee. How about you?"

"At this time of night?"

"Suit yourself."

"You used to keep decaf."

"I used to have a reason." Jesse set up the pot and turned it on. Behind her Ned was rummaging through the refrigerator.

"Look at this," he said, pushing the baby supplies aside. "There's not a single thing to eat."

"Who needs food when you can live on caffeine?"

"Is that what you do?" Ned slammed the door shut in disgust. "No wonder you look like you do."

"Oh? And what is that supposed to mean?"

Her tone was fair warning. Ned chose to ignore it. "It means that you could stand to gain some weight. I hate to say it, Jess, but you've let yourself go."

The words were untrue, but they still stung. "Whereas you, of course, are growing younger and more handsome by the moment."

"Give me a break. That wasn't an insult, it was an observation. If you ask me, you need someone around to take care of you."

So they were back to that, were they? Jesse poured herself a mug of hot dark coffee and watched the steam rise toward the ceiling. It was still too hot to drink. She set the cup on the counter to cool.

"All right, Ned. What's the deal? I doubt you're desperate for female companionship, so why are you here?"

"Desperate?" Ned choked the word out. His good looks had always been a source of pride. "That's a laugh."

"Maybe, maybe not." Jesse kept her voice deliberately casual. "Did you know your girlfriend is refusing to support your alibi?"

"Girlfriend? I don't . . . Oh, you mean Tiffany."

"Whoever." Tiffany, indeed. "According to Detective Maychick she says she was with you in the bar but not afterward."

Ned looked genuinely taken aback and Jesse found herself taking a perverse pleasure in his discomfort. "So much for having someone to keep you warm. You were so good, she doesn't even remember you."

"She's wrong." Ned frowned. "Or she's lying."

"Why would she want to do that?"

"I don't know." He jammed his hands into the pockets of his pants. "Shit. I suppose this means I'll be hearing from Detective Maychick again."

"Does that worry you?"

Ned looked up, meeting her gaze. "It's a pain, that's all."

Jesse reached around for the mug of coffee and took a cautious sip. Let him carry the conversation for a while.

"Look," he said. "You talk to Maychick. Put in a word for me, would you? The last thing I need is to be hounded by the police."

"Really?" she asked dryly.

"Jess, this is not funny."

"Believe me, I'm not amused. Either the woman was there, or she wasn't. One of you is lying, Ned. I have to wonder why."

"How should I know? Maybe she has a jealous boyfriend. Shit, maybe she has a husband."

Jesse stared at him incredulously. "Don't you know?"

"Why should I? It wasn't any big deal, just your basic one-night stand. If it had happened any other night, it would be forgotten by now."

"Right," Jesse said sarcastically. "Spoken like a true man of the nineties."

"I'm not an idiot. I used protection, in case you're wondering."

"I'm glad to hear that."

"Are you?"

"Of course." Jesse gazed at her ex-husband and wondered how it could have come to this: standing in the kitchen and discussing the birth control he'd used to sleep with another woman. "You're Amanda's father, and a man I once loved very much. Just because we're no longer married doesn't mean I want you dead."

"Well, that's comforting."

Jesse sighed. "I'm not trying to comfort you Ned, I'm trying to find out the truth."

"Dammit, Jesse, I told you the truth. You just don't want to believe it, and I think I know the reason why."

She was just too tired for this. Any moment now she and Ned were going to be screaming at each other like banshees. History was doomed to repeat itself and there wasn't a damn thing she could do to stop it.

"You're jealous, Jess. Admit it."

"I am not."

Ned started toward her, his expression intent. "We may not be together anymore, but I can still read you like a book. The thought of me in bed with another woman really eats you up."

"You're crazy, you know that? When I filed for divorce, I should have filed two petitions, one for you and one for your ego."

"Deny it all you like. *I* know the truth."

"Go to hell!" Jesse spun away from his continuing advance.

Ned grabbed Jesse's arm and whirled her back to face him. She stumbled as she turned, and fell against him. Automatically her hands came up to grasp for a hold. For a brief, startled moment she didn't move at all. She'd forgotten how he smelled; but now the scent of him, filling her nostrils, was wonderfully evocative. Their bodies fit together effortlessly.

"No," she said, pushing him away.

"Yes."

Ned's head tilted down and his mouth covered hers, the touch as warm as it was familiar. Instinctively she parted her lips. Or maybe it was habit. But how could she account for the sudden heaviness in her limbs? Until that moment Jesse hadn't known how much she needed to be held. Until Ned's tongue slid the length of hers and sent a shiver coursing through her she hadn't realized what a relief it could be simply to turn thought off and coast on sensation alone.

When he drew back, his hands remained, his palms cradling the sides of her face. Jesse opened her eyes and saw him gazing down upon her. Once upon a time she'd fallen in love with that look. But once upon a time was gone now.

"This is wrong," she whispered.

"Like hell." When she would have pulled back, Ned's hands held her in place. "It's the first right thing we've done in months."

He kissed her again, and Jesse gave herself up. Even when everything else was wrong between them, this had always been right. No doubt she was making a mistake; later there'd be plenty of time for regrets. But for now she no longer had the will to fight. Ned could help her forget. Even if it was only for a few minutes, how could she deny herself that solace?

Somehow they made their way into the bedroom. When Jesse would have switched off the light, Ned's hand stopped her. "I want to see you," he said softly. His fingers smoothed the robe from her shoulders and it fluttered to the floor.

His hand caressed her jaw, the long smooth line of her throat, then briefly cupped the weight of her breast—a promise for later. Then he stepped back and quickly stripped off his clothes. When Jesse hesitated over her gown, he bunched the cool pink satin and slipped it off over her head. In the light he studied the changes childbirth had made.

He was smiling when he reached out his hand. "Come to me, Jesse love."

Jesse went.

TWENTY-ONE

Day Five

The next morning Ned was gone. Predictable. Then again, thought Jesse, considering she'd just had her first real night's sleep in days, she wasn't about to complain. She'd used Ned, and he'd used her. For once they were even.

A note, dashed off in a hurried scrawl, was propped against the bedside lamp. "Good as ever. Call you later. N."

Jesse crumpled the paper in her fingers and let it fall to the floor. It wasn't as though she'd expected endearments. Still she'd have thought he could do a little better than that.

The sun was long since up, the sky a brilliant shade of morning blue. Jesse gazed at it through the window and sighed. The night's stars were gone, and her wish had not been granted. So much for magic.

Turning away, she closed her eyes and pictured her daughter's face. "Good morning, Amanda," she mouthed silently. "Mommy's thinking of you. I'm doing everything I can to make sure you come home soon, okay?"

Though she'd never believed in ESP, Jesse was sure her daughter could hear her. Even if Amanda didn't understand the words, surely she must be able to grasp their comforting message. The bond between them had been incredibly strong. Amanda had to know that her mother wouldn't abandon her, didn't she?

As usual Jesse had no answers, save the ones she gave herself. Amanda was warm, and safe, and being well cared for. And it was only a matter of time until she came home. Jesse had to believe that, because the alternative was simply unbearable.

She showered and dressed quickly, eager to get downtown and talk to Detective Maychick. Ned could hedge all he liked, but the fact of the matter was, either he had an alibi or he didn't. The whole situation was decidedly odd.

The kitchen reeked of spoiled steak. Jesse pulled out the garbage bag and took it outside, then dragged the can down to the curb for pickup. A brown Ford Fairlane turned the corner onto the road, and she stared for a moment, considering. She'd seen that car somewhere before. . . .

The car slowed as it drew closer, then nudged in to the curb in front of her house. Jesse recognized Detective Maychick behind the wheel and her heart flew into her throat. There was news, there had to be. Why else would he have come?

Dropping the garbage can, she dodged around the back of the parked car. "What?" she demanded, before he'd even had a chance to climb out. "What?"

"Now, Ms. Archer, don't get all excited." The detective closed and carefully locked the door behind him.

"You've heard something!" Jesse cried, grabbing his arm. "Do you know where Amanda is?"

"Just calm down," Maychick said firmly. Though

he didn't shake her hand away, it was clear from the look on his face that he'd have liked to. "I don't have any information about your daughter."

Jesse's hopes fell, and her face with them. "You don't?"

"No."

"Then . . . why are you here?"

"I have some questions. Maybe we'd better step inside."

"Questions?" Jesse looked at him blankly. "For me?"

Maychick let his gaze sweep up and down the street. At many of the houses people were up and around. "I don't want to do this out here, Ms. Archer. Do you?"

Jesse shrugged. What difference did it make if all he was going to do was ask more questions? She'd already told him everything she knew. Most things she'd told him more than once.

But then, she thought snidely, that was what police did when they weren't out actually solving crimes. *They asked questions.* No doubt it made them feel useful.

"Come on," she said with notable lack of grace. "We may as well go in."

Detective Maychick declined her offer of coffee, but he did ask if she minded if he smoked. "Be my guest," Jesse told him. There was an old ashtray under the sink. She pulled it out and set it on the kitchen table between them.

It seemed to take him an inordinately long time to find the crumpled pack of Marlboros and shake out an equally crumpled cigarette. Another minute was devoted to hunting down a match, and yet another to the lighting then to the inhaling of the first deep drag.

Jesse watched the ritual in silence, torn between jealousy over his obvious enjoyment and pride in her own willpower. Maychick seemed to be waiting for her to open the conversation. He had to think her very naive; either that, or not a fan of Steven Bochco. Instead she simply sat back, folded her hands in her lap, and waited.

When he did finally speak, however, his first question came as a surprise. "Do you have a lawyer, Ms. Archer?"

"No . . . yes." Jesse frowned. "Sort of."

Maychick tapped off a slender piece of ash. "Care to spell that out for me?"

"A lawyer in town prepared my will and handled the closing on this house, so yes, I do know where to get in touch with one. But I wouldn't exactly say I *have* a lawyer."

"You might want to call him."

"Why?"

"You're entitled to have a lawyer present during questioning. That's the law."

Jesse stared. "Those rights are for suspects, not victims. Am I a suspect, Detective Maychick?"

He took his time about answering. "Like I said, I don't like to rule anything out. You want to call your lawyer, I've got the time to wait."

"I don't need a lawyer."

"You want to waive your rights, that's up to you."

Irritation surged through her at his pompous, knowing manner. "I don't have to waive something I have no need for. Nothing is more important to me than getting my daughter back. *Nothing*. And if you have some questions for me that you think might help in that pursuit, I'll be very happy to answer them."

"All right." Maychick pulled out his pad and set it on the table. "Let's start with your husband."

"Ned?" Jesse's voice rose on a squeak.

"Are there others?"

"No—of course not."

"Ned Archer," he muttered under his breath, writing the name at the top of the page. Then he lifted his gaze and nailed her. "What was he doing here last night?"

"He came to see me. . . ." Jesse's voice trailed away, her eyes narrowing. "How do you know Ned was here?"

"You might say we've been keeping tabs."

"On me?"

"In part." Maychick set down his pen and took time for a drag. "On the neighborhood as well."

"Since when?"

"Two nights ago, when you called 911. One incident in a neighborhood like this is one thing. Two, you begin to wonder. So maybe we've been watching a little closer than normal."

"And have you seen anything unusual?"

"As a matter of fact we have." Maychick sat back and folded his arms over his chest. "Last night we saw your husband drive up and let himself in here. He stayed until this morning."

Indignation sharpened her tone. "I don't see what's so noteworthy about that."

"Really?" Maychick lifted a brow. "An overnight visit from a man you say you haven't spoken to in months? A man toward whom, only last week, you seemed distinctly hostile? I'd say that's a little unusual, wouldn't you?"

"Not at all," Jesse snapped.

"Why was he here, Ms. Archer?"

She wanted to tell him that it was none of his business, and would have, except she suspected it would only make things worse. "He came to see me."

"I figured that."

"Ned and I may be getting a divorce, but he's still Amanda's father."

"Umm-hmm."

"He wanted . . ." Jesse stopped, floundering. What *had* Ned wanted? A quickie with his ex? Probably. And he'd gotten it, too.

"Did you invite him here, Ms. Archer?"

Jesse looked up, surprised. "No."

"But you knew he was coming?"

"No, I didn't. In fact, when he arrived, I wasn't even here." She flushed then, remembering where she had been.

Luckily Maychick didn't pursue it. He was gnawing on the filter; the cigarette bobbled up and down in his mouth. "When was the last time you saw your husband before last night?"

"Friday."

"Last Friday?"

Yes."

"The day after your daughter disappeared."

"Yes."

Maychick's fingers strummed distractedly on the tabletop. "Maybe I misunderstood. I thought you said you hadn't seen your husband in almost a year."

"Before that I hadn't."

"Because he didn't want to have anything to do with your daughter."

"No," Jesse said impatiently. "Because he and I were getting a divorce. Amanda had nothing to do with it."

Maychick had reached the bottom of the page and flipped it over. "Who instigated the divorce proceedings, Ms. Archer?"

"I did."

"Then it was your idea not to continue with the marriage?"

"Forgive me, Detective Maychick, but I fail to see the relevance of these questions."

He looked up and smiled. His teeth were tobacco-stained. "Humor me."

"Is there a reason you're asking me these things?"

"There is. Otherwise I wouldn't be wasting your time and my own. Now, can we continue?"

"I suppose so."

Maychick stubbed out the cigarette. A thin spiral of smoke rose toward the ceiling. "I'll repeat the question for you. Were you the one who decided to end your marriage?"

"No." Jesse frowned. "Ned left me. He packed up one day and left while I was at work."

"Did that come as a surprise to you?"

"Yes."

"Maybe even a shock?"

"I guess so."

"And yet you just let him go."

"What choice did I have?" Jesse flared. It had been bad enough going through this with her parents. But to rehash the subject now, so far after the fact, with a man who was virtually a stranger, seemed perfectly useless. "Ned is a grown man, Detective Maychick. He wanted out. There wasn't much I could do to stop him."

"Did you try?"

"Yes, I tried!" Jesse's voice rose. Taking a deep breath, she brought it back down. "It didn't work. We agreed to separate, and then to divorce."

"Just like that."

"Yes, detective," Jesse said shortly. "Just like that."

Maychick looked around as though wishing for another cigarette. He settled for chewing on the top of his pen. "After you and your husband were separated, did you date much?"

"No."

"Why not?"

"I have a very demanding job. The hours don't leave much room for a social life, even if there had been somebody I wanted to date, which there wasn't. Besides, it wasn't very long after Ned and I separated that I found out I was pregnant."

"With a baby that he didn't want."

"We've been all over this before."

"Yes." Maychick flipped back through his notes, scanning an earlier page to refresh his memory. "You said at the time that your husband was Amanda's biological father. Did he have any quarrel with that?"

"No, of course not."

"Yet that didn't bring your marriage back together."

"Ned didn't want to be a father, Detective Maychick. Considering he left before he found out I was pregnant, that certainly wasn't going to bring him back."

"Did you hope it might?"

"Pardon me?"

"I said, when you found out that you were pregnant, Ms. Archer, did you hope that might do the trick?"

"Do the trick?" Jesse repeated incredulously. "Just what trick are we talking about here?"

"You've already told me you wanted your husband back. I'm just wondering if you thought that might be the way."

Anger ripped through her. For the first time she understood what it must be like to be a rape victim, violated once by an assailant and then, yet again, on the witness stand. What right did he have to go poking around in her life this way, invading her privacy with his intrusive questions? What right did he have to her dreams, her hopes, her fears?

"I'd like you to answer the question, Ms. Archer."

Her voice shook with suppressed fury. "The pregnancy was accidental."

"Birth control didn't work?"

"Something like that."

"And yet"—he looked down, consulting his notes once again—"you told me before that when the first child died, you wanted another baby."

"I did. Ned didn't."

"What kind of birth control were you using, Ms. Archer?"

Jesse leaped to her feet. "I hardly think that's any of your business."

"I was just wondering whether we're talking equipment failure here, or maybe human error."

"I said, *that is none of your business!*"

"Actually," Maychick remarked, "I think it is."

"The facts of Amanda's conception have nothing to do with her disappearance."

"On the contrary it's my opinion they may have a great deal to do with your daughter's disappearance."

Jesse's anger softened to confusion. "What are you talking about?"

Maychick flipped his pad shut and tucked it away. The chair scraped across the floor as he shoved it back and rose. "You had a baby, Ms. Archer, and now she's gone. You presented one scenario to explain that; now let me present another.

"You knew your husband didn't want that baby, didn't you, Ms. Archer? You knew that as long as the child was here, you could kiss your marriage goodbye. You told me yourself that you'd tried to win your husband back, and within days of your daughter's disappearance you'd succeeded."

Maychick leaned closer, his expression menacing. "So I have one last question for you, and I'd like you to think about it, because you can be damn sure that I am. Just how badly did you want your husband back, Ms. Archer? Suppose you answer me that."

TWENTY-TWO

Pale and shaken, Jesse watched Detective Maychick drive away down the street. If he had left a cigarette behind, she'd have lit up in a second. Though the sun shone brightly through the window, her hands were trembling and she felt cold all over.

How could the detective have said those things to her? How could he imagine, for even a moment, that she might have done something to harm Amanda?

He'd waited a moment after tossing out his accusations, expecting—no, daring—her to justify her actions. The fumbled explanation she'd offered had done no good. But dammit, how could she explain what had happened the night before when she didn't really understand it herself?

Ned had caught her at a vulnerable moment, and he'd taken advantage of it. Or maybe, needing someone, anyone, to hold her through the night, she'd taken advantage of him. What difference did it make? What happened with Ned had nothing to do with finding Amanda. Surely Detective Maychick would come to his senses and see that.

Jesse turned at the sound of a knock on the back-door. The hinge screeched as the screen was drawn open. "Jesse? Are you home?"

She was smiling before she even reached the kitchen. "I'm here, Kay. Come on in."

Kay was carrying a bundle under one arm. She dropped it on the kitchen counter. "You look better. Skinny, but better. Are you eating?"

"No."

"That's what I thought. This afternoon, I'm going to make you a casserole. Chicken tetrazzini, you'll love it. It's fattening as hell. Used to be one of my favorites before we all found out cholesterol was killing us."

"Kay, I don't want—"

"Don't want what?" Kay demanded so vehemently her curls shook. "To come over? To be a bother? To live through the week? What?"

"To impose," Jesse tried weakly.

"Fine, you're not." Kay waved a hand through the air. "You don't have to come and be sociable, I'll bring it here. All you have to do is put the dish in the oven." Her eyes narrowed. "You do remember how to use the oven?"

Jesse smiled. "I think I can manage."

"Good. And you'll eat it tonight, or I'll know the reason why." Kay reached for the brown-paper-wrapped parcel she'd brought and slit open one end. "I missed you yesterday. Sunday with George's folks, you know the drill. But I caught your interview in this morning's paper."

Jesse waited a beat. "And?"

"It was good. Forthright, honest, emotional with-out being maudlin. You did a good job."

"Rita Hollings did, you mean."

"All she really did was transcribe your words. The story itself does the rest. And speaking of that, has there been any news?"

"Nothing yet. Actually Detective Maychick was

just here. His latest brainstorm is that I got rid of Amanda myself."

"You're kidding." Kay stared. "Why would he think you'd want to do something like that?"

"To win Ned back."

"Right. The man's a fool."

"Which one?"

"Either, both. Take your pick."

Jesse pulled out a chair at the kitchen table and sat down. After a moment Kay left the package and joined her.

"Ned was here last night, Kay."

"I hope you threw him out on his butt."

"Actually . . . no."

"Uh-oh." Kay searched Jesse face. "You didn't."

"I did."

"I hope at least it was good."

Jesse stifled a giggle. "It was."

"Well, I guess that's something."

Jesse's fingertip doodled an aimless circle on the tabletop. "He said—not that I believe him—that maybe he made a mistake by leaving."

"Of course he made a mistake." Kay snorted. "That's not news. The question here is, why'd it take the dumb oaf all this time to figure it out? I just hope you didn't do anything rash."

"Like what?"

"Like tell him you'd take him back."

"Of course not."

"Well then." Kay looked pleased. "That's two somethings. So what's the big deal?"

Put that way, even Jesse had to wonder what all the fuss was about. Thank God for Kay, and her knack for putting everything in perspective. Relieved, Jesse changed the subject. "What's in the package?"

"Oh! Wait till you see." Kay jumped up, swept the parcel off the counter, and plopped it back down on the table. The brown paper wrapper was already par-

tially open. Now it tore the rest of the way, scattering a
sheaf of papers on the tabletop between them. "Look
at these. Aren't they great?"

Jesse lifted the top sheet and found herself looking at
a grainy picture of Amanda's face. Above the image, in
bold print, were the words "PLEASE HELP." Beneath
was a brief description, including the date of Amanda's
disappearance, followed by the hot-line number.

"So?" Kay prodded. "I got the idea when we were
talking about milk cartons that day, remember? Only
this didn't take nearly as much time to put together. I
used that picture you gave me. It's a little dated, but
close enough. I figured we'd take these out and plaster
the town. What the hell, it can't hurt. . . ."

Slowly Kay's voice trailed away as she realized that
Jesse still hadn't said a word. "Hey, I was only trying
to help. Are you okay?"

"Fine." Jesse's tone was unconvincing. "You're
right. This is a great idea."

Working quickly, Kay gathered the scattered papers
into a stack. "Then what's the matter?"

"It's so basic, it's so logical," Jesse said softly. "I
can't believe you thought of this . . . and I didn't."

Kay's hands stilled, then folded together on top of
the papers. "You can't be everywhere at once, Jess."

"But I have to be." Jesse's expression was stricken.
"Don't you see? That's the only way I'm ever going to
get Amanda back." Her hands curled into fists in her
lap. "I can't believe I overlooked something so simple.
And if I missed this, how many other things are there I
should have done that I haven't?"

"Jesse—"

"Do you know that yesterday I wasted hours walking around the neighborhood, just talking to people,
hoping that maybe someone might have seen or heard
something? What a stupid idea—"

"It wasn't a stupid idea. It was one plan of attack.
This is another."

"And last night with Ned . . . I can't believe he and I were making love when I might have been out doing something."

"Doing what?" Kay demanded.

"I don't know . . . anything!"

"It was the middle of the night."

"That doesn't matter." Jesse's voice dropped until Kay could scarcely hear her. "I wanted Ned to make me forget, if only for a little while, and he did. What kind of a mother am I, what kind of a monster am I, to want to forget her own child?"

"I want you to stop that right this minute." Half rising, Kay scooted her chair around the table until she was close enough to gather her friend in a hug. "You're not a monster, you're a human being, with perfectly normal needs. For five days you've done nothing but think about Amanda, am I right?"

Silently Jesse nodded.

"You're working so hard, I'm watching you fade away right before my eyes. I'm worried about Amanda, Jesse, but I'm also worried about you. You can't go on like this—not eating, not sleeping.

"Maybe you're feeling guilty because Ned was here, because of what happened between you, but that's a crock of bull. If Ned was able to give you a few hours' relief, then I say more power to him. I wish he'd come back and do it again."

"You don't."

"I do."

Already Jesse was feeling better. "I guess self-pity isn't going to gain me any points with you."

"Nope." Kay shook her head. "Not a one. Now, how about my brilliant idea? These fliers won't do us any good just sitting here on the table. What do you say?"

"Head 'em up and move 'em out?"

"That's the spirit." Kay split the pile in half. "How about if I head north and you go south?"

"Done. And Kay?"

"Hmmm?"

"Thanks."

Kay had made an abundance of fliers, so Jesse wasn't choosy about where she left them. She tacked some to street signs and handed others to strollers in the park, before going back for her car and driving over to the small shopping center on Newfield Avenue. From the dry cleaner, to the ice-cream parlor, to the beauty salon, everyone she spoke to was anxious to help.

By the time Jesse reached the supermarket at the end of the row, she only had a few fliers left. Two days earlier she'd run from the store in a daze. Now, though she steeled herself as she stepped inside the large, brightly lit expanse, no trace of the confusion she'd felt before remained. Determinedly she walked straight to the assistant manager's booth.

Today there was no line. The man she'd spoken to before was once again on duty. His shirt was white polyester, tinged with a faint shading of gray. A name tag, identifying him as ASSISTANT STORE MANAGER QUENTIN STONE, had been clipped to the pocket. He smiled at her approach, and his face took on the pleased, rounded countenance of a chipmunk storing nuts.

Jesse's gaze dipped to the name tag, then lifted. "Mr. Stone? I'd like to ask a favor."

"Of course, anything." He glanced at the fliers she'd placed on the counter. "It's about the baby, isn't it?"

He'd remembered her. Jesse had thought he might. She turned the papers so he could read what they said. "I'd like to post one of these in your front window, and maybe another on the bulletin board. Would that be all right?"

"I don't see why not," Quentin Stone said importantly. "Neighborhood participation, wonderful thought. How are the police doing? Any clues so far?"

"Some." Jesse gathered up the papers.

"Here, let me help you." In a deft move Quentin swept the pile from her hands. "That hot-line number is a good idea. I'll bet it's really humming."

"It is. Really, I appreciate your help, Mr. Stone—"

"Quentin."

Jesse blew out a breath. "If you'd just give me back my fliers, I can manage just fine."

"Nonsense." Quentin unlatched the half door to the booth and let himself out. "I'm happy to be of service. I'll bet you've been pretty busy following up on all the calls."

"Me? No."

"The police then."

"I suppose so."

For a moment Quentin looked as though he was going to press for more details. Then, instead, he bent back to look down beneath the counter. "I'm sure I've got some tape around here somewhere."

"I have a roll," Jesse said quickly, moving away. "I've got everything I need. You don't have to come with me."

"In times like these everybody has to do what they can to help." Quentin strode toward the front of the store, holding the posters in front of him like a shield.

For Pete's sake, Jesse thought as she followed along behind. You'd have thought the man was marching off to war.

Just inside the door was a bulletin board, already covered with cards and notices. There was one spot open, and it looked good to Jesse, but Quentin quickly overruled the site.

"Eye level's good," he pronounced. "But you want the right side, not the left. People always look to the right first, did you know that?"

"No." Jesse took a poster and began to place tape along the top edge.

"Well, it's true." Frowning, Quentin leaned in closer to peer at some of the listings that were in the way. "What drivel! And look at this. Here's a kid who wants a job raking leaves. This thing must have been here all year." With a flourish he reached up and ripped the offending notice from the board before continuing his inspection. "Free kittens, rooms for rent—there's no rhyme or reason to any of this. Who's in charge of this thing anyway?"

"Probably you," Jesse told him as she stood back, waiting for him to get out of the way. "Do you mind if I put this up?"

"Sure, go ahead. No . . . wait!" Quentin pounced back in, rearranging the signs and cards until he'd cleared a space that suited him. "There, that's much better."

"Much better," Jesse agreed, deciding to humor him. She stuck up the poster, then paused, her eyes resting on the picture of her daughter's face for a long, wistful moment.

"What about the window?" Quentin prodded, bringing her out of her reverie. "You'll want one there, too."

There was no getting rid of him. While Jesse held the flier up to the window on the inside, Quentin bounded out through the swinging door and stood on the sidewalk angling his head first one way, then the next, as he decided on the perfect placement. Finally they were both satisfied.

"You know," he said as he came back inside, "I've just noticed something. This flier lists the hot-line number, but not your home phone."

"That's right." Behind him Jesse saw Kay's babysitter, Denise, wheel her cart out the end of one aisle and start up the next.

"That's fine for regular people, but I'm thinking maybe you ought to give your number to me. You never know what I might be able to pick up. All sorts of things come my way. Why, a position like mine is the pulse of the whole neighborhood. . . ."

Jesse nodded, listening only halfheartedly. Denise, she could see, had stopped beside the baby supplies. As Jesse watched, the woman hefted a heavy case of premade formula off the bottom shelf and into her cart.

"So?" said Quentin. "How about it?"

Denise turned the end of the row and disappeared once more. Jesse frowned distractedly. "How about what?"

"Your phone number. You really ought to give it to me. That way, if I hear anything, I can come straight to you—"

"Sure," Jesse agreed. Anything to get him out of her face. "Why don't you go find a pen and a piece of paper?"

As Quentin hurried off Denise reappeared once more. This time she pushed her cart straight to the checkout line. A display of low-fat baked goods was just to Jesse's left. She swept a box of orange-pecan muffins off the top, then strolled into the express lane behind Denise.

Predictably the customer at the head of the line had snuck at least twenty items through. There was plenty of time. "Hi," Jesse said as Denise began unloading her cart. "Remember me?"

Startled, the woman dropped the heavy box of formula she'd had in her hands. "Oh, Mrs. Archer, it's you."

"Sorry. Do you want some help with that?"

"No, I got it." With practiced ease, Denise got a better grip and slung the carton up onto the counter.

"Kay speaks so highly of you as a baby-sitter, but I never realized you had children of your own."

"I don't." Denise followed the direction of Jesse's gaze. "The formula's for my job. Did Mrs. Samuel tell you? I'm a nurse over at St. Simon's. I work in the maternity ward."

"Actually Kay didn't mention it. Surely they don't make you bring your own formula."

"Yes and no." The woman in front of them finally finished, and Denise's groceries rode the conveyor belt forward. Pushing her cart up, she followed them along.

"You had your baby in a hospital, didn't you?"

"Umm-hmm." Jesse plopped the muffins on the counter, then promptly forgot them.

"I'll bet when you left, the OB nurses gave you all sorts of supplies—diapers, bottles, things like that."

"You're right, they did."

"It's kind of a tradition, lots of nurses do it. The problem is, over at St. Simon's we got a new administrator last winter, and she's cutting back everywhere, especially on the giveaways. A bunch of us nurses got together and decided to take up the slack."

I'm getting as bad as Detective Maychick, Jesse thought as the checker began to pack Denise's items with brisk efficiency. I'm wondering about everyone, whether there's a reason or not. First Laurel, and now Denise. Next thing you know, I'll be questioning Kay.

"Mrs. Archer? Over here!"

Whirling around, Jesse saw Quentin waving in her direction. Even after he caught her eye, the frantic motion didn't stop. Leaving the muffins to their fate, she stepped out of line and strode over to his booth.

"I just wanted to make sure I got your number before you left. He held out a pen and a piece of paper. "Here. Why don't you give it to me now?"

Hurriedly Jesse scribbled down the information he wanted. The self-important assistant manager was about the last person she could imagine being of any help. Still the number was listed in the phone book, so it wasn't as though giving it to him was any big deal.

When she was done, Quentin took the paper, folded it, and slipped it into his pocket. "Don't worry, Mrs. Archer. I'm sure it's only a matter of time before you get your baby back."

Jesse nodded distractedly, turning away to scan the checkout line. Though she'd only been away a minute, it was too long. Denise had already gone.

TWENTY-THREE

Since she was halfway downtown already, Jesse drove straight from the supermarket to the police station. Luckily Detective Maychick was nowhere around as she strode through the lobby and down the hall that led to Agent Phillips's office. His door was closed. She knocked twice, hard, then waited, tapping her foot impatiently.

"Come," yelled a voice from within. Jesse's hand was already on the knob.

Phillips was sitting at his desk, writing. For a moment, finishing what he was doing, he didn't look up. The afternoon sun shone through the window behind him, casting a bright streamer of light across his shoulders. It made him look somehow . . . chosen: the knight in shining armor.

Jesse blinked twice and the fanciful image was gone. Chosen, indeed. Who was she kidding? Nobody so far had come galloping to her rescue. At this rate maybe nobody would.

Finally Phillips set his pen aside. By now Jesse was standing with her arms folded over her chest. Ignoring that, and the piqued expression on her face, he waved her toward a chair. "I missed you this morning."

"Pardon me?"

"I expected you to check in."

"Why?"

"You haven't missed a morning yet." Phillips shuffled his papers, then shoved them back into a folder. "Was there a problem?"

"Not exactly."

"Oh?" He looked up. "Care to elaborate?"

"I didn't come here, because Detective Maychick came to me."

"Really?"

Jesse had no intention of explaining. She wouldn't have, either, except that he looked so genuinely surprised. "Don't you two talk?"

"Certainly. We compare notes, keep each other informed of progress, that sort of thing. But our investigations are totally separate."

"I imagine he'll mention it to you sooner or later himself. Detective Maychick's newest thought is that Amanda is missing because I did something to her."

Phillips leaned forward intently. His elbows rested stop the desk; his fingers were steepled together beneath his chin. "Why?"

"Because he's nuts."

He almost smiled, then settled instead for clearing his throat. "No—I mean what reason does he have for thinking that?"

"The detective has some sort of a crazy theory that I'm trying to get my ex-husband back."

"Are you?"

"No."

"Well, that seems clear enough."

"Try telling that to Detective Maychick."

Phillips gazed at her across the desktop. "Perhaps I will. Does he know anything I don't?"

"I sincerely doubt it."

"I see." Once again Phillips seemed on the verge of a smile. "Well then, let's set that theory aside for the time being."

"Bury it," Jesse said succinctly. "It's nonsense."

Taking her cue, he changed the subject. The morning paper was neatly folded beside his blotter. Phillips gestured in its direction. "I read your interview earlier. Nice job."

"Thank you." Jesse gazed past him and out the window. He was avoiding the one subject she wanted to talk about. She supposed there was a reason for that. "You haven't mentioned Andy Meehan yet. I assume that's a bad sign?"

"Well . . ."

"You haven't found him."

"No."

Anger surged through her. "I can't believe this. I thought the FBI was supposed to be able to do anything."

"These things take time—"

"So you said. But how much time are we talking about? Days? Weeks? Months?"

"Getting angry isn't going to solve anything."

"Maybe not, but it makes me feel better."

"Well then." Phillips sat back. "Be my guest."

"Dammit!" Jesse leaped up. "How you would feel if it was your daughter?" The hypothetical question wasn't enough. She added another. "Or one of your nieces?"

"I'd be outraged."

She balled her fists on the edge of his desk and leaned forward, straight-armed. "You'd be livid."

"Probably."

"You'd do a hell of a lot more than sit behind a desk and shuffle papers."

"Actually"—Phillips stared up into her eyes—"I wouldn't. The computer's a very valuable tool. Don't underestimate its worth to our investigation."

"It's turned up one lead so far. And you can't even find the man."

"That's where you're wrong." Phillips rose and walked over to a credenza. "It's true, we do want to question Mr. Meehan. But he's no longer our only lead." He gestured toward a stack of papers lined up beside the printer. "In the last two days the hot-line number has been flooded with calls. Some of them seem promising."

Jesse came up beside him. She lifted the top sheet and scanned the list of names, dozens of them, from all over the metropolitan area. "So now what?"

"Now we run them down." Phillips took the paper from her hands and replaced it carefully where it had been. "One by one. We'll be calling, conducting interviews where necessary. It'll take—"

"Time," Jesse finished for him. "I know." Like water racing through a drain, the fight went out of her. Weariness took its place. She sighed. "How much time?"

"It depends on how many calls there are. The response is biggest in the beginning. It'll taper off. And as usual we've drawn a bunch of attention seekers who will need to be weeded out." Phillips sat down on the edge of his desk. "By the way, does the name Karen Valez mean anything to you?"

Jesse thought for a moment, then shook her head. "No. Should it?"

"Her son, Ramon, goes to Piper Ridge with Amanda. Except that last Friday she pulled the boy out and seemingly disappeared. It's likely that our questions prompted her flight."

Jesse'd long since stopped jumping at every little scrap of information. That was all most of them turned out to be, scraps. But that didn't mean she wouldn't ask.

"Were the questions about Amanda?"

"Yes and no. We don't necessarily think her

response had anything to do with Amanda's disappearance. Special Agent Harvey seems to feel that it's probably an issue of citizenship."

"You mean she's an illegal alien?"

"Perhaps. At the moment that's what we're trying to find out."

Jesse stared out the window. Poor Karen Valez. They'd never even met, probably never would. But because of Jesse, she was on the run. Another life shaken up, then put back down, just slightly off kilter. All because everyone was a suspect.

She turned and said, "Yesterday I took a walk around my neighborhood."

"And?"

"Mrs. Manetti, who lives across the street, saw a green van parked in front of her house Tuesday night."

Phillips crossed the room to the file cabinet and pulled out a folder. "Is that unusual?"

"No. I mean, anyone is free to park on the street. It's just that we're not near much, so there's no reason to be there unless you live on the road or you're visiting someone."

He thumbed through the folder until he found the paper he was looking for. "Dark van, probably green, possibly blue. There at suppertime, gone an hour later."

"Oh," said Jesse. "You've got that."

"Yep. Anything else?"

"Bill Custer at number 198, told me that the Renfrews around the corner have a grandson who's always in trouble."

"Renfrew," Phillips muttered. Another file came out. "Zach, age seventeen. Suspected of vandalism over at the high school, no proof. Caught joyriding in a neighbor's car. Charges dropped. One count, possession of marijuana, pled guilty to the misdemeanor, serving probation now."

"He sounds like a lovely boy," Jesse said dryly.

Phillips snapped the folder shut. "These days he sounds like an average kid."

"And you sound like a cynic."

"When I have to be." He slipped the folder back. "The bottom line is, breaking and entering, assault, and kidnapping seem way out of this kid's league. Besides, his parents can account for his whereabouts all night. What else?"

"Not much. A robbery two or three years ago at the other end of the street. The people's name was Findley."

This time he didn't even bother to look it up. "Got it."

"I figured you might."

"That's it?"

"Umm-hmm. It's not much, is it?"

"Not this time. Next time you never know. It's good that you're keeping your eyes open. And if anyone says anything, or does anything, that seems suspicious to you, I want to hear about it. Don't worry about whether or not I already have the information, come to me anyway."

"With anything?"

"Anything at all."

Jesse sat back. Should she mention Amanda's doll? And what would she say if she did? That whole night had begun to seem like a figment of her overactive imagination. Bad enough that she'd panicked and called 911 over a man who had turned out to be Ned. Not only that, but having just dismissed her ex-husband out of hand, she had no desire to reopen the topic.

Jesse thought of something else. "This isn't suspicious exactly. More like weird."

"Go ahead."

"At the supermarket I go to, there's a man—the assistant manager. He saw Amanda on TV, and now he seems to think I'm some sort of celebrity. Every time I go in the store, he asks questions and follows me around. I mean, I guess he's trying to be helpful, but . . ."

"You wish he'd mind his own business."

"Well, yes."

Phillips frowned. He reached across the desktop and came up with a pen and a piece of paper, where he scrawled some notes. "Has he ever contacted you anywhere else?"

"No." Jesse was startled by the idea. "It's nothing like that."

"The questions he asks you, are they personal, or about the case?"

"Just about the case. You know, whether the police have any leads, things like that." Jesse began to feel guilty for even bringing it up. He'd told her to mention everything, but somehow she hadn't expected such a strong reaction. It was almost as though Agent Phillips was feeling protective of her. "I'm sure he's really only curious about something he saw on television."

"You're probably right. Every case that's publicized like this has been draws its share of groupies. But if he's bothering you, I'll send someone over to talk to him."

"Please, don't." Jesse could just imagine how that would swell the little man's ego. "He's already told me his job is the pulse of the entire neighborhood. He'd probably think you wanted to consult with him, and I'd never hear the end of it."

Phillips snorted softly under his breath. "I can arrange for him to leave you alone."

"It's all right. Really. I'm sure he's harmless."

Phillips's expression, as he looked at her, was oddly intent. Jesse found herself raking back her hair and looking around for her purse. She felt a queer flutter of recognition, more than enough to tell her it was time to go.

The pocketbook was sitting on the corner of the desk. She picked it up and slung the strap over her shoulder. Standing behind his desk, Phillips made no move at all. So why, suddenly, did he seem so close? Clutching the purse in front of her, Jesse backed toward the door.

"I'll help if you want," Phillips said gently. "I want to help . . . in any way I can."

Was it just her luck or was it general male perversity? When nothing was going on in her life, there wasn't a man around for miles. Now, when she had more than enough to think about already, here were two in twenty-four hours. What a bitch.

Jesse reached the doorway and paused. It seemed too abrupt just to walk out. "Thank you," she said. "I appreciate that."

"I know you have a lot on your mind right now."

"Too much."

"But later, when we've found Amanda . . ." Phillips let the thought dangle.

Jesse grabbed the knob and pulled on it, hard. At another time . . . in another situation . . . The possibilities were there. She just couldn't deal with them now.

"I have to go." The door was half-open. She slipped through the sliver of space and made her escape.

On the way home Jesse stopped at the hardware store. She'd never gotten hold of a locksmith. Last night, when there'd been a warm, solid male presence sleeping beside her, it hadn't seemed to matter so much. Feminists could rage all they liked, under certain circumstances there was a lot to be said for male protection. But that was last night. Now she was by herself again and she'd settle for better locks.

The hardware store was crowded, which meant she was on her own. One whole aisle was devoted to locks of various shapes and sizes. Jesse looked through the choices slowly. Dead bolt had the kind of nice, solid ring she was looking for. But what about installation? Parts? Did she even have the tools?

At the end of the row the merchandise changed. Security devices gave way to birdhouses. Jesse was about to go back when she heard the familiar rattle of plastic keys and the soft, delighted coo of an amused baby. She was already smiling when she turned around to look. Sitting off to one side was a dark blue Aprica stroller, much like Amanda's own.

The baby was all alone; her mother was nowhere in sight. That didn't seem to bother her, for she was looking down, rapt attention focused on the set of toy keys wound around her chubby fingers. Abruptly she flung her hand up and out, and the keys sailed through the air. For a moment she looked startled. Her mouth pursed for a cry. Then she turned her wide, blue eyes to Jesse and their gazes met.

Like a jolt of electricity, Jesse felt the shock plummet through her. Amanda!

It was impossible. She was wrong; she had to be. Had things reached the point where she was seeing her daughter everywhere?

Jesse shook her head and looked again. The baby wasn't Amanda, not really. But oh, the resemblance was there. This baby had the same blue eyes, the same downy soft blond hair. There was even a dimple in her left cheek, just as Amanda had.

Jesse drew a deep breath and looked away. She tried to conjure up her daughter's face, but couldn't. The image refused to come and confirm the difference. Even closing her eyes didn't help. All she could see was the infant in the stroller.

And still the baby's mother didn't appear. Drawn forward, unable to resist, Jesse found herself stooping down to retrieve the fallen keys. "Here they are," she said in a singsong voice. "Here's your toy."

The baby laughed delightedly. She extended her hand, then withdrew it, and laughed again. A natural coquette. How many times had Jesse thought the same of Amanda? How many times had she already anticipated the challenge of her daughter's teenage years?

"Come on." Jesse leaned closer and swung the keys enticingly. "You want these, don't you?"

This close, she could see that even the shade of blue in the eyes was the same: dark and smoky, rather than light and clear. But of course there were differences, there had to be. She had only to search them out. This baby's upturned nose was broad. Amanda's was much smaller . . . wasn't it?

The baby snagged the keys, then promptly dropped them again, this time inside the stroller. Jesse leaned closer still, reaching in a hand to fish them out. The fresh baby smell washed over her, its aroma achingly familiar. She inhaled deeply, her hand caressing the length of a soft, dimpled baby thigh.

"Amanda," Jesse whispered. Almost before she knew what she was doing, the strap around the baby's middle had been unfastened, and the child lifted up and into her arms. No, this wasn't her baby. But just for now, for the briefest of moments, couldn't she pretend?

Jesse laid the infant up along her shoulder, one hand beneath its padded bottom, the other supporting its back. The baby's cheek lay against her own, and the infant gurgled softly. Instinctively Jesse began to rock.

Dimly she was aware that a woman had rounded the end of the row, her arms filled with two large bags of birdseed. When the woman's startled gaze went directly to the empty stroller, then flew to her, Jesse knew her time was up. She couldn't bear for it to end just yet.

"What are you doing with my baby?" the woman demanded. The bags fell with a thud to the floor. One broke open, and a cascade of seed spilled out over her feet.

"Nothing . . ." Jesse mumbled, stalling for even a moment's time. If the woman hadn't advanced so swiftly, she'd never have backed up.

"What are you doing with my baby?"

T WENTY-FOUR

"Give her to me!" the woman screamed. "Give her to me this minute!"

Jesse moved to comply, but time seemed to stretch endlessly as she unwound the baby's tiny fist from her collar, lifted its grasping hand from her sleeve. Or maybe it was she who moved in slow motion, loath to give back the small warm body just yet. The woman had an entire lifetime to spend with her baby, how could she begrudge Jesse just a moment more?

"Is there a problem here?" A security guard moved swiftly up the aisle. In a glance he took in the two women, the empty carriage, the spill of birdseed on the floor.

"Yes, there's a problem! This woman has my baby and she won't give her back!"

"Ma'am?" The guard swung his gaze Jesse's way. "Is that your child?"

"No." Jesse gave the baby one last, fierce hug before finally passing her back. "I found her sitting here all alone. There wasn't anyone with her, or even anyone around."

"I was only gone a minute," the woman said defensively. She held the baby out, inspecting her closely, as though looking for possible damage. "How was I to know the ten-pound bags of seed were up at the counter? Katie was fine in her stroller." A glare came Jesse's way. "She had no right to take her out."

"The baby looks all right to me," the guard said soothingly.

"Of course she's all right now." The woman slid the child down into the stroller. "She's back with her mother, where she belongs. But who knows what might have happened if I hadn't come back when I did? My God, you hear the stories, but you never think it will happen to you! I should think about pressing charges."

"I'm sure that won't be necessary," said the guard. "It doesn't appear that any damage has been done."

Jesse's features were taut, her face flaming. She could feel the heat of humiliation scorching all the way up into her scalp. A crowd had formed at either end of the aisle as curious shoppers stopped to see what was going on. Turning to flee from their staring, she stumbled blindly over a floor display. The guard's hand came out to catch her arm. It kept her from falling and, at the same time, prevented her escape.

"Ma'am, if you could come with me for just a minute?"

Instinctively Jesse tensed against his hold. "Why?"

"That's it," the woman said loudly. "Take her in. Who can believe the kind of crazies you run into in the hardware store? And in a nice town like this, too."

The guard gave the woman a stern look as a clerk appeared with a broom to clean up the mess at her feet. "I suggest you move along and finish your shopping. And if I were you, I'd keep a closer eye on that baby."

"Well!" Kicking aside the sack of birdseed on the floor, the woman marched away with stroller and child.

"The office is this way," said the guard. "If you wouldn't mind?"

Though it was couched as a request, Jesse had no doubt she'd received a command. What was the alternative, causing another scene? Resigned, she followed the guard to the back of the store. The small office was empty. He went straight to the desk for a pen and paper.

"If you could just give me your name?"

"Why?" Jesse folded her arms over her chest. She hadn't done anything wrong, stupid maybe, but not criminal.

"It's for our files."

"I don't see why that's necessary."

The guard shrugged. "It's just procedure."

"I'm not a shoplifter."

"No."

"All I did was admire a baby."

The guard shrugged again, implacably, as though he had all day to wait for her to come around. No doubt he did.

"Jesse Archer," she snapped out.

"Address?"

"Portland Road." Jesse spun on her heel and let herself out, half expecting to be stopped. The guard must have gotten what he needed, however, for he didn't come after her. Though several people stared, nobody said a word as she left the store.

Back in her car Jesse fitted the key to the ignition, but didn't turn it on. Away, finally, from the derisive glances and curious stares, she let her head droop lower and lower until her forehead pressed against the steering wheel. Even now she could still feel them looking. She could hear them wondering, whispering among themselves, "There she goes. What's the matter with *her?*"

What *was* the matter with her? Only last week her life had had order and stability. Now everything she did was wrong, and nothing seemed to make any sense. Where was the reason in her life? Where was the logic? Was this was it felt like to go mad?

Jesse raised her head slightly, then let it fall, pounding again and again against the solid curve of the wheel. The ache she created felt good. This at least was something tangible, something she could control.

Minutes passed. Jesse knew she had to find the strength to sit up and drive home. But once she was there, then what? Would she be getting another call from Detective Maychick? Already he doubted her. Already he seemed to think she was on the edge. What would he do when confronted with this latest evidence of her instability?

How could she rationally convince him of her innocence when she'd forgotten what rationality felt like?

The first thing she saw when she reached Portland Road was Ned's car parked in front of her house. Great, that was just what she needed. Another confrontation.

Jesse pulled past him and into the driveway. By the time she got out of the car, Ned was already crossing the yard to meet her. In his arms were two large grocery bags.

"You're back," she said flatly.

"Sure." Ned juggled his parcels and tried out a grin. "What did you think?"

Striding past him, Jesse unlocked the kitchen door, picked up the casserole Kay had left on the step, and let herself in. "To tell you the truth I didn't."

"Didn't you see my note?"

"I saw it."

"I said I'd call."

Jesse stopped abruptly and turned to face him. "I've been fooled before."

"Jesus." Ned set the bags down on the counter. "You're prickly as a crab, aren't you? I thought we'd gotten past all this last night."

"Why? Because we went to bed together?"

"For starters."

"What else?" Jesse was truly curious.

"It was good, Jess. You can't tell me it wasn't."

"So?"

"So . . ." Ned let the word hang. Looking away, he began to unpack the bags. "I thought we might have dinner together."

"Tonight?"

"Of course tonight. When else would I mean?"

"Are you going to cook?"

"Possibly." Ned plopped a package of chicken breasts on the counter. "Maybe we'll negotiate."

"Dammit, Ned!" Jesse blew out a breath.

"Yes?"

"I like you better when I hate you."

"Pity."

"Don't you dare be nice to me."

"I wouldn't dream of it." Ned's smile was all innocence.

"I'll just bet." Jesse stowed Kay's casserole in the refrigerator, then pulled out a kitchen chair and sat down. Ned was obviously dying to be useful; let him go to it. She watched as he opened all the cabinets and began stuffing cans and boxes in at random. "Why did you come back?"

Ned turned and the cabinet swung shut behind him. "After I'd used you for your body, you mean?"

In spite of herself Jesse almost smiled. "Something like that."

"Gee, I don't know. Maybe because you looked hungry."

"I thought you said I looked like hell."

"You did, and if you don't mind my saying so, today's not much of an improvement."

"What if I do mind?"

Ned piled up the perishables and stuck them in the refrigerator. "Then you'll eat all your veggies at dinner and go to bed early."

"With you."

He glanced back over his shoulder. "Maybe."

"Maybe?"

"If you ask me nicely."

"How about if I don't ask you at all?"

"Then I guess you'll just have to hope you get lucky." Ned shook the last bag and four ears of corn fell out onto the counter. One by one he picked them up and tossed them to her. "Here, make yourself useful."

"Four? Are we planning on company?"

"Nope." Ned's brows waggled, Groucho Marx style. "We're planning on working up an appetite."

Jesse began shucking corn and didn't look up again until he'd gone out the backdoor, presumably to light the grill. She stared for a long moment at the empty doorway. Whatever had gotten into Ned, she had to admit she liked it. This was the man she had fallen in love with, a man who, more recently, had been only a memory from the giddy, early months of their relationship.

He was doing his best to woo her tonight, and dammit, he was succeeding. Sure, on some level she was still angry. Nor did she trust him an inch. But it was one thing to tell herself that the love she'd once thought would last a lifetime was gone. And quite another to be pushed into backing up the claim.

But how far would Ned be able to push her before she began to push back?

Back inside, Ned popped the cork on a bottle of chardonnay and poured them each a glass. While the chicken sat marinating Jesse went into her bedroom and pulled out the photo album from the nightstand drawer. She hadn't opened the book since Amanda had disappeared. She hadn't been able to bear seeing the innocence of their smiling, unknowing faces. Now it seemed like time.

Though Ned glanced at the album curiously when she set it down between them, he let her go at her own speed.

Jesse took a long sip of wine that nearly drained her glass. Without a word Ned filled it back up to the brim.

"You always were a picture taker," he said, running his finger over the embossed leather cover. "Did I ever thank you for those copies you made for me when we separated?"

"No."

"Then I should have."

"I bet they're still sitting in their envelopes."

"Well . . ." Ned didn't have to finish. Jesse had always been the caretaker of the memories in their family, and they both knew it. Casually he slid a finger under the cover and lifted. "Are there any of Amanda in here?"

"Only a thousand or so."

"She's wonderful," Ned said softly when they came to the end. He let the book fall shut. "I can't wait to get to know her."

Jesse leaned back in her chair. She liked the sound of that. Even more she liked the solid ring of certainty in his voice, as though he had no doubts at all that he would have a chance.

"Jess?"

"Hmm?"

"You will let me be a part of her life, won't you?"

She glanced up, surprised by the question. "Of course, you're her father."

Ned sat up slightly and inched his chair closer. "What about your life? Will you let me be a part of that, too?"

Jesse's mouth opened, but no sound came out. Surely there was an answer to that question, but right that moment she hadn't the faintest idea what it was. They were both Amanda's parents; and as such they would always share a connection that went beyond any personal disagreements. Of course Ned would have a place in her life. But whether or not it was the one he wanted . . .

Behind them the phone began to ring. Blessing the interruption, Jesse scrambled to her feet. She lifted the receiver and held it to her ear.

"Jesse Archer?" asked a vaguely familiar male voice.

"Yes."

"This is Special Agent Phillips."

"Yes?" Jesse inhaled sharply. "Did something happen?" Behind her she heard the scrape of Ned's chair as he rose and came to stand beside her.

"Yes and no. Now, don't get your hopes up." Phillips's voice was firm enough to quash any potential excitement. "I just wanted you to know that we've located Andy Meehan. He's in Massachusetts, and I'll be driving up to talk to him tonight."

T**WENTY-FIVE**

When the woman awoke in the night, it was as though it was all around her still: the crisp flash of napalm exploding in the dark sky, the sweet, sickly stench of blood that coated her hair, her clothes, and never seemed to wash away. Vietnam was a long time ago, but some things you never left behind, no matter how badly you wanted to.

Awake now, the woman tiptoed in and peeked at the sleeping baby. The child had a cough and that worried her. The woman didn't dare take her to a doctor. Now, with her picture posted in so many store windows, she didn't dare take her anywhere at all.

Instead she'd bought some cough syrup and added it to the baby's bottle. When the infant had drunk her fill, she was quiet. She lay in her cradle, deep asleep, and snoring softly. She didn't cough at all.

The woman decided she shouldn't have been so worried. A cough was really nothing serious, especially not compared with the things she'd seen in Tan Son Nhut. There was an orphanage there, run by the nuns. It was always filled. In Vietnam there were children everywhere: children with missing limbs and vacant eyes, children who'd been abandoned by their own parents and left to die.

She'd tried to help, but there was only so much one person could do. She'd certainly learned that quickly enough. She'd gone to Vietnam because she thought she'd be able to make a difference; she hadn't even made a dent.

She'd taken medicine and supplies, even though there was never much to spare. She worked her tail off at Long Binh, then spent what time she had off with the children. And none of it had done any good.

The children were still starving, covered with sores and flies. There were still those who fed themselves and their families by rifling through the rat-infested garbage trucks. Even worse she'd seen the ones who'd been blown to bits when the Viet Cong used them to carry their grenades.

So many children abused, neglected. She'd tried to steel herself against caring about those things that couldn't be changed, but she'd never really succeeded. Their eyes haunted her, chasing through her dreams until she screamed and screamed her frustration as though she'd never be able to stop. And still they wouldn't go away.

She'd done all she could, but it wasn't enough. Nothing was ever enough.

Until now, when she finally had a baby all her own. Now things would begin to change. This baby would cleanse her, make her whole. This baby would atone for all the others she hadn't been able to save.

The woman reached out a hand to stroke the small, sleeping form. The baby started, then lay still. Since her arrival she had yet to sleep through the night. The deepness of her slumber now was somewhat disquieting.

The woman snapped on a soft light and took another look. The baby's cheeks were warm, and flushed with pink. But then what could she expect?

The room was stifling. She'd have liked to open the windows, but she didn't dare. The baby might wake up at any time, and sound carried much too well.

It probably was nothing, the woman decided. Perhaps she'd given the baby too much medicine. Maybe she only needed more time to sleep it off. At least she wasn't coughing anymore, and that was something. Maybe, in the quiet early-morning hours of the long, dark night, maybe, just for now, it was enough.

Across the way Ruby Saunders saw the light come on. That was the problem with getting old, you couldn't sleep a wink. She'd never had that problem when she was young. So what was her neighbor's excuse?

Something was going on in that house, Ruby was sure of it. She wasn't the type to pry, but now she couldn't help but wonder. It wasn't natural for a person to lock herself up at home all the time. And it wasn't natural to sleep inside in the summer with all the windows shut up tight like a tomb, either.

It wouldn't hurt to keep an eye out, Ruby decided. No, it wouldn't hurt at all.

TWENTY-SIX

Jesse's fingers curled so tightly around the receiver that her knuckles whitened. "When are you leaving?"

"Almost immediately. I plan to see Mr. Meehan tonight."

"I want to come with you." Beside her Ned caught her eye and mouthed the word "where?" Shaking her head, Jesse turned away and waited for Phillips's response.

"That isn't possible. It's against policy and totally impractical besides. There's no sense in two of us making the trip. If Meehan has anything to tell us, I'll find out soon enough, and we'll go from there."

His tone made it clear she'd have to be content with that. "Will you call me after you've spoken to him?"

"It'll be late."

"I don't care."

"Probably midnight at least."

"It doesn't matter. I won't be asleep."

There was only a brief moment of silence as Phillips made his decision. "All right then, I'll be in touch."

197 ■

"Tonight," Jesse said firmly.

"Tonight."

When she hung up the phone, Ned was scowling. "What was that all about?"

"It was an FBI special agent who's been working on the case. He said they've finally managed to locate someone who may know something about Amanda's disappearance."

"Who?"

"A man named Andy Meehan. He was on the crew of painters that did my house in the spring."

"What's so suspicious about that?"

Quickly Jesse filled him in on the details. By the time she finished explaining, Ned was frowning anew.

"Jesus, Jess! What were you thinking, letting someone like that hang around here? Didn't you get references, for Christ's sake?"

She rubbed a hand across her eyes. A sudden stab of pain had her temples throbbing. "Yes, I got references. But they were for the company itself, not for each of the individual men in the crew. I had no idea that Mr. Meehan had any sort of a police record, and even if I had—"

"Don't tell me you'd have hired him anyway?"

"Let's just say I can understand how a parent who's been denied contact with his child might do something desperate to remedy the situation." Jesse turned on the tap and filled a glass with water. There was a bottle of aspirin in the drawer beside the sink. She shook out two, then added a third for good measure, and swallowed them down.

Ned watched as she turned away from him and went to inspect the chicken that was marinating on the counter. She picked up a fork and poked at the pieces desultorily. "Still and all," he said to her back, "you've got to admit things would be better if you had a man around to take care of you."

Jesse didn't even bother to turn. She'd had a man

around once, and it had been a toss-up who had taken care of whom. "Like who, for instance?"

"Guess."

He'd come up behind her so quietly that Jesse hadn't even heard him approach. Ned slipped his hands around her waist, and she felt herself stiffening. If he pressed, they'd end up having things out right now, and it was going to be hard enough filling the time until Agent Phillips called without that. Though she wasn't hungry in the slightest, all things considered, she'd just as soon cook.

"The chicken's ready. Why don't you go out and check on the coals?"

"Coward," Ned whispered. He was standing so close she could feel the warmth of his breath on the back of her neck.

"All right." Stepping away from him, Jesse deliberately ignored the goad. "I'll check them myself."

Ned muttered an expletive under his breath as he slipped the dish from her hands. "Keep your pants on. If you want to eat, we'll eat. But don't think that discussion's tabled indefinitely."

Alone in the kitchen, Jesse steamed the corn and made a salad. The twenty minutes of solitude came as a relief. Surely he must realize how much she had on her mind right now. Why, then, was he so intent on adding himself to the list?

Until she heard something, anything, about Amanda, everything else in her life had been put on hold. Because without her daughter's safe return, none of it mattered.

Over dinner they managed to keep what little conversation there was on neutral ground. Jesse lifted food to her mouth, chewed and swallowed mechanically, all while watching the minutes on the clock tick slowly by. When one hour had passed, she knew Phillips had reached Hartford. Two, and he'd crossed into Massachusetts. Compared with Connecticut, that state was huge. Why hadn't she thought to ask him where he was going?

After they ate, Ned cleared the plates, then rinsed and stacked them in the dishwasher. Jesse sat and stared out the window. She tried to picture Andy Meehan with her daughter, but the image wouldn't gel. Finally she gave up and concentrated on Amanda, seeing her daughter's face in her mind, imagining the sweet bliss of holding that tiny body once more in her arms.

"You're not going to sit there all night, are you?"

Roused from her thoughts, Jesse needed a moment to reorient herself. The table was cleared, the kitchen clean. Even the leftovers had been put away. At some point Ned had turned on the kitchen light. Now he was leaning back against a freshly wiped counter, his arms crossed over his chest as he regarded her with a bemused expression on his face.

"I guess not." Jesse pushed back her chair and stood up. She looked around in confusion. "Where did everything go?"

"Magic."

"Oh." Jesse smiled weakly. "Thanks."

"You're welcome. Coffee's almost ready. Why don't we take it into the living room?"

"Umm . . . sure." Jesse gazed around distractedly. What difference did it make where they waited—as long as the cordless phone was nearby.

"I've added the sugar. I hope you still take it that way."

"Fine."

Ned draped an arm over her shoulder and steered her, unresisting, toward the living room. The portable phone was on an end table. He watched as Jesse noted its position. "It could be hours before we hear anything."

"I know."

"Do you want to play backgammon?"

"No." Jesse sank down in the nearest chair.

"Cards?"

She shook her head. "I don't want to have to think."

"Right." Ned smiled. "TV it is."

The set in the corner was more or less intact. Ned found the remote control and switched it on. Immediately the sound of a noisy car chase filled the screen. People screamed and dived for cover as two cars careened through an intersection.

"No," Jesse said succinctly.

Ned hit the button again and found a sitcom.

"Just what my life needs right now. A laugh track."

"Has it occurred to you that you're awfully hard to please?"

Jesse shot him a look. "Has it occurred to you to stop trying?"

"Once it did." Ned pushed the mute button and the laughter vanished. "But not recently."

"Ned, don't do this."

"I have to."

Jesse shook her head quickly, fiercely. "No, you don't."

"Yes," Ned said softly. "I do." He left his chair and came to hunker down beside her. "I think we should give our marriage another chance."

"What?"

He knew she'd heard him. Instead of answering, he gave her a moment to let the idea sink in. "We had our problems, sure. But a lot has happened since then. We're different people than we were." Ned paused, then played his ace. "We have a child now. I think we should give it another go."

"Why?"

"What do you mean, why?"

Jesse looked him straight in the eye. "What's in it for you, Ned?"

"Shit." He rocked back on his heels. "You *are* in a mood, aren't you?"

"I just don't understand. Why this sudden burst of

attention? We've been apart for months, Ned. Why now?"

"Maybe it's precisely because we have been apart for months. Did that ever occur to you? When we weren't together, I could tell myself that we were wrong for each other. I could even make myself believe it. But once I saw you again, I couldn't keep on pretending." Ned reached up and took her hand. "I love you, Jess. You knew that was true once, didn't you?"

She nodded slowly.

"Do you believe it's true now?"

Jesse didn't know what to believe. She didn't need to be a cynic to realize that Ned had always loved her most when she was the neediest. Was that what this was all about; had she roused his protective instincts? Or had he simply realized that life was a good deal tougher without her cushy income to fall back on?

"Come on, Jess," Ned wheedled. "Think back—"

"No!" Jesse pushed him aside and sprang to her feet. "That's exactly what I can't afford to do. Maybe we can salvage something together, Ned. Maybe we can't. But now isn't the time to try. I'm not looking back and I can't look ahead. The only thing that matters to me is getting Amanda back. And until that happens, I can't even think about the rest."

"Right." Ned braced both hands on the floor behind him and pushed himself up. "Well, I guess you've made yourself clear."

He was wearing that expression of hurt bewilderment Jesse'd provoked all too often in the past. Until that moment she'd forgotten all about it. Now one look brought all the memories back. Deliberately she turned away.

"Do you want me to go?"

And leave her alone to wait by herself? No, she didn't want that. Tonight, of all nights, she needed someone with her. That someone could be Ned. If only he didn't push so hard.

When she didn't answer, Ned tried again. "Do you want me to stay?"

"I don't know what I want, Ned. Sometimes I'm so confused . . . it's as if I can't even think straight anymore."

"I'd like to stay, Jess. I want to be here when Agent Phillips calls. She's my daughter, too."

That tipped the scales, neatly, in his direction. Just as he'd probably known it would. Jess turned and saw her movement, and Ned's, had placed the entire length of the room between them.

"See?" he said, holding up his empty hands. "You couldn't be safer. I won't touch you. I won't even come near you."

Reluctantly Jesse found herself smiling. "Don't be an ass."

Ned saw the smile and knew he'd won. He sank down onto the couch. "I'll do my best."

"That may not be good enough."

"Then you'll just have to cut me some slack, won't you?"

Jesse glanced down at her watch. Though it seemed like aeons had passed since Agent Phillips's call, it wasn't even ten. It could still be hours before they heard.

There was a deck of cards in an end-table drawer. Jesse crossed the room and pulled them out. "What are you up for?"

Ned raised a brow. "Honeymoon bridge?"

"I don't think so."

"Gin, then."

"You're on." Jesse tossed the cards to Ned, who dealt while she pulled up a chair.

"I'll keep score," he informed her. "You cheat."

"I do not!"

"Only when you're losing, but still ..."

"I've never lost," Jesse told him haughtily. "At least not to you."

"And don't think I don't know the reason why."

The argument carried them through the first dozen hands and kept the game lively when Ned finally pulled ahead. Though Jesse would have let the issue die, Ned purposely goaded her, keeping her mind on the game as the hours passed. He knew how heavily the waiting weighed on her, and he was creating the best diversion he could. For her part Jesse saw what he was up to, and was grateful.

The call came at one A.M. Ned beat Jesse to the phone, then lifted the receiver and handed it to her.

"I'm sorry," said Agent Phillips. "It didn't pan out."

Jesse heard the words, but her mind refused to accept the information. For days she'd clung to the fragile hope that this was the lead that would bring Amanda home. She couldn't give up that hope. She simply couldn't.

Blood drained from her face, leaving her feeling suddenly light-headed. Jesse braced a hand on the tabletop for support. "You've been to see him?"

"I've just come from Mr. Meehan's house now. I'm satisfied he had nothing to do with your daughter's disappearance."

"You're satisfied. . . ." Jesse stumbled over the words, then pushed on. "What does that mean? What if you're wrong?"

"I don't believe—"

"What if you *are?*"

There was a long pause before Phillips spoke. "I'm sorry. I know how hard this is for you. But there are other leads, other avenues to explore. This is only the beginning."

"But it's been five days. It's been too long. . . ."

The receiver fell from her fingers and bounced onto the floor. Tears were already gathering in her eyes as Ned picked up the phone and disconnected the call. "She wasn't there," Jesse choked out. Tears spilled over and ran unchecked down her cheeks. "Amanda wasn't there. She isn't anywhere."

"Of course she is." Ned turned her around and folded her into his arms. "Of course she is. We'll find her, Jess. We'll bring Amanda home."

One hand came up to stroke her hair. The other held her close as sobs racked her body. Jesse turned her face inward and tried to absorb Ned's warmth.

She couldn't go on like this. How much more was she expected to take? There had to be an answer. Somewhere, there had to be someone who knew where her baby was. Jesse clung to Ned and he held her tight, rocking her gently until the worst had passed.

Dimly she was aware that he had walked her into the darkened bedroom. The hands that had soothed her while she cried continued their caresses now, sliding up and down her body to remove her clothes. Naked, they came together on the bed: needing, seeking, reaching for each other with a violence that surprised them both. There was desperation in their lovemaking, but it was better than nothing at all.

Afterward Jesse fell asleep almost immediately, only to waken hours later, just before dawn. Ned was asleep beside her, one arm curled beneath her breasts, one naked thigh thrown casually over hers. He was snoring softly into her ear, and the sound made Jesse smile.

She'd done her best to discourage him and yet, when she'd needed him, he'd been there. Ned wanted her to believe that he'd changed, and maybe he had. Certainly she couldn't fault his newfound interest in Amanda. Even that first day when she'd visited his apartment and they'd done nothing but argue, he'd still asked to see a picture of his daughter.

Abruptly Jesse felt a chill as she remembered what had happened next. Ned had commented on Amanda's doll. The same doll that was still lying upstairs in

Amanda's crib. Even now Jesse couldn't explain how it had gotten there. She'd tried to forget the incident, worked to put it out of her mind. Now the questions came flooding back.

As the first soft light of day spilled in over the sill, she found herself struggling to push off Ned's weight and roll to the other side of the bed. Hardly anyone knew of Amanda's attachment to that doll. Hardly anyone would have realized how seeing the toy, placed just that way, would have rocked her to the core.

And now, as she lay in bed beside him, Jesse realized that Ned's name had been added to the list.

TWENTY-SEVEN

Day Six

Jesse had been in the police station so often recently that for the most part no one took note of her arrival at all. That morning, however, as she strode through the reception area on her way to Agent Phillips's office, there was an imperceptible change in the air. Conversations grew muted, or stopped entirely. Several of the officers turned to stare. When Jesse met their glance inquiringly, they quickly looked away.

Phillips's door was closed. Jesse knocked, but there was no reply. She tried the knob and found it unlocked, but when she pushed the door open and poked her head inside, the room was empty.

"Damn," Jesse muttered under her breath. She'd been hoping he'd be back from Massachusetts and she wouldn't have to see Detective Maychick. Now, however, if she wanted information, there was no choice. As she pulled the door shut a pair of uniformed officers came walking down the hall.

"Excuse me," she said. "Would either of you know when Agent Phillips might be expected back?"

The two officers exchanged a look. "Back from where?" asked one.

"Massachusetts. He was there last night."

"Was he?" The officer scratched his head. "Well, I wouldn't know anything about that."

"Fine," Jesse replied, puzzled by their demeanor. "Do you know if Detective Maychick is in?"

"Oh, he's in, all right." The other officer grinned broadly. "You're Mrs. Archer, aren't you?"

"That's right."

"Yeah, he's in." He poked his buddy in the upper arm and the two of them shared a laugh as they continued on down the hallway.

Baffled, Jesse watched them walk away. They seemed to be sharing a joke at her expense, but if so, she hadn't any idea what the punch line was. She was halfway to Detective Maychick's office on the other side of the building when another officer approached.

"Ms. Archer, could you come with me, please? The chief would like to see you."

"The chief of police?"

"Yes, ma'am."

In all the time the investigation had been going on, Jesse hadn't met the chief of police. Why now? "What does he want to see me about?"

"I'm sure he'd rather explain himself."

Chief Stockton's office was larger than those she'd been in before, but hardly more plush. Instead of one small window there were two large ones. They even seemed to have a view. Louvered blinds had been drawn up haphazardly, letting in streaks of sunlight that fell across the floor.

As the officer announced her the chief braced a pair of meaty hands on the desktop and rose to his feet. Jesse guessed his age as late fifties. Though time had taken a toll on his waistline, his bearing was still erect

and firm. His eyes a steel-gray color and very direct.
Jesse doubted that much escaped his notice. As she
looked at him he was studying her with equal care.

She crossed the room and held out her hand.
"Hello, Chief Stockton, I'm Jesse Archer. I was told
you wanted to see me."

The moment of hesitation was brief, but definitely
there. Then Stockton lifted his hand, shook hers per-
functorily, and let it drop. As he sat down once more
behind his desk, he motioned her to a chair.

"Let me say up front that this is a difficult situation
all the way around, and I sympathize wholeheartedly
with your predicament. That said, however, I have to
admit that I'm adamantly opposed to your solution."

Jesse started to speak, but Stockton held up a hand.
"I understand your frustration, Ms. Archer, and perhaps I am partly to blame for not taking a more active
role in the investigation. This was not an oversight on
my part. I was assured by Detective Maychick that he
and Special Agent Phillips had the situation well in
hand."

"Chief Stockton—"

"Please." A stern look nailed her. "Let me finish.
Obviously you were dissatisfied, maybe you had reason to be. To tell the truth I don't know the answer to
that yet. Nevertheless, no matter how things shook
down, I wish you had come to me and voiced your
displeasure before publishing it for the world to see."

Jesse stared at him, growing more bewildered by
the moment. "What on earth are you talking about?"

"Your letter." Stockton's hand skated across the
desk to one side. There was a newspaper there. On it
was a creased sheet of white paper. "The one you
wrote defaming this department, my men, and the
whole investigation. The one in which you called the
Keystone Kops a more effective law enforcement
agency.

"I'm sure you'll be pleased with this morning's

Journal. They printed that particular quote in bold print. I suppose the fact that they got you published so quickly means that their copy arrived yesterday. Unfortunately mine didn't come until this morning. It was sitting on my desk when I got in. Had you had the decency to speak to me directly—"

"Wait!" Jesse leaned up and scooted her chair closer to the desk. "Wait just a minute! I haven't the slightest idea what you're talking about. I haven't written a letter to anyone, much less you or the *Cranford Journal.*"

"No?" Using just the tips of his fingers, Stockton lifted the offending paper from his desk and handed it to her. "Then what is this?"

Quickly Jesse unfolded the letter and skimmed the page. It was addressed to Chief Stockton and it was neatly typed; she noted that in a glance. Then she began to read and her stomach lurched. The contents were rude, disparaging, and purposely inflammatory. They criticized every facet of the investigation and the men who were handling it. Even Agent Phillips came in for a slam or two. Worst of all, when Jesse reached the end, her signature was scrawled across the bottom of the page.

"You say this came this morning?" she asked slowly, trying to make sense of what she was seeing.

"It was on my desk when I arrived."

"And the *Journal* has a copy of it?"

"Ms. Archer," Stockton said with exaggerated patience, "the paper printed excerpts in this morning's edition. Not only do they have a copy, but they're having a field day with it. You couldn't have made the department look worse if you'd taken a billboard downtown."

"But I didn't write this letter," Jesse protested. The paper dropped from her fingers and slid across the top of the desk. "I've never seen it before in my life."

Stockton folded his hands in front of him: prosecutor, jury, and judge, all in one. "Do you mean to tell me that isn't your signature?"

"No. Definitely not. I mean, it looks like my signature." Jesse picked up the letter and peered at it closely. "But it isn't. How could it be? I didn't write this letter, and I certainly never signed it."

"What you're trying to say then is that someone else sent it?"

"Yes." It was about time he got the point.

"Who?"

Jesse shrugged helplessly, searching for an answer and finding none. "I don't know."

"Can you think of anyone who might have something to gain from writing a letter such as this, besides yourself?"

"No, but—"

"Anyone else who has as high a stake as you do in seeing this investigation resolved?"

"Well, no, but—"

"Do you have any explanation at all for where this letter might have come from if you were not the person who wrote it?"

This time, when he gave her a chance to answer, Jesse had nothing to say at all.

"Ms. Archer," Stockton said after a moment, "you did an interview with the *Journal* a day or two ago, didn't you?"

"Yes."

"I believe it appeared on page two."

"Umm-hmm."

"Obviously you must have connections at the paper."

"No, I don't. A reporter who'd been following the case called and requested an interview. I thought the publicity might help, so I agreed."

"So if a little publicity is good, more must be better, right?"

"That's not what I said."

"And if you could make page two with an interview, imagine where you could go with a story like this."

Jesse leaped to her feet. "Chief Stockton, I did not write this letter."

His eyes were steely beneath the bushy brows. "So you said."

"I've sent nothing to the newspaper, or to you."

Stockton just looked at her.

Deflated, Jesse sank back down. "You don't believe me."

"No."

"Is anything I say going to change your mind?"

"At this juncture probably not."

"So," she said. "Now what?"

"What do you mean?"

Jesse waved a hand angrily at the offending letter. "In light of that what happens next? Does the investigation continue as is? Do you hand it over to a new team? Do you take me out and shoot me? What?"

Stockton regarded her with renewed interest. "Is that what you were hoping for, a change of personnel?"

"I wasn't *hoping* for anything. I'm merely asking where we go from here."

Stockton picked up some papers and shuffled through them, busywork for his fingers. "I understand that you and Detective Maychick have had your differences."

"Did he tell you that?"

"Regardless of what you may think, Ms. Archer, I am not entirely unaware of what goes on. I do keep myself apprised of the important cases."

"I'm sure you do." She'd meant it as flattery; it came out sounding more like an insult.

Stockton looked up. "Letter or no, there will be no changes made. We're not New York. We don't have access to unlimited manpower. You and Detective Maychick may not see eye to eye, but he's a good man. I trust his judgment and his ability. The investigation will go on as it has."

Except that now, thanks to that letter, she'd been alienated from the very people on whom she was dependent for help. It didn't matter whether or not she was responsible; they believed that she was. From Chief Stockton on down, the condemnation would be unanimous. The police hadn't been able to find Amanda when they'd been on her side. What hope did she have that they'd be able to accomplish the feat now?

Jesse gathered her purse and rose to her feet. Automatically she offered her hand before realizing what she was doing and quickly pulled it back. "Do you know if Agent Phillips has returned from his trip?"

"He's back," Stockton said shortly. "But he's not here. I believe he's in Bridgeport for the day."

"Did he . . ." Jesse stiffened her shoulders. "Did he see this morning's paper?"

"He did."

"I see." Jesse turned away. She tried telling herself that Phillips might have had a legitimate reason for being at his home office. Just because this was the first day since Amanda's disappearance that he hadn't been available was no reason to go jumping to conclusions.

Still she couldn't help but realize that whoever had written that letter had known exactly what he was doing. Someone was out to make sure that Amanda was never found. And he was doing a damn fine job.

"Ms. Archer?"

Stockton's words stopped her at the door. Jesse turned and looked back.

"Now that we've had this talk, I trust we understand each other. You want to say something, you come to me. There won't be a need to write any more letters."

She almost told him to go to hell. She settled for slamming the door behind her instead.

TWENTY-EIGHT

Kay was out in her front yard when Jesse drove past on the way home. She was barefoot, in shorts and a halter top, watering the flower beds with a hose. Jesse slowed to wave, then found herself pulling over to the curb. Before she was even out of the car, Kay was treading carefully across the squishy lawn to meet her.

Kay directed the stream of water toward their feet. "I'm considering turning this thing on myself. Want to join me?"

"It's a thought." Jesse closed the car door behind her, then changed her mind, pulled it back open, and kicked off her sandals onto the floor.

"That's the spirit. That skirt's cotton, right?"

"Right." Jesse hopped across the hot sidewalk and onto the grass. "But don't get carried away. Wading is more my style."

"Then you've come to the right place." Kay turned off the water and tossed down the hose, then led the way around back. Her yard was small and cluttered with the twins' toys. Off to one side sat a plastic wading pool, filled to the brim with cold water. "Voilà!"

"Perfect." Jesse pulled up a lawn chair as Kay did likewise. "Some people have all the luxuries."

"Some people have four-year-old boys. Think of this as a form of self-defense."

Jesse sat down and dangled her feet in the icy water. By contrast the warmth of the sun felt good on her face. "Now that you mention it, where are the twins?"

"Socializing with their peers for the entire morning. Thank God for summer camp."

"When do they get home?"

Kay opened one eye lazily. "It gets out at noon. Usually I'd pick them up, but today I wanted to try and get some work done, so I asked Denise to take them to the park for a while afterward."

Jesse smiled at that. She nudged a plastic boat with her toe and watched it skim across the surface of the water. "Working hard, are you?"

"Of course. Can't you tell?"

Minutes floated by. Jesse felt herself begin to relax. "Speaking of Denise, I ran into her at the supermarket yesterday. Did you know she's a nurse at St. Simon's?"

"Sure."

"She seems to be around a lot during the day," Jesse mused. Another toy boat floated within range and she sent the two sailing toward each other. "Does she work nights, or what?"

Kay shrugged and sent a rubber ball bobbing into the sea battle. "I don't know. I guess I never gave it much thought. But whatever she does, I think she's going to be quitting, because she told me she wouldn't be able to do any more baby-sitting after this week. Her mother died and left her some money and she's going away. A long vacation, or something like that."

"A long vacation." Jesse sighed. "That sounds nice."

Kay cocked her head in Jesse's direction. "Maybe you should take one."

"Now?"

"Of course not now. Later . . . you know."

Jesse did know. Later, when Amanda was home. Later, when she'd finally been sprung from this horrible limbo. Later, when real life began again. She and Amanda could go to the mountains. Or maybe the beach, it was that time of year. She'd always loved the water; Ned had, too. Amanda was probably a natural.

"That reminds me," said Jesse. "I meant to thank you."

"For what?"

"The chicken tetrazzini."

"Yeah." Kay grinned. "Can I cook, or what?"

"Actually . . ."

"Don't you dare tell me you didn't eat it. I swear, Jesse, don't even try."

"I would have eaten it. Really. But—"

"No excuses accepted."

"Ned came over again."

"Oh." Momentarily silenced, Kay considered the ramifications of that. "He doesn't like chicken?"

"He brought dinner with him."

"He didn't!"

"He did."

"Bad sign, Jesse." Kay reached up with her foot and sank the whole fleet with one blow. "I tell you, I don't like it."

Jesse watched in silence as the boats bobbed back up to the surface.

"Sex is one thing, food is something else."

"Well, that's a revelation."

"I'm serious. He didn't cook, did he?"

"Actually we both did."

Kay groaned. "Worse and worse. The two of you, pressed up side by side in that little kitchen—"

"The night before we'd been pressed together a lot closer in bed, and that didn't seem to bother you."

"There's a difference. Do I have to tell you everything? Sex is lust. Food is seduction."

"He wants us to give our marriage another try."

"See? I knew no good would come of it."

"I told him no."

"Of course you did," Kay's tone was soothing. "You're not stupid."

"But you know, I have to admit—"

"Oh God. Here it comes."

"He did give me something to think about. After all, he *is* Amanda's father."

"Sure. And he's made a hell of a job of it so far."

"Kay." Jesse dragged the word out until she was sure her friend had gotten the message to shut up. "I know Ned isn't perfect. But neither am I. And there's something else. Now, more than ever, I need some stability in my life."

"You're doing fine, Jesse."

"I'm not doing fine."

"You're in the midst of a terrible situation. Lots of people would have cracked. But you're handling it."

"I'm *not* handling it!" Jesse said vehemently. She paused and pulled in a long breath, searching for calm. "I haven't told you everything."

That got Kay's attention. She pulled her feet out of the water and sat up. "Like what?"

"Things have been happening."

"What kinds of things?"

"This morning I went down to the police station," Jesse said slowly. Even the remembered humiliation was enough to bring heat to her cheeks. "The chief of police wanted to see me. Have you read today's paper?"

"No. We don't have it delivered. George usually brings one home from work."

"There's a letter in it, on the front page. It says all sorts of terrible things about the investigation and the people who are handling it. Chief Stockton got a copy, too."

"Where did it come from?" Kay asked, looking puzzled. "Who wrote it?"

"That's just it, I don't know. But it had my signature at the bottom."

"*Your* signature?"

Jesse nodded. "Close enough that even I couldn't tell the difference."

"But you didn't write it?"

"Of course not!"

"All right, all right!" Kay held up a hand. "I'm just trying to sort this out. Why would anyone want to write a letter like that and forge your signature on it?"

"I've come up with one reason. Maybe it's crazy. . . ."

"Go on."

"What if the kidnapper was trying to make me look bad, you know, so that the police would be angry and they wouldn't work so hard on the case?"

"I guess it's a possibility," Kay said slowly. "But what if the opposite happened and the negative publicity goaded the police into working even harder? Do you think the kidnapper would take that chance?"

"I don't know."

"And where would he get your signature?"

"I don't know."

For a long moment silence stretched between them. Finally Jesse spoke. "There's some other stuff as well."

"More letters?"

"No, not letters. It's me. I think I've been seeing things, or hearing things. . . ."

Kay held up her hands to bracket a headline. "Aliens Rescue Stolen Child?"

"Kay, I'm serious!"

"Good God." Kay looked at her friend closely. "You are, aren't you?"

Jesse nodded slowly. "Yesterday I was in the hardware store. There was a baby there, a little girl with blond hair and blue eyes. She was sitting in a stroller all by herself, no mother anywhere in sight. I looked at her, of course—how could I not? And for a moment, I swear, I was sure it was Amanda."

"But then you realized it wasn't."

"Rationally, yes. But emotionally . . . " Jesse shrugged helplessly. "She started to fuss and I picked her up. Just my luck her mother chose that moment to appear. Talk about screaming, she nearly brought the roof down. And the worst thing was, in spite of the scene she was causing, I didn't want to give the baby back."

"You didn't still think she was Amanda?"

"No, I knew the difference by then. But don't you see? I should have known the difference right away. I should have taken one look at that baby and walked away."

"Not necessarily," Kay pointed out. "You saw a baby all by herself, just like—in the back of your mind—you're thinking your own daughter might be. Of course you're going to take another look. Besides, at that age lots of babies resemble each other.

"Think about it, Jesse. You've never been separated from Amanda before, and you're missing her terribly. It's only natural, under the circumstances, that you might think you see her—"

"Is it natural to be hearing her, too?"

The question brought Kay up short. "You didn't."

"I did."

"When? Where?"

"The other night. I was outside lighting the grill. I heard a baby crying. The sound was faint. I couldn't even tell where it was coming from. But it sounded just like Amanda."

Kay stared for a moment, then looked away. "This whole area is filled with families. There are lots of other babies around."

"I know that." Jesse sat up, pulled her feet out of the water, and wiped them dry on the grass. Somehow the idea of wading didn't seem so appealing anymore.

"You're letting your imagination run away with you."

"You don't believe it was Amanda I heard."

"Let's just say I'm not entirely convinced," Kay said carefully.

"To tell the truth neither was I. It was just that I wanted so badly for it to be Amanda." The sun had shifted to create a shadow and she stood up to drag her chair out of the shade. "And if I wanted it that badly, how could it not be?"

"When I was little," said Kay, "I refused to believe my mother when she told me there was no Santa Claus. I figured it was like that part in *Peter Pan* where Peter says that if you believe in Tinkerbell, she'll be there. Of course it didn't help that the presents kept coming anyway. I just figured that I was right, and my mother was confused."

"You would."

"Of course I would." Kay grinned and was relieved to see Jesse smile with her. "Is that everything?"

"Almost."

"There's more?" Kay teased gently as she tilted her face to the sun. "If I'd known we were going to be out here this long, I'd have put on my bathing suit." Eyes closed, she adjusted the halter top to expose more skin. "Tell me the rest."

"It's a little weird."

"I'm a mother." Kay opened one eye balefully. "I can take it."

"The night after Amanda disappeared I brought her favorite doll down from the nursery. I slept with it that night and the next night, too. But the night after that, when I looked for it, it was gone."

"Gone, like vanished, and never seen again?"

"Not exactly. That's the weird part."

"Go on."

"Well, I searched the whole house looking for it. I mean, I'd just had it, so how far could it have gone? Finally I knew it wasn't downstairs anywhere. The only place I hadn't looked was the nursery. I hadn't been back up there since . . . you know, that night."

Kay reached up and brushed a damp strand of hair off the back of her neck. "I thought you just said you went up for the doll."

"No, actually Officer Rollins brought it down to me. I didn't want to be in the nursery when Amanda wasn't there. I didn't want to see the crib and know she wasn't in it. That's why I know for sure I didn't do it. I couldn't stand to be in that room."

Kay turned to look, alerted by Jesse's tone. "Do what?"

"I found the doll, Kay. It was in the crib. It was wearing one of Amanda's nightgowns and sleeping under the blanket, just like a real baby."

"*Sleeping* under the blanket . . .?"

"You know what I mean," Jesse said, feeling suddenly defensive. "It was swaddled, just like a baby would be. Just like Amanda always had been. And I had no idea how it had gotten there."

"You didn't put it in the crib?"

"I just said that, didn't I?"

"Well, yes," Kay said slowly. "But . . ."

"But what?"

"Maybe it was like seeing Amanda in the stroller, or hearing her crying at night. Maybe you were trying so hard to bring her back that you—"

"Dressed up her doll and made a substitution?" Jesse asked sarcastically. "And then totally forgot about doing it?"

"I'm not saying it happened exactly that way."

"All right." Jesse made a conscious effort to pull her anger down a notch. "What exactly are you saying?"

"You have a vivid imagination, Jesse."

"Not that vivid, believe me."

"And you've been on edge lately. Who wouldn't be?"

"You're saying I'm crazy."

"No, I'm not."

"Unhinged, unbalanced—"

"Maybe a little confused," Kay broke in. "That's all."

"I didn't dress up the goddamn doll."

"All right," Kay said reasonably. "Then who did?"

"I tell you, I don't know!"

That shut both of them up. Ten minutes passed before Kay spoke again. "Does Ned have a key to your house?"

"No." The answer came much too quickly.

"All right," Kay said, sitting up. "What aren't you telling me?"

"It's not important."

"Of course it is. Otherwise it wouldn't be making you nervous."

"Ned doesn't have anything to do with this."

"But?"

"It's just that I showed him a picture of Amanda a few days ago. The doll was in the picture, and we talked about it. I mean, it doesn't make any sense that he would want to do something like that. But still, I couldn't help but wonder."

"It might make more sense than you think."

Jesse looked up. "How?"

"Ned's apparently decided he wants you back. Two weeks ago, even a week ago, he wouldn't have had a chance, right?"

"I guess so."

"Now at least he's got you thinking about it. If Amanda's disappearance has done anything, it's pushed you two back together."

"That's crazy. Ned wouldn't kidnap his own daughter." The words didn't come out sounding nearly as convincing as she'd hoped.

"There's something else, too."

Jesse frowned. "Now what?"

"That letter that was sent to the police with your signature on it. The one that's got them backing off but good. Most people wouldn't even know what your signature looks like. Ned would."

"Oh shit."

"Yeah, well." Kay shaded her eyes from the sun. "It's something to consider."

"I don't believe it," Jesse said firmly. "Ned would have to know that if he ever pulled a stunt like that, I'd never forgive him, not in a million years. Not ever."

"Maybe. Or maybe he's not as smart as he thinks he is."

Abruptly Jesse rose to her feet. "I've got to go." She needed to be alone to sort things out in her mind. And as soon as she was finished doing that, next on the agenda would be a long overdue talk with Ned.

"Don't leave yet. If you do, I'll have to go in and work. How about an early lunch?"

Jesse shook her head. "Some other time?"

"Sure." Kay lifted out her feet and shook them dry. "Another time."

Jesse saw the envelope as she turned into her driveway. It was manila, and too large to fit in the mailbox by the front door. Even folded sideways, it still stuck out the top. She gathered it up as she let herself in.

The envelope was hand-lettered and bore no return address. She dropped it on the kitchen table and stared at it a long moment before finally slipping a nail under the flap and slitting it open.

A single sheet of paper fell out. The words on it were mismatched, and cut from the pages of a magazine. Its message sent a chill racing through her.

"I HAVE YOUR BABY. SHE IS SAFE. IF YOU WANT HER BACK, YOU'LL HAVE TO PAY."

TWENTY-NINE

Detective Maychick arrived almost immediately. Agent Phillips took longer; and by the time he got there Jesse and the detective had covered the same ground twice and were no closer to agreeing than they had been in the beginning.

"I want to pay the money," Jesse was saying, for what seemed like the tenth time, when Phillips walked in the door. "I want Amanda back. I don't care what it takes."

"We all want to get your daughter back," Maychick replied. "But that's not the best way to go about it."

Greeting neither, Phillips walked between them and went directly to the ransom note on the table. He glanced at the envelope lying beside it, then lifted the note, holding it carefully between the tips of his fingers. "This it?"

Maychick nodded. "Don't worry, it's already been done. The only prints on it are hers."

Agent Phillips skimmed the contents of the note quickly. Beneath the bold headline were two more lines cut from smaller print. Fifty thousand dollars in cash was to be gathered. A call would come Wednesday morning with further instructions.

Jesse watched as Phillips finished reading. When he turned and looked at her, the warmth she'd grown accustomed to was gone. Wariness had taken its place. "It arrived this morning?"

She found herself stiffening to match his rigid stance. "Yes, but I'm not exactly sure when. I left around nine and didn't get home until an hour ago. It was sticking out of the mailbox when I drove up."

"The mailbox is where?"

"Hooked to the wall beside the front door."

"Did you check it this morning when you got up?"

"No. Usually the mail doesn't come until noon."

Phillips replaced the sheet of paper on the table. "Which door did you go out when you left?"

"The back . . . like always. It's closer to the car. And no," Jesse added, seeing where he was going. "I didn't see it on my way out."

"Did you look?"

"I don't remember."

Jesse was accustomed to this kind of questioning from Detective Maychick, but until now Phillips had been her ally. It wasn't hard to figure out what had brought about the change. She'd hoped to have a chance to talk to him about the letter. Now it was too late. Obviously he'd condemned her without even hearing her side.

"Think about it," Phillips prodded.

"I am thinking." Jesse shook her head, hard. "No, I didn't look at the box on my way out."

Phillips turned to Detective Maychick. "It could have come during the night."

"Or even yesterday, for all we know."

"I got the mail yesterday," Jesse said. "It wasn't there then." Neither man paid her much notice.

"What about follow-up calls?" asked Phillips.

"Nothing yet," Maychick replied. "The trap's on,

and the recorder as well. So far, we haven't got a thing. You want my gut reaction on this, it stinks."

Phillips glanced at the note again. "You think it's a hoax?"

"I'm leaning that way." Maychick pulled out a cigarette and lit up. "When was the last time you heard of a kidnapper that waited six days to try and collect?"

Phillips paused, considering. "Maybe it wasn't a kidnapping to begin with. Maybe we're dealing with someone who wanted the child; only now, with all the attention, they're afraid to keep her."

"Could be," Maychick allowed. "Or maybe it's someone who's never been within ten miles of this baby, but he's read the press and seen the TV and thinks maybe there's a quick buck in it for him."

Jesse felt as though she was watching a play about her own life. It was her daughter whose welfare was at stake and nobody seemed interested in her opinion at all. "I want to pay the money," she said loudly.

At least that got their attention. They stopped speaking and exchanged a glance. "Go ahead," Maychick said to Phillips. He reached over to tap a long cylinder of ash into the sink. "I was all over this before you got here. You may as well give it a shot." The detective levered his bulk up from the chair. "If you don't mind, I think I'm going to have a look around outside."

By unspoken agreement they waited until the screen door had snapped shut behind him. Putting off the inevitable, Jesse watched the screen vibrate until the rattling stopped. "You're angry," she said finally.

"Hell yes." Phillips yanked out a chair and sat down. "What did you expect?"

"I didn't write that letter."

"I've been told that was your defense."

Jesse bristled at his tone. "It's not a defense, dammit. It's the truth."

"But you don't know who did write it. Or anyone

else who might have had a motive for pushing the investigation along."

"If that was the motive."

Phillips looked up. "Explain."

"What if the kidnapper was trying to make the police angry at me?" asked Jesse. "Suppose he was hoping to undermine the investigation, not help it along?"

"We've considered that possibility."

"And discarded it?"

"Tabled it," said Phillips. "Due to lack of supporting evidence. Now, any other thoughts?"

Jesse hesitated. The conversation she'd had with Kay was still depressingly fresh in her mind. "I guess there are one or two possibilities," she said carefully.

"That's not what you told Chief Stockton."

"No."

His muttered expletive was brief and to the point.

"I hadn't had a chance to think things through then. Now I have."

Phillips's hand was resting on the table. Jesse felt the urge to reach out and cover it with her own. She wanted him to believe her. She wanted him to understand. Most of all she wanted him to reach back.

As if he'd read her thoughts, Phillips glanced down at their two hands, separated by a space of inches. Deliberately he drew his away. Then he looked her square in the eye and dropped a bomb. "Are you sleeping with your ex-husband?"

"What?"

"You heard me."

"I don't think that's any of your business." Jesse felt outrage, but heard distress in her voice instead.

"It is if it bears on this investigation."

She looked down, away, anywhere but at him. If his interest was strictly professional, she'd eat her chair. No wonder Phillips had been so angry. The letter in the newspaper was only half of it.

"According to Detective Maychick, Ned Archer has spent the last two nights in this house. Is that true?"

"Yes."

The word was scarcely louder than a whisper, but the effect it had was written all over Phillips's face. "I see."

Abruptly Jesse recovered her voice. "The hell you do! Amanda is Ned's daughter, too. He has a right to know what's going on."

"When I called you last night from Massachusetts, was he here?"

"Yes, but—"

"But you didn't think that warranted mentioning."

"No, I didn't."

"Yesterday in my office you told me point-blank that Detective Maychick's suspicions were wrong, that you had no intention of reconciling with your ex-husband. And yet you'd apparently just spent the night with him. Was that something else you didn't think warranted mentioning?"

"Detective Maychick was wrong . . . is wrong," Jesse corrected herself hastily. "Yes, Ned was here, but that had nothing to do with Amanda's disappearance."

"A moment ago you said his presence had everything to do with your daughter's disappearance."

"You know what I mean."

"Frankly, Ms. Archer, I'm beginning to doubt if I've ever known what you meant."

Angrily Jesse scraped her chair away. She wanted to be up and moving, not sitting there passively, listening, while he twisted her words in an effort to soothe his own ego.

"You can't do this to me," she snapped. "You can't make me the heavy. I'm the victim. I'm the one who was beaten, tied to a chair, and terrorized. I'm the one whose daughter was taken. Whether you understand me or not makes no difference. Right from the beginning I've only had one concern, and that's to find my daughter and bring her home. The rest of this"—she stabbed a hand through the air—"is just bullshit!"

Phillips looked at her for a long moment. "Thank you for spelling that out for me."

All right, so maybe she should have been more tactful. One look at his face was enough to tell her it was too late now. Under the circumstances the only thing she could think to do was change the subject.

"I want to pay the ransom."

"That's not your best idea."

"Oh?" It was an effort not to sound sarcastic. "What is?"

"Stall while we try to figure out where the note came from, and whether the person who sent it is on the level."

Jesse hugged her arms tightly around her chest. She'd been marking time for days. Now, finally, a course of action had presented itself. Stalling was the last thing she wanted to do.

"And if you decide they are on the level, then what?"

"When that happens, we'll take it from there."

Well, that told her a lot. "The quickest way to find out is to pay the money."

"No," Phillips said bluntly. "If this is our man, that's the quickest way to get your daughter killed."

"The kidnapper wants the money."

"Yes. And once he has it, he'll have no more use for Amanda."

"Which is why he'll return her."

"Possibly, more likely not. Returning her is risky. All sorts of things could go wrong. From the kidnapper's point of view, it'd be much safer to kill your daughter and just dump the body somewhere. Remember, kidnapping's already a capital offense. He doesn't have much more to lose.

"Once you pay, you give up your edge. Now you both have something the other wants. You have to delay for as long as you can."

"While Amanda's life hangs in the balance."

"*If*"—Phillips leveled her a look "—the whole thing isn't a hoax. And to tell the truth I'm inclined to agree with Detective Maychick on that."

"It doesn't matter." Jesse planted both palms on the table, leaning against them, stiff-armed, as she looked down at him. "I still want to go through with it. Don't you see? This is the first opportunity I've had to act, to do something positive that might actually bring Amanda back. I have to give it a try. I couldn't live with myself if I didn't."

Phillips frowned, but didn't answer. He lifted a hand, massaging the bridge of his nose with thumb and forefinger, then took a moment to settle his glasses back in place. When he finally glanced up, Jesse hadn't moved.

"Do you have the money?"

"Not right now, no. Not in cash anyway."

"Can you get it?"

"Yes." Jesse nodded with more conviction than she felt.

"According to the note you've got twenty-four hours."

"I'll manage."

Phillips looked as though he wanted to say something, then changed his mind. He pushed himself to his feet. He looked older than he had when he'd arrived, as though arguing with Jesse had worn him out. "I imagine you have some calls to make."

Detective Maychick stuck his head in the door and looked at Agent Phillips. "Everything settled?"

"She's going to get the money. If the call comes, we'll make the drop."

The detective threw up his hands, an eloquent gesture that more than expressed what he didn't say. He shouldered aside the door and let himself in. "I'm heading back downtown. I want to get that paper to the lab. Maybe they can turn up something."

"It said Wednesday morning." Phillips watched as Maychick picked up the note and slid it carefully into its envelope, then from there into a small plastic bag. "That gives us a day to assemble a team. I'd like someone here in the meantime, though, in case the call comes early."

"Officer Rollins is outside." Maychick glanced in Jesse's direction. "That okay with you?"

She'd hoped it would be Agent Phillips who stayed. Maybe she'd even counted on it. She needed a chance to try to smooth things over. It didn't look like she was going to get it.

"Ms. Archer?"

"Fine." Jesse nodded quickly. It wasn't as though she had a choice.

Maychick took the note and let himself out. Phillips followed him to the door. He'd already pushed it open before he stopped and looked back. "Get everything lined up. If the call comes—and that's a big if—we're going to have to move fast." He paused, then added, "You're sure you don't want to tell him you need more time?"

"I'm sure."

"Fifty thousand dollars is a lot of money."

"I'll find it."

"In the meantime don't go tearing yourself to pieces over this. That note may be the extent of it. We may never hear another word."

Jesse knew what he said was true, but that didn't make it any easier to hear. "Whatever happens," she said softly, "I have to be ready. I have to try."

Phillips nodded and let the screen door close behind him. "I'll send Officer Rollins in."

THIRTY

After he left, Jesse slumped down in a chair. *Fifty thousand dollars.* I'll manage, she'd said. Who was she kidding? Where was she going to get that kind of money?

Of course she had something stashed away in the bank. But that was three or four thousand, tops. There was her pension plan at work. She'd been a faithful contributor for years. But even citing family emergency, she couldn't get to it quickly, and certainly not overnight.

The problem was, almost everything she had was tied up in the house. When she and Ned had separated, selling the home they'd shared had been a wrench. Jesse had felt rootless and unmoored. At the time nothing had seemed more important than finding a new house and making it a place that was all her own.

When Jesse saw the little Cape on Portland Road, she knew it was exactly what she needed. She liked the community and the neighborhood. Best of all, even with Amanda coming along so quickly, she could afford the mortgage, taxes, and upkeep on her salary.

The downside was there hadn't been much left over to put aside. That hadn't seemed to matter much . . . until now.

She glanced up as Officer Rollins let himself in the backdoor. He took one look at her face and, with his gift for making himself scarce, kept right on going into the living room. Jesse stared after him thoughtfully. Fifty thousand dollars. The number had a familiar ring. Why was that?

Abruptly she remembered; the answer was right in front of her. While she'd taken her half of the proceeds from the sale of their home and put it back into real estate, Ned had rented an apartment and banked his. Of course, knowing Ned, he could have squandered it since. But fifty thousand dollars in less than a year? Even for him that was pushing things.

Immediately Jesse went to the phone and dialed. She let it ring five times, then another five. She was just about to give up when Ned finally picked up. "Yeah, what is it?"

"Ned? This is Jesse."

"Jess." His voice dropped an octave. "I was just thinking of you . . . and about last night."

"Oh." Flustered by the insinuation in his tone, it took Jesse a moment to pull herself back together. "Well, um, that's nice. But listen, you have to pay attention. This is important. There's been a ransom demand."

"You're kidding!"

Just that, as though his favorite television show had taken an unexpected turn. "No, Ned, I'm not kidding. The kidnapper wants money to return Amanda. I have to come up with it by tomorrow."

"What do the police say?"

She'd been hoping he wouldn't ask that. "Actually they're not convinced the note came from the kidnapper."

"Why not?"

"There are a couple of reasons, mostly the fact that it's been six days."

"But they think you should pay the ransom?"

There it was, the sixty-four-thousand-dollar question. Or, in this case, the fifty-thousand-dollar one. "Not exactly."

"Then what exactly?"

"They think I should stall," Jesse said in a rush. "They want more time, which is exactly what they've wanted from the beginning. They've had time, Ned. It's been almost a week. I want Amanda back and I don't care what it takes to accomplish that."

"Why do I sense there's a reason for this call?"

"Of course there's a reason. You're Amanda's father. You have a right to know what's going on."

"Um-hmm," Ned said slowly. "What else?"

"I need to borrow some money."

"For the ransom."

"Yes."

For a moment neither one spoke. "How much?" Ned asked finally.

"Fifty thousand dollars."

"*What?*"

Jesse held the receiver away from her ear. "The note says I have to come up with the money by tomorrow, Ned. Where else am I going to go?"

"Jess, I'd like to help, you know I would."

"But?"

"I don't have that kind of cash available. You know that better than anyone."

"What about the money from when we sold the house?"

"What about it?"

"Fifty thousand dollars, Ned. We both got the same amount."

"I can't give you that."

God, how she hated the role of supplicant. "I'm not asking you to *give* me anything. All I want is a loan. I'll pay it back, with interest, if you like."

"Interest isn't the issue, Jess. Paying it back is.

Something like that would take time, and I need the money now. You know I'm not working."

"Yes, but—"

"I didn't want to say anything until things were all set, but I've had a chance to get in on the ground floor of a new venture. I need the money for start-up capital. That's what I'm bringing to the deal. Without it it's no go. Don't you see, Jess? If I can make this work, I won't have to answer to anyone ever again. I'll be my own boss, create the kind of work environment where I can thrive. . . ."

Jesse couldn't believe it. "While you're thriving, Ned, your daughter may be dead. That's what's at stake here. I'm not talking career opportunities. I'm talking about Amanda's life."

For a moment Ned said nothing. When he finally spoke, his voice was quiet. "You're always so sure you're right, Jess. But what if this time you're wrong? The police don't think you should pay the money, and neither do I. What if the kidnapper takes the money and still doesn't bring Amanda back. Have you thought about that?"

"Yes."

"Has it occurred to you that once you pay off this maniac, Amanda becomes expendable?"

"Yes, Ned, but—"

"But nothing. I, for one, don't think of my daughter's life as expendable. If the police want more time, I think we should give it to them."

"Then you won't let me have the money."

"No."

Well, that was final enough. Jesse had known the chances weren't good, but still she'd had to try. So much for the strong, supportive Ned of the last few days. She'd wanted to believe that he had changed, but she should have known better. When it came right down to it, Ned would always think of himself first.

Jesse didn't even bother to say good-bye; she simply placed the receiver back on the wall. One call down. And bad as that one had been, she hated to think about who was next.

She got up and walked around the counter. Mixing a pitcher of iced tea used up fifteen minutes. Offering some to Officer Rollins took five more. Finally she'd just about run out of excuses.

Lifting the phone, Jesse punched out a number she hadn't called in over a year. "Hello, Mother," she said when Beth Ross picked up.

"Jesse, is that you?"

As if there were options. "Yes, Mother, it's me."

"If you're calling, there must be a reason. Is there news about our granddaughter? Hold on a minute, let me go get Howard."

Jesse waited while her mother left the line. It would be better if she spoke to her father anyway. Beth had always been old-fashioned when it came to defining a woman's place in the home. She knew little about the family's finances and had no desire to know more. If the money was there, and available for a loan, her father would be the one to give it to her.

A long time seemed to pass before Beth returned. "Howard wants me to ask you if you're still getting divorced."

Jesse's first impulse was to lie. Certainly, under the circumstances, that would be the expedient measure. It would also be the coward's way out. "Ned and I have been seeing each other," she said carefully, then waited while her mother passed the information along.

"But you're still separated?"

"Mom, why don't you just put Dad on and I'll explain it to him myself?"

"I'm sorry, Jesse, but he doesn't want to talk to you," Despite her words Beth's voice held more censure than regret. "He says as long as you're still planning to go through with the divorce he has nothing to say to you."

"Isn't he even interested in his own granddaughter?"

Again there was a pause. Jesse heard the faint sound of a door slamming and wondered if her father had just left the room.

"He doesn't know Amanda," Beth said slowly. "But he does know you. And he knows that things you've done have disappointed him terribly. And until that can be made right—"

"I didn't call to rehash all this," Jesse blurted out. "I need money." It wasn't the way she'd meant to ask, and the shocked silence on the other end of line confirmed that she'd made a mistake.

"For the baby?" Beth asked finally.

"Yes."

"The police have found her then? Everything is all right?"

"No, it's not all right. There's been a ransom demand. I have to come up with fifty thousand dollars by tomorrow morning."

"But Jesse, we couldn't possibly. . . ." Beth's voice trailed away as she stopped to think. "I don't know. You heard how Howard was. I'd have to talk to him. Just convincing him could take longer than that. And then to get the money . . ."

"I'm desperate. I wouldn't ask if I weren't."

"Well, that's a fine state of affairs, isn't it?" The momentary softening Jesse had heard in her mother's voice was gone. "When I offered to help before, you wouldn't even let me come. Now, suddenly, you're desperate and I'm supposed to be impressed."

Jesse tilted the receiver away so Beth wouldn't hear her sigh. "I'm not trying to impress you, Mother. I'm asking for a loan. I'll pay you back."

"Pay me back? Is that all you think I'm interested in, the money? Well I've got news for you. . . ."

The tirade went on for several minutes. Resigned, Jesse let it run its course. Whether or not her mother might be willing to make the loan wasn't an issue: she didn't have access to the money. And her father wouldn't even speak to her.

Jesse waited until Beth was finished, then hung up the phone and headed into the bedroom. Going to family hadn't helped. It was time to see the professionals. She took off her casual skirt and top and pulled open the closet door. A dozen "dress for success" suits hung on the rack: exactly what she needed.

Jesse chose a lightweight gray wool suit and a shawl-collar silk blouse. She hated the thought of panty hose, but yanked them on anyway. For the first time in days she made up her face and styled her hair. When she was finished, she looked every inch the calm, competent businesswoman, just the sort of person banks would want to lend money to.

Leaving Officer Rollins in the house, Jesse headed straight downtown. Cranford had its share of banks. One by one she hit them all. All expressed initial interest. All were willing to consider the possibility of giving her a second mortgage on her house. None, however, cared to move with the unseemly haste her situation required.

Indeed, the mere fact that she needed the money right away branded her as suspect in their eyes. Nor did explaining the situation help. Jesse tried that once, appealing to the loan officer's human instincts. In the space of an instant she saw the change. She went from being a customer with potential to being a victim. She wasn't stupid enough to try it again.

Even the Cash Store that advertised on TV, flaunting outrageous rates that in more discriminating times she'd have thought of as usury, couldn't give her money to go. Every place she went had one thing in common. They all required time, and that was the one thing Jesse didn't have.

Back at her own bank once again she arranged to take a cash advance against her Mastercard that would push her credit right to the limit. The bank agreed to have the cash ready in the morning. Five thousand dollars there, plus the three from her savings account. It wasn't nearly enough. When Jesse found herself wondering whether the kidnapper might be convinced to take a down payment, she knew it was time to pack it in and head home.

Don't worry, Amanda, Jesse told her daughter silently as she maneuvered through the busy streets. I'll get the money somehow. Whatever happens, I'll find a way.

And she would. Jesse promised herself that. If she had to spend the entire night on the phone, making calls to every person she'd ever known, then that was what she'd do. It was impossible that something as inconsequential as money was all that was standing between her and her baby.

Back at home Jesse spent the remainder of the afternoon making a pitifully short list of people she might call. None looked particularly promising. At six she fixed Officer Rollins a haphazard dinner, which he was kind enough to eat without comment. By eight o'clock they'd both given up on the idea of a call coming in from the kidnapper.

Rollins left and Jesse tossed the dishes in the sink. She was sorely tempted to leave them there, except that as yet, she hadn't figured out what else to do. And as long as she had to stop and think, she might as well wash at the same time.

She'd just finished the last pot when there was a knock on the screen door. Jesse squinted from the light out into the darkness. A shadowy form was visible on the step. "Who is it?"

"Ned. Can I come in?" Without waiting for her reply, he opened the door. "You know you really ought to keep this locked."

"I can see why." Jesse looked him up and down. "Locking the door might keep out all sorts of undesirables."

"Now, Jess, don't be that way." Ned moved toward

her, arms outstretched. She ducked at the last minute and his kiss glanced off her cheek. When his arms would have circled her, she spun out of his grasp.

"Don't be what way? Upset? Disappointed?"

"Angry." Ned made no move to follow her. Instead he leaned casually back against the counter as if that had been his intention all along. "I don't want you to be angry."

"Oh. But upset and disappointed are okay?"

There was a bowl of fruit next to the sink. Ned reached in and selected an apple. "Of course you're upset. You have every right to be." He examined the apple, then polished it on the front of his shirt. "All I'm trying to say is that what's happening isn't my fault. You don't have to take it out on me."

Not his fault? Jesse stared at him. Did he really think that was what mattered here, assessing the blame? Amanda couldn't be rescued and brought home, but that was okay because it wasn't Ned Archer's fault.

Jesse watched as he bit into the fruit and chewed slowly. This was a man who had loved her once. It wasn't, apparently, the "for richer, for poorer, till death do us part" kind of love, but still, what he felt must have counted for something. Now she needed his help more than she'd ever needed anything in her life. He had to be made to see that. He had to be made to give her the money.

"When I spoke to you earlier, I had options. Now I have none. You're it, Ned. You're the only one left who can do this for me."

Ned finished the apple and dropped the core into the sink. "We've been all over this, Jess. I need that money."

"Not as badly as I do."

"The police think you should stall while they do their job. I think they're right."

"Why? Because this time it suits you to agree with

them? What about when they decided you were the chief suspect, were they right then? How about when they decided I was, what about then? The police haven't been right yet, Ned. They've had six days to try every trick they know and so far they haven't come up with anything but dead ends. I'm tired of waiting. It's time for me to act. But I can't do it without your help."

"Without my money, you mean."

Jesse shrugged eloquently. The semantics meant nothing. "What will it take? Just tell me. A promissory note? Do you want me to sign over the deed to my house?" She moved in closer and ran a teasing hand up the front of his shirt. "How about if I seduce you on the kitchen table, will that help?"

This time it was Ned who spun away. "You're disgusting!"

"No, I'm desperate. I'll do anything to get that money, Ned. Anything at all."

He stared at her from across the room. "You know what you're asking me, don't you? This is my shot at the brass ring, and you're asking me to give it up."

Weighed against their daughter's life, Jesse could hardly see a comparison. Somehow, though, she suspected that wasn't what Ned wanted to hear. "Not give it up. Just delay it a bit. Even if the money is lost tomorrow—which it won't be, if the police do their job—I can still have it back for you in a couple of weeks."

Ned shook his head stubbornly. "The opportunity is here, now. There are other investors interested, Jess. It's not going to wait."

"There'll be other opportunities—"

Ned held up a hand for silence and Jesse gave it to him. She'd have crawled to him on her hands and knees if that was what it took. Let him think, she had time for that. After all, she had nowhere else to go.

The dishes in the drainer were dry. One by one

Jesse took them out and put them away. She knew that Ned was watching her; the back of her neck tingled with awareness. He'd been the one who wanted silence, let him be the one who broke it.

"Jesse," Ned said finally. "Look at me."

Slowly she turned.

"If I give you that money, I could be setting myself back years. Even knowing that, it is still what you want?"

Yes! she wanted to shout. Yes and yes and yes! But Ned would have hated her for that, perhaps even with reason. Instead she forced herself to wait a moment before replying. "It is."

His face went hard then, harder and colder than she could ever remember seeing. Even from across the room she could feel the chill.

"The banks open at nine," he said. "I'll do the best I can." The screen door slammed behind him as he walked out into the night.

THIRTY-ONE

The TV repairman didn't show up until Tuesday noon, and Ruby Saunders figured it was about time. Then, when he'd finally gotten there, he looked at the television and laughed, saying it was made before his time, which was probably about right. After that he'd gone outside and looked at the antenna where she showed him.

They'd agreed that that was probably the problem right there and Ruby had shown him the old ladder in the garage. He'd dragged it out himself, then grumbled his way all the way up to the roof. These old antennas were like dinosaurs, he'd told her. Outdated and unreliable. Why didn't she just get cable like everybody else?

And where was she supposed to get the extra twenty-five dollars a month for that? she'd wanted to know. Not from Social Security, thank you very much.

Anyhow, he'd managed to patch the thing up. The snow had disappeared from her screen and the picture had come back. While he was putting away the ladder she'd gone inside for her wallet. She'd asked him how much, but he'd looked around and shaken his head. It wasn't really much work, he said, and he'd been in the neighborhood anyway, so this one was on the house.

Then he'd laughed so long and hard at his own joke that Ruby had wondered if he'd given her the freebie just so's he'd have a chance to use it. Still, free was free, and she'd taken it. Not that she'd be starving anytime soon: years ago she'd put the family nest egg into IBM. But the repairman didn't have to know that, did he?

So he'd climbed in his van and left, and Ruby had gone inside to catch up on all the soaps she'd been missing for nearly a week. Sure, you could keep up by reading all about them in the *TV Guide*. There was even a number you could call. But that wasn't the same as watching them yourself. That wasn't the same as pulling your chair up next to the set and hanging on every emotional scene. Ruby didn't know about other people, but she'd never yet been moved to tears by a synopsis.

There was a fan in the living room on the corner table. Mornings, it was cool enough to go without, but by noon the air was still and heavy. When Ruby went in, it was time to turn it on. One year her daughter had wanted to spring for an air conditioner and Ruby had liked the idea fine, until an electrician had told her that the wiring in the house was just too old to support the extra usage. That was the problem with these old houses. The modern amenities were just too much for them.

Well, Ruby had lived without having her air artificially conditioned for sixty years; she figured she could go a few more. The only problem was that in the summer all the windows had to be wide open to let in the breeze. Had the world gotten noisier recently? Or did she just notice it more?

There were screeching tires and blaring radios from the teenagers roaring up and down the block. And now that new baby next door. At first she hadn't been sure. She'd seen the baby carriage, but that was hardly conclusive. But now, a couple times recently, she'd heard an infant crying. Ruby knew all the neighbors; most of them were her age. So where was the sound coming from if not next door?

The only problem was, she knew for a fact that that woman had never been pregnant. Sure, she knew there were some who didn't show until late, but this woman had never shown at all. And in summer clothes, too.

All right, so maybe she'd adopted. Plenty of people did these days. But then where was her husband anyway? In all the time she'd been looking, Ruby'd never seen one. And she knew full well that young, healthy infants went to families, not single mothers. Not unless they were movie stars, which the woman next door definitely was not.

Ruby turned on her set, picked up the remote control, and settled back in her chair to watch. Of all the newfangled inventions that had come around, surely remote control had to be the best. That way, she didn't have to watch one soap and tape another for later viewing. Instead she could simply switch the channels back and forth during commercials and all those boring hospital scenes.

Her husband had died in a hospital. Ruby'd been there for that. She didn't have to watch some handsome TV actor who looked far too rosy to be on his last legs do the same.

Usually Ruby watched the news at five. Once a day was more than enough to catch her up. Any more than that and it got depressing. But now she'd been out of touch for the better part of a week. When the news brief came on, Ruby let the channel stay.

The newscaster looked scarcely older than her grandchildren. Certainly he'd never had a thought serious enough to develop wrinkles over. He talked some about the Middle East and then told her that the Consumer Price Index was rising. Ruby shook her head at the predictability of it. Five days off and she hadn't missed a thing.

She was about to change the channel when she could have sworn she heard the newscaster mention her hometown. The picture of a baby was now filling up the screen and Ruby squinted for a closer look. Her fingers were stiff and she had to hit the volume button twice before the sound really came up. She missed part of the middle, but she caught the ending loud and clear.

"If anyone has any information about Baby Amanda, missing from her Cranford, Connecticut home since June sixteenth, they are asked to please call the hot-line number listed below. All calls will be kept strictly confidential."

Well, thought Ruby, wasn't that something? Imagine Cranford getting itself on TV like that. Imagine someone losing her baby. She glanced toward the side window and frowned. Imagine someone finding a baby. It certainly was something to think about, wasn't it?

Ruby finished watching her soaps, but all the time she was thinking. Just because she was old didn't mean her brain had gone bad. Something funny was going on next door. She'd known it for days. Then she counted back on her fingers and realized maybe she'd even known it since June 16.

Babies didn't just appear out of nowhere, like this one seemed to have done. She'd bet her boots she had information the police wanted.

At five o'clock she was ready with a pencil and a piece of paper. She turned back to the channel where she'd seen the baby's picture before and had to wait through nearly the entire broadcast before they got around to showing it again. This time she was ready, and she got the phone number copied down before it went away.

The first two times she dialed the number it was

busy. Well, that was to be expected. After all, they'd just shown it on TV, hadn't they? No doubt everybody wanted to get in on the action.

The third time she got through. The man who answered the phone sounded bored before she even got a chance to open her mouth. "Now, listen here," she said, hoping to snap him to attention. "I have some information about that missing baby."

"Yes, ma'am. Could I have your name, address, and telephone number, please?"

Dutifully she supplied the information. "Now, let me speak to somebody who knows what they're doing."

"That would be me, ma'am."

"Not you," Ruby snapped. When she was younger, she'd had patience. Now she was simply too old to be bothered. "Someone in charge."

"There's no one else who can speak to you right now. However, someone will be getting back to you shortly. If you'd like to give me your information, I can write it down."

"All right. Write down that I know where the baby is."

"Yes, ma'am."

He still sounded bored. Hadn't he heard what she said? "You need to send somebody out here. Right away."

"Have you seen the baby"—there was a pause while he searched out her name—"Mrs. Saunders?"

"No, not exactly. But I heard it crying."

"Thank you for calling," he said, cutting her off. "One of the detectives will be getting back to you soon."

"Wait!" cried Ruby. "What do you mean by soon?"

"As soon as possible, ma'am. We have a lot of calls to answer."

"Yes, but I'm the one who knows where the baby is."

"Yes, Mrs. Saunders. I understand. Someone will be getting back to you."

To Ruby's chagrin he disconnected her before she even had a chance to hang up on him. She went back over to her chair and sat down, staring at the TV irritably. She'd only had it back one day and already it was causing her problems.

But if that young policeman thought she was going to take a brush-off like that sitting down, then he didn't know Ruby Saunders. She'd call back, that's what she'd do. When was his dinner break likely to be? Seven o'clock? She'd try then. And then again at ten before she went to bed. Sooner or later somebody was going to listen to what she had to say. Who knew? Maybe after she found this baby for them, they might even stop the teenagers from roaring up and down the street.

THIRTY-TWO

Day Seven

At nine-thirty the next morning Ned was back.

By then Detective Maychick had already been there an hour, waiting in the kitchen beside the phone. When asked, he'd told Jesse that Agent Phillips was readying a team. Beyond that neither of them had felt like talking. They were making inroads into their second pot of coffee when Ned arrived.

He didn't bother to knock, but simply opened the backdoor and walked in. Jesse watched Maychick frown and knew her husband's lack of formality had been noted. Ned, as usual, was oblivious. He strode across the room and hefted a brown leather briefcase up onto the table. "Here it is. Fifty thousand dollars. All the money I have in the world."

This last was added for Jesse's benefit, but it was Detective Maychick who answered. "You're having second thoughts," he said, opening the case and flicking a finger through the stacks of bills. "Get them out of the way now. Both Special Agent Phillips and I have recommended against this course of action, as your wife well knows. We'll do our best to safeguard your money, but there are no guarantees. You got that?"

"I got it," Ned said grimly.

Hastily Jesse stepped between them. "Do you want a receipt?" she asked Ned.

"No, I don't want a receipt." Reaching over, he slammed the case shut. "Unlike some people, I know who I can trust. Just watch what you're doing, okay?"

He might have been concerned about her. Or then again, maybe it was the money. Jesse couldn't help but notice the way his hand lingered on the handle. Given the slightest opening no doubt he'd change his mind about the whole thing. Slipping past him, she pulled the briefcase toward her across the table. Lord, it was heavy. Another good yank, and she was cradling it in her arms possessively. "Don't worry. I'll take care."

"See that you do."

Ned left as quickly as he'd come. Perplexed, Jesse stared after him for a moment before turning back to Detective Maychick. If he had a reaction to the family drama he'd just witnessed, it wasn't visible on his face.

"Now what?" she asked.

"We wait. Maybe a call will come, maybe it won't. Either way there's nothing we can do about it."

"But what about . . .?" Jesse knew what she wanted to say. It was just that she also knew it was bound to set Maychick off again.

"What?"

"On TV they mark the money." She saw him wince and remembered his earlier reference to Kojak. Ignoring it, she pushed on. "You know, so that if it shows up again, they know where it's from."

"They who?"

Was the man dense? "The authorities."

"I'm from the authorities, Ms. Archer." Maychick started to say something else, then stopped and shook his head. "Look, you want to mark it, go ahead."

"Me?"

"You're holding it in your hands."

Jesse let the briefcase drop. The thud it landed with was hard enough to make the table shake. "What do I do?"

"Get a red pen, make a dot. Yellow shows up, too. Or if you want, you can copy down the serial numbers."

Maychick was grinning. It wasn't hard to figure out why. "Get a red pen?" Jesse repeated incredulously. "That's *it?*"

"Yep."

"I thought you had something scientific, something electronic."

"Like what?"

"I don't know." Jesse threw out the first thought that came to mind. "Ultraviolet."

"Dots work just as well. Marked is marked."

"But there must be five hundred bills in there. It would take me all morning."

He glanced at the still-silent phone and the implication was obvious. She might have all morning. She might even have all day. Except that as they were staring at it the phone began to ring.

Jesse and Maychick moved at the same time. He hit the record button on the machine, then quickly picked up the receiver, holding it tilted between them so that both could hear. For a moment nothing happened. Maychick glared at Jesse and she found her voice.

"Hello?"

"You got the money?" The voice was low and guttural; clearly it was being muffled.

"Yes."

Stall! Maychick mouthed urgently.

"I've got your money," Jesse repeated. "Is my daughter all right?"

He continued as if she hadn't spoken at all. "There's a playground on Hope Street, just north of the school. In the back, near the picnic area, there's a big rock. Leave the money behind it."

"I don't know where that is," Jesse improvised.

"You'll find it."

"I want to know about Amanda—"

"When I get the money, you'll get her back."

There was a sharp click as the connection was severed. Maychick was already shaking his head as he hung up the phone. "It was too short. I don't think we got a trace." He pushed down the lever, waited for a dial tone, then immediately dialed again. "Joe? What'd we get?" He frowned. "That's what I thought. Give me Lou, okay?"

Jesse paid scant attention as Detective Maychick made arrangements to have the playground covered. Her head was filled with the kidnapper's voice, and the conversation they'd just had. He'd sounded so rough, and so impersonal. As if he wouldn't know how to snuggle a baby if his life depended on it. He hadn't mentioned Amanda at all. How could her tiny daughter possibly be all right in the care of a person like that? And what if Amanda wasn't all right? What if—

"Ms. Archer!"

Maychick's hand was on her shoulder, shaking hard. When Jesse looked up, she saw both worry and irritation on his face. "Are you okay or what? Hell," he swore, answering his own question. Using the hold he had on her shoulder, he pushed her back until her legs connected with the chair. Gratefully Jesse sank down into the seat.

"That does it," said Maychick. "I'm getting someone else to deliver the money, a woman officer. Let me make another call."

He was reaching for the phone when Jesse grabbed his arm. "No!"

Maychick stopped and stared. Slowly Jesse's fingers fell away. "Look," he said sternly. "This was a bad idea to begin with, but we're into it now, the least we can do is get it right. Our man's not stupid, picking a playground. I know the place he's talking about. There are woods on one side, the road on the other—in other words plenty of escape routes.

"On top of that there are only so many ways you can plant men in such a situation. Not to mention the risk factor to innocent bystanders. Take all of that together, and I've already got enough to worry about. If you're not one hundred percent, you're staying here."

Jesse was already rising to her feet. "What if he knows who I am?" The thought was abhorrent, but it had to be considered. "And what if he's watching for the drop to be made? He'll know if it isn't me."

"We'll take that chance."

"No." Jesse lifted the briefcase in both hands and started across the kitchen. "We won't take any chances." By the time she reached the door, Maychick still hadn't moved. "Now what's the matter?"

"It'll take some time to get our people into position."

"Oh." Deflated, Jesse set the heavy case back down. "How long?"

"Half an hour, maybe more."

"*Half an hour?*"

Maychick scowled at her tone. "What do you want us to do, run them all in there together in a bus?"

"No. I guess I hadn't thought about it."

Be glad someone's thinking, Maychick's look said. He didn't say a word.

Jesse used the time to wash their few dishes, then followed that by scrubbing the sink and counter. She was giving serious thought to doing the floor when the call came.

"All right," said Maychick, hanging up the phone. "Time to roll."

"Was that Agent Phillips?"

The detective nodded. He headed toward the brief-case, but Jesse got to it first.

"Where is he?"

"In a van two blocks from the playground." May-chick followed her out. "We'll be coordinating the surveillance from there. What you do is simple. Drive to the playground, find the rock, leave the money. Nothing fancy about it. Don't hang around to see what happens next. Come straight back here."

"But I want to know—"

"You will know." Maychick opened her car door and handed her in. "If anything happens, we'll send someone over to tell you. Don't be tempted to stick around, Ms. Archer. I mean that. All those fancy hero-ics you see on TV mean nothing out here. Just leave the money and go. You'll only jeopardize your daugh-ter's chances if you don't."

It was less than a five-minute drive to the play-ground. Other times, pushing Amanda's stroller, Jesse had walked. Now it seemed as if only seconds passed before she was there.

Though the morning was warm and sunny, the park was mostly empty. Two toddlers were being pushed on swings by their mothers. Another woman was exer-cising her dog along the edge of the field. Out by the road an elderly man sat on a bench, reading the news-paper. At the end of the parking lot a telephone repair truck was parked beside a pole. One man was up and working. Another waited below.

At first glance everyone looked as though they belonged. Any other day Jesse wouldn't have given them a second thought. Now, however, as she parked her car and got out, she glanced around surreptitious-ly, wondering which were Detective Maychick's men.

Probably the telephone repair crew. Possibly the woman with the dog. The mothers she ruled out immediately. No one would bring children into a situ-ation like this. But what about the old man? Was he friend or foe? Which of these people could be trusted? And which, if any, was the one who had her daughter?

Head up, shoulders straight, Jesse made her way over to the picnic tables. There was only one large rock in the area. She stepped behind it and wedged the suitcase in underneath. A casual passerby probably wouldn't notice it. Someone who knew what to look for would see it immediately.

The woods were to her back now, and Jesse wondered if she was being watched. Was the kidnapper already in place, or would he come later, after she had gone? Nobody seemed to be paying any attention as she crossed the field and got back in her car.

Slowly she pulled out of the parking space and then up the hill and out of the lot. It wasn't until she was on the road that Jesse paused and looked back. Firm as Maychick's instructions had been, she hated to drive away. Any moment now Amanda's kidnapper might reveal himself. Perhaps it was even someone she might recognize. Or maybe she'd be able to be of assistance—

Jesse gasped as the door on the passenger side was jerked open. "Drive!" Agent Phillips ordered tersely. He hopped in and slammed the door shut. "Move it, now!"

Without thinking, she obeyed. Her foot came down hard on the accelerator and the car sped away up the street. "You nearly scared me to death."

"Good."

Wonderful. He was still angry. Irrational as it had been, she'd hoped that somehow they might be able to return to the comfortable working relationship they'd had in the past. Obviously that was not to be. At least not yet.

"You were thinking of going back, weren't you?"

"Certainly not."

Phillips pointed to a road on the left and Jesse made the turn. "Detective Maychick told you to leave the money and get out."

"How do you know that?"

"Because that's what I would have said if I'd have been there." Phillips pointed again. "Here, pull over to the curb."

There was a van parked there, dark gray and nondescript. Jesse pulled in behind it. "Shouldn't you be somewhere?" she asked pointedly.

"Yes. I should be inside that van attending to my part of the surveillance, not out here baby-sitting you."

"Baby-sitting?"

"I don't know what else you'd call it." Phillips jerked up the door handle and climbed out. "Wait here." Leaving the door open, he went around the side of the van and spoke through one of the windows. A moment later he was back. "Nothing yet," he said, sliding back onto the seat. "Come on, let's go."

"Where?"

"Your house, where you should have gone to begin with."

Jesse reached out and turned the key. "I know the way. You don't have to come with me."

"Maybe I'd like to be sure you actually get there."

"I'll get there," she gritted.

"Yes, but will you stay put?"

Jesse pulled out into the lane. "For how long?"

"As long as it takes. This isn't a game. And if you insist on treating it as one, I'll have to remind you that it's your daughter's life you're playing with."

They drove the rest of the way in silence. Jesse parked beside the house and climbed out. "Well?" she asked, looking back. "Are you coming in?"

"For a minute."

Phillips watched from the doorway as Jesse tossed her purse on the counter, then went to the sink and splashed cold water on her cheeks. That done, she straightened and turned to face him. "Let's get this over with. You're still angry. I know you think you have your reasons. That doesn't change the fact that you have a job to do."

"No." Phillips crossed his arms over his chest. "It doesn't."

"Are you going to help me find my daughter?"

"We're doing everything we can."

There it was, the company line. It told her everything she hadn't wanted to know. Phillips was through confiding in her, finished working one-on-one. And if he'd turned away from her, that meant he'd aligned himself with the police. Jesse hated to think what that would mean: the investigation would continue to plod along by the book, just as Detective Maychick wanted it to.

She couldn't let that happen. And wouldn't, Jesse vowed. There was simply too much at stake.

"Do you think the ransom money will be picked up?" she asked.

"Possibly. It's too early to tell."

"Or you don't want to tell me."

Phillips didn't reply.

"Gut feel," Jesse prodded, desperate to get through to him.

"No."

The brevity of the answer surprised her; the content didn't. Jesse grasped the edge of the counter as the air seemed to rush from her lungs. As each avenue of possibility closed off it was as though a vise was tightening around her, hemming her in until there was nowhere left to turn.

"There must be something—anything—that I can do."

"You can wait here and stay out of our way. Don't come back to the park, Ms. Archer. Believe me, if something happens, we'll be in touch." Even as he spoke he was already turning to leave.

"How will you get back?"

"Walk. It's not far."

"I could drive you."

"No."

There wasn't anything left to say. And if there was, Phillips had no intention of hearing it. By the time Jesse reached the door, he was already halfway down the driveway.

Now she was really on her own.

THIRTY-THREE

Since she hadn't gotten to it earlier, Jesse washed the kitchen floor. When she finished with that, she cleaned the rest of the downstairs, room by room. By noon she was washing windows, and by two o'clock she was ready to scream.

Agent Phillips had promised he'd call if anything happened. She had to believe that he'd keep his word, but it had been hours, and she hadn't heard a thing. How could a briefcase filled with fifty thousand dollars in cash sit for the better part of a day in a children's playground? Where was the kidnapper? Why hadn't he come to collect his money? *What was he doing with her daughter?*

Moaning softly, Jesse cradled her head in her arms. She couldn't go on like this. That morning she'd felt so close to Amanda. It had seemed so right to be out and doing something rather than sitting back waiting for the police to act. But now it looked as though all her efforts had been in vain. Amanda was slipping farther and farther away, and nothing she'd done so far had changed that. The more time passed, the less likely it became that she would ever see her daughter again. Jesse couldn't just sit there and accept that. She had to do something, anything. It was better than nothing at all.

She got in her car and drove back to the van. It was still parked by the side of the road where she'd seen it that morning. Jesse had to knock twice before the door was finally opened a crack.

"Is Agent Phillips—"

The door slammed shut in her face. A moment later it opened again, and Phillips slipped out.

"I told you not to come here."

"No, you told me not to go to the park." Jesse was determined not to be cowed. Still she found herself leaning back against the hood of her car. The engine was warm beneath her. "And I haven't. Has anything—"

"Nothing," Phillips said curtly. "If it had, you'd have been told."

"The money's been there for hours. If he was coming, wouldn't he have done it by now?"

"Maybe. Or he might be waiting for school to let out and add to the general confusion." Phillips paused, considering the rest of his answer. "The bottom line is, you're probably right. It doesn't make sense for the money to have been left this long where anybody could find it. If the kidnapper had intended to show, he'd probably have been there by now."

"Then it really was just a hoax." The last, fragile hope Jesse'd clung to slipped away. As soon as it was gone, anger took its place. She'd wasted an entire day and a half, and all for nothing. "I don't understand. Why would anyone be so cruel? What could they possibly have gained?"

"I guess that depends on what you're looking for." Phillips flicked a piece of dirt from above the headlight. "We've already made the front page of the daily paper as incompetents. A thing like that puts ideas into

people's heads. You'd be surprised how many supposedly upright citizens would find it amusing to make
fools of the authorities."

Something in his voice alerted her. He was referring
to the letter, but he was also talking about himself. It
was too late now to wish that she'd explained about
Ned from the beginning, but at the very least she
could set the other record straight.

"I told you I didn't write that stupid letter."

"So you did."

"Do you believe me?"

"Does it matter?"

"Of course it matters." Jesse slid down off the hood
and landed on her feet. "That letter made everyone
angry, just as it was probably intended to. I told you I
thought the kidnapper wrote it. Have you given that
any more thought?"

"I have."

It wasn't much, but it was something, probably
about as big a concession as she was going to get. At
least he was talking to her again. Jesse pressed her
advantage before his goodwill faded.

"Tell me about the hot line."

Two days ago he would have, in detail. "We're getting tips. As I told you before, they're coming faster
than we can get to them. Within a few days we should
be on top of it."

"Do any of them look promising?"

"I'm sorry, I'm not at liberty to discuss specifics."
Before he'd even finished speaking, Phillips was
already turning to go. "I'd better be getting back
inside. Go home, Ms. Archer. That's the best thing all
the way around. There's nothing you can do here."

Jesse let her anger surge. "Apparently there's nothing anyone can do."

Phillips's hand was on the van door. He twisted the
handle downward. "You were the one who wanted to
go through with this. Like it or not, it's our duty to

carry it out. So for now, we wait. That's the way it works."

He climbed into the van and closed the door behind him, leaving Jesse standing outside on the street. She balled up a fist and smacked the hood of her car, hard. Agent Phillips might be content to sit around waiting for something to happen, but she most certainly was not. And if delivering a ransom was not going to bring her daughter home, then she'd just have to keep trying until she found something that did.

Jesse set out toward home. Two blocks later she turned and circled back. An idea had begun to germinate, but it wasn't until she'd pulled into the lot beside the police station that the plan emerged full-blown. If Agent Phillips wasn't willing to discuss the hot-line calls with her, then she'd just have to have a look for herself. He'd admitted that the department was swamped, and under those circumstances who knew what might be overlooked? It was her duty—no, her responsibility—to follow up.

Just because she'd justified the action in her own mind didn't mean that Jesse was about to ask permission. Instead she sailed into the police station as though she knew exactly what she was doing, and as she had hoped, no one even looked up. The power of positive thinking carried her through the reception area and down the hallway to Phillips's office.

She knocked on the door, just in case. As she'd expected, nobody answered. Jesse waited a moment, cast a furtive glance up and down the empty hallway, then turned the knob and let herself in. Quickly, quietly, she closed the door behind her.

As always Phillips's office was neat. The file drawers were closed, and the few papers on his desktop were arranged in tidy stacks. Jesse went there first, rifling through the sheets from top to bottom, then straightening them again before moving on.

Though she saw her own name in several places,

she didn't stop to read. Now was not the time to satisfy her curiosity, not when the risk of discovery was so high. The sooner she got out of Phillips's office, the better. Finding the hot-line list was top priority. Anything else would have to wait.

Two of the drawers in the desk were locked. Of the remaining four two were empty and the others held only supplies: a ruler, paper, and an assortment of pens. Jesse hesitated over the locked drawers for only a moment. Even if she could have pried them open, it would have been a sure giveaway that someone had been there. Besides, there was no reason to think that the list was confidential. No doubt it was simply tucked away somewhere, probably in the last place she'd think to look.

Leaving the desk, Jesse turned to the file cabinet. Again only two of the drawers were filled, and she thumbed through their contents quickly. Nearly all the file headings related to the case in one way or another. None, however, contained the list of names.

Frustrated, Jesse shoved the second drawer back. It rolled inward on its oiled casings and smacked soundly shut. It was then, when the vibrations stopped, that she heard the sound of footsteps approaching outside in the hall.

In the space of an instant Jesse went totally still. There were other offices in this wing. Surely whoever was coming would simply walk on by. They wouldn't be coming here. They couldn't. . . .

The footsteps stopped. For a brief, horrified second Jesse could only stare as the metal knob on the door began to turn. Reason fled. It was instinct alone that made her drop to her knees behind the desk.

The chair had been partly pulled back. If she scooted down, there was just enough room to wedge herself into its well. She'd barely finished pulling herself in before the door pushed open.

"Sam?" asked an inquiring voice. "You in?"

Jesse's breath lodged painfully in her lungs. From her vantage point she couldn't see a thing. Tucked up tight in the small space as she was, even the pounding of her heart seemed impossibly loud.

She pressed her forehead to the top of her knees. What an idiot she'd been! She should have remained standing, told a story, tried a bluff. She could have brazened her way through. Now, if she was discovered, how on earth would she ever be able to explain this?

She heard him cross the floor, coming closer. At least he hadn't closed the door behind him. Maybe that meant he wasn't staying. Then adrenaline rushed through her as he stopped in front of the desk and a pair of shiny-toed wing tips appeared beneath the lower edge.

Another step and he'd have kicked her. Another half inch and he'd know that she was there. Holding her breath, Jesse scooted fractionally away. Sweat broke out on her forehead. Every breath, every heartbeat echoed in her ears. It was a miracle he hadn't discovered her yet. If he stayed much longer, it was only a matter of time.

Images flashed through her brain. She could see herself being hauled out ignominiously. And then what? Arrested? Fingerprinted? Or maybe just turned over to Detective Maychick. If he'd doubted her before, now he'd know she was unhinged.

The man shifted position as he reached around behind the desk and opened the top drawer. Jesse had been leaning back; now she quickly edged forward. She heard his fingers scrambling through the pens. A moment later he tore off a sheet of notepaper.

Above her he braced against the blotter and wrote. Beneath him Jesse hugged her knees to her chest and waited. It seemed like an eternity before he was finished. He replaced the pen, then slammed the drawer shut.

As the shoes disappeared from beneath the desk

Jesse's whole body slumped in relief. She listened as he crossed the room, then let himself out and closed the door. Still a long minute passed before she could finally convince herself to move.

That was it. She'd taken her shot and she'd failed. Detective Maychick was right about one thing: police work was best left to the police. She wasn't an amateur sleuth, and she wasn't invincible. She was only a mother, and it was time to go home. In the morning she'd talk again to Agent Phillips. In the meantime she'd just have to accept her limitations and go quietly away.

Carefully Jesse rolled back the chair and gave herself room to maneuver. One leg had cramped up. Even as she straightened her knee it threatened to give out. To compensate Jesse leaned awkwardly on one arm.

And found herself staring at the printer on the back edge of the credenza.

A coil of paper dangled beneath it: several sheets of newly printed material. Ignoring her throbbing leg, Jesse hauled herself up. Rubbing helped; she kept it up as she hobbled with indecent haste across the floor.

"If you've ever been with me on this, God," she whispered, "now's the time."

Maybe he heard her. Or maybe her luck had finally changed. Jesse slipped in her fingers and pulled up the roll of continuous paper. At the top of the first sheet was a phone number. Jesse'd seen it so many times she knew it by heart.

Beneath the hot-line number followed a list of more than a hundred names. Many near the beginning were crossed off, or followed by comments. Those at the end were untouched.

It made noise, but she didn't care. With a quick flip of her wrist, Jesse tore off the sheets and stuffed them into her purse. She stopped at the door to listen, but didn't hear a thing. When she let herself out, the hallway was deserted.

Purposefully Jesse strode back out the way she'd come in. Her purse tucked tightly beneath her arm, she contained her grin until she'd reached the outside steps. By the time she was back in her car, she was laughing out loud.

Reaction, no doubt, from her narrow escape. Jesse didn't care. Now she had choices; now she had a way to go.

Hold on Amanda. Just hang on a little longer, baby. Mommy's on her way.

THIRTY-FOUR

Back at home the surge of euphoria faded. Now that she had the list, it was time to get down to work.

Twenty minutes of searching turned up a pair of atlases, one for Fairfield County and the other for Connecticut and the surrounding states. Jesse took everything and spread it out over the kitchen table. Though some of the hot-line entries were anonymous, most listed a name, a telephone number, and an address.

Starting at the top, she began plotting the locations on her maps. With luck she'd be able to finish them that night. Then tomorrow morning she'd begin making calls, starting with those people who lived closest to her and working outward in an ever-widening circle.

Jesse was on the third entry when the telephone rang. Quickly she pushed the sheets aside and scrambled to her feet. She'd told herself repeatedly that Agent Phillips wouldn't call, that there wasn't going to be any news, but still her heart leaped. She grabbed up the receiver and fitted it to her ear.

"Mrs. Archer?"

The voice was wrong, Jesse knew it immediately. It wasn't Phillips, or Maychick, either. Disappointment had her sagging back against the counter. "Yes?"

"This is Quentin Stone. You know, from down at the supermarket?"

It took her a moment, then she realized who he was: the mousy little assistant manager who'd been so interested in the investigation.

"I just wanted you to know that I'm still following the case for you. I've got my ears open, and even though I haven't heard anything yet, you never know what might come up."

Jesse murmured something she hoped didn't sound encouraging and looked longingly at the papers she'd left on the table. She didn't have time for this. But how to get rid of him gracefully?

"Anyway," Quentin continued, "I was wondering whether the police are doing a better job than they were. I mean, I read your letter and all, and I think it's a real shame that they're not working harder for you."

She started to protest, then held the words back. Of course he would think she'd written the letter. Everyone else certainly had. Trying to convince him otherwise would only prolong the conversation. "Everything is going fine. The police are doing their job. Is there a reason for this call?"

"Well, actually, as it happens, I got to thinking of you being alone and all, especially at such a terrible time, and I realized that you could probably use some cheering up. Why don't I stop by and pick you up . . ."

Jesse closed her eyes and stifled a groan.

". . . and maybe you and I can go out and grab a bite to eat?"

Oh shit. As if she didn't have enough to deal with. Exasperated, Jesse threw out the first excuse that came to mind. "I'm afraid that won't be possible. You see, I'm a married woman."

The silence on the other end of the line was long and telling. "I'm sorry," Quentin stammered finally. "I didn't realize. I mean, your check-cashing application didn't list anybody . . . that is, I never saw a ring."

So much for privacy, Jesse thought with irritation. But then again, stuck as he was behind that counter all day, what else did he have to do beside read people's files?

"Actually I haven't been wearing my ring. My husband and I were separated." Jesse held up her hand, two fingers crossed. If a lie would smooth over the awkward moment, she wasn't above it. "But now we're going to be getting back together, so you see, it really would be out of the question."

"Out of the question," Quentin echoed firmly. "Yes, indeed."

No sooner had she managed finally to hang up than the phone rang again. This time it was Kay. "George is out of town, so it's just me and the boys. I'm on my way over to Doyle Street to get them from Denise. I figured while I was there, I'd pick up Chinese. How does moo-shu pork sound to you?"

"Great. And another time I'd love to take you up on it. But not tonight, okay? I have some work I want to get done."

Kay paused, then whispered dramatically into the phone. "Are you alone?"

"Yes, Kay, I'm all alone. Somehow I suspect Ned won't be dropping by again anytime soon."

"Really?" Kay's voice, and interest, perked up. "Did you two have a fight?"

"We always have a fight. This one just covered a little more ground than most. It's a long story, and I'll tell you all about it sometime, but not now, okay?"

"All right, I get the message. You want to work. Anything I can do to help?"

"No, I'm all set."

"Right. I'll eat an egg roll in your honor, then."

"Do that," said Jesse. "I'll talk to you soon."

After that the phone stayed silent, and Jesse got down to serious business. One by one she worked her way down the long list, marking off each address she found with a red star. She hadn't thought there'd be many calls from Cranford, but there were. Norwalk and Bridgeport came in for their share as well.

Several names came up more than once. One was listed five times over a two-day span. The first several entries had been crossed off, with a note beside them dismissing the woman as a habitual caller. Jesse left it for the time being, more interested in those people who were still under consideration.

The sky outside darkened. She got up, switched on the light, then returned to the table and continued working. By now Agent Phillips and his team must have retrieved the money and given up their wait. Though she'd told herself he wasn't going to call, somewhere deep inside a small kernel of hope had remained. Now even that was gone. The list, and the maps that went with it, were all she had left.

She'd gone two thirds of the way through before her stomach began to rumble; but when it did, it wanted to be fed. Pushing her chair back from the table, Jesse surveyed her progress with satisfaction. At the rate she was going, even with a break for dinner, there'd be plenty of time to finish the maps that night.

Kay's casserole was still in the refrigerator. As she covered it with wax paper and stuck it in the microwave, a sudden wind kicked up outside. The papers on the table swirled up and around, then slithered onto the floor.

On her hands and knees, Jesse gathered them up. She could smell the moisture in the air. It hadn't rained for days, but a storm was coming now. If the winds outside were any indication, it was going to be a big one.

Hurriedly she slammed the window shut and locked

it. The screen door rattled in its casing and she pulled both doors firmly closed as well. Even without the breeze it felt as though the temperature in the room had dropped ten degrees. Jesse hugged her arms over her chest and decided she needed a sweater.

She was almost to the bedroom door before she saw that it was shut. Funny, she hadn't noticed it earlier. Usually, when she got up in the morning, she left the door standing open. Why would that morning have been any different?

Had that morning been any different?

Jesse froze where she stood. You're imagining things, she told herself sharply. Don't be ridiculous. No doubt the wind had blown it shut.

Still she couldn't seem to make herself move. She'd thought she was chilly before, but that was nothing compared with the tremors that rippled through her now. She had to do something. But what?

She couldn't very well remain standing there, staring at a closed door. Nor could she call for help. Kay and George weren't home, and the police had already had their fill of her "false alarms." Jesse couldn't see explaining to them that she needed someone to look inside her bedroom.

Besides, Jesse told herself, taking a halting step forward, she'd been home for hours. Surely if anyone was inside the room, she'd know it by now.

She saw that the door wasn't latched, merely pushed shut. She didn't have to turn the knob, just reaching out and pushing with her foot would be enough.

Jesse gave the door a quick kick, then jumped immediately back. She was halfway across the kitchen before she realized that nothing had happened. The door swung partway open, then stopped. The room within was dark and quiet.

It took her several more minutes to work her way back to the doorway. Thoughts raced like lightning through her mind. Like she ought to have a dog. Like she ought to have a gun. Like she ought to have her head examined.

Finally she reached the light switch and flicked it on. When she saw that the room was empty, Jesse didn't know whether to be relieved or disgusted. No wonder Detective Maychick had his doubts. Her imagination was running wild, and she was doing nothing to stop it.

Irritated, Jesse strode across the room to the dresser. Sweaters were in the bottom drawer. She'd pulled one out and straightened to slip it on before catching her own reflection in the mirror.

Then she saw what was behind her and screamed.

The glint of the knife caught her eye first, and then the smear of red splashed below it. Slowly Jesse turned and saw Amanda's doll, impaled on the back of the bedroom door. The hilt of a carving knife stuck out of the doll's chest; the blade was driven through her body and into the panel behind. Something red was splattered across her, and it had dripped down onto the door beneath.

Legs trembling, Jesse forced herself to cross the room.

The doll's eyes were open and staring blankly. The nightgown she'd been wearing was gone. In its place was a child's T-shirt, which covered her from neck to toes. Jesse could see that something had been stenciled across the front.

Slowly she breathed in, and then back out. And again. Oxygen flowed to her brain. At least for now she wasn't going to faint. Her hand shook as she lifted it. Using just the tips of her fingers, Jesse grasped the edge of the T-shirt and pulled it outward to smooth away the folds. Below the hilt of the knife was a name.

CHRISTINA.

Jesse had thought she had no more emotion left to give, but now outrage washed up from the depths of her soul. The feeling was strong and sharp. Braced by it, Jesse wrested the doll away from the door and flung it across the room. It landed in a heap beneath the window. Turning away, she left it, and the room, without another glance.

Her first thought was to call the police. This time they couldn't tell her she was imagining things. Or could they? After all that had happened recently, after the day they'd spent guarding a ransom that was never touched, no doubt Detective Maychick would be filled with questions. And what if he asked her who might have done such a thing; what would she say to that?

As if on cue an image of Ned's grinning countenance surfaced. Jesse closed her eyes and shook her head, but it wouldn't go away. Apart from Ned there were very few people—her parents, Kay, Maychick, Phillips—who would know what the name Christina meant to her.

Ned was the one without an alibi.

Ned was the one who knew her signature.

Ned was the one who knew about Amanda's doll.

All day long she'd been bursting with the need to act. Now, finally, Jesse knew what to do. Her car keys were on the counter. She swept them up and hurried outside. Earlier she'd questioned why somebody would demand a ransom then make no effort to retrieve it. Now she knew.

It had been more than a year since she'd been victimized by one of Ned's insidious little games. Maybe that was why she hadn't recognized it sooner. The demand for money was a hoax, all right: Ned's hoax. Once again he'd set her up. Once again he'd engineered a test for her to fail.

And what about the doll? Was that meant to be her punishment? While she'd been out trying to deliver the ransom had he been here, in her house, doing this?

Both the parkway and the thruway would take her to White Plains, but at this time of night back roads were quicker. As Jesse crossed the line from Cranford to Greenwich, the storm that had been gathering burst upon her. Rain splattered against the windshield. Jagged lightning creased the sky. The roll of thunder suited the anger boiling within her. Even on the slick roads it was an effort not to push the gas pedal to the floor.

Visibility was low, but here in the back country, it scarcely seemed to matter. Except for a car behind her she was alone on the road. Jesse caught the flash of headlights in her mirror once, and then again. On the straightaway they dropped back. When she turned, they seemed to catch up. Jesse slowed; they did, too. She speeded up; the other car remained with her. In the rain-soaked darkness of the quiet country roads it was just the two of them, moving in tandem.

Once again Jesse cursed her imagination. She'd been spooked by the doll, and this was the result. Obviously her shadow was someone who knew the same shortcut she did. Still it wasn't until she'd reached the edge of White Plains with its wide, lighted streets and busy thoroughfares that the car disappeared and Jesse felt her shoulders relax. Minutes later she pulled up before Ned's apartment. Lights were on inside; his car was parked out front.

She rang the bell and pounded on the door simultaneously. It was a lot of noise, but it suited her frame of mind perfectly.

"What the fuck . . .!" The door flew open. Ned peered out into the darkness. "Oh," he said, calming. "Hi, Jess. I didn't expect to see you tonight."

"Like hell." She pushed her way past him and went inside.

T HIRTY-FIVE

"Sure," Ned said, closing the door behind her. "Come on in. Make yourself at home."

Jesse whirled to face him. "You bastard!"

"Well, I guess that sets the tone of the conversation. Thank you for not leaving me in doubt."

"You did it, didn't you?"

He raised a brow. "Did what?"

"For once don't be stupid, Ned. Just tell me."

"Maybe we should sit down and discuss this like adults."

Deliberately Jesse looked around the room. "I'm not sure I see any adults here, and I don't feel like sitting."

"Suit yourself." Ned dropped into a chair. "In case you're interested, I'm not in the best of moods myself. So if there's a point to this, I'd appreciate it if you'd get to it."

"I don't give a damn about your mood."

"I gathered that from your entrance. Why don't you tell me what's wrong?"

Oh, she'd tell him, all right, but now that she'd

finally come to get some answers, Jesse figured she might as well start at the beginning and do it right.

"Tell me about your alibi, Ned."

"You've heard it before."

"It's filled with holes."

"Nobody's perfect."

"Damn it, Ned. This isn't a game."

Abruptly he sat up straight. "All right then, I'll tell you about my alibi. Maybe I don't have one. But I can't see how that matters when I'm not the person who kidnapped Amanda. I wouldn't do something like that to you, Jess. You know I wouldn't."

Jesse wasn't sure she knew anything of the sort, but she let it go for now. There were plenty of other points to be made. "A letter was sent to the *Cranford Journal* two days ago. What do you know about it?"

"Nothing." Ned frowned. "Why should I?"

"What was interesting about this letter was that it had my signature on the bottom. Only I didn't send it. I've been trying to figure out how that could have happened."

"Damned if I know."

"You remember my signature, Ned. We shared a lot of credit cards in our day."

"Of course I remember your signature. What the hell was this letter about anyway?"

"About the incompetence of the Cranford Police Department, for one."

"Here, here."

Idiot that he was, he sounded delighted. But what he didn't sound was smug. If Ned had had a hand in defaming Detective Maychick, no doubt he'd be happy to take the credit. "There's something else."

"I thought there might be."

Jesse glared him down before continuing. "Someone was in my house today while I was out. They took Amanda's doll, splattered it with red goo, and drove a knife through its chest. It was dressed in a T-shirt that said 'Christina' on it."

"No shit!"

"Right," Jesse said flatly. "No shit."

"Who would want to do something like that?"

"That's what I'd like to know."

Ned's eyes widened. "You can't mean me."

"Why not?"

"Because that's crazy, that's why not."

"Think about it for a minute. How many other people even know about Christina?"

"Dammit, Jess!" Ned sprang to his feet. "If you can even imagine that I'd do something as perverted as that, then this whole mess has driven you right around the bend. The last thing I'd want to do is hurt you or Amanda. You know that's true. I gave you the money for the ransom, didn't I?"

"Ah yes." Her movements calm, unhurried, Jesse folded her arms over her chest. "The ransom. I was working my way around to that. You haven't even asked me whether the money was picked up. Why do you suppose that is?"

Ned swallowed heavily, his discomfort obvious. Then abruptly his expression changed and he was once more on the offensive. "I would have asked, but you hardly gave me a chance, did you?"

"I'm giving you a chance now, Ned."

"Fine. Tell me how it went."

"It didn't." Spinning away, Jesse began to pace. "It didn't go at all. But then, you already knew that, didn't you?"

"I don't know what you're talking about."

"Sure you do, Ned." Jesse stopped and stared. "We're talking about a ransom note that appeared in my mailbox right after you'd just spent the night. We're talking about a phone call that came less than half an hour after you'd dropped off the money and left. We're talking about lying and cheating and playing games. Tell me it wasn't you, Ned. And try and make me believe it."

She'd expected him to argue. Maybe she'd even hoped he would. Even as Jesse threw out the ideas she was no more than half-convinced herself. She wanted Ned to tell her she was wrong, that he'd had nothing to do with Amanda's disappearance, that it was all just some sort of awful coincidence. But instead, when she'd finished, he said nothing at all.

And it was his silence that gave the game away.

"I did what I had to do," Ned said finally.

Jesse was shaking so hard, it was an effort to push the words out. "Which was?"

"I had to find out where you stood. I had to make sure it wasn't going to be like before. Back then you were always putting other things first—your career, your pregnancy. It was our relationship that should have been important. I thought maybe now you'd realize that. After all this time I thought you had changed."

She couldn't believe he could sound so earnest, as if what he had done made perfect sense. "So you thought you'd give me a little test, is that it? And if I passed, you might consider taking me back?"

"Now, Jess, don't be like that. What are you talking about, tests? It wasn't like that. . . ."

All at once standing seemed like too much of an effort. Jesse sank down on the arm of the couch. "My God, what on earth could you have been thinking? Don't you know how you got my hopes up? Don't you know how you made me feel? And even if that means nothing to you, how could you not realize that what you did was illegal?"

"Great." Ned snorted. "Is that what's next? Are you going to turn me in?" When Jesse didn't answer, he found himself continuing, trying to make her understand. "I didn't think it would be such a big deal. How was I to know things would go as far as they did?

"The police told you not to pay the money. Most people would have listened. But not you. You had to carry the damn thing through. Go on, tell on me if you like. I doubt that I could be arrested for extorting my own money, but I guess you can find out."

Jesse couldn't even look at him. Did he have any idea at all how childish he sounded? Tell on him? He thought she was going to *tell on him?* She drew in a long breath and let it out slowly.

"Tell me one thing, Ned. The truth this time. What was all this business about the two of us getting back together?"

"You know what it was. It was mutual attraction, the same thing that brought us together in the first place. I still have feelings involved here, and I know you do, too. I thought we could make another go at it. At the very least it seemed worth a try."

He gave her that endearing, lopsided grin, the one she loved, the one that had always covered a multitude of sins. But by now they'd been down this road once too often. Every time Ned screwed up, he was always contrite afterward. And every time he apologized, she'd fallen for his heartfelt words and forgiven him.

But not this time.

Jesse swept a glance around the meager apartment. "Funny how you managed to forget all about our mutual attraction when you walked out eleven months ago. It doesn't look to me like you're doing so well on your own. Is that what brought it flooding back?"

"Don't be absurd."

Jesse shook her head wearily. He didn't even have the grace to sound convincing. "Was there ever really a start-up you needed the money for?"

"Well . . ."

There was no use in prompting him. She simply waited until the awkward silence forced him to continue.

"Something will be coming along. You know how it is."

"Sure," Jesse said bitterly. Once again she was up and moving. "I know how it is. Time passes, but nothing ever changes. You'll never grow up, Ned. You'll always be looking for someone to wipe your nose and cover your back. Well, I'm not going to be that person anymore."

"I don't know what made you think you ever were. Even when we were married, especially when we were married, I could never depend on you to be there for me when I really needed you!"

The volume of his voice had risen. Jesse matched it effortlessly. "I was there, all right, just not in the way you wanted me to be. Not to the exclusion of everything else. Did you think I was stupid? I saw right through your charades and your idiotic games. You thought you were so clever. You thought you were the one who pulled all the strings, but I knew what you were up to all along."

"Ha!" Ned spat out. "You think I tried to manipulate you? That's a laugh. You were the one who was a master at manipulation."

"What are you talking about now?"

"Let's discuss how you got pregnant, shall we?" Ned's features were twisted into something hard and ugly. His voice grated across her nerves. "Why don't you tell me about the diaphragm you swore you were using?"

He started toward her and Jesse found herself backing away. "I see you've been talking to Detective Maychick," she said, striving for calm even as panic bubbled within her.

"I sure as hell have. You knew I didn't want another baby, but did you let that stop you? No, just like always, you had your own agenda. First your career, then a child. It all happened right on schedule, didn't it?"

"No." Jesse shook her head. She looked down, away, anywhere but at him.

"*Didn't it?*"

"It wasn't like that." She heard herself say the words he'd used earlier and hated herself for it. "After Christina died, I couldn't stand it. I felt as though I was dying, too. It wasn't a matter of choice, it was a matter of survival. I needed another baby again to make me whole."

"Bravo!" Ned clapped his hands together. "What a convincing performance."

"Dammit, Ned! I'm not acting."

"Really? I seem to recall being told with equal conviction that you were taking care of the birth control."

Jesse went cold all over, whether from rage or despair she wasn't sure. "What does it matter anymore? It's all old news. Amanda's here. She's our daughter. The only thing that matters is finding her and bringing her home."

Ned held up his hands, fingers extended as if to frame her face. "Caring Mom Makes Heartfelt Plea. Keep it up, Jess. You're doing great."

She didn't know how the vase found its way into her hand. Once there, the only thing left to do was throw it. Her aim was only fair, but anger lent strength to the effort. When Ned ducked to one side, the vase sailed over his shoulder and hit the wall with a satisfyingly loud crash.

"Jesus, are you crazy?"

"Yes!" she screamed. "That's exactly what's the matter. You're perfectly sane, and I'm the one who's crazy."

She reached for a book, but Ned was quicker. In two long strides he'd crossed the room and grabbed her wrists in his hands. "Stop it! Do you hear me? Stop it!"

He shook her hard. Her head snapped back, then forward again. As her chin connected with her chest she bit her tongue. Immediately tears sprang to her eyes. Her hands encased in his, she couldn't even brush them away.

"Dammit, Ned," she said, her voice trembling. "Don't you know what you did? Don't you even care how you made me feel? I thought I'd found a way to get Amanda back, and all I'd found was nothing. Another empty promise, just like our marriage turned out to be."

He hit her then, his palm coming up full across her cheek. For a moment Jesse wasn't sure which of the two of them was more shocked. Furious, she wrested her hands away.

"Jess, I'm sorry. I never meant to—"

She wasn't listening, she didn't want to hear. Already Jesse was spinning away and wrenching open the door. "Don't you dare come near me. Not now, and not ever again. If you do, I'll kill you."

She slammed the door so hard the windows rattled.

THIRTY-SIX

Bath time was the woman's favorite part of the day. She'd fill the tub with warm water, then strip off their clothes—her own first, then the baby's—and climb into the tub. The infant's skin was slick and slippery as she cradled her between her naked thighs.

The child laughed with delight at the flotilla of rubber toys and brightly colored plastic boats that bobbed up and down in the water. Her chubby fingers reached for them, her full round mouth squealed with glee. She was such a happy baby. Of course she still cried sometimes, but not nearly as much as she had. She knew the woman was her mother now.

When a boat floated by, the baby snatched it up and lifted it, dripping, into the air.

"That's it, Christina," the woman said. "Reach for the things you want. Then hold on tight, so that no one will ever be able to take them away."

The woman loved looking at the baby's plump body with its rolls of fat. She could spend hours just staring, and sometimes she did. Every piece was as it should be. Every feature was just right.

Lying back in the water, the baby bobbing on her breasts, she remembered the doctor who had visited her in the hospital after the last miscarriage. She supposed he'd tried to be kind when he'd explained that miscarriages were nature's way of dealing with defective babies. He'd mumbled something about Agent Orange and the inadvisability of trying again. He'd told her she'd never have a child of her own, and then all but run from the room.

The woman's husband had taken the news stoically, which was the way he took everything. When she'd married him, the woman had seen only that outer strength. She'd hoped he might shore up her fears and insecurities, but instead he'd saddled her with his own.

A baby might have made the difference, but they never had a chance to find out. After the third miscarriage the woman had stopped holding things together. Bit by bit they fell apart. The marriage ended a year later. She wasn't really sorry to see it go.

The baby cooed loudly, and the woman looked down and smiled. She had a child of her own now. So what did that doctor know?

She and Christina were a team, mother and daughter. They had their whole lives ahead of them. It had been a week already, and the woman was starting to feel safe. If someone was going to find them, they'd have done it by now.

Besides, there were just a few loose ends left to wrap up and then she'd be leaving. No one would follow them. No one would ever suspect a thing.

The woman chuckled at her own cleverness. If she'd learned one thing in Vietnam, it was that the system didn't work. Let the police follow false trails until they were blue. By the time they came knocking on her door—if they ever did—she'd be long gone.

Look out for number one, baby. That was the American way.

One by one they'd all deserted her. Her parents, her

husband. Now even her brother was gone. But this child would be different. This was the one person in the whole world who would never, ever, leave her.

The woman gathered the infant to her and began to sing. Sound bounced off the enclosed bathroom walls. The baby cocked her head to one side then began to laugh. After a moment the woman laughed with her.

Their bodies rose and fell together in the buoyant water as the merriment bound them together and filled the room. The laughter grew and grew, until it became all there was, and the water sloshed over the rim of the tub and onto the floor.

THIRTY-SEVEN

Day Eight

Jesse awoke with a throbbing in her head and the taste of bile in her mouth. Though the sun was up, she felt as though she'd barely slept. Awake, half-awake, even dreaming, the scene with Ned haunted her. It was one thing to suspect her husband of such treachery, and another to confront the reality. How could she have ever thought Ned had finally grown up? She'd been needy, but she wasn't stupid. How could she not have seen through him?

Fortified by a hot shower and a mug of strong coffee, Jesse went back to her maps. There were still more than twenty names to get through. Slow as the work was, at least it was something. That it was the only thing, was something she didn't even want to think about.

Two hours passed before she looked up again, and only then because someone was knocking on the front door. Slowly Jesse rose, stretched the crick out of her neck, and headed into the living room. Before she could reach the door, the pounding started again, punctuated this time by the shrill ring of the bell.

Through the front window, Jesse could see Detective Maychick's brown Ford Fairlane parked at the curb. After she had unlatched the lock and pulled the heavy door inward, he strode inside.

"Ms. Archer." His nod was curt.

"What is it? What's happened? Is there news about Amanda?"

"No, nothing about your daughter." Maychick helped himself to a long, slow look around. "Sit down, Ms. Archer. We're going to talk."

Last time he'd come to see her, there'd been an edge to his behavior. Now that hostility seemed to have intensified. From the look of him the detective had come to do battle.

Jesse sank down into the nearest chair. "All right, I'm sitting. Now please tell me what's going on."

Still standing, Maychick towered over her. Jesse knew their positioning wasn't accidental. His face was set in hard lines. His voice, when he spoke, was harder still.

"I've just come from White Plains. I'm afraid I have some bad news. I've been at your husband's apartment. He's dead, Ms. Archer."

Shock swept through her system. "But that's impossible. I just saw him."

"He was murdered sometime during the night. A neighbor discovered the body this morning."

The news itself was horrible enough, but this flat, emotionless recounting made it somehow worse. "No," Jesse said firmly, as if by denying the fact she could make it go away. "No, it isn't true."

"I need to ask you some questions."

Jesse barely heard him over the pounding in her head. Ned wasn't dead, how could he be? He'd been the love of her life and the thorn in her side. He'd taught her how to laugh, and eventually how to hate.

He couldn't be gone. Not now, not like this. Yes, she'd despised him, but she hadn't wanted him dead. Like it or not their lives were irreparably intertwined.

"Ms. Archer?"

Jesse looked up. Maychick was holding a glass of cold water. She had no idea where it had come from.

"I think you'd better drink this."

Jesse took the glass and gulped from it. It didn't help. She still felt queasy and slightly ill, crushed down by a weight so immense she could barely breathe.

"Feel better now?"

"No."

"I'm still going to have to ask you some questions."

Jesse didn't bother to answer. Let him do what he wanted. What difference could it possibly make?

Maychick reached inside his coat. She thought he was going for a cigarette, but instead he came up with a pen and a pad of paper. "When was the last time you saw your husband?"

"Last night."

Her voice caught in her throat. It was an effort to push the words out. It all seemed unreal. Any minute now she was going to wake up, blink her eyes, and it would all go away. Any minute now she'd hear Amanda fretting in her crib and go to fetch her. None of this had really happened. It couldn't have. It was all some sort of a terrible dream—

Jesse realized the detective was talking again, that he'd repeated his question more than once. "I'm sorry?"

"What time did you see him?" Maychick asked for the third time.

She couldn't remember. It was an effort just to collect her thoughts. She tried to concentrate and block out all the rest. "It was dark when I got there—maybe nine or so. I guess I left about half an hour later."

Maychick noted her answer, then abruptly switched gears. "You're probably wondering about your money.

It's down at the station. You can pick it up later, if you want."

Ned's money, thought Jesse. Now there'd be no way to give it back.

"We searched his apartment this morning." This time, when Maychick had finished patting his pockets, he'd come up with a cigarette and a lighter. "You mind?"

Jesse shook her head. She got up, opened a drawer, and pulled out an ashtray.

"Your husband was behind the phony ransom demand. We found evidence to support that during our search."

She drew in a deep breath and waited. There didn't seem to be much to say.

"You don't look surprised."

"No."

A thin wisp of smoke curled from the tip of his cigarette. Its scent was incredibly enticing. God, if it wasn't for Amanda, she'd go back in a second. Her fingers itched with the need. Her body craved the release. With her baby in her arms she'd thought she'd put the urge behind her. Now it was back, stronger than ever.

"Could be that's something you already knew."

Jesse's grunt was noncommittal.

"When did you find out?"

More questions. Was that all the man knew how to do? She wanted to be alone. She wanted to nurse the pain, and marshal the confusion, in solitude. If answering would get rid of him, so be it. "Yesterday afternoon I began to get suspicious. That was why I went to see Ned last night. I wanted to confront him. I did confront him. He admitted he'd sent the note and made the call."

"Any idea what he hoped to gain?"

"I didn't understand what motivated Ned when I was married to him. I certainly don't pretend to now."

Maychick blew out a coil of smoke. "I hear you were pretty angry when you went to see him."

"Wouldn't you be, under the circumstances?"

"I don't know, Ms. Archer. It's your reactions we're concerned with here. You said you went there to confront him. What did you plan to do then?"

"I didn't have any plans. I didn't need any. I was only trying to find out the truth."

"Which you did."

"Yes."

"And just what exactly was that truth?"

Warning bells went off in her head. If she hadn't been in shock, maybe they'd have gone off sooner. This man had never been a friend; at times he'd been an adversary. She'd do well to remember that.

"That Ned had been the person who made the ransom demand," she said carefully.

"That's all?"

Jesse watched him stub out the cigarette in the ashtray. Smoke curled toward the ceiling; its aroma eddied around her. Even as the temptation was snuffed out she could still feel its pull. "Just what exactly are you getting at, Detective Maychick?"

"I'm sure you must have discussed other things while you were there."

"I imagine we did."

"Care to enlighten me?"

She felt herself grow warm, remembering Ned's angry accusations, and worse, the fact that they were right.

"No."

Maychick gave her a long look. "Then let's go on to something else. Was your husband planning on going out after you left?"

"I don't know."

"Perhaps he had plans to meet someone, or someone was coming there?"

"I don't know. He didn't mention it."

"So as far as you know, after you left, your husband was alone. Maybe he watched some TV, read the paper, went to bed."

"I wouldn't know what he did after I left."

"Then you didn't return."

The question was slipped in just as casually as all the rest, but the bells in Jesse's head had begun to peal like fire sirens.

"No," she said, slowly and distinctly. "I did not return to my husband's apartment."

"You came straight back here?"

"Yes."

"And then what?"

"I went to bed."

"Sleep well?"

"As a matter of fact, no."

Maychick took his time scribbling some notes. Finally he looked up. "By later today we should have the approximate time of your husband's death. I suggest you be able to account for that time."

"I just told you, I was asleep."

"So you did."

He stared at her as though trying to bore holes straight through to her brain. Jesse found herself shifting uncomfortably beneath his gaze. When was this going to be over? Why couldn't he just leave?

Abruptly Maychick flipped his pad over and snapped it shut. "I'll tell you what I think, Ms. Archer. I think if you set aside all the confusion and the running around, what this case boils down to is pretty simple.

"We have a woman whose husband has run out on her because she's had a baby he doesn't want. Maybe it's his, maybe it isn't, we don't know. The child disappears, the husband comes back. Everything's hunky-dory, right?"

Jesse tried to speak, but no sound came out.

"Then, for some reason, the husband does a bunk

again. Maybe he decides he never really loved her. Maybe he begins to wonder where the child's gone—"

Finally she found her voice. "No!"

Maychick didn't even pause. "So now we have a woman who's been twice scorned, and you know what they say about that. She goes to his apartment late at night. Is it one last effort to get him back, or is she looking for revenge? Probably the latter, because she's boiling mad when she gets there. So mad that the neighbors can hear them arguing through the walls. Now they don't make walls like they used to, but still—"

"You're wrong! It's all wrong! You have no idea what you're talking about!"

Maychick stopped then and gazed directly at her. "Oh yes, Ms. Archer, I do. Because whatever went on last night in that apartment, it was loud enough to make the neighbors sit up and take notice. They heard a crash and plenty of yelling. And they heard something else. They heard you tell your husband that you were going to kill him."

THIRTY-EIGHT

Jesse paled as the blood rushed from her head to her feet. A sudden, debilitating weakness accompanied its descent. If she hadn't been sitting, she might have fallen. As it was, she clutched the arms of the chair, squeezing them hard for support.

She remembered the damning words all too well. At the volume they'd been spoken, no wonder the neighbors had heard. She'd said them, and she'd meant them. But she hadn't acted on them.

Sitting across from her, Maychick was waiting patiently. What he'd wanted was a reaction, and he'd gotten that in spades. Now he had all the time in the world. It was Jesse whose time was running out.

"I did not kill Ned Archer." She meant to sound forceful, but it was hard when the words were scarcely louder than a whisper.

"We have motive. We have opportunity. We damn near have witnesses." Maychick snapped his pad shut. "We'll see."

He got up to leave. Jesse felt curiously detached, as if this wasn't her life at all, but rather a movie she'd been forced to watch. Only moments earlier she couldn't wait to be rid of him. But now some small spark of self-preservation pushed her to her feet. She couldn't let him go like this, not believing what he did.

"Detective."

Maychick stopped by the door.

"How?" The word stuck in her throat, choking her with its ramifications. She didn't want to know, didn't want to have to picture the scene in her mind. But none of that mattered. If it helped, she would ask. "How was Ned killed?"

He might have cleaned it up for her, but he didn't. "Your husband was stabbed, Ms. Archer. Six times. Random hits, lots of blood. An amateur job all the way around."

"But . . ." Hope bubbled within her. A reprieve. "But then you must know I couldn't possibly have done it."

"And why is that?"

"Ned is . . ." Jesse stopped, swallowed, made the effort to correct herself. "Ned was much stronger than I am. There's no way I could have overpowered him."

"Straight out, probably not. But there was a blow to the base of the skull, too. Preliminary look says he hit it when he fell, but we could be wrong. We'll know later what came first, and what sorts of possibilities we have to consider."

Maychick reached for the door and pulled it open. "Six hits, Ms. Archer. Lots of blood. Whoever stabbed Ned Archer was mad at him. Nobody makes that big a mess unless they're either crazy or looking to get even.

"Believe me, I'm going to find out what happened to your husband. And until I do, I want you around. No sudden, unexplained trips, understand?"

Anger steeled her, brought purpose into her voice. "I'm to keep myself available, isn't that what you mean?"

"Yeah, that's it. You might try finding a lawyer, too. Next time we talk you're going to need one."

"What about my daughter?"

That stopped him where he stood. For the first time since his arrival she'd managed to surprise him. "What about her?"

"You said you're going to be investigating Ned's . . . death. While you're busy there who will be looking for her?"

Maychick's silence was long enough to provide an answer of its own. "We may not know where your daughter is yet, but believe me, we're going to find her. Somewhere at the bottom of this whole sorry mess we'll find her. And when we do, I suspect we'll have the evidence we need for an indictment. Like I said, you'd better be getting yourself a lawyer."

Jesse fought to hold on to that blunt edge of anger, even as fear brought a sheen of sweat to her brow. The threat to herself was bad enough, but for Amanda the ramifications were disastrous. "You're wrong. I don't care what you think, you have to believe me about that. Investigating me won't find my daughter. I want to know who you have that will still be working on the case."

"We'll all be working on the case," Maychick said meaningfully. "If I were you, I wouldn't do anything stupid."

She'd slammed enough doors recently to know that it didn't help. This time, after Maychick walked through, Jesse merely pushed it shut behind him. Deliberately she turned away from the front window and stared out the back.

After the night's rain the yard looked obscenely lush and green. To one side was the garden she'd never gotten around to planting. Jesse focused her gaze there. The dry, untilled dirt looked every bit as barren as she felt.

Jesse swayed on her feet, then began to rock. The age-old mothers' rhythm was strangely comforting, even as it reminded her of all she had lost. Poor

Amanda. Poor tiny baby. Now her father was gone, and she'd never even had a chance to know him. Who could do these things to a helpless child? What sort of monster could conceive of these acts, much less carry them out?

Jesse had no answers, and standing there, wallowing in pity, wasn't going to provide them. If nothing else, the events of the last two days had taught her one thing: if anyone was going to save Amanda, it was going to have to be Jesse herself.

In the kitchen she laced a fresh cup of coffee with a shot of brandy big enough to give her a good jolt. Then she picked up her maps and went back to work. She was almost to the bottom of the page when she came upon the fifth listing for a Mrs. Ruby Saunders at 226 Doyle Street.

Jesse plotted the address, then stared at it thoughtfully, wondering why it sounded familiar. Looking back up over the list, she saw that Mrs. Saunders had made all her calls to the hot-line number over a two-day span. Though the number had been on TV for almost a week, her response had started only recently. A note beside the woman's name at its prior listings tagged her as a habitual caller.

Wonderful, thought Jesse. Apparently the police had heard from Ruby Saunders before, and they'd hear from her again. The case didn't matter, nor the people involved. Like the rest of the attention seekers, she was somehow able to get a kick out of the misery of others. Jesse's head began to throb. She pressed the heels of her palms against her eyes and took several deep breaths before pushing on.

Four more names, and Jesse was done. She took the pages of the Fairfield County atlas, ripped them out, and spread them over the table. Maps covering the rest of Connecticut, New York, and New Jersey were placed beyond that.

One hundred names, give or take a few. One hundred people to call. Jesse glanced down to see which were the closest, who were the first people she'd be contacting. Once more the name Ruby Saunders leaped out at her.

Five calls, Jesse mused. The police had discounted her, but maybe they were wrong. The woman might be a regular caller, but that didn't mean that this time she might not know something.

Irritation spiking through her, Jesse pushed the maps away. She might be desperate, but she wasn't that naive. When she started grasping at straws, it was time to take a break.

She pulled open the refrigerator. Its shelves were as every bit as bare as they had a right to be. The one lone hunk of cheese was hard; containers of milk and yogurt had long since expired. Kay's casserole, now that she thought of it, was still in the microwave.

In no mood to face that, Jesse turned to the cupboard, which yielded three cans of vegetables, a box of noodles, and a jar of peanut butter that looked like manna from heaven. She dug it out, rolled off the top, and went in fingers first. The peanut butter was dry and stuck to the roof of her mouth. Too bad she'd let the casserole spoil. . . .

Abruptly, hand poised on its way for seconds, Jesse went still. That was why Doyle Street had sounded familiar, because Kay had mentioned it the night before. *I'm on my way to Doyle Street to get the kids from Denise.*

Jesse set the jar of peanut butter down on the counter, her appetite gone. Denise Connelly lived on Doyle Street. Denise Connelly, who'd been in the supermarket buying formula. For the hospital, she'd said. Supplies for new mothers. It all made sense, except . . .

Jesse frowned, pushing herself to remember. Her thoughts had been so centered upon Amanda lately, she hadn't been paying nearly enough attention to everything else. Hadn't Kay mentioned something about Denise inheriting some money and going away? And if she was quitting her job, why would she need so many supplies?

Jesse grabbed up a towel, wiped off her hand, then reached across the counter for the phone. She let Kay's number ring five times, then another five. Still there was no answer.

It didn't matter. There were other ways. Slamming down the receiver, Jesse yanked opened the drawer and pulled out the phone book. Hastily she skimmed through the flimsy pages.

"Connelly," Jesse muttered to herself. "Connelly, Connelly. Denise." There it was. She ignored the phone number and went straight to the address. Her breath caught as the tiny print seemed to swim before her eyes. She blinked twice, rapidly, then checked again to make sure there was no mistake.

Connelly, Denise. 228 Doyle Street.

Right next door to Ruby Saunders.

Jesse flew around the counter to the table. Papers scattered as she grabbed the one she sought and carried it back to the phone. Her fingers shook as she punched out the number. The phone was picked up on the second ring.

"Ruby Saunders?" It was a struggle to hold her voice steady. "Is this Mrs. Ruby Saunders?"

"That depends. Who wants to know?"

"I'm—" Jesse began, then stopped. The woman had contacted the police. Perhaps it would be better if that's who she thought she was speaking to. "I'm calling in response to your hot-line tip concerning the kidnapped child."

"Well, it's about time. I've called that number repeatedly. I was beginning to wonder if anyone even wanted to know."

"Know what, Mrs. Saunders?"

"Where the baby is, that's what."

For the space of a second it was as though everything stopped: her heart, her lungs simply ceased to function. Waves of shock eddied through her. Jesse sagged back into the counter. If it hadn't caught her, she'd have crumpled to the floor.

After all these days, after all this time, it couldn't be just this simple. Could it?

"Are you still there or not?"

"Yes!" Jesse fought to recover her equilibrium. "I'm here. I'm listening. Please tell me what you know. Have you seen the baby?"

"I've seen *a* baby. Not close up to tell what it looks like. But you don't have to be close up to know when there's a baby where it doesn't belong."

"I don't understand."

"I don't either." Ruby cackled into the phone. "That's the problem. One day the lady next door doesn't have herself a baby, the next she does. A body has to wonder where it came from. A body has to wonder why it never leaves the house."

It never left the house? Agent Phillips's dismissive attitude toward groupies hovered, unwelcome, at the edge of her thoughts. He hadn't given them any credence. Nor had the police. They'd dismissed Mrs. Saunders as an annoyance. Jesse couldn't afford to be so cavalier. Ruby Saunders might be all she had.

"Mrs. Saunders, if you haven't seen the baby, how do you know it's there?"

"I hear it, that's how. I'm a mother myself—grandmother, too. Don't think I wouldn't recognize the sound of a baby crying. Once I even saw a baby carriage. I just happened to be looking out the window, you understand."

Jesse understood, all right. The woman was a busybody. More power to her, if it got Jesse the information she sought. "Mrs. Saunders, what is your neighbor's name?"

"Connelly." Ruby smacked her lips in satisfaction. "Denise Connelly, that's the one."

The news should have excited her, but if anything, the opposite was true. All at once Jesse felt remarkably calm. She had no intention of making any mistakes. "Mrs. Saunders, how do you know your neighbor isn't baby-sitting for someone?"

"The baby's been here a week, maybe more. Besides, if you were baby-sitting, would you leave that child locked up tight all day inside the house? She comes and goes, I've seen her. She does the marketing. Who's looking out for that baby then, I'd like to know?"

"She leaves the baby all alone?"

"I just said that, didn't I? It's not normal, that's what I say. I may be old, but I keep up with things, and I know babies don't just appear. There's a shortage, that's what I hear. So who's going to give one to her?

"You get somebody up here," Ruby continued without pausing for breath. "And don't waste your time, either. While you're at it you might try handing out some speeding tickets, too."

"Speeding tickets?"

"To those crazy teenagers. You know what I'm talking about. I've called about them before."

"Yes, of course," Jesse broke in. "We'll get right on it. Thank you for your help."

Slowly Jesse hung up the phone. Her hands clenched on the counter as she stared out the window and forced herself to concentrate. She had some of the pieces of the puzzle, but she certainly didn't have them all. Suppose Ruby Saunders was right. Suppose Denise Connelly did have a new baby. It could have come from anywhere. It didn't necessarily have to be Amanda.

But it might be.

Jesse closed her eyes and pictured her daughter's face. Of course Amanda was the most wonderful baby in the world, but then every mother thought that.

What could there have been about her daughter, or about herself, that might have caused Denise to fixate upon them? Denise had never even seen Amanda. The baby had been born at Cranford Hospital, not St. Simon's. Not like Christina . . .

The name called up an image: the doll impaled on the back of her bedroom door. "Christina," its shirt had said. Christina who'd been born at St. Simon's where Denise had been working. Was that the connection? Had Denise somehow known about Jesse's first baby? Had she been at St. Simon's when Jesse was there?

She needed more answers. Once again Jesse found herself heading for the phone. She dialed the hospital and asked for personnel. She'd been in business long enough to know how information was obtained. One low-level bureaucrat to another. In a nasal voice she identified herself to the clerk who answered as a sales rep for Citywide Life Insurance. For her records she needed to verify the employment record of one Denise Connelly. Would the clerk be so kind as to help her out?

The clerk would. Two minutes later Jesse found herself listening to Ms. Connelly's file. Denise had been employed at St. Simon's for the last four years. The first two had been spent in the ER. After a leave of absence, attributed to professional burnout, she returned to work in the maternity ward.

"Professional burnout," Jesse repeated. "Do you know what that was in reference to?"

"I'm afraid I can't give out that information. You can speak with her doctor, if you like."

"No, thank you, that won't be necessary."

Jesse already had what she needed. And though the information didn't make perfect sense, at least it was beginning to take shape. Apparently she and Denise had shared a connection of sorts. Not enough of one for Jesse to remember, although for some reason she'd made an impression on Denise.

Enough of an impression to keep her coming back, to make her haunt Jesse's house, Jesse's life. To make her covet Jesse's daughter.

The receiver was still warm when Jesse picked it up again. This time, when she called Kay, she simply let it ring. Two minutes passed. She clocked them on the microwave. Sheer determination told her Kay had to be home. Finally the phone was picked up.

"This had better be important. I'm dripping water all over the floor."

"It's important," Jesse said tersely. "You told me Denise Connelly was going away, remember?"

"Sure, I remember. Why? Is something wrong?"

"Yes. Maybe. I don't know." Jesse was humming with impatience. "The thing is Kay, I need to know something. When exactly is Denise going?"

"That's easy." Kay chuckled in relief that the question was so simple. "She's all packed and ready. She's leaving tomorrow, first thing."

THIRTY-NINE

She had to find Agent Phillips. His lousy opinion of her be damned. This was important. This was vital. And he would just have to grow up and deal with it.

But when Jesse called the police station, he wasn't there. She tried his office first, then the main switchboard. The first yielded no answer; the second an operator who didn't know where he was and didn't care. Reluctantly Jesse settled for leaving a message, reminding the operator twice to tag it urgent.

That left Detective Maychick, a very poor second choice indeed. He didn't like her, and he didn't believe in her. But Phillips could be gone for minutes or for the rest of the day. Jesse didn't have time to wait. With luck the strength of her information would be enough to temper the detective's hostility.

This time her call was put right through.

"Maychick," he barked into the phone.

"Detective? This is Jesse Archer. I have to talk to you. I know where my daughter is."

If he was surprised by the news, it didn't show in his tone. "Have you consulted a lawyer, Ms. Archer?"

"A lawyer? No. I don't need a lawyer. I need the police."

"You want to come down and make a statement, is that it?"

It took her a minute, but Jesse finally realized what he was getting at. "This isn't about me," she snapped. "It's about Amanda, my baby who was kidnapped. Later we'll work out the rest, but right now I need your help. There isn't any time to waste. I know who has Amanda, detective. You have to help me get her back."

"Do I?" There was a pause, accompanied by the sound of an indrawn breath. Jesse pictured Maychick sitting back and lighting up. "Suppose you tell me where you think your baby's coming back from."

"There's a woman named Denise Connelly. She was a nurse at St. Simon's Hospital, and she works as a baby-sitter in the neighborhood. We have to hurry, detective. Denise is leaving town tomorrow."

"And you think she has your baby."

The question was calm, curious, and totally devoid of urgency. Jesse's hand folded into a fist on top of the counter. In another minute she'd be pounding. "Yes, I do."

"Mind telling me why?"

"There are several reasons." She'd known she'd have to explain. Still she couldn't help but begrudge the time it took. "Let me backtrack a minute. Do you remember when we discussed my first daughter, Christina?"

"Sure."

Sure was the last thing he sounded. Jesse pressed on regardless. She described what had happened to Amanda's doll and finally succeeded in getting his attention.

"Did I hear you right, Ms. Archer? Someone splattered blood on your wall?"

"It wasn't real blood, it just looked like it. At the time I thought Ned was responsible, but he wasn't."

"How do you know that?"

"He told me. Anyway, it doesn't matter, except that it's all part of the bigger picture." If she'd had more time to prepare, she might have made more sense. Now all Jesse could think about was getting the information across. "You see, not that many people even knew about Christina. But Denise Connelly did—"

"Let me get this straight," Maychick interrupted. "Are you telling me that yesterday there was another intruder in your house?"

"Yes, I am, but—"

"I don't recall seeing a report."

Jesse sighed. "That's because there wasn't one."

"Someone enters your house, throws blood around, and you don't call the police?"

"Yes . . . no. Usually I would. I had other things on my mind," Jesse finished lamely.

"What other things?"

"Ned." They'd covered this before. Why was it necessary to go over it again? "At the time I thought he was the one behind everything, but he wasn't."

"What makes you so sure?"

"Because he's dead!" Jesse all but screamed.

"Yes, indeed, Ms. Archer. Your husband is dead."

At least they agreed on something. Jesse squeezed her eyes shut and prayed for patience. Somehow she had to convince him that she knew what she was talking about.

"The important thing is that Denise Connelly knew about my first baby. She was working in the maternity ward of St. Simon's Hospital when I delivered Christina there."

"Did she tell you that?"

"No."

"Then who did?"

"That's not important."

"On the contrary I think it may be very important. Where did you obtain your information?"

Was he questioning her veracity, or her source? "It came from the personnel department at the hospital."

"You just called them up and asked."

"Yes."

"And they told you what you wanted to know."

"Yes." Jesse was damned if she'd elaborate. Let him wonder.

"I'm curious, Ms. Archer. What led you to call St. Simon's in the first place?"

"I spoke with Denise's neighbor, a woman named Ruby Saunders. She'd been making calls to the hot-line number, but nobody had gotten back to her. She says something strange is going on next door, that there's a baby living there now who's never been there before."

"Ruby Saunders," Maychick repeated slowly, as though writing the name down. "You say she was one of our call-ins?"

"Yes!" What did the name matter? It was what came after that was important. "Did you hear what I said? She says she's sure Denise Connelly has a baby in her house."

"Yes, Ms. Archer, I heard what you said. But I'm curious about a few other things as well. How did you happen to come up with Ruby Saunders's name?"

"I told you before, it was on the list."

"I wasn't aware that you had access to that list."

Jesse swallowed heavily.

"Would you care to explain how you happened to come across it?"

Seconds passed. She had no defense, only the lesser option of a good offense. "Actually I wouldn't. What I would care to do is accompany someone in authority to Denise Connelly's house. I'm sure we can iron out the rest of the details later. But right now there isn't time. Denise is packing to leave."

"As far as I'm aware, Ms. Connelly is free to come and go as she pleases."

Jesse bit down on her lip, hard. He couldn't possibly be so obtuse; no one could. "Don't you see? If she takes Amanda away, we may never find them again. We have to do something now, before it's too late!"

"Oh, I see, all right. I see plenty, Ms. Archer. I see a woman getting a little bit nervous about how things are going, as well she might. I see someone trying to interfere with our investigation. I see—"

Jesse hung up on him. She took the receiver and placed it back down on the hook. It was as simple as that. So much for help from Cranford's finest. Why did she keep believing that the authorities were going to step in and save her? Maychick wasn't about to. As for Agent Phillips, she couldn't even find him.

So she would deal with Denise on her own. She would brave the specter that had haunted her dreams with its dark, soulless eyes and long-bladed knife. She would take on the person who had stolen her child and her life.

Last time they'd come together on Denise's terms. Jesse had been taken by surprise and scared half to death. This time she'd have to do better. This time the surprise would be hers.

If Jesse had had a gun, she'd have taken it. There were knives in the kitchen, but nothing she could slip into her pocket. She wasn't planning on carrying a purse. She was going to be moving much too fast for that. Denise was strong, but Jesse would be smarter. One way or another she was going to get her baby back.

Doyle Street wasn't far. She cruised her car slowly down the block, noting the addresses. The area was residential, much like her own. The houses were small and of postwar vintage. They sat up close to the road on small, well-tended lots.

Ruby Saunders's house was a Victorian, with gables and turrets, and a porch that extended across the front. The Connelly house next door was a Cape. The front doors to both were closed. The shades upstairs at Denise's house were drawn. There was no movement anywhere. The house looked quiet, and deathly still.

Jesse felt herself grow cold all over. Denise had to be there. Tomorrow, that was the plan. She couldn't have gone already. Jesse couldn't have come so close to finding Amanda, only to lose her again.

Then as she eased past the driveway she saw a van parked behind the house, in front of the detached one-car garage. It was of boxy make and shape, dark green, with no commercial lettering of any kind. A Dodge.

A horn blared behind her and Jesse realized she'd slowed to barely better than a crawl. Immediately she pushed down on the gas. Now was not the time to be stopping or drawing attention to herself. At the end of the block she turned right and circled around again.

This time, at the top of the block, she eased over to the curb and parked. If anyone came out, Jesse would know. Surely someone planning a long trip might need a few last-minute supplies. Mrs. Saunders had said that Denise left the baby home alone when she went out. Five minutes, that was all Jesse needed. Five minutes with Denise's attention elsewhere so that she could get into the house and get her daughter out.

With excruciating slowness the afternoon passed. Nobody came or went; nothing stirred at all. By evening, daylight had faded enough to make the surveillance difficult. Jesse had started her vigil certain that it would present an opportunity. Now she wasn't so sure.

Amanda was so close, Jesse could feel her presence. Her baby was in that house, she just knew it. And so was Denise. Denise, who might never be coming out until morning when it would be too late. Full darkness might have been better, but Jesse couldn't wait any longer. Dusk would have to do.

Jesse slipped out of the car and began to walk. As she neared the house a light flicked on inside. She melted into the shadows and waited. After a moment

Denise crossed the path of the lighted window. A reflection seemed to move behind her. Jesse squinted, trying to determine its source. Then the shade came down, and the light was gone.

At least now she knew that Denise was in the front of the house. Jesse slipped up the driveway and around the back. A quiet hand on the back doorknob told her it was locked. The window beside it was also secured. Heart in her throat, Jesse looked for alternatives.

By the side of the house a big old oak tree spread its branches over fully half the yard. Several nestled up close to the house. Jesse measured their size against her weight and decided they'd do. She hadn't climbed a tree in years. Maybe it was like riding a bicycle, something you never forgot.

A jump and a swing put her on the bottom branch. Immediately she remembered why she'd left tree climbing behind. Bark skinned her palms and scraped her legs. Looking only up, Jesse began to climb.

The windows on the second floor were dark, their curtains drawn. As Jesse neared the closest one she could see that it was shut, but not latched. Maybe her luck finally had begun to change.

She reached out a hand and grasped the sill. The branch jiggled and swayed beneath her. Waiting until it had steadied, she flattened her palm against the window frame and pushed upward. The window stuck at first, then finally gave, scratching in its grooves.

Jesse cleared six inches, then nine. Needing better purchase, she eased out carefully to the end of the branch. She'd just reached out her hand once more, when there was a crash from inside.

Jesse pulled back so quickly she nearly fell. One foot slipped from its perch as she grabbed frantically for a new hold. Someone was yelling, arguing. The sounds were loud and strident. Though they came from inside, from downstairs, Jesse could hear each shout as it was followed by the next.

The words didn't matter. Jesse didn't bother to listen. It could have been the TV, or then again, maybe not. She'd assumed that Denise would be alone, but there was no going back now. At least with Denise occupied downstairs there'd be less chance of a confrontation.

One last push eased the window up the rest of the way. The branch creaked and dipped as Jesse levered herself carefully up onto the sill. She didn't even want to think about what the return trip would be like, with a baby in her arms.

The curtain was thick and heavy; it smelled of mildew. Cautiously Jesse pushed it aside. The room was dark, but her eyes had already adjusted. Within lay a nursery, fully equipped. The wall nearest her held the changing table and a child-sized dresser stenciled with bunnies. In the corner opposite was a cradle.

Even as Jesse's gaze fastened upon it she was already hoisting herself up and over the sill. She pushed off the branch and hovered for a moment, suspended, half in and half out. Then her balance shifted and she dropped quietly to the floor.

Scarcely daring to breathe, Jesse strained her ears to listen. The shouting had stopped. But all at once she could hear the tread of heavy footsteps moving across the floor. Were they coming closer? Maybe up the stairs? She shrank back against the wall, looking for cover where there was none.

Abruptly a door downstairs opened, then slammed shut, and the footsteps were gone. Moments later the van in the driveway gunned to life. Jesse heard the *whoosh* of wheels as it passed beneath the window and turned out onto the road. Then all was quiet once more.

In seconds she was up and moving. A floorboard creaked beneath her sneakered feet. Jesse didn't care. She was drawn, inexorably, toward the cradle in the corner. No sound at all came from the small bed. No movement caught her eye. Lace-trimmed sheets spilled up and out over the sides. A pink cotton blanket was bunched at one end. But the tiny mattress was empty.

A wail rose up within her. Jesse jammed a fist into her mouth and choked it back. Amanda had been there, in this house. This was her room.

Where was her daughter now?

Flattened against the wall, Jesse crept toward the door and eased it open. The hallway outside was dark. There was another door opposite, closed as well. A narrow flight of stairs led down to the landing below.

She waited. Seconds ticked by, but still she heard nothing. The silence in the house was oppressive. It surrounded her like a shroud. A bead of sweat trickled between her shoulder blades and down her back. When she grasped the banister, her palm was wet and clammy.

Step by cautious step Jesse went down the stairs. Had there been two people below, or only Denise? Had they both left in the van, or was one still there, waiting to trap her in the quiet and the dark?

The front door was to her right, the living room on the left. Jesse reached the bottom and turned stealthily. A scream gathered in her throat; her legs buckled beneath her. Her hand, braced against the wall, was the only thing that kept her upright.

Denise was there, waiting for her.

Only one light in the room was on, and it cast long shadows over a mishmash of furniture that filled every available space. Backlit, Denise loomed over her surroundings. She was standing beside a wing-backed chair, one hand resting heavily on its curved top. The look on her face was decidedly odd; her eyes were flat and empty of expression. She should have been surprised to see Jesse, but the emotion didn't seem to register.

For a moment Denise didn't move at all, neither toward Jesse or away. Then slowly she raised her hands, fingers spread, palms empty.

"You came for your baby," she whispered. "But you can't have her. Nobody can. She's gone."

FORTY

"*Where is she?*"

The sound of Jesse's voice seemed to ricochet off the walls of the small room. Denise let her arms fall to her sides. She shook her head slightly, but didn't answer.

Jesse took a step forward, then stopped. All her instincts counseled caution. Something was very wrong. She knew what kind of strength, what kind of violence, Denise was capable of. So why was she just standing there? Warily Jesse eyed the other woman's hands. "Tell me where my baby is."

"She's not your baby." Denise's voice was hollow, and as flat as her eyes. "She's mine. She'll always be mine. You don't deserve her, any more than you deserved the other one."

"Christina," Jesse said softly.

Denise nodded.

"What do you know about her?"

"I knew everything about your daughter. I knew her better than you did. I was the night nurse in charge of her care. But we never met. Not back then.

How could we, the way you acted? Waltzing in at nine and out again at five, like having a baby was nothing, a job you could turn on and off whenever you felt like it."

It wasn't like that, Jesse wanted to cry. She remembered those anguished weeks with a clarity so sharp it still hurt. Juggling Ned's needs, and Christina's, and her own. Trying to satisfy everyone and, in the end, succeeding in nothing but coming up short. But she wouldn't justify what she had done. Not now, and certainly not to this woman.

"I loved my daughter."

"Hah!" Denise snorted. The sound was followed by a hacking cough. "Don't tell me that was love. People like you have everything, and you take it all for granted, even babies."

Jesse took another step closer. Adrenaline was humming through her body, drawing her tight as a bow. And still Denise didn't move.

Jesse cast a hurried glance around the room. Where was Amanda? What had happened to her? Her gaze skimmed back to the woman standing in the middle.

"Tell me where she is, Denise."

"Gone. All gone."

"Gone where?"

Denise thought for a moment, as if trying to find an answer. "My brother took her away."

Jesse hadn't expected that. She'd heard the van leave only minutes before. Had she missed her daughter by that little?

"Who is your brother? Why did he take Amanda?"

"My brother is a shit." Denise seemed pleased by that revelation because it made her laugh, a dry, rasping cackle that sounded as though it hurt.

"I don't understand. Why did he take Amanda away?"

Denise shrugged; the movement was awkward, jerky. "I tried to stop him, but I couldn't. He wouldn't listen. He never listened. He wanted to be the hero. I thought he was going to save me, but he only wanted to save himself. . . ."

Denise's voice began to fade away. One hand came up, clawlike, to grasp the back of the chair. Her skin was white as chalk. As Jesse watched, the muscles in her face seemed to slacken. A drop of spit dribbled from the side of her mouth.

"Who is your brother?" Jesse demanded. "Where has he taken my baby?"

Denise didn't answer. She swayed back, then forward; the motion was jarring, puppetlike. As Jesse watched in horror a drop of something dark and wet fell to the carpet. A second drop followed the first.

Blood.

Jesse tried to move, but couldn't. She could only stare, fascinated, like a deer caught in the glare of oncoming headlights, as Denise swayed one last time, then crashed forward onto the floor. The thick, black hilt of a carving knife stuck out from between her shoulders.

"Shit!" Jesse scrambled backward, overbalanced, and fell into the wall behind her. Her shoulder wrenched at the contact, and the pain felt good. It was real. It was alive. And so was she.

She ought to call the police. She ought to check for a pulse. She ought to get the hell out of there. Thoughts ricocheted at random through her brain. Jesse braced her back against the wall and pushed herself up.

And still Denise didn't move. Jesse stared, unable to do anything else. Denise couldn't be dead. How could she be dead? Injured certainly, but not dead.

Jesse told herself that once, then ten times, even as blood soaked through the back of Denise's shirt and traveled in a sluggish stream down her outstretched arm. She told herself that as Denise's eyes, open, staring, and vacant, followed her around the room.

And she told herself that as she ripped that room apart.

Denise had a brother. Her brother had Amanda. And somehow, somewhere, Jesse had to find out who he was. As for the rest, nothing could be changed; it was better not to think about it.

Jesse finished in the living room and moved on. The bulletin board in the kitchen held clippings, cartoons, and recipes, but not a single clue as to Denise's family. Nor did the short list of numbers tacked beside the phone. Jesse rifled drawers and cabinets alike. Quickly and methodically she searched the downstairs and came up with nothing.

Denise's bedroom was at the top of the stairs, opposite the nursery. The bed was double size, four-poster, and neatly made up. Jesse passed it by and went to the dresser. Its top held only a silver comb-and-brush set and a single bottle of hand lotion. Drawer by drawer she took it apart. Clothing scattered around the room. Jesse kicked it out of the way and kept going.

The night table beside the bed had two drawers. The top one held several bottles of pills. The bottom drawer stuck. Jesse jiggled in vain, then stood up and gave it a good kick. That worked. On her next try it fell open into her hands.

There were papers on top. Jesse skimmed through them quickly. Underneath were pictures. They tumbled through her fingers as she had a look.

Kneeling, she scanned the faces, looking for a clue, a sign, anything at all. Denise, in nurse's whites, graduating from school. Denise in army fatigues, arm around a female buddy. A smiling Denise, wearing a suit and corsage, standing next to an equally happy young man. A wedding picture?

Jesse flipped it over. There was nothing written on

the back. She laid it to one side and went on. The pile of discarded photos around her grew. Near the bottom was a group shot. Jesse took her time and examined it carefully.

There were eight or nine people in the picture. They were grouped around a picnic table and mugging for the camera. Slowly Jesse looked from face to face.

That the picture was old was obvious. Denise, who was sitting to one side, looked at least ten years younger. The rest of the group around the table were people Jesse didn't know, had never seen before. And yet . . .

She started to set the picture aside, but something drew her back. Jesse angled the picture into the light and stared at the three men. One of them looked vaguely familiar. Something around the eyes . . .

She took her finger and placed it over the man's hair, making it recede high up into his scalp, and the pieces fell into place. He was younger, thinner, definitely hairier. But Jesse knew the face. She'd seen him only days before.

Quentin Stone.

The pictures scattered as Jesse leaped to her feet. Quentin Stone? Until he'd started badgering her about Amanda's disappearance, Jesse'd barely even noticed him. He'd seemed like such a mild man, always helpful, self-effacing. Was he the person behind all this? And what did he want with Amanda now?

Stopping only long enough to dial 911 and report a disturbance at Denise's address, Jesse let herself out of the house and ran back to her car. Hang on, Amanda, she willed the thought outward as she sped down the narrow street and rounded the corner.

If only she'd gone into the house earlier, she might have Amanda now. Quentin had been there when she arrived; she was sure of it. It was he she'd heard arguing with Denise. And when he'd left, he'd taken Amanda with him. She'd been *that* close.

Tires squealing, Jesse pulled up into her own driveway. She had to stop. She had to think. It was one thing to take on Denise by herself. Quentin was another matter entirely. Obviously he was getting desperate. Who knew what he might do next?

It had been hours since she'd left her message for Agent Phillips. Surely she'd be able to find him by now. He couldn't still be unavailable. . . .

The house was dark, even the porch light was off. Jesse had her key out, but the knob turned easily in her hand. Pushing for speed, she shouldered the door aside and was into the kitchen before the thought even registered.

The door should have been locked.

The screen slammed shut behind her. Jesse jumped and reached for the light. She didn't make it. In the dark a hand came up to cover hers. A second closed over her mouth.

"Don't scream," said Quentin. "I won't hurt you."

She gasped for air that wasn't there and tasted his fingers instead. He smelled of smoke and sweat as he pressed his body next to hers.

"Tell me you won't scream." The whisper was low, guttural. The sound of it grated in her ears. "And I'll let you go."

She couldn't think. She couldn't speak. Eyes wide, staring, Jesse shook her head from side to side and the pressure against her face loosened.

"Promise."

"Yes," she rasped out, and the hand fell away.

The effort to drag in air made her dizzy. Jesse spun around and away, backing until her spine pressed up against the sink. She braced her hands and held herself steady, measuring the distance between them.

The scene had a horrible familiarity to it. Determinedly Jesse pushed the thought from her mind. This time she would be the one to take control.

"You surprised me, Quentin. What are you doing here?"

"Waiting." He blinked uncertainly, unsure of his reception. "I was waiting for you."

"In the dark?"

As though it was the most natural thing Jesse reached around the cabinet and turned on the switch. Above them the kitchen light glowed. Quentin was standing in the middle of the room, his body blocking any escape she might try to make. On the far counter the message light on the answering machine was blinking.

"Yeah, well, I didn't want to disturb anything. I just used my own key and let myself in."

Jesse didn't say a word, but her expression made Quentin smile.

"You didn't know I had one, did you?" he said smugly. "That's because I'm smart. I took your key and copied it, and then I brought it back. I'll bet you never even missed it. I am smart, aren't I, Jesse?"

Nodding, she let her gaze slide past him. Where was Amanda? She'd been so sure Quentin had the baby. But what had he done with her?

"I have good news," Quentin said, and his smile widened.

"You do?"

"I found your baby. I know where she is."

"You found Amanda? How?"

She shouldn't have asked that, Jesse saw that immediately. But the question had slipped out and she watched Quentin struggle with how to deal with it.

He shook his head and it lolled from side to side. "The police and everybody, they think they're so smart. They're not so smart. They don't know everything. I saw how unhappy you were. I knew how badly you wanted someone to fix things for you, so that's what I did."

Jesse didn't look at the knife rack, but she was thinking about it. "What did you fix?"

"Everything," Quentin said gleefully. "I fixed everything."

"I'm so happy you could help. And now you have to help me again. You have to tell me where Amanda is."

"Oh, no!" cried Quentin and Jesse's stomach plummeted. "I'm not going to tell you. I'm going to take you there."

"Where?"

He leaned closer across the space that separated them. "It's a secret."

"I don't like secrets, Quentin."

"You'll like this one."

Jesse didn't answer and he leaped suddenly toward her. Before there was time to move, he'd grasped her arm. "Tell me. Tell me you'll like this one."

"I will." Jesse pushed the words out. He dropped her arm as suddenly as he'd taken it. Her skin was striped with red from the pressure of his fingers. When she reached up to rub it, he looked down and saw what he'd done.

"That's your fault," he said accusingly. "I didn't want to hurt you. I'd never want to hurt you. You know that, don't you?"

"Yes, of course." She let her hands fall to her sides. "I understand. It was my fault. It doesn't really hurt."

"Enough talking. It's time to go. I'll take you to Amanda, and we'll all be happy."

"Please, Quentin, tell me where she is." Jesse couldn't just go with him, not like this. And yet what choice did she have? "At least tell me where we're going."

"Can't do that!" Quentin grinned as though he'd said something impossibly clever. "It's a surprise. You want to see your baby, don't you?"

"Yes, but I—"

"Then come." Abruptly his mood changed, his features hardening as he headed for the door.

Jesse took one step after him, then another. "Just tell me," she said, her voice low, pleading. "Is Amanda all right?"

Quentin stopped, turned. "She is now. You wouldn't want that to change, would you?"

FORTY-ONE

They were just outside the door when the phone began to ring. Quickly Jesse turned back. "I'd better get that."

Quentin's hand stopped her. "Leave it."

The phone rang a second time, and then a third.

"It might be important."

"It doesn't matter."

"It might—"

"Come *on.*"

As his fingers closed around her wrist and he pulled her down the driveway, Jesse heard the ringing stop. The machine had picked up. With her luck it was probably Agent Phillips. Even now the recording was telling him that she wasn't home, that there was no way to reach her, that everything was just fine. Damn.

They reached the curb and kept going.

"Where are you taking me?" Jesse asked.

"Over there."

Quentin inclined his head and Jesse saw his van. By mistake he'd parked in the driveway on the other side of her house, the one that belonged to Mary Stewart.

Or maybe it hadn't been a mistake. If she'd seen the van when she pulled in, she'd have known not to go inside.

"This is my neighbor's driveway."

"Who cares?" Quentin steered her around to the passenger side and opened the door. "These houses are right on top of each other. How am I supposed to know the difference?"

"Look, there's Mary now." Jesse could see the older woman standing, silhouetted, in her front bay window. She lifted her hand and waved frantically. "Wave, Quentin! She's looking at us."

"What the hell?" Quentin turned to look, his expression stormy. "She's just some old lady. Let's go."

"Wait, she's coming to the door. I have to say hello, otherwise she'll think something's wrong."

Leaving Quentin behind, Jesse approached the porch. As the door opened she called, "How are you, Mary? It's me, Jesse, from next door."

"I can see that, dear." Mary squinted vaguely in their direction. "And is that your nice young man? Aren't you lucky to be getting out. I hope you're going to be moving that van."

"We are. Right now." This was Jesse's chance to leave a trail. It wasn't much, but it was the only one she was going to get. "Quentin and I are going to pick up my daughter. Isn't that great?" She reached back and drew him, resisting, into the light. "I don't believe you've met Quentin? Quentin Stone?"

"Fenton, you say? What a lovely name. I once had a beau by that name, myself."

"Not Fenton." Jesse emphasized the words carefully. "Quen—"

His arm circled her shoulder roughly and pulled her back. "Sorry," said Quentin. "We've got to go."

"You two have fun!" Mary called out gaily. She went inside and shut the door behind her.

Quentin didn't say another word as he pushed Jesse into the van, then walked around to the driver's side. He started the engine, gunned it briefly, then pulled out onto the road. Jesse stared straight ahead, out the window, and saw nothing. She couldn't believe she was going with him. It was lunacy. But then so was the fact that he had Amanda.

Soon, anytime now, she'd be seeing her baby again. Soon she'd be holding Amanda in her arms. As for the rest she'd just have to figure it out as it came. Quentin knew where Amanda was, and he was going to take her there. For now it was enough.

The drive was longer than she'd expected as Quentin drove north for more than twenty minutes. Here in back-country Cranford the houses were farther apart, and set back from the road on large plots of land. Finally Quentin slowed, then turned in at a driveway that was little more than a dirt track. It meandered through a copse of trees, then came out into a lawn. A large house was on one side, a three-car garage on the other.

Quentin saw her look of surprise. "I live over the garage," he said, pulling up beside the outbuilding. "The owners travel a lot. They like to know that someone's around. They're in Italy now. Won't be back for weeks. Don't worry, we'll have plenty of privacy."

He parked the van, then hopped out and came around. Jesse was slower getting out. Except for the one opposite she saw no houses at all. No lights were visible through the trees. No other homes were within shouting distance. Quentin had chosen his lair well.

"Come on." He took her around the back of the building. "This way."

Even as he put the key in the latch and sprang the lock, Jesse could hear a baby crying upstairs. She pushed past him and flew up the narrow stairway. It opened out into a sitting room. Though the wails were louder here, the room was empty.

Coming up behind her, Quentin flicked on the light. Jesse saw that two doors led off from the room. She tried the first and found a bathroom; the second was a darkened bedroom. As light from the sitting room spilled inside, the crying stopped momentarily.

Amanda was lying in the center of the double bed. She looked at Jesse, blinked twice, then began to scream again.

Jesse flew across the room and scooped Amanda up in her arms. Tears streamed down her cheeks as she nestled the infant to her breast. "It's all right, it's all right. Mommy's here."

She began to rock and Amanda quieted. A tiny hand reached up, fingers grazing Jesse's chin. Then Amanda turned her face inward and closed her eyes. With a quiet sigh she snuggled in against her mother as if she'd never left.

Sobbing quietly, Jesse sank down onto the bed. Emotion poured through her and left her weak. She curled both arms protectively around the tiny infant and murmured nonsense syllables under her breath. Her hot, wet tears covered them both.

She had no idea how long she stayed that way, rocking, crying, singing in the dark. Time didn't matter; nothing did, except the tiny baby she held in her arms. Her fingers were gentle, tracing every inch of Amanda's body as she slept, until Jesse was finally satisfied that the infant was all right.

Slowly peace crept over her. She was whole again. She had her daughter back and life could go on. For days she'd thought of nothing but Amanda. Now it was time to look ahead.

Jesse glanced up at the empty doorway. It was also time to get the hell out. She drew in several deep breaths and slowly let them out. The back of her hand, lifted to her face, smeared away the tears. She stood, shifting Amanda so that the baby rested up along her shoulder. Then she walked out into the sitting room.

Jesse wasn't sure what she'd expected to find, but it certainly wasn't this. Quentin was there, of course, as she'd known he would be. But to her surprise he was sitting in an easy chair, reading the newspaper. When she entered the room, he looked up and smiled.

"I've made some coffee," he said, setting the paper aside. "I'll get you some."

"I don't want any coffee, Quentin."

"Sure you do." He rose and walked past her into the kitchenette. "I know you like it."

Frowning, Jesse watched him go. He was acting so normal. As though there was nothing unusual about the situation at all. As though she was simply a friend who'd dropped by for a visit, who'd stopped in for a goddamned cup of coffee. Jesse cradled Amanda closer.

"I don't have time for coffee. Amanda and I have to be going home."

He took a cup from the cabinet and filled it before turning back to face her. "No," he said simply. "You can't leave."

"Sure I can." Jesse edged toward the stairs. "Don't worry, you don't have to drive me. I'll just walk back to the road. I'm sure I can pick up a ride."

In one quick move he was between her and the steps. Coffee sloshed over the rim of the cup, scalding his fingers. With a yelp Quentin let go. The cup shattered on the floor at his feet.

"Now look what you made me do."

"I'm sorry." The look on his face had her backing away. "I'm sorry, I didn't mean to—"

"Clean it up!"

She hurried into the kitchenette. There a roll of paper towels on the counter. Still holding Amanda, Jesse tore off several.

Quentin had moved back several feet to the top of the staircase. He stood, arms crossed, and watched her mop up the mess one-handed. "That's better." Unexpectedly he grinned. "In fact that's very good. We're going to do very well together, you and I."

"Quentin, I can't stay here with you."

"Of course you can." The smile on his face never even wavered. "I've got it all planned. Everything's going to be perfect. Nobody ever takes me seriously. But you will now. You'll have to, won't you?"

Amanda woke and began to fret. Jesse jiggled her up and down, then slipped a finger in her mouth. The baby sucked happily. "I don't understand. What do you have planned?"

"Everything!" Quentin clapped his hands. "You'll see!"

Casually Jesse checked out the room, looking for another way out. One wall held a picture window—a single, solid sheet of glass. Beyond that was a set of bookshelves, its contents neatly aligned according to size. She went on, then stopped, and came slowly back.

On the top shelf was a small picture, framed in silver. Even as Jesse stepped in for a closer look, she knew what she would see.

"Beautiful, isn't it?" Quentin came up beside her. He lifted the heavy frame and hefted it in his hand. "I've always loved this picture of you."

"That's Amanda's picture."

"I look at it every day," he continued on as though she hadn't even spoken. "I can see you here, happy, laughing, the sunlight shining on your hair. We'll take pictures of our own like this, you and I."

"No." Jesse backed away. "We won't."

Quentin looked up suddenly. "Your hair will grow back. I like it better long. But this time when it grows, it will be only for me."

Jesse lifted a hand to her head, then let it fall. A shudder rippled through her body. It was an effort not to let him see. She'd thought she'd been so clever, following Denise's trail. She'd thought she had everything all figured out. But now, too late, Jesse saw that she'd missed the point entirely. Amanda wasn't the target, she never had been.

It was Jesse he'd been after all along.

"Don't you see?" Quentin said earnestly. "Everything's going to work out now. Nothing stands in our way anymore. Not my sister, and not your husband, either. I thought he might be a problem, but he wasn't. I took care of him. It was easy."

Jesse's eyes widened as she remembered the pair of headlights that had tailed her to White Plains. "You followed me."

"I certainly did." Quentin chortled with satisfaction. "I'm a very good follower. I was doing you a favor really. You didn't want to get back together with him, I could tell. He wasn't right for you. Not like I am. That's what I told Denise. She didn't believe me, either, at first." He began to laugh, a high, manic sound that seemed to bounce off the walls. "But I convinced her, all right."

Jesse backed away, knocked into a floor lamp, and caught it as it began to swing wildly. "You killed her."

"I had to. She made me do it. She wanted to keep Amanda for herself. She thought that was the plan. But all the time I knew better. I needed the baby to make you come to me. And you did. I got your baby back for you. Now I'm the hero, aren't I?"

If it wasn't for Amanda, she'd have made her move then, as Quentin walked past her calmly and headed back to his chair. He was comfortable in his own house, and as long as she kept agreeing with him, he was comfortable with her. He didn't think anything about turning his back on her. She could use that against him. It might be the only advantage she had.

Carefully Jesse laid Amanda on the floor in the corner. It hurt, physically, to put the sleeping baby down, but Jesse forced herself to do it. She wasn't sure what she was going to do next, but whatever it was, she'd need her hands free and Amanda safely out of harm's way. There had to be a way to incapacitate Quentin so that she and Amanda could make their escape.

"The baby's diaper's wet," Jesse said casually. "I'll have to go out for some."

"Later." Quentin bent to pick up his coffee. "I'll take care of it."

Behind him Jesse advanced slowly. As she passed the shelf a bookend came into her hand. Its thick, solid weight was comforting. "That sounds good. Why don't you just relax awhile first? Maybe I'll join you in some coffee and we can read the paper together."

"Perfect."

Smiling, Quentin looked up over his shoulder. Then he saw her upraised arm and his expression changed. Just in time he lifted a hand to ward off the blow. The bookend glanced off his shoulder and Jesse heard him grunt. He fell back into the chair, but in seconds he was up and coming at her.

"That wasn't nice," Quentin said softly. One hand rubbed his shoulder as he came toward her. The other he held outstretched. "Give me the bookend."

"No!" Her quick dodge put the couch between them. She circled it warily, her eyes never leaving him.

"Really, Jesse, there's nothing to be gained by this kind of behavior."

She didn't bother arguing with him. She needed her breath for other things, like filling her lungs. A bookend wasn't much, but it was the only weapon they had between them. Unfortunately, now that he was on guard, she'd never get close enough to use it.

"You're going to be sorry." Quentin skirted one end of the couch as Jesse came around the other. "Very, very sorry."

Instinctively Jesse leaped back as he lunged toward her across the couch. Too late she realized she should have gone forward instead and struck while he was off balance. Think, she told herself. Think! It was time for a change of tactics. Humoring him hadn't accomplished anything. Maybe making him mad, would.

"You can't keep me here, Quentin. I don't want to stay."

"You have to." The statement was uttered with childlike simplicity, and the complete assurance that she would do what he wanted. "I love you, Jesse."

She couldn't help but stare. "You don't love me, Quentin. You don't even know me."

"Sure I do. I've known you for almost a whole year."

The amount of time she'd been coming to the supermarket. Had he been watching her that long?

"I'm not staying, Quentin."

"You have to," he repeated stubbornly.

"I don't!"

"Don't talk that way, Jesse. It isn't right. Not when two people feel the way we do—"

"I don't feel anything!" Jesse yelled. "And I certainly don't love you!"

A cry was dredged up from deep inside him: the sound of an animal in pain. His features twisted into an ugly grimace. "You shouldn't have said that."

"I don't love you." Jesse rocked back and forth on the balls of her feet. She'd found his weakness, now all she needed was an opening. "I don't love you, and I won't stay here with you."

Quentin shook his head sadly. "This isn't how things were supposed to be."

"I don't love you, Quentin."

"This is all your fault!"

She was getting to him, all right. "Amanda and I are leaving."

"You're going to stay. We'll be like a family—"

"No."

"We'll be happy forever—"

"No!"

"Don't keep saying that, Jesse." He covered his ears with his hands. "Don't keep saying that!"

"Let us go, Quentin."

"I can't."

"Yes, you can."

"Be quiet! Don't make me do this!"

"You have to let us go," Jesse pushed. "You don't have a choice."

"There are always choices." Quentin stared in her direction, but it was as though he was looking right through her. "Denise made hers. And now you've made yours."

FORTY-TWO

His tone was so so matter-of-fact that it took a moment for his words to register. When they did, Jesse sucked in a harsh breath. So much for making him mad. Her eyes were drawn to Quentin's hands. They were big and meaty, fingers flexing, as though in readiness. Her teeth began to chatter.

"You don't want to hurt me, Quentin."

"I have to. It's all your fault." He was whining now. His eyes were unfocused, beginning to glaze.

"You said you loved me."

"I do love you. That's why I can't let you leave."

Jesse felt her diaphragm contract, squeezing the air from her lungs. Her legs, her arms, even her hair felt tense, as though it was standing on end. She hurt all over.

"Don't do anything stupid, Quentin. You're in enough trouble already."

She saw her mistake when he nodded in agreement. "One more isn't going to make any difference."

Dread shuddered through her. "You don't know that. One more won't help."

"If I can't have you," Quentin said softly, "no one will."

Unconsciously she'd bent closer to hear what he said. When he lunged, the movement was so quick Jesse barely had time to react before he was upon her. Up and over the couch he came, slipping, scrambling, grabbing for a hold. He tackled her and they fell to the floor together.

Jesse landed rolling, and was briefly on top. Then he spun her down and her head hit the floor with a crushing blow. Lights flashed in front of her eyes; the sound of cymbals rang in her ears. She heard him grunt with satisfaction and willed herself to focus.

One of her hands was trapped between them. The other, holding the bookend, was stretched back above her head. Quentin shifted his weight to reach for it.

Jesse saw her chance and acted purely on instinct. Her upraised knee was meant to do serious damage. Instead, as he levered himself up, the blow glanced off his thigh and sent him flying over her shoulder.

Jesse didn't stop to celebrate the small victory. Freed of his bulk, she scrambled to her feet. The bookend fell from her hand and she left it behind without a glance. There was no time to go back. Half up, half down, Quentin just kept coming. She pushed the lamp down in his path, then tumbled a chair between them. He never even paused.

"You can't run forever," Quentin gasped. "You'll never escape."

Jesse blocked out the words. She threw his own coffee at him, then followed it with the cup. He slowed only briefly. By now she'd retreated nearly all the way across the room. Cornered on the landing, she had only two ways left to go: into the kitchenette, a dead end of its own, or down the stairs.

Once that option would have been appealing. But not now. Not without Amanda.

He had her and he knew it. Jesse brought up her

hands and spread her feet apart, wanting to be ready. But what good would readiness be against Quentin's superior strength? She tried to pray, but her mind wouldn't form the words. There was nothing left to say.

Then, as she braced back against the half wall that separated them from the stairs and waited for him to make his move, Jesse heard the siren. One, or maybe more, she couldn't tell. The wail was faint at first, but within seconds it grew louder.

Quentin heard the sound the same moment she did. His features contorted with rage. "Bitch!" he screamed. His mouth was open, teeth bared. Coffee matted his hair to his head. "You'll be sorry! I swear you'll be sorry!"

If he'd come at her from the other side, she'd have been lost. But Quentin was beyond thinking things through. He simply launched himself into the air, a human missile. Jesse's hands reached up to ward him off; they had no effect at all.

She grunted with the impact as his body slammed into hers. Together they fell backward, Jesse stretched over the waist-high wall. Her hands flailed outward, reaching for a hold that wasn't there. The ceiling spun before her eyes.

She heard a scream and wouldn't have recognized it as her own except that her breath was suddenly gone, and her throat hurt from the effort. He'd hit her too high and Jesse knew she was going over. Her legs snapped up, propelling them both into empty space. She saw the look of startled surprise on Quentin's face as he somersaulted past her.

Her hand found something hard: the banister. Fingers scrambling, she dug her nails into the wood and grabbed it and held on. The hold wrenched her around with sudden force. Jesse landed, aching and dazed, on the top step.

Beneath her came a series of thumps, then a final,

solid crash. The front door rattled in its frame. Her neck hurt when Jesse turned to look.

Quentin's body lay sprawled on the landing in an ungainly heap. His arms were splayed outward. One hand still reached in her direction. Recoiling with revulsion, Jesse tried to rise. Then she saw his neck. It was cocked backward at an odd, unnatural angle; a stain spread slowly across the front of his pants.

He wouldn't be coming after her again.

Jesse slumped where she sat, but only for a moment. Then she was up and running. Her legs were too weak to support her. Her body still trembled from shock. Half crawling, half stumbling, she made her way across the room to Amanda.

The baby was lying where Jesse'd left her. Her lips were parted; her eyes closed. Her tiny fist was tucked up tight beneath her chin. Oblivious to the world around her, Amanda was peacefully, blissfully asleep.

Moaning softly, Jesse lifted the baby up and into her arms. Her head bowed down as she cradled Amanda to her. Their faces were so close she could feel Amanda's breath, warm and sweet, upon her cheek. Jesse nuzzled the baby with her nose and let the tears fall.

Dimly she was aware of the noise outside, the flashing lights whose reflection spun in the window above her. Jesse heard the pounding on the door below, but it didn't seem important, not enough to do anything about. With a crash the door broke, then flew open.

"Police!" yelled a loud voice, abruptly stifled. She supposed they'd found the body. Jesse drew herself inward and continued to rock.

She heard someone call her name, but the sound seemed misty, and so far away. It slipped briefly through her consciousness and then was gone. Humming under her breath, Jesse let it go.

"Jesse!"

The voice was louder now, more insistent. Then

Agent Phillips was kneeling down beside her. Gentle fingers grasped her chin and turned her face to his.

"Are you all right?"

She found no words and settled instead for a nod.

His hand touched the front of her shirt and came up bloody. He saw her questioning look and said, "Your nose. I think it's broken."

She must have done it in the fall. She hadn't known, hadn't felt the pain. Jesse shrugged. When his hand lowered to Amanda, she levered the baby protectively away.

"I'm not going to take her. I just wanted to make sure she was all right."

"She's fine." For Amanda's sake Jesse would find her voice.

Phillips's hand withdrew as he sat down beside her. An officer approached from behind. With a quick wave Phillips sent him away. Behind them, through the rest of the apartment, the police did their job noisily. In this one small corner nobody said a word.

Finally Agent Phillips expelled a heavy breath. "You'll have to give me a minute. My heart's still going a million miles an hour. I was afraid we'd be too late."

"I was afraid you weren't coming at all." His leg had settled in along hers. Jesse thought about it for a moment, but didn't move away. "How did you know where I was?"

"We got a call about the Connelly house. You?"

Jesse nodded.

"I thought so. Detective Maychick was briefing me on your tip about Ruby Saunders when it came in. You going to tell me how you got hold of that list?"

"No."

Phillips lifted a brow. "Someday?"

She found herself smiling. With Amanda in her arms it came easily. "Maybe."

He nodded and went on. "Anyway, the detective and I went out together. I assume you know what kind of mess we found. Maychick dived right in and decided you were responsible."

"I was responsible." Jesse cleared her throat. "For some of it. Before she died, Denise told me that her brother had Amanda. I tore the place apart trying to figure out who her brother was."

"But you didn't kill her."

To Jesse's relief he phrased the words as a statement, rather than a question. "No, Quentin did that. While I was upstairs. Denise wouldn't give up Amanda." Instinctively she cuddled the baby closer. "He told me Denise made him kill her."

"Too bad he won't be able to testify to that. There'll be questions, you know that."

"Yes."

"Think back. This is important. What did you touch?"

Jesse remembered the hurried, frantic search.

"Everything."

"Denise?"

"No . . ."

"The knife?"

She shook her head and saw him release a pent-up breath.

"We should be all right then. The weapon probably has Stone's fingerprints on it. With luck it may even be the same one he used on your ex-husband. . . ."

Jesse closed her eyes and let the words flow over her, around her. Of course she'd be all right. She had Amanda back, didn't she? The rest could be sorted out, dealt with, explained. Now that she had Amanda in her arms, she could do anything.

Long moments passed before she realized Phillips had stopped speaking. Somehow, in the intervening time, he'd moved closer, so that as she'd relaxed, her head had come to rest on his shoulder. The support he offered was warm, and solid. With effort Jesse opened her eyes and sat up.

"You still haven't told me how you found out where I was," she said.

"Your neighbor Mary Stewart. By the time I saw what had happened at the Connelly place, I was good and worried. You hadn't answered my calls, so I went to your house. You were gone by then, but Mrs. Stewart came out and flagged me down."

"I talked to her when we were leaving. I tried to make her see that something was wrong, but I didn't think she understood."

"She didn't." Phillips smiled faintly. "We had quite a chat about an old boyfriend of hers named Fenton."

"Then how . . . ?"

"You had left a message. You just didn't realize it. It turned out Mrs. Stewart had copied down the license number on the van. It was parked in her driveway, and after what you'd told her about Amanda, she was concerned about strangers in the neighborhood. She gave me the number and I traced it here."

Jesse looked past him. Her gaze came to rest on the silver-framed photograph. "He was crazy, you know. I still can't believe the things he said . . . the things he did. All this time he's stalking me, playing with me, backing me into a corner. I was beginning to think I was the one who was nuts." She shook her head angrily. "And then he said he loved me. He actually seemed to believe he could make me love him back. I just don't understand. . . ."

"There aren't always easy answers," Phillips said quietly. This time, when his hand reached out, Jesse didn't angle away.

"But I've seen him in the supermarket for months. Somehow I should have known. I should have realized—"

"No," Phillips broke in. He wouldn't have her blaming herself. "I'm the one who should have known. You'd told me about him before. I should have sent someone out to talk to him. I should have talked to him myself."

"It wasn't your fault."

"It wasn't yours, either." His voice was firm. "With everything that happened, with all that was going on, you never once stopped fighting. That's something to remember and always be proud of."

Jesse started to protest, then closed her mouth without saying a word. Maybe he was right. Maybe it was time to stop being a victim and start the process of healing. In her arms Amanda stirred, then opened her eyes. Her chubby fingers clutched at the front of Jesse's shirt. She was ready for a meal. She was ready to go home.

Jesse brushed a soft kiss across her daughter's nose, then levered herself to her feet. As Phillips started to rise beside her she extended him a hand. "Agent Phillips?"

"Hmm?"

"Do you mind if I call you Sam?"

His grin told half the story right there. "Somehow, I think you'd better."

"Good." She cradled Amanda in one arm and linked the other through his. "Let's go home."

Laurien Berenson, who holds a B.A. degree from Vassar College, breeds and shows Miniature Poodles. She lives in surburban Connecticut with her husband and son.

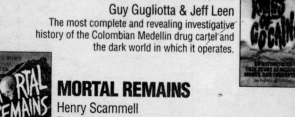

PAINTED BLACK

Carl A. Raschke

Carl A. Raschke, America's leading authority on subcultures of darkness, documents an invisible wave of evil that holds America's children by their minds and parents by their hearts.

PRIVILEGED INFORMATION

Tom Alibrandi and Frank H. Armani

The gripping story of an attorney who risked everything—including his life—to protect his client's horrifying secrets.

VALHALLA'S WAKE

J. Loftus & E. McIntyre

John McIntyre, a young Irish American falsely branded a spy, became the innocent victim of an incredible international conspiracy involving the IRA, CIA, KGB, British SAS, and the Mafia.

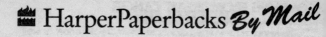
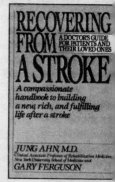
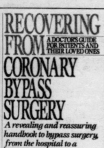

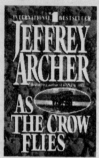